END OF UPSETTING GAMES

END OF UPSETTING GAMES

Lucien Nzeyimana

Rev. date: 01/14/2014

To order additional copies of this book, contact:
Xlibris LLC
1-888-795-4274
www.Xlibris.com
Orders@Xlibris.com
140587

CONTENTS

PART TWO

This book is a product of experiences interacting with different categories of people in difficult circumstances. It has been crafted over time and includes life experiences in Africa as well as in North America. Through the character of Jacob, the author shows that we can survive loss of loved ones, a country, a home, and all our worldly possessions and still find strength to start over. He reminds us that we are much more resilient than we think are. Although this captivating story tells of the world many cannot even imagine, it will resonate with many a reader. It prompts us to consider what we would do in similar situations and where we would find the strength and courage to carry on. The story brings to the fore the injustice people of Burundi faced for decades. As Jacob grew up, he understood that his homeland, often referred to as *Heart of Africa*, had become *Land of the Dead*. Despite losing many members of his family, he struggled to retain a sense of normalcy, gained education, and even started a family, all in hope that one day he would make a change for his fellow citizens. His life journey took him into many dangerous situations, forced him to cross borders in order to escape certain death, and finally brought him to Canada, where he hoped to start anew. However, his resolve was tested yet again when his former enemies were brought back into his life, forcing him to make some difficult decisions.

Master of his own craft, Lucien Nzeyimana managed to interweave Jacob's life experiences into the beautiful narrative that will capture mind and soul of all the readers whose lives will be touched by his words. *End of Upsetting Games* is a true masterpiece that will be hard to put down and will stay on long after the last lines are read!

An Unforgettable Message from an Evildoer

Jacob, why do you keep clutching at straws? It is no use studying so hard. Secondary schools were not built for children like you. Your place is in the village, not in school. You are here by mistake and you are wasting your time, brain and energy. What makes you think that people like you will ever lead Burundi? Go to the village, where there are jobs that suit you. You are good at tilling the soil, cleaning latrines and chopping the wood. Look at yourself . . . I mean . . . look at your muscles . . . your biceps . . . your face. What are you still doing here? Go home for God's sake.

—Dickson Rushatsihori to Jacob Barak
Mugera High School, 1988

Message to Evildoers

Democracy is the only hope to the problems of Burundi. By killing President Melchior Ndadaye, you, Evildoers, thought that you assassinated democracy for good. As human being, Ndadaye was only a messenger. You killed the messenger, but you will never kill the message he delivered. Ndadaye's message will never die. You killed millions of messengers, yet the message of peace and justice is still spreading and the light of hope is shining. The wind and water carry the message farther and faster than we humans do. Even if you kill everybody and burn them to ashes, the smoke will convey the message that you are evildoers. It will take away your inhumanity and all your negative forces that are harmful to human species. It will purify the country and lead it to democracy. By killing the pro-democracy activists, you sent more ammunition to the freedom fighters.

—Lucien Nzeyimana, September 29, 2008

Ap 23, 2007
Is the very first day
I carried a torch for a human rose
I was so desperately in need of caring love
I was searching for a golden pillar to support my true love
I was expecting more than peace, joy, happiness, comfort, and gentleness
I was longing for caring, warmth, sympathy, strength, affection, and soft heartedness
I was expecting support, familiarity, encouragement, respect, compassion, and tenderness
Her arrival ended my dreams. She brought a harsh, a bitter destiny and sadness upon me
She came with fierce competition, troubles, abuse, embarrassment, and hopelessness
She demonstrated her true face, her unwomanly behavior, and unfaithfulness
She left discomfort, concern, anxiety, dejection, and unhappiness
She left pain, tears, sorrows, depression, and stress
She treated herself as a horrible mess
My hopes were screwed up
By Nikita Chissocco
Mushatsihori
Rushatsi
Geram
Rose
Loves
MiDick
Juvenhack
Zim Anan Mus
Lucien B. Nzeyimana
Tend of Upsetting Games
"Peace is not an absence of war; it is
a virtue, a state of mind, a disposition for
benevolence, confidence, and justice" Baruch Spinoza
Dick Rushatsihori, M. R. Mush, Juvenhack Zim Anan,
The Empire Studio 16 Country Hills, North E, Alberta, Canada

ACKNOWLEDGMENTS

I am deeply grateful to a wonderful array of people that inspired me to the writing of this book. I cannot fully record my indebtedness to all of them, though. However, a select few deserve special mention.

First and foremost, my heartfelt thanks are addressed to my four little children with whom I shared both enjoyable and upsetting experiences. They provided me with strength, courage, and determination throughout the writing process to the completion of this work. They gave my life a purpose, a direction, and more joy ever they can imagine. Edgar-Frank Izodukiza's week in the banana plantation of Bujumbura at the age of two weeks left a mark on me. Adneth Marie Kaze Nzeyimana reminds the welcome received as refugee on Tanzanian soil when my home country was persecuting me. Léon Jonêl Nzeyimana revives in me my parents and relatives left in the *Heart of Africa*. Bryan Malcolm Nzeyimana brought the smile back to my face. He was named after Malcolm Little aka Malcolm X as symbol of the freedom that Canadians of African descent have to pursue their happiness in the western hemisphere. As they know what we as a family went through and how I had to struggle through hell to save their lives, they always remained nice, wise, and loving children. They became so close to me that our bond is much deeper than that usually developed between a parent and children. Without my beloved children, this book would never exist. I love you so much, and I am proud of you.

I also wish to extend my profound gratitude to Jean Chrisostome Harahagazwe, Eugene Nindorera, and Kapata Ntaho for their protection when my family, relatives, neighbors, and friends were being killed by the Burundian army. Hadn't they hidden me in their families, I would have suffered the tragic fate of millions of other innocent citizens. Though my presence among their children disturbed their daily activities for some time, I was nonetheless always treated with kindness, patience, and love. I shall be forever grateful to you.

I cherish people that do the right thing—those who fight against acts debasing human dignity. In particular, I refer to honest men and women who liberated Burundian citizens from the hands of assassins and dictators. Committed supporters and defenders of democracy and human rights did an extraordinary amount of work without which Burundian citizens would still be held in bondage in their own country. By fighting for freedom and democracy, freedom fighters liberated citizens who so richly deserved long lasting peace. Freedom fighters, you honestly deserve a bouquet of orchids!

My deepest gratitude goes to Ange-Michelle Musharatsi and her most enthusiastic, indispensable, and faithful friends, Michel Rushihori, Juvenal Hakizimana, Gerald

Sinzayivaho, and many others that liberated me from the terrible circumstances I found myself in. I am especially thankful to these people, as they enriched my life at the same time when I was fighting against man's evilness. By unknowingly organizing and guiding my rescue, they liberated me when I was being beaten at my own game. I would never have so thoroughly enjoyed writing this book if Ange-Michelle and her friends did not exist. Disillusioned by fallacious promises of true and faithful love, I recovered my strength and jotted down notes of upsetting events that made my heart stronger. If there are unforgettable occasions to mark, Ange-Michelle, you are the focal point of at least one of them and the instrumental part of my life's journey. Like Michel, Juvenal, and Gerald, you deserve special thanks.

I want especially to thank, Nestor Bizimana and Ema Florida Bankuwiha, Emmanuel Manirakiza, Cécile Nduwimana, Patrick Kataryeba, Esperance Mukamarara, and Philippe Nsingi Kalukembelako who were there for me when I needed someone to rely on. They proved to be more than just friends, for they gave me the greatest support one can give to a friend. Désiré Hezumuryango and Sophonie Batwenga taught me how to build a house with grass and plastic sheets in the refugee camp to shelter my family. I will always be grateful for that. Randolf Yetman, Sam Ahora Singapuri, Gigi, Jean Bray, Tamiru Kassa, and Monique Bergeron were moved by my story and advised me to write this book for which I will forever be thankful. Special thanks go to Alain Kayiranga and Tamakloe Togbui, Essayas Gabremariam and Allan Ewankow, Velma Parrill and Oswald Francis, Osman Rashid and Cosmas Thebe, Abdi Burale and Sassan Abadid, Abdiradak Farah and Su Yun Seo, Paul Blank and Lionel Duguay, Jean Paul Joncas and Biruk Belay.

I am indebted to many others; thus, grateful acknowledgement is due to all my friends and relatives for their love and their moral support that made my days enjoyable. I think particularly of Emmanuel Gahungu, aka Cuma, who was my pillar of support whenever I needed him. Your wisdom and gentle guidance are deeply appreciated.

The list of people to whom I will eternally be grateful would not be complete without a word of recognition to all and one that made my life in Burundi, Rwanda, Congo, Tanzania, and Canada an enriching experience and cherished memory. I think particularly of Dominique Nsanzerugeze, Tharcisse Nibarirarana, my coworkers at Diversified Transportation Ltd, Fort McMurray, Alberta, Canada, and of course, you, my reader.

As always, the best is left for the last. I feel much obliged to God who protected my family and led us from the ordeals of Burundi to the land of open blue skies, gull of hope and promise. I would never have gone through the exodus without the hand of the Lord. Like my ordeal in Tanganyika Lake, most of my dangerous tests were not under my control. Yet I was always rescued in the nick of time. Thank you, Lord, for liberating me from evils! I am so grateful to you. Amen.

Lucien Nzeyimana

INTRODUCTION

The world in which we live is full of greed, capitalism, selfishness, inhumanity, and betrayal. The powerful people of our world combine their materialistic interests with enmity to condemn citizens of good will to everlasting misery. Most political leaders feign love for their countries and their people. In reality, they are chiefly concerned with economic interests, and they invest little to no energy and resources into the prosperity and well-being of humankind. Only some democratic governments work for the common good of the governed. Jacob Barak witnessed the more typical form of government in his homeland. He was born and raised in a country ironically referred to as the Heart of Africa—a country where politicians used the army and police to kill their own people. After witnessing people being slaughtered, Jacob called that country the Land of the Dead. For decades, governments persuaded civilians, many of whom had been making their livelihoods cooperatively and in peace, to turn against one another. Officials successfully convinced civilians to harbor suspicions against one another. The love that united these extended families and friends for centuries disappeared and so did their humanity.

Jacob is a person of four small worlds. In his first world—like that of many other infants—he was born white, naked, wet, tired, and hungry, in a garden of sorghum and bananas, behind the backyard of the family's home. Back then, very few Burundians were born in maternity clinics as there were few hospitals in the region. He was raised and educated in the village.

His second world was marked by the school in which he grew up, where he learned of man's greed and inhumanity. He spent most of his life in Burundi as a student: eight years in primary school, four years in junior high school, three years in high school, and four full years at the university. He also spent several months in the Major Seminary and the Military Academy.

His third world—like that of the overwhelming majority of citizens—was the period during which he lived a ghastly life, experiencing man's animosity. He learned to sleep on the grass under trees, covering his baby with banana leaves. Many a time, he witnessed his country fellows grazing like cows. He helplessly watched his schoolmates stabbing innocent citizens to death.

In his fourth and final world, he lived a life of a betrayed man as his classmates and his close friends wanted to kill him.

Like everybody, Jacob thought he was born to enjoy life, rather than to suffer. For a quarter of a century, he looked forward to the time when Burundians would live in harmony with one another. He hoped to be able to fulfill his dream of a happy life with his family. Just as a watched pot never boils, Jacob realized that his dreams would never come to fruition—he was condemned to live an absolute nightmare, a life of quiet desperation. Little by little, his hope to enjoy life in his motherland faded from memory.

Although he was always on friendly footing with everyone, not all people showed him soft hearts. During the day, people had a smile on their faces, whereas from sunset onward, they became as tough as leather. Friends turned into monsters. Jacob saw people partying and congratulating one another after slaughtering hundreds of their country fellows. Military officers quickly rose to high ranks when politicians got promotions. Jacob wondered if Burundi was really his home or a cemetery of innocence and justice.

Enemies of peace behaved like hungry and angry dogs with rage syndrome. During forty years since declaration of independence in 1962, the army, police, and rulers rarely behaved as their duty would call upon. They succumbed to murderous rage during more than twenty years in that period. Burundi of the time was synonymous with hell with Satan as Head of State. In fact, people that led the country before 1993 behaved like Adolf Hitler. They put the country on fire. There was only one slight difference between Burundi and hell. Unlike in hell, in Burundi, only honest citizens were suffering while the others lived a happy life. People were slaughtered, not as a form of punishment, but because of greed, selfishness, and inhumanity.

Jacob recalls all the occasions that marked his life, most of which he spent among bad people. His father in heaven recommends him to love them as they too are his children. Still, although they are his brothers and sisters, Jacob cannot help but hate them for doing wrong. He hates the sins, including his own. When talking about his country, he does not reveal what little birds told him. He is a victim of injustice, survivor of a series of massacres and crimes of genocide. He has been around the blocks of Bujumbura a few times to confirm what he read in books. He is an eyewitness of some of the misery innocent citizens had suffered. His feelings were hurt in school as well as in his own house. Therefore, he speaks of what he saw with his two eyes and what he smelled with his nose. Not only did he experience the ghastliness of his life on the Land of the Dead, he also recalls memories from elders who witnessed much more.

From the very first day he went to primary school, until the day he was forced to leave his home country, Jacob only saw, read, and heard of dreadful things about the so-called Heart of Africa. Everything else was one big lie. Fallacious arguments that Burundi was a country of milk and honey were invalid. They had no resemblance to the truth. Jacob saw a land of betrayal, hatred, violence, injustice, tears, and sorrows. Some of the hardest misfortunes humankind had to bear included embezzlement of public funds, spoliation, mass killings, genocides, war crimes, arbitrary arrests, and illegal and inhumane detentions, amongst many other social ills. Survivors of genocides were forced to pass under the yoke of the enemy. If they had to choose between two evils, they would choose the least. Unfortunately, they did not have much choice. None of the evils would be easier to bear, for the only options would be bullets, grenades, butcher knives, machetes, fire, sharpened bamboo branches, and poison. If there was another choice, it was either a sledgehammer or a rope. People found themselves between a rock and a hard place. Like the majority of citizens, Jacob humbly yielded to submission. By so doing, he threw in the oppressor's hand and lived a desperate life. Citizens were so oppressed that they became slaves on their own land. Like Jacob, many survivors sought asylum in neighboring countries only to see their situation worsening. They were continuously harassed by foreign troops that terrorized the African Great Lakes Region.

In addition to the dramatic history of Burundi, other sociopolitical evils undermined relations between the four ethnic groups of people. The most recent violations of human rights include war crimes and many atrocities of the army fighting democracy, freedom, peace, and justice for all. The army dominated the sociopolitical scene for many a decade.

All the tragic flaws ended with the beginning of the third millennium after a twelve-year war between freedom fighters and proponents of the status quo. That war, one of the most ravaging histories has witnessed, was perceived as a fight for liberation on both sides. On one hand, it liberated minds and spirits of Burundians who had resigned their consciences to support oppression and tyranny of a small minority on power. Many civilians lost their lives in the fight for democracy. Others were executed on the premise that they did not support the actions of the bad leaders. On the other hand, the war liberated citizens from all kinds of mistreatments. Most importantly, all parties signed a peace agreement in which they reaffirmed their faith in fundamental human rights and equal opportunities for all citizens. Though casualties were high on both sides, the war marked the end of the domination of a minority over the rest of the citizens. It also marked the end of the mistreatment of innocent citizens by military, political, and economic powers. The end of the dictatorships gave rise to a new era of democracy where human rights are protected by the rule of law.

The democratic governments inherited from different forms of struggle proved that neither Hutus nor Tutsis were in the wrong. Burundians are by nature a peaceful people willing to live in harmony with one another. Selfish people were at the origin of all crises that made Hutus and Tutsis suspicious of each other. Those troublemakers lost their original identity, only to become immoral beings or—as I choose to call them—*Evildoers*. They chased Jacob from his home, his country, destroyed his marriage, and even sought to kill him on a number of occasions.

In this book of occasions to mark, Jacob revives some of the hard moments of his life. In October 1993, an Evildoer, whose only desire was to kill, pulled him out of his rescuer's vehicle. A few days later, he was about to be drowned in Tanganyika lake but was miraculously saved. In 1995, he was arrested by the Evildoer in towering rage. His name was Juvenhack Zim Anan, the same soldier who wanted to kill him two years earlier. While three other captives were executed, one of the executioners ordered assassins to let Jacob free.

In Burundi of 1995, executions were taking place in broad daylight. The hate for Hutus and Tutsi moderates had no boundaries. From infants to elders, no one was free from the brutality of the Evildoers. The situation was no different from the suffering in the past, during the four decades of darkness of oppression, when three regimes of terrorists ruled the country. The same year, as Jacob was quenching his thirst with his friends in Rutana province, an old schoolmate of his recognized him. His name was Dickson Rushatsihori. Without any reason whatsoever, the soldier decided to put an end on his days. Jacob narrowly escaped the killing. In Gitega, his hometown, soldiers did not even allow him to see his family. As soon as he reached his family home, they tried to put their hands on him. Once again, Jacob was saved by the miraculous power of the Lord.

Upsetting events did not stop there. Jacob got married to Nikita Chissocco, a woman he knew from his youth. Within two months, she was flirting with Dickson and Juvenhack, the same Evildoers who had killed her first lover, as well as her father and brothers. Shockingly enough, she knew that they had tried to kill Jacob. At night, she would disappear from home for several hours at a stretch. Worse still, she welcomed her lovers in Jacob's home and allowed them to take important decisions pertaining to their family. Jacob was condemned to spend days and nights out of his household for his safety. As the Evildoers became Nikita's lovers, they acted like masters of his house too. They controlled his life and Nikita. Yet one more time, Jacob was saved by the hand of the Lord. Many more incidents happened without any respite.

In 2014, Jacob sleeps in his empty queen-size bed, wondering what helped him survive all these incidents. What strength did he have to escape death a dozen of times? He grew up as a poor, peaceable, and courteous boy. He obeyed the law and respected all people. But even the victims of the brutality of the army were as innocent and courteous as he was. They longed for lasting peace and justice for all. Still, Jacob had one weakness—a rather significant one: he trusted everybody. He ignored the fact that people were just people. He met Evildoers and treated them with kindness and respect. He could not treat them otherwise. His parents taught him to love and respect everybody, no matter what they were. He forgave and befriended with the Evildoers who sinned against him. When they were not killing people, they appeared to be nice. Jacob joined them and shared social activities. They found him so nice, and they obliged him to share his possessions including Nikita. Jacob refused and Nikita said yes. In their eyes, she was the nicest person in the world. She took advantage of Jacob's absence and kept the door wide open for the Evildoers. When Jacob closed the door, she changed her mood and complained to her new boyfriends. The latter ordered her to kick him out of the house, which she did without mercy. As he feared the Evildoers' interventions, Jacob ran faster than their bullets. Yet he still had a positive attitude toward the Evildoers as human beings with human weaknesses. He never stopped loving his country and his people. His only enemies had always been the evil acts rather than the Evildoers.

Although some Burundians wanted to kill him, Jacob never failed to acknowledge that he owed his life to some of their kinsmen. Jean Chrisostome Harahagazwe and Eugene Nindorera are knights in shining armor. They saved him from a terrible mess. He saw them at his greatest moment of need. In fact, October 1993 was not an easy time for those that supported democracy, peace, and justice, especially promoters of human rights. Jacob could find neither shelter nor refuge in his own country. Even cemeteries had become so precious that victims had no right to the funeral. Throughout the country, dead bodies were decaying on sidewalks. Jacob saw hundreds of them. Like many other innocent civilians, he managed to escape the killings with the help of honest people. He learned the hard way the truth of the saying that a friend in need is a friend indeed.

After several years in what looked like a bandit territory, Jacob got obliged to wave good-bye to the remains of his beloved family. Twenty years later, he still did not trust Evildoers with their greed and inhumanity. Although democracy came as a glimmering ray of hope, wounds of dictatorship and oppression are still fresh. They are being healed by the rule of law now that Burundians see justice as more important than law.

Jacob's life was marked by the conflict between folly and resignation. In this novel, folly is portrayed by evils of oppression and dictatorship of Evildoers who ruled the postcolonial Burundi. Citizens inherited a corrupted country where the Evildoers related to innocent citizens as immoral beings. Burundians became victims of all kinds of injustice.

In this novel, the character of Dickson Rushatsihori is presented as the symbol of evil, the prototype of Evildoers. He is a rigid, corrupted individual that would not wish anything good to his fellow citizens. Rather than seeing his country fellows living a peaceful life, Dickson and Juvenhack would set the entire country alight. They are proponents of the status quo, the kind of persons that would only wish evil, chaos, and anarchy to their mother land.

The theme of folly is also depicted in Jacob's relationship with Nikita Chissocco. It is illustrated by Nikita's betrayal of his love for her. Nikita expresses her folly through abusive language, domestic violence, infidelities, and her collaboration with Evildoers such as Dickson, Juvenhack, and Geram whose earthy desire was to shade blood. She collaborated with Evildoers to destroy Jacob's dignity. After the liberation of democracy kept in bondage for decades, the new composition of Evildoers forced Jacob to another war to liberate his mind imprisoned in his own house. He hoped that folly and resignation would eventually coil up. He would not accept that his destiny was to suffer all his life. He decided to speak the truth, and he liberated his conscience held in bondage by Nikita and her Evildoers.

Owing to the determination to build a brighter future for the generations to come, young patriots defended their honor and their dignity. Folly and resignation collided and gave rise to a revolt. Citizens stood up to fight for their democracy. They forced the Evildoers to abide by the will of citizens of goodwill. Not only did the fight for democracy liberate Burundians' minds, it also gave rise to an egalitarian society. Citizens now relate to one another in a spirit of unity, goodwill, and brotherhood. Nikita's folly was defeated by Jacob's patience and honesty. By breaking up with her folly, he liberated himself from a heavy burden. After liberating his mind from a coalition of Evildoers, Jacob pulled himself together to rebuild his life with more strength and courage.

PART ONE

CHAPTER I

The Game with Devils

1. Loving Evildoers

God loved humankind so much that he created people in his image. He told each and everyone to love one another as he loves them. Love is very strong. Without love, people not only disobey moral laws, they also hate one another and are thus willing to fight one another. In all his teachings, Jesus Christ focuses on love and respect among humans.

Jesus is not concerned with the intimate and romantic love known as Eros—the sexual love and beauty. He does not even teach Philia—the brotherly love, the imitative affection between friends. In the New Testament, he teaches the parental love that surpasses all other types of affection. It is agape, the love of God for humans as well as the human reciprocal love for God. It extends to the love of one's fellow. While the Old Testament invites us to love one another as we love ourselves, Jesus goes even further. He invites us to love our enemies as well.

"But I tell you: Love your enemies and pray for those who persecute you" (Matthew 5:44).

Like our neighbors, friends, and relatives, our enemies were created in the image of God. God cares for them regardless their sins. He invites us to follow his example, to forgive those who sinned against us, to love every person—not because we like their manners or actions but because they are members of our human family.

Although Jesus invites us to love our enemies, some people do not even love their own families, let alone their neighbors. Others hate their own children, parents, or spouses. The case of Jacob illustrates both situations. He had friends who took advantage of Nikita's vulnerability. When he found out that Dickson, Juvenhack, and Geram were fulfilling their needs with Nikita, they treated him as their bitter enemy. Nikita herself betrayed him by selling his secrets to her new partners. If people harm their beloved ones, how can they love and forgive enemies who keep hurting them? Evildoers do not find it easy to love someone who put their lives in jeopardy. Even if they do nothing to hurt them, they fear for their own safety. They anticipate the danger. Because of the fear, people leave their personal belongings and beloved ones to seek asylum outside their motherland. Refugees are tempted to retaliate and hate the enemy who chased them from their homes. They hold on to anger, resentment, competition, and thoughts of revenge.

Many people were hurt so much that they found it too hard to forgive. The case of Peter is illustrative case in point. Peter had an issue with his brother who could not help sinning against him. He took the matter to Jesus and said, "Lord, how many times shall I forgive my brother when he sins against me? Is seven times enough?"

Peter had been patient; still, at times, he found the situation too hard to bear. Even his tolerance had limits. Jesus's answer was that Peter should keep forgiving his brother, no matter how many times he sinned against him. Jesus put his principles to practice. He prayed God to forgive soldiers that had been ill-treating him and were planning to kill him on the cross. The Bible quotes him as saying,

"Father, forgive them, for they do not know what they are doing" (Luke 23:34).

One cannot love God and still hate his children. If we believe in our Father in heaven, then we agree that our enemies are not evils but just Evildoers. As our brothers and sisters, they are members of our human family and thus God loves them unconditionally. If we hate them, we hate children of our Father. Consequently, we hate our own family. Therefore, we hate ourselves. Thus, by loving others unconditionally, we demonstrate our goodwill and understanding toward one another.

Love is very important in man's life. In this book, Eros is represented by Jacob's love toward Nikita. His attraction to Nikita embodies the force of love. The counterpart was hate as Nikita's feelings were all directed to the Evildoers. Philia and agape too helped Jacob get along with his rivals. He saw Dickson Rushatsihori, Geram Murara and Juvenhack Zim Anan as human beings worthy of respect. He forgave and loved the very people whose desire was not only to destroy his life, but also to annihilate some human species.

Jacob's case is an example of true forgiveness. Though he never liked their actions since childhood, he still treated the Evildoers with patience, kindness, love and respect. Jacob is also fond of people who do the right thing. Before Nikita, Geram Murara looked like someone one could count on. If there are betrayals in human life, Geram is one of them.

God created human beings and gave them all good things. He expected them not only to love one another, but also to extend that love to all living things—to protect the environment around them. Many abide by His wishes and enjoy living with animals in nature, growing all kinds of plants. Others put plants and animals in their houses. In some societies, people live with pets under the same roof. Jacob used to live in the same house with mice, cats, rabbits, goats, sheep, pigs and cows. That was back in the 1970s. Cocks were crowing underneath his bed. In most families, people shared rooms with their pets. In western societies, some folks share their beds with dogs and cats. If people can live with animals, why do they fail to live in harmony with one another? The love for animals indicates that men can transcend their differences and love all living things. They should respect one another as the most valuable creatures on earth.

Some may say that Jesus's teachings are not satisfactory if one has to live in this materialistic world. Men compete in order to earn their living and improve society. Jesus's thoughts are directed toward another world that has nothing to do with the modern life on earth. Materialistic interests set people apart. In this world, however, we are faced with many obstacles and challenges. Such evils as wars, oppression, jealousy, competition, ethnic stereotyping and other human rights abuses cannot be solved by man's spiritual affairs. As long as our world is full of misery and suffering, there will always be something to fight for. If people don't compete for a better living, they fight for their survival. They face enemies that try to keep them in abject poverty. They have to struggle in order to solve their problems. In doing so, they keep themselves alive and strive toward a better future for younger generations. In Burundi as in many other countries, the oppressed citizens had to shed their blood for the liberation of their democracy. Rémy Gahutu, Melchior Ndadaye, Melchiade Ngurube, and others did not sacrifice their lives because they hated themselves. They died for a cause they believed to be noble and just. They died for peace, freedom, and democracy. They agreed with King when he said, "If you have never found something so dear and so precious to you that you will die for it, then you aren't fit to live."
Martin L. King, Ebenezer, April 4, 1967.
The Burundian heroes believed with King that nothing was more precious than peace, freedom, and democracy. They did not seek to destroy their enemies though. They sacrificed their lives for the country they loved so much.

When trying to understand the meaning of love, one encounters a kind of contradiction. The Bible teaches us to love our enemies when the enemies hate us. At the same time, scriptures invite us to hate Satan as our bitter enemy. Everybody agrees that Satan is bad. Evildoers are said to work for him. However, our problems are caused by people we know. Evildoers are responsible for the misery of humankind. They slaughtered people, raped women, and destroyed our countries and our values. Satan did not do worse than that. He was not the one to condemn one group of Burundians to suffer all their lives while Evildoers enjoyed their full rights. Burundians did not blame Satan for their problems; they blamed the Evildoers who committed the crimes. The Evildoers proved to be worse than Satan can ever be. Satan did not destroy the World Trade Center on September 11, 2001, to kill thousands of innocent people. Evildoers did. Satan did not cause the wars that claimed millions of victims in Burundi, Rwanda, and the Democratic Republic of Congo. Men and women triggered the genocide. Satan did not kill President Ndadaye and his entourage; it was the evildoing of Jean Bikomagu, Pierre Buyoya, and their clique. Satan did not shoot down the Falcon plane that killed two presidents in 1994 and triggered genocide in Rwanda—the Evildoers did. Satan did not provide equipment and military training to Rwandese people to kill one another. He does not have any military base on this earth, and he does not manufacture weapons. Humans are responsible for their immoral acts. Yet God invites His people to love Evildoers and only hate their evil acts.

Jacob should not be concerned with hate as he hates nobody. Even when his friends were destroying his dignity, he still treated them as good friends. They did not rape Nikita. She took herself to their places, and she was happy about it. Jacob only hated the bad actions. He does not find it a problem, as most people do, to love and hate at the same time. As the story unfolds, it will become clear that there are circumstances in which this kind of situation is unavoidable. In this situation, love and hate complete with each other, rather than being in conflict, as life and death are. One cannot live and die at the same time. Yet love and hate are somewhat intertwined.

One may find the argument awkward though. Some folks may find it impossible to love peace and war at the same time. Yet this is what is happening all around us. Some people want to live in peace at home and still instigate or fight wars outside. They love their peace and love war against their enemies. There are people that believe in something yet also accept its opposite. In other words, they hate war at home and love it somewhere else. As a case in point, powerful countries assist the poor in building infrastructures, educating people, and feeding the hungry. At the same time, they aid governments with armored vehicles, military tanks, and other heavy weapons and ammunitions to fight their own people or terrorize their neighbors. Similarly, they back rebel groups to fight the same governments. Jacob could not believe it until he found himself in such a paradoxical situation. He asked this question when he was spending sleepless nights with his two-week-old son under banana trees, covered with banana leaves. There was no one to answer the question. All of his kinsmen were in the same boat, struggling to survive the hardest moments of their lives. Thus, he decided to put off the question for another time.

People needed food, medicines, shelter, education, and other necessities. In addition to the basic needs, they were assisted with heavy weapons and ammunitions. The world loves citizens, and yet they give them guns and bullets to kill themselves! How can a parent love his children and give them ropes to hang themselves? They even provide training on how to use the weapons.

Still, if people hated the sin, rather than the sinner, they would not keep peace with weapons. Weapons destroy lives. To put it in other words, only Evildoers need weapons. Those who use them to protect themselves can only destroy the Evildoer, not the evil. In that case, evil replaces evil, and the guns became masters of man's destiny.

For a long time, it has been clear that many governments defend human race on their own soils while promoting weaponry race elsewhere. They respect democracy in their countries while supporting dictatorship and oppression elsewhere. They even use their power to suppress other democracies. In 1993, Burundi had the first experience with democracy, after many decades of oppression and dictatorships. When citizens were happy to enjoy peace, outsiders sponsored a military coup against the young democracy. At the same time, they were plotting against Rwandese government that had refused to back aggression against their neighbors of Congo. Rwandese citizens started fighting one another. Rather than bringing them together through peaceful solutions, the international community sent a peacekeeping force with heavy weapons. The heavy military equipment did not save lives. Politicians that sent troops purported that weapons and human beings would complete each other, although they knew they were wrong. Experience showed that military interventions threatened innocent citizens' lives. There are, of course, some instances when military equipment saved lives. Jacob still dwells on his conviction that weapons do more harm than good. In Burundi, the army wiped out entire villages of thousands of people. Rather than securing everybody without shedding blood, the Evildoers imposed their power and forced innocent citizens to exile. Logically, people should hate guns and gunmen for their evil acts. Still, our worse enemy is not the Evildoer but rather the evil itself. The evil violates known moral rules. Therefore, the best way to deal with Evildoers is to fight their evils and remove them from their minds, in particular when Evildoers are our relatives, friends, or country fellows.

Jacob lived in Burundi where Evildoers hated other citizens as their bitter enemies. He saw soldiers and civilians pounding their country fellows with sledgehammers and rocks or stabbing them with butcher knives and bayonets. Soldiers and cops could just shoot innocent people dead while they buried others alive. Most of the time, killers did not even know the victim's identity. Jacob saw the killers. Some of them were his schoolmates, classmates, neighbors, or friends. Others were their parents or relatives. Victims were Jacob's relatives, friends, or just acquaintances. They were innocent civilians. They were of all ages—infants, toddlers, adolescents, men, women, elders, and handicapped. Professionals were the main target of the Evildoers. Assailants and their victims had something in common. They were human beings, and they were Burundians. Most of all, they were created in the same image of God. They were taught to love and respect one another. All of them wanted to live a happy life and bring up their children.

Although Jacob's schoolmates were stabbing his relatives with butcher knives, he never considered retaliating with force as that would only bring more bloodshed. Jacob wanted a remedy to reconcile all people and turn Evildoers into friends. If one were to hate Evildoers, one would hate the long network of Evildoers—manufacturers, suppliers, buyers, shippers, receivers, and users of the weapons that commit mortal sins. One still has to love those people, for God's sake. They build public infrastructures. They improve the well-being of their people. Concisely, they contribute to the development of their countries. Jacob loves them in spite of their countless crimes against humanity. He only hates their evil actions.

After escaping death a dozen of times, Jacob asked himself why Burundians killed one another when they loved one another. Those who wanted to kill him did not even know him. He did not know them either. They did not even know his tribe. They betrayed their best friends and relatives for selfish economic interests. In the beginning, they killed out of nastiness and selfishness. They did not want to share poverty. Greedy politicians decided to kill their opponents. They could then take control of the country unopposed.

Because of the fear of retaliation, assassins decided to deal shrewdly with survivors. For many years, employers invited soldiers to kill their employees. School headmasters offered their students to assassins. Married people offered their spouses or children to assassins. The case of a certain Louis Kaveshanga, aka Mituragaro, is an illustrative case in point. In 1993, he betrayed his parenthood by offering his first son, Monford, to the assassins in a towering rage. They killed him, as well as his wife and their children. This tragedy took place at the time when Louis was supposed to be mourning the death of his second son, Privat, killed in Bujumbura a few days earlier. The entire village of Makebuko was in a state of shock. By betraying their beloved ones, Louis proved that killings had nothing to do with hatred.

Every individual has something they hate or dislike. Even Evildoers would not wish to be killed. They keep their families in a safe environment and go to kill those who are not related to them. These criminals are human beings who deserve good treatment. They do to others what they would not wish to happen to their own families. What is worse, they attack and kill peaceful citizens. In doing so, they kill innocence. By destroying innocent lives for years on end, killers invite survivors to self-defense, resistance, and retaliation. As attack is the best way to self-defense, many criminals became victims of their own acts. The case of Dickson's father illustrates it better.

In spite of their differences, people converge on one point—they hate evil. However, disagreements appear when it comes to defining an evil. As a case in point, a crime is an evil, no matter who commits it. For Evildoers, however, the evil is a crime only when it is inflicted on their beloved ones. Such people forget their own evils and project them to the victims. They blame others for their actions. In Burundi and Rwanda, enemies attacked and killed the presidents and destroyed their governments. Citizens organized themselves for self-defense to avoid even worse outcome. Victims of the tragic events became the ones to be blamed for the genocide that followed their assassination. As the world prefers strength to innocence, the victims are treated as killers. No one in the world can dare assume for granted that the victims of the attack on the World Trade Center were responsible for the attack. When Evildoers said that Pres. Juvenal Habyalimana planned the genocide in Rwanda, some folks seemed to believe the big lie. Very few remember that President Habyalimana was the first to die. In other words, he is among the victims of the very act he is being accused of committing. There is no reason one should believe lies. The lie is an evil.

In fact, it is very ugly. Jacob does not condemn those who love it though. He would only appeal to people to consider doing right and telling the truth.

People don't have to hate or love the same things. One can love what everybody else hates—it is a matter of choice, which explains the numerous wars around the world. Honest people are obliged to fight for justice. By so doing, they proclaim their hate for injustice, rather than the unjust persons. They want their opponents to look in the same direction of love, truth, and justice. Unjust people hate justice. They fight to destroy the political system that runs against their personal interests. Some do wrong and think of their wrong to be right. They clang on the belief that might is right. By killing people, they label them as enemies.

In Burundi, as in most countries of the African Great Lakes region, bad people killed innocent citizens. They called themselves Hutus, Tutsis, or whatever. Jacob calls them Evildoers purely and simply. As Hutus and Tutsis, they killed nobody. Only Evildoers did wrong. They destroyed Jacob's family and killed his parent, brothers, uncles, and cousins. They wiped out entire villages and set citizens' personal belongings alight. They forced Jacob and hundreds of thousands of citizens to either exile or total submission. In 1993, Evildoers went too far and killed the goose that was laying golden eggs. Melchior Ndadaye was a president of unbelievable charisma. His assassination hit the nation like a bombshell. Burundians became like orphans. Evildoers are responsible for all the social evils and the aftermath of Ndadaye's death. Still, Jacob does not hate the killers. He cannot hate his own people. As citizens— whether Hutu or Tutsi—we are Burundians. More importantly, we are human beings. We cannot be anything else. We belong to the ethnic groups only if we do right. If we do evil, we are Evildoers and enemies of the people. The values of human beings transcend ethnic prejudices and stereotypes.

2. Early Thoughts and Souvenirs of Childhood

Jacob was born and raised in the rural area of Gitega. His home village of Nyamagandika gave an accurate picture of the country. As a little boy, he enjoyed life as if it were a bowl of cherries. Life was good and harmonious. In fact, he knew nothing of injustice. Families were neighborly with one another. People were never at cross-purposes. They loved one another and cooperated in times of happiness and misfortune. Everybody was like his brother or sister. In Jacob's mind, life was but a rose. It was about self-indulgence and pleasure. He could not see farther than his hometown, which itself seemed to be a paradise.

On weekdays, Jacob could play different kinds of games with kids of his own age. He played soccer with village children, all of whom were barefoot. Jacob would make his own balls out of grass and rags to play on the dusty or muddy streets. His toes were always bleeding as he would knock his bare feet against rocks. Every now and then, as he walked to school each day, he would lose a toenail. He never sought treatment, as no first aid was provided to children wounded at school. Even at home, not a single family owned a first aid kit. Yet reaching a clinic would have been more painful than the wound itself. The nearest dispensary was in Makebuko, several miles from Nyamagandika. Usually, the wound was left to dry with the dust. With fresh wounds, one could still perform other tasks, such as tilling the soil or chopping the wood. Wounded kids would play in muddy or dusty roads, cleaning their open wounds with dirty water in creeks. Still, Jacob never complained about life.

In the nearby village of Mwanzari, people were worlds apart. On the one hand, there were the Evildoers, rich families from Bururi, who held all the positions in the District Commission of Bukirasazi. They were the headmasters of schools, the accountants, the police officers, the communal administrators, and occupied other prominent positions. They enjoyed the rights that were denied to common people outside of their sphere. They behaved as members of a high class. These newcomers ruled the territory as their own colony. Although their children went to the school with the common people, they were noticeably cleaner compared to the others. Their clothes were pressed, and their shoes were polished. They had houseboys to take care of their dirt. As they were well-off, they would change clothes every day.

Jacob studied with one of them, a boy named Dickson Rushatsihori. He was always the last of the class. He was sent in Mwanzari as punishment because he did not like school. His parents had to keep him away from home so he could learn how to live.

The rest of the students had worn-out clothing and walked barefoot. They were too poor to have shoes. They even had difficulty finding a soup. Jacob was trained to dress like them, just to avoid jealousy. He would put on his shoes on Sundays, the time to go to church.

When Jacob heard of colonization for the first time, he thought these newcomers were the colonizers. Soon enough, he learned that they were not the European colonizers. They were part of his people. They spoke his language as their mother tongue. They practiced the same religions, shared the land, and other facilities. However, they had special names. Although the names sounded like Kirundi, the mother tongue, some of them appeared strange. Names like Rushihori, Kandikandi, Ryogori, Bijonya, Fyiroko, Manwangari, Rusuku, Kinigi, Kidwingira, Fyiritano, Rushatsihori, etc., were not common in the country. One had to dig deep to understand their meaning.

On the other side were the local people. They lived on their land and depended entirely on it. Only a few of the local people had jobs, working for the rich of Mwanzari as houseboys, babysitters, cleaners, gardeners, garbage removers, and so on. Their children would not go to secondary school as they used to do before. Jacob did not know why until he was mature enough to understand the situation.

The first worry was that—being a part of the local people—he would never go to secondary school. He would be condemned to spend his entire life in the village, tilling the soil in his bare feet. He would get a job as houseboy or street cleaner. This prospect ate him alive. What was worse, he would not complain about it. It did not matter, though, as there was nobody to complain to. That was the way things were. Nobody could change them. The local people lived in fear of the strangers who had full control over them.

Jacob learned that his family had moved from Mwanzari. His elder brothers and sisters had been born in Mwanzari. Although Jacob was the first born in Nyamagandika, he liked Mwanzari more than the other place. From an early age, he would go there to gaze upon the white Beetle automobile of the District Commissioner, Gabriel Kandikandi. That was the first vehicle he had ever seen in his life. That was sometime in the 1980s. Commissioner Kandikandi had since changed vehicles twice. After the Volkswagen, made in Germany, he was seen behind the wheel of a yellow pickup—a Chevrolet. Jacob loved it so much. The color itself attracted him. Actually, yellow was his favorite color. Gabriel would drive from Mwanzari to his hometown of Ryansoro at least three times a week. As it was the only vehicle in the neighborhood, most kids ran down the streets to wave a greeting to their ruler.

The road was not paved. In the dry season, the vehicle raised a cloud of dust and the kids liked it. They even enjoyed the smell of the air pollutant emissions. As village children, they knew absolutely nothing about diesel gas exhausts. They enjoyed playing in the vehicle emissions because of the strange and rare smell. To them, it was perfume. They inhaled the gas emissions mixed with the dust.

After the Chevrolet, Gabriel Kandikandi had another pickup, a Peugeot 404, made in France. Those were the only vehicles Jacob would see in the neighborhood for several years. In many other families' compounds, there were carcasses of old car. Jacob wondered how car frames ended up in villages where not a single individual looked like someone who might ever have owned a vehicle. No one of them had ever sat behind the wheel either. Little by little, he learned that there used to be rich men and genuine intellectuals. That was before the holocaust of 1972. There was even a very nice bungalow, the nicest in the region. It was one of the nicest houses in the country. Jacob had never seen a nicer villa in his life. The house had always been vacant, even before he was born. Only birds lived in there. Kids used the beautiful bungalow as their playground zone. In the yard, there were many kinds of fruits— guava, avocadoes, oranges, and many others. In short, there was a lot to enjoy. After school, kids would play hide-and-seek in the villa. They would also catch birds. The nice villa was left by Emile Bucumi, chairman of the Parliament. Emile was one of the parliamentarians killed by Evildoers in 1965.

The house was too beautiful for the survivors of Emile's family to live in it. As his brothers were killed in the genocide of 1972, the survivors could not imagine occupying such a beautiful house with such a tragic history. They feared the killers and preferred to live a modest life. In any case, they had no means to maintain such an extensive property. There was neither water nor electricity. The generator and the furniture had been looted since Emile's death. No one in the family could afford utilities, and there was no modern infrastructure.

In the 1980s, Jacob's family decided to demolish the house. They needed construction materials to build smaller houses. Jacob never understood how his family could have decided to destroy one of the most beautiful houses in the country, the only legacy late Emile Bucumi left to his family as his other house in Bujumbura was still occupied by one of his assassins. Yet no one would talk about it for safety reasons. Emile's house was a great monument, a big treasure.

A striking element held Jacob's attention. The majority of families had something in common. They had no fathers. The vast majority of parents were single moms, as there very few men around, most of whom were all illiterate. Jacob noticed this lack of intellectuals and young men when he was in grade four. In fact, not one of the older boys was in secondary school. At first, he did not bother asking why only a few of the children had both parents. He thought there had been a plague that killed male children a few years earlier. Therefore, as he grew up, he feared that the end of his days was approaching and death was imminent. Later on, Jacob became curious to know what really happened to men, especially the educated ones. Other kids did not seem to worry about such matters, probably assuming that they were busy working somewhere in the offices of Bujumbura. This was partially true as young men who did not like the village life were applying for odd jobs in towns, just to earn their living and make ends meet. Others could find jobs in Kibuye, Makebuko, and Gitega.

Soon enough, Jacob learned that the intellectuals and schoolchildren of his tribe were killed. As a result, survivors lived in fear that the military and police would crush them too. People were still treated unfairly because of their ethnical backgrounds, which deepened misunderstanding between citizens. Because of the continuous killings, the two groups became deeply suspicious of each other. As early as 1965, relations between the two communities were so tense that their disagreements grew. This tension lasted all the four decades of domination of Evildoers over the rest of the citizens. To increase their power, rulers used divisions by making ordinary people fear one another. At the same time, Evildoers were preaching that they were born to rule, whereas others were born to till the soil. This collective belief of superiority increased Evildoers' self-confidence.

As a young boy, Jacob used to hang around with his friends, one of whom was a girl named Nikita Chissocco. Although the Chissoccos lived a few blocks from Jacob's family, Jacob's mother did not want any of her children to hang up with them. Whenever Jacob was with Nikita in their hideaways, his mom would give him some work to do. When Nikita offered to help him, Jacob's mother would send her home. Jacob would finish the work and return to play hide-and-seek with Nikita. One day, he asked his mother why she hated to see Nikita. His mother said with vehemence that Nikita would only teach him bad manners.

Jacob grew up and became curious to learn more about his country. One afternoon, he and Nikita came from school together. They passed by Pierre

Birahinduka's house, who was Nikita's cousin. Pierre had survived the killings of Hutu students in Bujumbura. Jacob asked Pierre about the events of 1972. Although many years had passed, Pierre described the horrible situation as if it had happened a few hours earlier. Jacob and Nikita listened carefully as they wanted to learn more.

"Soldiers erupted in the College Saint Esprit with lists of students and teachers to kill. All the people on the lists boarded onto military trucks and they pulled away. No one returned. I believe they were killed." He paused and wiped tears from his eyes with a handkerchief.

"How did you manage to escape then?" Jacob asked.

"Well . . . I was new in the school and very young. Thus, I was not on the lists of students to kill, as they targeted older students and teachers. Still, I know that some of my classmates were taken. I would say that I was lucky that no one knew me."

"How did you get home?" Nikita asked.

Pierre did not want to go through everything. "It was a long nightmare. Killings were happening everywhere. Soldiers were combing the country. When I arrived home, my dad and my brothers were taken away. The rest of the family was ordered to vacate our house. We lived temporarily in a grass shack until we built a small cabin in the farm. We still fear to return to that house."

Jacob and Nikita were shocked by the revelations, and Nikita wanted to know the reasons behind such atrocities.

"Why did they kill people?" she asked.

Pierre sat down, put his head between his knees, not wanting them to see tears in his eyes as he answered, "So far, no one has been able to understand what happened and why it happened. Evildoers were determined to let no man to tell the story. They killed all the educated. Look, there is nobody here who can tell us what really happened."

"If I had power, I would hang the goddamned Evildoers on trees. I would cut their tongues hanging out of their throats and throw them in the dumpster," Nikita said.

"Don't say that. If they heard you, they would cut your tongue," Jacob warned her.

After these revelations, Jacob understood that he would be dead were he a student in 1972. He leaned against a tree and reached for a handkerchief. After clearing his eyes and nose, he sat down with his hands on his cheeks, elbows on the knees. Pierre stood up and forced a weak smile at Jacob. With his hand on Jacob's shoulder, he tried to hide emotions.

"It is okay, Jacob. I'd rather not to continue this story. Let's go home," Pierre motioned.

Jacob was overawed. He stood up and leaned against the tree again. He thought for a while and then hung his head, crying. Pierre took him by the hand and led him to his house. Nikita did not seem to understand the implications of the revelation as she was two years younger than Jacob was.

As Jacob was growing up, he thought the same situation might happen to him. Pierre's story aroused in him a keen desire to learn what really happened to his country fellows. He started reading books about Burundi. He started looking for books about Africa. He was only interested in the chapters about Burundi. He never cared about authors or titles of the books. He was eager to learn about his uncle Emile Bucumi and other relatives who were killed back in 1972. Whenever somebody came to see what he was reading, he either closed the book or put it away to avoid questions and potential trouble. He could only share ideas with a few close friends. From the books, he learned that genocide in Burundi was still a disaster waiting to happen.

Whenever Jacob spoke to elders, they always shared the same stories. They spoke of dead people, how the army arrested and executed them. As the assassins were still holding high positions in the army and government, every story had to be off the record. People rarely spoke of great achievements of their governments as they were rare. Civilians lived in this situation for many years. They were not shown how to develop themselves or get involved in the affairs of the state in any way. The government needed them just to pay taxes.

The more books Jacob read, the more he realized how people were different. There were Democrats and Evildoers, and he could not tell them apart. The Evildoers were responsible for the tragic events. They dominated the sociopolitical life of the country for centuries. Jacob read how they executed Emile, many of his relatives, and thousands of innocent civilians. He realized that Burundi was not the paradise he thought it was.

Jacob enjoyed life in the village. On Sundays, he could take Nikita for a walk to Kibuye, around three five from his home. A trip to Kibuye could change their routine. Kids could collect empty cans of lotion and other old items lost in the garbage area. Kibuye was a nice city. There was a Free Methodist Church, a bookshop, a hospital held by American missionaries, a primary school, a woodwork workshop, and a few shops. More importantly, there were white people, American families. Jacob had never seen Whites before.

The church was organizing Sunday schools and Christian Bible activities intended to help children grow spiritually as they could perform different activities that helped them learn the Word of God. Kids liked attending the Sunday school, and most would come just for the fun of it. They worshiped God with joy and thanksgiving. They sang, listened to stories, and exchanged experiences. At the end of lessons, kids could play, sing, draw pictures, and eat candy. Each week, Jacob could hardly wait for Sunday schools.

In addition to what the school provided, the children looked forward to watching white children riding their bicycles or tricycles. It was amazing to see American toddlers on tricycles when even the local workers could not afford bicycles. Moreover, the kids were speaking a language no one else could understand. Jacob often played with them though they could not communicate. As time went by, he learned his first word in English—"Hi." As it was less complicated than "Good morning," he had to make sure that he was the one to greet first. It seemed that the Americans had many greeting formulas and Jacob knew only one. By the end of primary school, he could utter a few more words.

There were many things to do in Kibuye. Kids could gather ripe fruits such as guava, oranges, and avocadoes that had fallen down. They also checked the garbage area to pick empty bottles or cans for decoration. At the end of the day, they could return home with a whole bunch of useless items. They distributed them to other kids who did not get the chance of going to Kibuye to collect them. One man's trash is another man's treasure. Empty bottles and cans of lotion were very precious objects to the village children who knew no other toys. Some other days, they had to go to Makebuko parish, several miles away from the village. Makebuko, too, enriched memories. It was very far for kids who had to walk barefoot on hot and sunny days. They got accustomed to the trips. They enjoyed fooling around, gazing on vehicles in the parish parking lot, or counting cars passing by. As usual, they would check the garbage area. Unlike in Kibuye, little was found in Makebuko. It was a big church with more children. On their way back, they had to spend a few hours panhandling in the market of Mwaro Ngundu. It was a way of killing the time as there was nothing to occupy young children in the village.

In week days, things were different. Jacob had to wake up early. He would help his mother to till the soil. Tilling the soil gave him headaches. He never got used to that activity. He wanted to stay home and sleep. His mom was an industrious worker who kept him busy. Every single day, Jacob was assigned chores to perform before and after school. He had to fetch water, to collect wood, to weed, to hoe, to harvest crops, and so forth. Performing such tasks reluctantly did not mean that he was a lazy boy. He only needed some time to hang out with other kids. He lived this lifestyle until 1983, the day he went to a boarding secondary school.

Apart from too much work for such a young boy, Jacob did not complain too much about life. There was no racism, no xenophobia, no hatred—nothing bad at all. Jacob, too, praised Burundi. In his village, ethnic groups were on good terms. Only a few knew what was going on outside the school. Even when President Bagaza built a military camp in Mwanzari, one mile from Jacob's home, he was still happy. He enjoyed seeing soldiers in their uniform, carrying guns on their shoulders. He liked to see them jogging, playing volleyball, and chanting. He decided to become a soldier when he grew up. The military career became his dream. The soldiers usually visited his family to have a talk with his sisters. They could also offer him a ride in their trucks. Jacob never realized that they were the ones who had been killing members of his family since 1959. Until he left his hometown for secondary school, he never knew that the handsome men like Emmanuel Ntunguka were capable of wiping out his village in a couple of hours. They appeared innocent. Jacob never believed that they could kill Léonard Gihinangongo, a prosperous businessman, who had been treating them as his own sons. To Jacob, these men looked as if butter would not melt in their mouths.

3. U and I

Jacob spent the first four years of secondary school in the Cycle d' Orientation de Mweya, around thirty miles from his hometown. He made many friends from different areas of the country. As they were growing up, they started exchanging views on the political situation. The majority of his schoolmates were orphans of the genocide of 1972. Jacob learned from his classmates that Burundi had never been a country of milk and honey. Désiré Hezumuryango told him how students had to change schools in order to pass the screening test. Others had to lie about their ethnic group. In fact, the intellectual genocide was still in effect. It was enforced by establishing segregation in public schools. Since the carnage of Hutus and Tutsi moderates in 1972, only children of Evildoers were allowed to go to secondary school. In the last year of primary school, which ended in grade six, students were identified with letters U and I according to their ethnic background. This identification was useful in selecting children of Evildoers to further their education while Hutus, Twas and Tutsi moderates were sent back home.

Jacob witnessed this segregation in his School District. When he was in grade six, at the eve of the screening test, a delegation from the Ministry of Education visited his class with a list of the students. It was submitted by Firmat Nahayo, the headmaster. The head of the delegation took the floor and told the students the aim of the visit—they were there to update lists of candidates for secondary education. As the names were read out, every student called had to stand up, whereby he was identified as I for Evildoer and U for unknown or other. Jacob doubted the truthfulness of the information received. The funny thing was that they already had lists of all students in their hands. He wondered why it was necessary for the government to see faces of all students of the country. They did not even know anybody. In Burundi, the gender and the ethnic group are the only personal characteristics that could be discerned from one's face. Democrats and Evildoers are as different as cheese. Using names, one cannot tell which is which. Both groups carry the same names and speak the same language—Kirundi. The longstanding conflict between them has nothing to do with land or religion. In Jacob's understanding, if the Ministry of Education needed to update lists of students at the eve of the National Test, this activity would be performed by head teachers who knew their students. The lists were updated anyway. Jacob had never seen this anywhere else. The fact that they did not show the final copy to the teacher, Antoine Barindambi, made the process even more suspicious.

The inspections had detrimental consequences not only to the students but also to the nation as a whole. When results came out, it was evident that no one of Jacob's classmates was on the list of successful students. Clearly, it was not the case that all students of his class were stupid. No one would believe that 100 percent of students could fail exams five or six times. Only Evildoers would agree with this paradox. In the modern societies, if 100 percent of students failed examinations, the problem would not be attributed to the students but rather the teachers. School authorities would investigate the matter and bring in corrective measures. The situation was the same in many schools throughout the country and remained so for decades. Yet little was done to improve the education system. Nobody seemed to care. Neither parents nor teachers could say a word.

The next year, the process was repeated, whereby most of Jacob's classmates were obliged to give up on further education. However, Jacob's family encouraged him to hang in there and persevere, which he did. He tried a second chance and a third one. Many students tried five to six years to no avail. They thought that they would eventually make it, which was a terrible mistake. Jacob always wondered what might have happened had he failed the third time. He never had a plan B. This time, only two names were on the list of successful students—Jacob Barak, who was among the best students, and Dickson Rushatsihori, the last one in the class. That day was one of Jacob's salad days. Really, he was as happy as a Larry. He would not be tilling the soil all his life, which was a destiny of all the other unfortunate classmates who were condemned to stay in the village. The best students of the class never got the chance to further their education beyond primary school when the last of the class passed. The following year, none of the students of Jacob's old school passed the screening exams. Jacob wondered if he passed by mistake or by chance. He reckoned that he was not the best of the class. For example, Léopold Chissocco was a kind of genius. The boy was fearfully intelligent. Unfortunately, although he was the best of the class, he was a democrat. During the eight years Jacob spent with Léopold, there was not a single occasion when Léopold did not get the highest mark of the class. He was always the one to demonstrate tricky exercises. Nobody could believe that Dickson was on the list of successful students when Léopold failed. Jacob even doubted that Dickson wrote the exam. During the screening exams, he even forgot to put his name on his blank answer sheet. There were no answers anyway as he had never been able to do any math. But he was a son of an Evildoer, an officer in the army at that. Somebody probably took out Léopold's name from the list and replaced it with Dickson's. Or rather, they erased Léopold's name on his answer sheet and replaced it with Dickson Rushatsihori. After losing four times, Léopold became disheartened and finally surrendered. Jacob became one of the rare children who knocked on the door of secondary school after the genocide of 1972—and that was in 1983, ten years after the genocide. When the news came out, the whole village spoke about it. Having an educated person would definitely change their lives.

The event created a lot of commotion. Jacob was the first student in his hometown to further his education in secondary school in ten years. Evildoers still believed that secondary schools were only built for them and not the others. The others advised Jacob's mom not to let her son go to what they called the slaughterhouse. They still had memories of all secondary school children slaughtered in 1972. Jacob's mother had never revealed to Jacob anything about the genocide. She did not even know that her son had some knowledge of what had happened.

Although Jacob's success was a big event, it was not celebrated. The event did not bring pleasure to the family. They were certain that their son would be killed as all intellectuals were still being reported dead or missing. Thus, there was no reason for the family to celebrate.

On the first day to secondary school, Jacob was overwhelmed with joy. His mother took him to school. They went tens of miles on foot with a wooden box full of school materials and clothes. Rich families took their children by cars but could not even give Jacob a ride. Once more, Jacob felt the dire consequences of the 1972 genocide. He was certain that if his people were not killed, he would not be going to school on foot with a heavy wooden box on his head under rain or heavy sun. He knew his family used to be well-off and owned vehicles. He wished members of his family were still alive to help. He hopelessly watched Evildoers taking their children to school in nice SUVs and brand-new pickups. He felt ashamed of his wooden box as other schoolmates had fashionable schoolbags. When he waved his mom good-bye, she burst into tears of happiness and sorrows. On one hand, she was happy and proud that her son was gaining education. He would use that education to improve her life and that of the entire community. Still, she was worried for his safety and feared that she might not see him again. In fact, his elder brothers were killed.

Jacob was surprised to see his mom on the verge of tears when he, himself, was joyfully happy for the opportunity. The situation left a bad taste in his stomach, especially that the tears were not shed in joy. His mom remembered the fate of her other sons who left home for secondary school and never returned. She feared that the same destiny was awaiting Jacob and that she would mourn again. In that part of the country, going to secondary school marked the beginning of a long and deadly ordeal. Only children of Evildoers could enjoy their right to education. As a young teenager, Jacob saw no difference between people. There was no reason to kill one another. He had seen all kinds of people. They were like him, and he liked them.

Under the circumstances, Jacob was not supposed to go to secondary school. He was allowed in by mistake. Usually, pupils like him—those who could finish grade six—were sent home. Jacob was lucky. He, therefore, needed a lot of support and encouragement. To him, starting secondary school marked the end of the village life in a shrinking world. He was entering the modern world, the world of intellectuals. He would wear pressed clothes with polished shoes, just like the Evildoers. He would no longer work on the soil barefoot. More importantly, he would study with those privileged to be born in maternity ward, those who had been in day care and kindergartens. Jacob knew nothing of those things and had to discover a new world. The event would definitely be life-changing.

Whenever Jacob returned to the village for vacation, it was a shock to see the brilliant Léopold tilling the soil. This event, though not the only one of the kind, left its mark on him. The dramatic situation persisted for several years, affecting all students who lived in Hutu dominated regions. Hutus and Tutsis were put in the same boat. In order to get around that problem, some parents decided to send their children to study with children of Evildoers. Otherwise, they had to stay home and cultivate the land. Jacob saw a young unfortunate Evildoer from Gishubi. Roderick Nziza spent twelve full years in primary school. He stayed seven years in the same class because he could not pass the screening exam. Like all his schoolmates, he was victim of injustice. As an Evildoer studying with the unprivileged children, other Evildoers took him for one of the oppressed people. The government could not allow somebody from Gishubi to further their education. Fortunately, Gishubi was close to Bururi. The poor boy got obliged to change school and joined other Evildoers. He was then allowed to secondary education. Unfortunately, it was too late for him to go any further. At the age of twenty, he was too old to be in the same classroom with twelve-year-old children. He got ashamed of himself and dropped school.

Although he understood that the screening was unfair, as it did not recognize Léopold's brilliance, Jacob was still disillusioned that he had to study with students who could neither read nor write. It was hard to understand how Dickson happened to be sitting in secondary school. He could hardly write his name. For a whole year, he was never able to copy a full sentence written on the blackboard. He could not enumerate days of the week, let alone months of the year. One day, the teacher of Geography by name Félix Gakwaya did something funny. As he was teaching the class about continents, he encouraged Dickson to say something. Félix put the list of continents on the blackboard, with their names presented in alphabetical order. All of them, except one, start and end with the letter A:

1. Africa
2. America
3. Antarctica
4. Asia
5. Australia
6. Europe.

He asked the easiest question he could come up with, posing it to the entire class: "How many continents are there on the Earth?"
The answer was marked in black-and-white in front of students' eyes, given that all their names on the list were numbered. To help Dickson, the teacher underlined the answer in red. The entire class answered the question in unison. As the teacher thanked the class, he turned to Dickson.

"Dickson, I have a question for you. If you give a correct answer, today will be the happiest day of my life." All students were curious to hear the question.

"How many continents are there in the world?"

Dickson hesitated a little bit. He dug into his memory and finally came up with his answer, "Ten, at least."

Everybody was taken aback. Félix thought he confused him by replacing the word "earth" with "world." He repeated the question, making sure he used the right word "earth." The outcome remained the same.

Jacob wondered how a boy who could hardly write his name could pass the exam at the national level when brilliant students had failed. He understood that someone was studying under somebody else's file. Successful students were replaced by Evildoers who actually failed the exam. Usually, students who failed the National exam were given a second chance to try.

Nikita was Jacob's sort of girlfriend. After school, Jacob could spend his spare time teaching her mathematics and helping her to do her homework. She was two years younger than he was, but she looked more mature. They were in their teens at the time. After failing four times to gain entry to secondary school, Nikita finally surrendered and stayed home. Things changed when a certain Francois Kadende was appointed as new Education Officer of Mwanzari School District. Francois did not allow anybody to try more than once. It was useless anyway. Jacob tried to negotiate a fifth chance for Nikita as he wanted her to further her education. In spite of his insistence, Francois responded with a categorical refusal. He pretended that there was no room at all. Schools were built due to the contributions of the community. Local administration supervised the activity, and all residents were required to bring in their contribution. Still their children could not take advantage of the schools. The Education Officer welcomed outsiders, shunning the local children.

At that time, no one could dare claim their rights. Citizens were trained to acclaim whenever an Evildoer speaks no matter what he said. They could never claim their right to education. Jacob was not happy about Nikita's staying home when she wanted to be in school. As Jacob was doing well and Nikita staying home, the gap between them widened. Nikita became shy, and she feared educated people. Jacob had to work hard to help her overcome her shyness. He remained close to her for another two years. As Jacob was in boarding school, the time and distance finally drew them apart. After a while, Jacob started spending most of his vacations with his cousins in Bujumbura.

Still, on many occasions, he spoke to Francois about equal opportunities for all children. He did not want the situation to continue. The Education Officer always avoided discussing the matter. Jacob's voice was never heard. Worst still, nothing would improve. When Jacob reached the university, he started expressing his opinions in public meetings. As the only educated person in the village, he wanted things to change for the interest of his community. He cried for justice. He wanted his voice to be heard. If he did not speak up his mind, no one else could.

Jacob decided to bring the matter to the governor of Gitega Province, Yves Minani. The governor himself was another accomplice in the injustice. During a public meeting held in Mwanzari in June of 1992, the governor praised the regime of Pierre Buyoya and his government. His speech was propaganda to the ruling party for upcoming election. He droned on for a full hour, and the audience appeared to be bored. After his boring speech, Yves opened the floor to the audience, allowing only fifteen minutes for hundreds of people to ask questions. As citizens lived in fear of the Evildoers, no one dared ask a question. Jacob was the first to take the floor. In line with the tradition, the governor expected everybody to fall in line with his ideas. In fact, there had not been any instance when a citizen would contradict an Evildoer, especially a ruler. Jacob took the floor and publicly denounced injustice in the education system. It was not the time to beat around the bush when the children's right to education was violated. Jacob denounced how the government was stopping children from pursuing their education. He called upon the government to allow equal opportunity to all children of Burundi. Jacob also reacted to the governor's speech, which was full of contradictions. People cheered at Jacob's speech more than they did at the governor's. Rather than making his argument clear, Yves rebuked Jacob with a violent attack on his personality. A friend of his, Joseph Nduwimana, a primary schoolteacher, member of the opposition, stood up to support Jacob's point. Gabriel Kandikandi, then communal administrator, advised the governor to cancel the meeting as the period of questions was making him uncomfortable. He feared interventions in support of democracy, given that 90 percent of citizens were suffering from injustice.

The meeting ended abruptly. The governor apologized and announced that he was booked up and had to call it a day. Governor Yves Minani was used to speaking to an audience that would only applaud him. Like all other Evildoers, he was not prepared to hear a different opinion. This time, he learned that democracy was knocking on his province. As for Francois Kadende, who had never agreed to discuss any issue pertaining education of children, he invited Jacob to his office to show him evidence that everything was going fine. As they were heading to the office, a crowd of people cheered to Jacob's argument and appointed him as their spokesperson. Covered with shame, Francois pretended that he did not have the office keys handy and postponed the meeting cine die.

4. Burundians and Their Fallacy of Ambiguity

Burundian schools taught bad consequences of colonization. However, teachers omitted to reveal that colonization produced Burundian free men and women that betrayed the independence. Rather than leading the country to freedom and justice, Evildoers plunged the citizens into submission. Jacob was born in the silent majority of the oppressed. He still has fresh memories of the police and army brutality. He describes the acts of violence as atrocious.

Terrorists ran the country and turned the situation upside down. They killed honest men and women, and they blamed the victims. The fallacies of ambiguity created confusion to the outside world that never knew the truth about the country. As the entire system was corrupt, no legal action was taken against the Evildoers. The killers continued to take things easy and lived without a care in the world. Not only did they behave as if nothing happened, they would do nothing to improve the situation.

The situation was awkward and somewhat bizarre. After killing top leaders, survivors were wrongly accused of plotting against the Evildoers. Thousands professionals were sentenced to death, and they were executed. Others were killed without trial. Executions targeted innocent civilians since late 1950s. For more than forty years, the army and police arrested and killed people. In Jacob's village, only three students survived the killings. Pontien Karibwami and Emmanuel Gahungu sought asylum in neighboring countries while Pierre Birahinduka hid himself on the mountain. In many cases, young Evildoers constituted militias the aim of which was to crush innocent citizens. The government maintained death squads and armed them like the army. They created many more casualties. It took several decades for survivors to overcome their feeling of hopelessness.

Like Jacob and all other survivors, Burundians lived with distressing emotions aroused by fear and terror. They suffered great distresses caused by their horrifying experiences with Evildoers. Even outside the country, refugees feared that the army would cross the border to kill them. As refugee in Tanzania, Jacob used to spend nights in forests for fear that the Burundian army would attack the refugee camps to kill the refugees. It happened in Eastern Congo from 1996 to 2003, when millions of refugees were slaughtered. Knowing that Burundian refugees were killed in Congo and Rwanda, Jacob's hopes for survival languished.

When genocide survivors were down and out struggling for survival, Evildoers were enjoying their full rights in urban centers. Few of them could sympathize with their fellow citizens. On the contrary, they spoke evil against them. Innocent citizens were prejudiced against and were invariably considered ugly, lazy, stupid, untrustworthy, greedy, selfish, and so forth. On the other hand, Evildoers claimed to be intelligent, handsome/beautiful, strong, and smarter.

Because of segregation in public schools, in the security forces and in the administration, the overwhelming majority of intellectuals and soldiers were Evildoers. Jacob wondered how it happened that Evildoers dominate the institutions of the country, including the army and police. Evildoers' answer was always the same.

Democrats fear to join the army. They cannot run fast. Their feet are too big and boots cannot fit them. They don't even like school; thus, they prefer to till the soil.

The Burundian status was often associated with occupations regarded as scornful, such as rubbish and waste removing. They only worked as manual laborers, cleaning streets, markets, and latrines. In short, the discrimination and prejudice against citizens was evident.

Jacob never believed the stereotypes. Democrats never feared to join the army. They did not hate school either. Jacob searched hard in libraries, interrogated people to learn about the stereotypes. The only physical differences had nothing to do with values as human beings. He continued to read about Burundi. Through his readings, he discovered that Evildoers believed in fallacious things. Horrible killings happened not because people hated one another, but because stupid and selfish Evildoers ruled the country.

Democrats were so terrorized that it became virtually impossible for them to break through negative stereotypes. They had difficulty changing their ways and values. They were victims of emotional, verbal, and physical abuse. The bullying combined with intimidation, physical and mental mistreatment to humiliate Burundians. The latter found themselves in an inferior position and unjustly diminished. Clothed with shame and humiliation, they dropped out of school and showed no interest in joining the army. One could not blame them for this lack of interest. In 1972, Evildoers killed all Hutu soldiers, students, and professionals. Since then, anybody who happened to join the army would be forced to quit. In Burundi, ethnic stereotyping meant that Evildoers were born to rule while others had to till the soil or perform odd jobs. In realty, Evildoers were born to kill. Only Evildoers believed in these stereotypes as honest people respected all Burundians as human beings.

The ethnic stereotypes had bad consequences on citizens. They made them feel a terrible inferiority complex, which seemed to confirm the stereotypes. They made them fear the Evildoers as monsters and supermen. In all public institutions, Burundians constituted a small minority surrounded with the majority of Evildoers. Jacob confirmed it though he could not recall exactly who was who. He could only tell by their evil acts. He was still too young to know of the difference between Democrats and Evildoers. He never looked at evil as black or white. He calls Evildoer anybody who does evil acts.

Jacob worked hard to understand the events taking place in his country. He pursued studies far enough to know why his people were persecuted. He read how the Evildoers executed his relatives and members of his own family. Hundreds of thousands of others were slaughtered as well. Jacob concluded that stereotypes existed and he had to fight them. He refused to believe that Evildoers were superior to 95 percent of the citizens. They were not more intelligent than others were. Thus, he could not understand how the overwhelming majority of people were reduced to lowliness and submission. With this passive acceptance, they were doomed to suffer forever. Even God helps those who help themselves.

Jacob still remembered his classmates, from primary school to university. In primary school, Léopold Chissocco had always been the best of the class. Nikita too had been one of the ten top students. Like Léopold, she was not an Evildoer. In Mweya Secondary School, no one could beat Emmanuel Karikumutima or Zephirin Bigirimana. In Mugera High School, a certain Paul Hakizimana was fearfully intelligent. Jacob himself was doing well. He finished university with distinction and always had the highest marks of the class. Students from all over the country met at the same university. When segregation was abolished, Burundians filled the university. Still, it was easy to know who was who as Evildoers were gathering to plot against their fellow schoolmates. Innocent students too had to get together to decide whether to leave school for their safety. Jacob was in school when segregation was still in effect. Throughout his studies, classrooms had an average of thirty students, most of whom were Evildoers. Thus, Burundian students had to accept insults and humiliations of all kinds. When crises broke, they had little chance to escape massacres.

Hypocrisy and irony played an important role in the destruction of Burundi. When the majority of the citizens were mourning or burying theirs assassinated by the army, assassins kept lying to the international community that Evildoers were nice people, and Burundi was one of the beautiful places on earth, a country of milk and honey. They assumed false appearance of goodness, honesty, and kindness. To the outside world, Evildoers were generous people with excellence of quality. By dissimulating their real character and by turning the situation upside down, the Evildoers gained sympathy and support from the international community. They provided more weapons to oppress citizens even harder. Very few cared about the oppressed. Musicians sang the beauty of Burundi, praising their rulers, the republic and the Head of State. In schools, teachers spoke highly of the country and the rulers. Survivors and orphans alike sang the beauty of Burundi and so did Jacob.

5. Burundian Education: The Legacy of Chaos

Education has a formative effect on the mind, character, or physical ability of an individual. Through education, society transmits knowledge, skills, and values to their children. Parents and teachers direct the education of children. They prepare them for a better future, which is also, the future of the nation. Life experience has a stronger impact on the mind and character. It guides the actions and behavior. It contributes to the type of person a child develops into as he or she grows up. In Burundi, education was provided to one group of citizens. It was directed to the strengthening of injustice and segregation.

Sociopolitical experiences shaped Burundian citizens. Children witnessed soldiers and civilians of the same background killing innocent people. They also watched their parents and siblings slaughtering people and looting their properties. Some even took part in the game of killing. This life experience shaped their personality as they grew up. At a young age, they formed negative attitudes toward other people. Such prejudices were passed on from generation to generation.

Usually, young children accept, trust, and respect everybody. Some parents input in children attitudes and prejudices that will make them hate their neighbors as they grow up. They taught them to resent and mistrust their neighbors. Thus, young Evildoers believed the ethnic stereotypes and ideas passed on by their parents. They held their parents' convictions to be true. They learned to value what their parents held valuable. They scorned what their parents scorned. Essentially, they emulated their parents' behavior and attitudes.

Parental messages are encouraging. They give permission to behave in a certain way, positive or negative. If parents and grown-ups boast about killing people and destroying their properties, their children learn that those acts are good. They will follow their parents' examples to destroy others' belongings. One day, Dickson reported to Jacob the killing of 1972. He was only thirteen. As an innocent boy, Dickson did not know that the people killed were human beings like him. He knew only of Evildoers. He was taught that there used to be species called Hutus, Tutsis, and Twas but did not know what that meant. He never knew that those species were human beings. When he spoke to Jacob, he did not know that he was talking to a survivor of the genocide, even though there were many other children whose entire families were wiped out. Dickson was praising his dad for his great contribution to the annihilation of what he termed as *bad species*. He never realized that he was hurting the orphans of the genocide.

"You know what!" he said. "Daddy told me that he killed many Hutus and Tutsis. How many did your father kill?"

Jacob was not only hurt but also shocked. He would not wish to tackle that subject with an Evildoer. As Dickson insisted, Jacob replied, "Well, I don't know what you are talking about. Are you suggesting that your father is the one who killed everybody in my family?"

"No. My dad did not kill your family. He killed members of a bad species."

"What is a 'bad species'? It is the first time I hear that expression."

"There used to be people called bad species. Haven't you heard about them? My dad worked hard for their extinction."

"Where are they now?" Jacob asked.

"That is what I am telling you, buddy. They died. I told you how the army killed them in great numbers. My dad was a young military officer at that time," Dickson concluded.

"I am not interested to hear your story. Leave me alone," Jacob interrupted the conversation and moved away.

If parents raise their children in a society that preaches with good examples, they will grow up with good manners. They will likely be good citizens. On the contrary, if parents and teachers are terrorizing their neighbors in presence of children, chances are that the children will show no respect for their neighbors. In Bujumbura as in many other areas of the country, young Evildoers could kill like adults. They were trained on how to use weapons. During the 1972 and 1993 genocide, young Evildoers terrorized the country with weapons. They imitated their elders who trained them and provided all the support needed.

These kids were as safe as houses and behaved accordingly. At the age of twenty-six, Jacob witnessed a twelve-year-old boy knocking down a forty-seven-year-old man. The child did not fear to attack two adults. The two men were walking downtown Bujumbura when the young boy halted them. The young Evildoer asked for money. Jacob and his colleague did not want to stop and ignored the boy. The boy persisted. They did not pay any particular attention to him. They just ignored him and went their way. The boy threatened them with a butcher knife. He pulled the man by the shirt collar to force him to stop. "Give me money."

"Leave me alone. I don't have money to give you," the teacher replied as he tried to stand up and continue on his way. The child knocked him down again. He started searching his pockets. By the time the victim was struggling to free himself, three adults came forth and ganged up on him. They pushed him down repeatedly while searching in his pockets. Jacob did not even try to call police to rescue his colleague. There were police officers watching. The nearest police station was just at one block from there. In Burundi of 1995, calling police to rescue a citizen would make the situation even worse. It was akin to adding fuel to fire. They could never rescue the victims. On the contrary, they encouraged assailants to hurt more. These kinds of incident were happening even at the gates of the police stations. Jacob discovered that the assailants were police officers undercover. They used children as their instruments.

The hatred against Burundians was encouraged by the government. Politicians, police, and the army offered support and benefits to young Evildoers. They trained the youth and sent them to terrorize the entire country. They killed people and destroyed their properties. When threatening lives, the youth paramilitary and terrorist organizations operated hand in hand with the army. The gruesome scenes took place across public and private institutions, where all of the Burundian elite, mainly Hutus, were liquidated. Throughout the country, teenagers and adults arrested people and led them to military barracks where the army performed extrajudicial execution.

The Evildoers ignored a common cause. They blindly assaulted innocent citizens. They could not even question the orders. They took for granted that all democrats were born to die. They never tried to check what might be the actual cause of the killings. Very few knew that economic interests were the true cause of disagreement. The coming of democracy meant the end of their privileges. Therefore, they had to kill everybody who supported it. Evildoers looted victims' personal belongings. During the ethnical cleansing, soldiers and the youth were seen carrying mattresses, television sets, and many other items of great value. After looting others' belongings, they forced residents into the houses and set them alight.

This education explains why, during the genocide, young children were as violent as adults were. Violence was commonplace in schools. Young Evildoers terrorized their classmates and forced them to quit. Students, headmasters, and teachers were killed in front of their students.

In Nyakabiga, as in most suburbs of the capital city, citizens died a horrible death. After clothing them with plastic sheets and tires, assailants invited each and everyone to watch the scene of desolation. Parents could pour gas on the victims' clothes and bodies and set them alight. Children were among onlookers, watching the victims burning and crying helplessly. They even participated in capturing runaways.

As no one was tried in connection with the crimes, the children understood that the life of Burundians had little value. In fact, all lawyers, prosecutors, and judges were corrupted Evildoers. They could not prosecute their own children and siblings. They themselves were the product of injustice in a country where justice had been one-sided. The children also learned that all prisons and detentions centers were built for the victims of injustice. Since the atrocities were performed with the consent of the army that provided supervision, training, weapons, and ammunitions to terrorists, the children believed that Burundians were born to be killed.

Although the Ministry of Education was one of the most organized institutions, little was done to suppress violence in public schools.

Dickson Rushatsihori grew up after the genocide of 1972, and he was brought up in a foster family. In that part of the country, there were no professionals left to kill. As a child, he did not witness much violence as the killings ceased by that time. He did not even appear to be violent like his father. In junior high school, he was not yet trained to do evil acts. He was only interested in smoking, drinking, and sex. He was always surrounded with bad boys and beautiful girls. People wondered why he was so famous when he was stupid, dirty, and grotesquely ugly.

Sharing a dormitory with him was a form of punishment for his classmates. In secondary school, students were sleeping on twin over twin bunk beds with metal frames and old small mattresses. Jacob shared the bed with another boy, and their bed was next to the bed Dickson was sharing with a certain Nene Ntahonsigaye.

Although Dickson was not from a poor family, he was stealing money from other students. He was drinking and smoking too much, and he never had enough money to buy cigarettes and beer. Thus, he would either steal it from his schoolmates or do shoplifting. One afternoon, Jacob arrived from sports and found the lock of his wooden box broken. His money was stolen. He suspected that Dickson was responsible for the theft since he was the only one left in the dormitory. Jacob asked the Discipline Master to search for his money in Dickson's pockets and bags. The Discipline Master, however, feared searching an Evildoer, a child of an officer at that. He did not even venture investigate on the theft. The same day, Dickson left school and went to share smoke and drink with a hooker. He did not get the chance to satisfy his sexual needs. He returned to the dormitory still aroused. Being so excited, he could not sleep without masturbating.

Nene had difficulty sleeping on the same bed under Dickson who would masturbate every single night. Dickson made a hole in the mattress that he would use the hole in his role-play. He had a nine-inch-long organ when his mattress was only six-inch thick. Thus, when he was masturbating, the bunk bed shook violently with loud jiggle sounds. Nene could see Dickson's organ protruding from the mattress. He complained about the situation to Patrice, the Discipline Master. The latter did absolutely nothing except to let Dickson know that he was disturbing Nene. Dickson would never stop. Nene warned him that if he did not stop masturbating with their bed, he would teach him a lesson.

Nene himself was another Evildoer and was as tough as leather. Like all Evildoers, he had a butcher knife and a piece of metal under his pillow. He was pissed off that he could never sleep with Dickson masturbating on the same bed. One day, as Dickson was enjoying with his mattress, he ejaculated. As he had no protection, his sperm fell like pouring rain. It dropped on Nene sleeping naked on the bottom frame. Nene got mad and decided to fulfill the promise. With his left hand, he snatched Dickson's organ and twisted it against the bedspring. He grabbed the piece of metal and pounded Dickson's organ. In the end, he picked up the butcher knife to cut it. Dickson was screaming loud trying to pull it from Nene's hand. At that time, it was shrinking in the mattress. He lost consciousness and fell on the ground. He lost a tooth during the ordeal. Students heard him crying for help and ran toward him. As he was bleeding in the mouth, they called Patrice to take him to the dispensary.

Patrice arrived with first aid kit and asked what happened. "What happened?" he asked.

"It is a ghost," Dickson said.

"Where is the ghost?"

"I dreamed being attacked by a ghost."

"You are bleeding. Who attacked you?"

"I tried to save myself from the ghost, and I fell down."

Patrice turned to Nene. "Is that true?"

"Yes. I tried to jump down and hit my mouth on the metal," Dickson cut in. He did not mention his bleeding organ. Still naked, he remained lying on his stomach. Patrice helped him to stand up, but he resisted. There was blood all over him, and he preferred to keep it a secret. Patrice finally realized that something more must have happened. Even if Dickson had lost his tooth, Patrice saw no reason why he could not stand up.

Patrice knew about the conflict with Nene, and he investigated on it. He helped Dickson to sit and saw that his underwear was wet with blood. He thought it was the blood welling from his mouth.

"Nene, did you see him falling?" Patrice asked.

"I was asleep when his screams woke me up. I did not see him falling down," Nene said calmly.

Patrice provided first aid and watched him until the morning by which time Dickson could not stand up and was crawling like a baby. The story of ejaculating on Nene and the latter hitting and crooking his organ remained secret. Dickson could not hide it forever when he needed medical treatment. He could no more walk normally. Besides, he was sharing the dormitory with other students who failed to understand why he was crawling when he was wounded to the mouth. They watched him day and night to understand what really happened. One day, Jacob surprised him just as he was changing Band-Aid on his organ.

"What happened to you? Did the ghost attack you again?" he asked.

"I was circumcised a few days ago," Dickson said.

Jacob seemed to believe it, knowing that it was normal at their age. Then he remembered that Dickson was already circumcised in Kibuye Hospital.

"Don't lie to me," Jacob said, refusing to believe the claim.

"It is true. Why should I lie to you?"

"I know that Joseph circumcised you last year. You can't be circumcised twice."

Dickson was lost for words. Jacob checked with Dickson's close friends who confirmed that they were circumcised the same day. From that day on, they kept bugging him about his wounded dick. They knew that he was okay at the eve of the incident and he had not been out again.

"Dickson, tell us what happened," Jacob insisted.

"I was hurt when I fell down from my top bed," he revealed.

"This is the biggest lie I have ever heard," Jacob said. The others only laughed, knowing that he only lost his tooth.

"How could he fall down and break his organ?" Raphael objected. Raphael was Dickson's best friend.

"He would rather break testicles," Jacob replied.

"I think that somebody caught him with his wife and castrated him," Raphael thought.

Few weeks later, Nene revealed a part of the hidden truth.

"Dickson was pleasuring himself using the bed, and in the process, his organ somehow got stuck in the metal bedsprings. I was awakened by the scream," he said.

"Is that true?" Raphael asked.

"I saw him struggling to pull his thing from the springs. I even helped him to take the springs apart," he said.

"How did he end up on the floor?" Jacob asked, not seeming to believe the story.

"He needed to justify the incident, and he jumped down. He pretended he fell off the bed," he concluded.

As Nene appeared to be an eyewitness of the incident, everybody believed him. They already knew that Dickson liked pleasuring himself using the bed.

The news that Dickson had a broken organ spread among students. Some women made funny jokes of him, thinking that he would not disturb them anymore. They even started tempting him, just to see what a nine-inch-long organ with a 145-degree angle looked like. They got him to go to the woods to see how big the broken thing was and how it worked. They were surprised by what they saw. They found it extraordinarily incredible. They were now the ones to advertise it, claiming that it was unique in the world.

6. Burundi, Land of Memories

Jacob did not forget the problems he encountered in Burundi. Every year, his community commemorates assassinations of heroes of democracy and thousands of innocent citizens. Among the victims, Jacob remembers his parent, siblings, relatives, close friends, neighbors, classmates, coworkers, employers, and many others. A friend of his asked him how he felt about the situation. Jacob expressed gratitude to his savior.

"I thank God for protecting me against all crimes of genocides. I did nothing to escape death a dozen of times in a country where hundreds of thousands of innocent people were killed. It was terrible to live a hopeless life after my beloved ones were slaughtered."

Like Jacob, many survivors found the situation unbearable. They vainly appealed to the international community for help. Nobody cared. All supported the terrorists that shed blood of the citizens.

After decades of sufferance, most patriots believed that God helps those who help themselves. They thought that a suffering through a short war would be better than a lifetime of sorrows. Jacob's generation decided to put their destiny into their own hands. By sacrificing their lives, they paved the way to democracy.

Although Jacob was forced to leave his country, he knew the importance of his homeland. It is always good to be home even if Burundi was not the place of happiness. His classmates from secondary school to university, teachers, soldiers, and police officers had given him hard times for many years. Only the poor village people could live their lives in remote land locked mountains with no interference of the army or police. Things could suddenly change as one moved from one's village to a place dominated by Evildoers. Woe betided those who lived in close proximity with them.

For young children, happiness could vanish on the day they left their villages for secondary schools. They would undergo hardships all the way to university, with their classmates yelling on them. The situation could worsen with security forces securing one group of people when they were supposed to protect all citizens. Whenever an innocent person had to suffer injustice, he was never alone. Everybody with the same background would undergo the same hardships.

Jacob is one of the unfortunate people who happened to be born in a country that hated its offspring. Evildoers spoiled his childhood. They killed people who would have lit his way. It was unfortunate because as a child, he deserved a better life in an environment free of violence. Jacob was lucky though. At least he was not killed as were millions of other innocent citizens.

Jacob was born too early. If people had to choose, very few would choose to be born under Micombero, Bagaza, or Buyoya regimes, in a country where parents feared to bestow their family names to their beloved children. Jacob would never have wished to live his life in a country where governments cherished hatred and wished evil to their own people. He would not have watched bloodshed. He would never wish to watch children of his age and friends he used to hang out with stabbing his relatives to death. Nor would he choose to live a life full of memories of his beloved relatives killed by Evildoers. If he had to choose, he would have waited a couple of more decades. Were he born forty years later, he would enjoy the beauty of his beloved homeland. He would never have watched his people living a miserable life, a life traumatized by Evildoers of all kinds.

During his stay in junior high school, Jacob did not notice any acts of injustice. The students were still young, and they lived in harmony with one another. The headmaster, by name Gerald Nduwingoma, commonly known by Mufozi, was so tough that nothing could happen without his knowledge or prior approval. Like all other headmasters in the country, he was an Evildoer from Bururi. Teachers and students feared him for his toughness. In other schools, however, Hutu students were either killed or forced to leave school. In most big schools of Burundi, students were dropping like flies. Many students joined refugee camps in Rwanda, Tanzania, and Congo. They left the College Notre Dame de Gitega, the College Don Bosco de Ngozi, the Ecole Normale de Rusengo, and the University of Burundi. Jacob did not even know much about what was going on. He had no idea that human beings, say, his schoolmates, could threaten their fellows and force them to leave school.

After the four years in Mweya, Jacob went to high school in Mugera Seminary. In 1986, Pres. Jean Baptiste Bagaza found himself at odds with the church. He considered the church as an implacable enemy of his regime. Priests and missionaries were held in jail for several months. Church activities were suppressed. Key symbols of the church were destroyed. Religious schools were either nationalized or closed. By so doing, the power of the church was reduced drastically. The conflict between the church and the state was linked to the sociopolitical situation in the country. The government wanted to take control of everything. It was a way of punishing the church that was providing education to all categories of citizens contrary to the vision of the government. In fact, the church was recruiting the best students to follow their education in seminaries, regardless their ethnic background. As there was no segregation in the church schools, Hutus and Tutsis were treated fairly and equally. They could complete their education without Evildoers to disturb them. In a few words, the church became a refuge for the oppressed people to farther their education. As seminaries offered quality education, they produced intellectuals who might be a challenge to the oppressor. The situation angered President Bagaza. Thus, through nationalization of catholic schools, the government took seminaries out of control of the church. Consequently, the students would be subjected to the rule and brutality of the government.

The Mugera Seminary was nationalized as well. Jacob was in the first year of senior high school when one day, Jean Baptiste Basomingera, then governor of Gitega, visited the school. The bell rang and students gathered in the yard to be confronted by new faces. Their headmaster and teachers were standing behind the strangers. Students quietened down and waited for a special message. The governor and his delegation were standing at the platform, talking among themselves. All the personnel of the seminary—priests and members of the teaching staff—were there, waiting to hear what the governor had to say. The headmaster of the school, Dr. Pascal, otherwise known as Maru, was not allowed to introduce his guests. The governor moved forward and took the floor. His announcement was directed to the students. Jean Baptiste was so mean when he tried to introduce himself. His first message was a question to the students.

"Do you know me?" he asked.

"No," the students chorused. Although they all knew him, they still wanted him to introduce himself as they were curious to know why he was there.

"Whatever. You don't have to know me. I am not the sun shining everywhere." There was a stretched silence. It was not the message that bothered everybody; it was rather the way it was conveyed. The governor was so rude. Without further ado, he went straight to the point.

"Anyway, I am here to shine like the sun. I want to inform you that this school is now in hands of the government. From now on, the headmaster of the school is Celestin Misigaro." He presented a tall man as the new headmaster. Celestin moved forward to greet the students. There was deep silence. The ceremony took less than five minutes. Priests were given few hours to stuff their personal belongings and leave the premises. All religious activities were suppressed from that point.

With the new headmaster, no trouble was recorded in the school. Celestin treated everybody with a heavy hand. He knew that teachers and students did not approve of the change. Thus, he cracked the whip to make sure everybody respected him. Thus, rather than respecting him, they feared him. He was the eye of the government. Even extremists like Dickson, Patrice, et al., were obliged to act with discipline. Teachers danced to his tune. Nobody could question what Celestin said.

Few months later, Celestin was appointed to a higher position in the Ministry of Education. A certain Francois Mubereza replaced him. This Evildoer proved to be a bitter enemy of innocent students whom he looked down upon like dogs put in quarantine. They were constantly humiliated. During nights, Evildoers were gathering for nightly meetings the aim of which was not communicated to other students. The situation not only embarrassed but also terrorized students, who were already traumatized by oppression and segregation. It worsened when, one day, students went to peel potatoes and found that the knives had disappeared. In a situation like that, it was no wonder that the knives were in hands of Evildoers. This new discovery came as a pain in the ass. Jacob and his friends could not sleep when their roommates were armed with knives. Close friends were turned against one another. They could not talk to one another. The situation was confusing.

Young students shared dormitories—Hutus, Tutsis, and Evildoers alike. High school students lived in the main floor, two in each room. Jacob shared the room with Cyriaque Ntirandekura, otherwise Masayi, who appeared to be nice and kind. Jacob did not expect any harm from his roommate. In truth, Cyriaque was attending secret meetings with other Evildoers. As he was often away, Jacob had to keep the room open but could not sleep out of fear. He joined his friends in Melance's room, which provided him with some sense of comfort. Melance was a stout man that was practicing martial arts. He was determined not to let anybody put their hands on him. He would fight for his safety. Jacob did not see how he could protect himself against a crowd of terrorists armed with bayonets and other weapons. He was so peaceful that he could not even kill a snake. He could not even slaughter a chicken or a goat for food. He had not been able to break eggs for omelet. Peaceful as he was, he could not fight a war with terrorists a hundred times stronger and expect to defeat them. Some of them had undergone military training, and they were equipped with guns. The army and police, who were much more dangerous, supported them.

The secret meetings scared many students into leaving school. They spent sleepless nights for fear of being assaulted and put to death. Soon, everything started falling apart. Friends of different background could not speak to each other. Jacob could not see Nicolas Hajayandi, one of his good friends. Nicolas did not even inform him that something bad was to happen. Students still had to use the same washrooms and eat in the same refectory. Apart from that, no other activities were performed together. Even if old friends or roommates met in the corridors, they could not talk to one another. They could not even ask their friends what was going on. They only waited for the worse to happen. Evildoers had total control over the rest of students.

Jacob and his friends feared being killed. When they met in Melance's room to talk about the situation, the Evildoers accused them of planning an assault. The claim was a goddamned lie as would be evident by their sheer number. If unarmed children were to assault their armed schoolmates a hundred times more numerous, the result would be dramatic. It would not be an assault but a mass suicide. While the undisciplined Evildoers were planning the assault, Mubereza did absolutely nothing to bring them to heel. Rather than knocking some sense into the Evildoers, he took part in the conflict. He could be seen giving instructions to Dickson and Patrice Ntadohoka—the ones who were in charge. As chairman of the youth movement, Dickson was narrow-minded when it came to politics, and he was in command of the entire situation. At that time, Evildoers would threaten citizens just to make a name for themselves. Politicians assumed the power beyond the throne. They controlled the country, and they had strong influence over any authority. It was the case of the tail wagging the dog. Suspicious activities went on for several days. Finally, the students put their feet down. They exerted the headmaster to prevent the worse from happening. They revealed the suspected activities and urged Mubereza to put the squeeze on Dickson and his clique.

There were few honest intellectuals Jacob could turn to for support or even just some conversation. In fact, throughout his childhood, he never encountered any intellectuals in his region until he finished his junior high school. As he later learned, after the genocide of 1972, most surviving students had to quit schools to seek asylum in foreign countries while others were reduced into slaves. The only intellectuals Jacob knew of were Pontien Karibwami, otherwise known as Kirimanyi (for whom he had great personal admiration and affection) and Emmanuel Gahungu, nicknamed Cuma. They had just returned home from exile after the genocide that wiped out intellectuals of their tribe. As children of his age were not used to seeing intellectuals, Jacob was happy to learn that these newcomers were neither foreign diplomats nor tourists. They were members of his family. Jacob had to meet them on a regular basis to learn about the people killed in 1965 and 1972. Having miraculously survived, they could give him an account of the dramatic events.

Pontien assisted Jacob in many ways. Apart from sponsoring his studies, he provided him with strength and courage without which he would never have pursued his education. He taught him to tackle some of the tough problems Burundian citizens were facing. He developed in Jacob an awareness of what was happening around him all his childhood. Jacob had, therefore, to report to him every situation he encountered at school.

One day, Pontien asked him how things were going in Mugera High School. Jacob briefed him how the youth, members of the Rwagasore Revolutionary Movement, were terrorizing their schoolmates. Dickson, the Evildoer extremist from Bururi, who grew up in Mwanzari, led them. Dickson never made a secret of his dislike of people different from him. Divisionism was one of the things he cherished. As Pontien was teaching Jacob about the ruling party, Jacob showed no interest to join the movement that was acting against innocent citizens. He was expecting Pontien to encourage him when he revealed that he was boycotting activities of the youth movement. He knew that Pontien hated injustice inflicted on citizens by the Uprona ruling party. To his great surprise, however, Pontien encouraged him to join the youth movement and participate in all their activities.

"It is the only way you will learn about your country," Pontien said. "The majority of citizens were not politically educated. Great involvement in politics is the only remedy to this lack of education. We take part in political activities, not because we support the dictatorship of the ruling party but because we need to know about our country," Pontien continued.

Jacob listened carefully and waved his head.

"I cannot imagine sitting with Evildoers like Dickson to discuss political issues. They would never listen to me anyway," Jacob objected.

Pontien noticed that Jacob was doubtful and tried to convince him some more.

"These Evildoers ruled the country for years and years, and they have a wide experience in politics. Their children have become inveterate politicians too. You guys had better approach them and learn from their experience. Never ever boycott their political activities," he concluded.

Jacob saw a different Pontien. They were used to talking about school but never politics. As Jacob was growing up in school, Pontien believed that he was mature enough to start thinking about the future of his country. From that moment on, Pontien did not talk to Jacob as a relative. He spoke in terms of a spokesperson of the oppressed. He regretted that the majority of citizens were not conscious of their situation. He emphasized the importance of political consciousness as a psychological weapon to right the wrong.

"Political consciousness constitutes a first step to fight dictatorship and oppression. It is our only weapon that will develop citizens' awareness of the injustice," Pontien said later.

Jacob expressed his pessimism, given the historical background of the country. Pontien's answer was straightforward.

"We must not keep worrying all our lives. This is the time when the oppressed must take their own responsibilities as patriots. We must be masters of our own destiny and take action before it is too late. Where there is a will there is a way. We count on the power of the citizens and their strong commitment to peace and justice. Together, we will fight for democracy using our great weapon of justice. If needs be, we will die for that ideal."

As pioneers of democracy, intellectuals returning home from asylum were taking steps to right the wrong. Jacob was surprised to hear that citizens could fight oppression single-handed. The great majority of citizens were never complaining of anything. The problem of segregation was like an elephant in the room. All knew about it, but a few could dare talk about it. Citizens could not even claim their rights. They had neither knowledge nor education to increase their awareness of the terrible situation they were living in. As all intellectuals were killed and others forced into submission or exile, survivors were not well equipped to address the socioeconomic concerns of their community. The few who had tried to speak against injustice were tortured to death. Others lacked knowledge and understanding of political processes and the means through which to bring their contribution. They even ignored that they had the same rights as other human beings. Pontien preached that the oppressed people had the responsibility to refuse obedience to the unjust government.

"It is their imperative duty to fight dictatorship and replace it with a democratic government," he concluded.

Jacob usually trusted Pontien, and he never questioned his ideas. At this point, however, he was scared. He feared to be tortured at his age. He tried as much to stay away from politics for safety reasons. As he trusted Pontien more than he trusted any other politician, he sat down and thought about his ideas. He could not imagine sitting among Evildoers to plot against his brothers. It is true that he was not old enough to know much about politics. He simply didn't need it. Moreover, he could not convince Paul, Melance, Bernard, et al, to join the movement of killers who were terrorizing them. He believed they would treat him as a traitor or a collaborationist. Jacob knew that they were not welcomed in their political activities anyway.

After a couple of days of soul-searching, Jacob finally made up his mind. He would not join the youth movement acting against him. He knew that, even if he were willing to join them, they would exclude him from their private meetings when plotting against him and his friends. After weighing all the facts, his conscience told him not to collaborate with the Evildoers at all. Instead, he joined his friends and reported the talk he had with Pontien. The conversation had to be off the record.

Paul and Melance were more politically conscientious than Jacob was. With the creation of the Burundian People's Liberation Party in 1980, Burundians were getting more and more conscious of their situation. The party had been developing an awareness of the injustice among citizens and was teaching the oppressed how to fight injustice. Jacob noticed that his friends were much more informed than he was. They simply did not know Jacob enough to discuss anything about the situation in the country. As Jacob was now the one to introduce the subject and suggested them what to do, they trusted him. They told him much more than Pontien did. They had read much about opposition. Jacob, however, hoped that new ideas of revolt would remain castles in the air. Evildoers would oppress them as usual.

Soon enough, it was proved that Pontien was right. Together with Melchior Ndadaye, they had plans to liberate the country from the hands of Evildoers. They invited all Burundians to join Uprona party so that they could know it in detail. Thanks to political meetings of the ruling party, they would discover the injustice. They would see what to improve in order to transform society. More importantly, joining the ruling party and its wings would offer a good opportunity to citizens to learn of their evil acts.

"It is easy to fight the system from within," Ndadaye muttered one day.

The strategy worked perfectly. Pontien and Melchior did not have any trouble convincing citizens of the need for a democratic change. They educated the already educated. They awakened people who were already on standby, waiting for spokespersons. The more educated refugees returned home, the more citizens realized their political interests and aspirations. Thousands of citizens quit the ruling party to join the new party of hope.

In Mugera High School, Jacob learned something extraordinary. Of the thousands of Evildoers, everybody had five roles—a student or a worker, a politician, a secret agent, a soldier or terrorist, and a killer purely and simply.

As schoolmates or coworkers, Burundians could be friendly and perform activities without discrimination. They could share social events and treat one another with respect. In sum, they could act well toward one another.

As politicians, Evildoers believed that the country belonged to them and only them. It was their private property. They were trained to rule over the rest of the citizens. The bad thing is that they would never let anybody else advance in business or move up in any activity. Evildoers kept cutting down the tall poppies. They forced students to leave school. Those who persevered could rarely get jobs. If they did, those who stood up from the crowd were terrorized and forced to resign or give up their responsibilities. Others were bounced into leaving the country. The aim of the terrorism was to stop the increasing number of intellectuals. Evildoers feared that educated people would outnumber them and start claiming power. The example of Dickson is illustrative. Dickson was a person who loved to lord it over other students. One day, as Jacob was working on his assignment, Dickson motioned to Jacob's desk and closed his book. He made him understand that he was burning his brain for nothing,

"Jacob, why do you keep clutching at straws? It is no use studying so hard. Secondary schools were not built for children like you. Your place is in the village, not in school. You are here by mistake, and you are wasting your time, brain, and energy. What makes you think that people like you will ever lead this country? Go to the village. There are jobs that suit you. You are good at tilling the soil, cleaning latrines, and chopping the wood. Look at yourself . . . I mean . . . look at your muscles . . . your biceps . . . your face. What the hell are you still doing here? Go home for God's sake."

Jacob stood up and whispered to Dickson, "Dickson, you don't have to hammer it into me over and over again. I know it."

Evildoers were repeating these words to any of their classmates. Top leaders of the youth movement were the ones to take the lead. Jacob and his friends had to bear up under the abusive language.

As secret agents, Evildoers worked hand in hand with intelligence services to threaten civilians. They would spy and check up on everybody. They could arrest any unwanted person and lock them up in jail. They could torture them to death.

As soldiers and terrorists, every Evildoer would receive military training that would provide them with physical strength and skills needed to terrorize citizens. They would take part in military activities. They formed terrorist organizations the aim of which was to kill, rape, destroy, and loot people's private properties. The Rwagasore youth movement, one of the wings of Uprona party, was the biggest death squad for many years. In 1990s, however, the political movement developed into other terrorist organizations that killed innocent people shamelessly.

As killers, Evildoers treated everybody as their bitter enemies. They did not need orders to kill. They were indoctrinated that killing was their major activity. Doctors and nurses would kill their patients. Midwives killed babies on the delivery stool. Workers would take part in killing their coworkers. In short, the main activity of Evildoers was to threaten lives of innocent citizens.

7. Jacob Was Not Cut Out for the Army

After high school, the defense ministry made an announcement on the radio inviting students desirous to join the army to enlist. Jacob joyfully responded to the announcement. The army had been his dream since young age. He did not inform anybody of his ambition. He feared that his family might oppose him. He only informed Denis Begenyeza, one of his mentors. Denis paid for the trip to Bujumbura for enrolment. Jacob prepared all the paperwork required to submit to the secretariat of the military headquarters. With documents ready, he headed to the army headquarters to complete the enrolment process. When he got there, other candidates were sitting in the waiting room. All candidates came under scrutiny. One by one, they were called to meet Col. Pascal Ntako for a personal interview. Jacob sat on a bench and waited for his turn. When his turn came, he entered the office.

"Good morning, Officer," he greeted him as he laid his binder on the table in front of the officer.

"Good morning, sir. How is life treating you today?" the officer asked.

"Mustn't grumble," he answered with a smile.

"Excellent! Please, have a seat."

"Thank you." Jacob took a seat facing the officer. He reached the binder, pulled his file, and handed it to the officer.

"Good boy. You want to be a soldier, right?" the officer asked.

"That is why I am here, sir," Jacob confirmed, still keeping his smile.

"The country needs good soldiers ready to die for it if needs be. Are you ready to die for your country?" Colonel Ntako asked.

"My dream is not to die. I merely wish to defend the honor of my country. I will have to make sure I am alive to keep everybody safe. If I die, I won't be able to defend my country. Besides, I am expecting quality training that will help me to defeat the enemy. The enemy will be the one to die, not me."

"Good boy. I will be happy to have a soldier like you," the officer responded.

The officer double-checked the documents one by one and confirmed that everything was in good order. Then there was the time for questions, which were rather straightforward. Only the last question embarrassed Jacob somewhat. Colonel Ntako asked him if he was related to any of the officers of high rank. Jacob thought he was joking, but it was serious. The question embarrassed him. He paused for a while to consider his response. Clearly, he could not be related to an officer of high rank when all soldiers were Evildoers. Jacob had never been an Evildoer. The officer himself knew that he was just a citizen. He noticed that the question bothered Jacob and tried to put it in other words.

"Did any military officer refer you to the army?" Jacob turned his head down and said to himself.

"Why does he ask me this question? Doesn't he see that I am not an Evildoer?" then he answered the question. "No. I decided myself. I have been thinking about it for a long time, and the army became my dream."

"Do you have any relative in the army? I mean, any officer who knows you."

As he insisted on the question, Jacob knew that he had to answer. Still, he did not expect the question as it was his first interview in his life. He answered in a negative. In fact, Jacob didn't know any military officers of high rank. He knew that there were some soldiers in their neighborhood, but he was not related to any of them personally. Even if he were asked about a corporal as reference, he could not find any. It was one of the first the first non-Evildoer trying to join the army. Thus, Colonel Ntako knew that Jacob could not have relatives in the army of Evildoers. It was akin to asking George Bush's children if they have siblings in Al-Qaeda. Yet throughout the years, the same question was asked to every recruit. Jacob had been expecting it, but he could not lie. If he answered with an affirmative, he would have to provide a letter of reference. He understood that lying would be futile. When he could not provide any name, Colonel Ntako reassured him,

"Never mind, you can give a name of any professional related to you. He must be somebody known in the city."

Jacob knew some people and hesitated to give their names to soldiers. He feared he might betray his relatives by selling them to the army, especially that they were just returning home from exile. If soldiers had put a hand on them, they would not have lifted them with velvet gloves. Thus, Jacob was reluctant to reveal their names. He became curious to know why the officer needed to know his family at all cost.

"For what purpose do you need that person, if you don't mind my asking?" The answer was straightforward.

"The army needs a reference of a person they can contact should anything happen to you. One never knows. You may get sick, and we would need somebody to contact." Jacob seemed convinced and gave the reference of Pontien Karibwami.

After the meeting with Colonel Ntako, Jacob went straight to Pontien to inform him of the situation. Pontien told him that he made a mistake by giving his name as reference. He should have named Gabriel Toyi, then Minister of Rural Development and member of Uprona party as his reference instead. At any rate, it was too late; there was nothing to do.

The following Monday, Jacob went to the military academy as scheduled. With all of the candidates, he sat for exams in Mathematics and French language. After exams, they had to stay in the military camp for several days waiting for results. In the meantime, candidates were free to partake in different kinds of sports. Results of the exams were never shown to candidates. Students, thus, had no way of knowing who passed or failed the exam. Major Didace Nzikoruriho, who was the headmaster of the military academy, was the one to decide which candidates to keep and which ones to send back home. The decision was not based on results of the exams but rather on references.

Every morning, he summoned a meeting with all cadets. Everybody had to go to the playground with all their personal belongings. The officer told them that cadets who had failed the exams had to exit the camp immediately. The officer read names on a sheet of paper. Everybody on the list had to pick up their baggage and exit the camp. Most Hutus and some Tutsis were sent home. Those who stayed had no problem. The next morning, Major Nzikoruriho came again with a new list of cadets to send back home. Curiously, some students who were sent home a few days earlier were brought back. That is why a good reference was important. Day after day, Major Nzikoruriho would come with new lists. One day, the same scenario happened. This time, the name of Jacob Barak was in his black book. He, and all the others named that day, were ordered to leave the military camp as soon as possible. As usual, no explanation was provided. It was a military order. Together with a dozen of other cadets, Jacob exited the camp.

As Jacob was going home, he wondered why the officer decided that he was not cut out for the army. If he had failed exams, he would have been sent home in the first round. At a given time, students were confirmed that everybody who was still there had no problem whatsoever. Thus, it was certain that the reason for sending Jacob had nothing to do with results of the screening exams or the medical tests.

Jacob sat down wondering why he should not be a military officer. Could the reference of Pontien be a problem if Jacob performed well? He reckoned that at that time, Pontien was known for supporting ideas of democracy. Together with Melchior Ndadaye, he had started expressing views of democracy at the time when it was a taboo word in Burundi. Democracy was a bitter enemy of the military dictatorship of Major Pierre Buyoya. Being related to Pontien or Melchior was perceived by political authority as an inborn sin.

Jacob missed a chance to be judged by his character and ability. If, however, they could judge a book past its cover, they would have seen that he would be a terrific soldier. The country did not need good soldiers anyway. Their main job was to threaten lives of innocent citizens. Jacob hoped to change the situation. Unfortunately, the country only needed Evildoers. Other cadets had given Léonard Nyangoma as reference. Some of them, like Jean Bosco Ndayikengurukiye, were allowed to stay while others, like Gradien Bizimana, suffered Jacob's fate.

Injustice in the army affected Tutsis too. During Jacob's stay in the military academy, he was acquainted with a certain Denis Ciza. Denis was an athletic young

Tutsi, very good at sports. Most of the time, Jacob and Denis were side by side. They were beating everybody. In long race, Denis was the one to take the lead. In sprinting as in many other sports, Denis and Jacob were side by side. That is why Jacob was interested in him.

Major Nzikoruriho kept sending cadets out. Jacob was expecting it since it was believed that Democrats were not cut out for the army. Yet the case of Denis left him breathless and tongue-tied. He was a Tutsi who happened to be born somewhere in the north of the country. Like Jacob, he did not have a good reference. All officers of high rank were southerners.

Finally, Jacob and Denis found themselves at the same university. Jacob could not dare make any comment on what happened in the military academy. The question would cost him a lot. At any rate, Democrats and Evildoers could rarely discuss anything pertaining to injustice in Burundi, let alone in the army. In fact, what was injustice to the majority of citizens was justice to the minority of Evildoers. The University of Burundi was one of the most corrupted institutions of the country. Segregation was as high as everywhere else. Although Denis had become a friend of Jacob's while in the military academy, the situation at the university set them apart.

8. Evildoers with Their Inhumanity and Animosity

In addition to the segregation at the University of Burundi, especially in the Law Faculty and the Faculty of Economics, Jacob witnessed the animosity amongst his fellow students. Once in a while, Jacob and Bernard Ntahiraja could stay with Jean Claude Ndoricimpa in his room. In Jean Claude's room, they had a bigger picture of the compound. They could watch everything happening all around. They watched Evildoers arresting pedestrians and torturing them to death. It happened several times right in front of their eyes. One day, a pedestrian in his twenties was arrested in the campus of Mutanga. He was wrongly accused of stealing a shirt and severely beaten. The boy was passing by, and nobody had seen him stealing a shirt. It was not even certain that a shirt was stolen as not a single student had reported a missing shirt. Even if a shirt was stolen, there was no evidence that the passerby was responsible for the theft. Besides, the theft of a shirt is not worth a horrible death. Yet some of the students responsible for the beating were Jacob's classmates or friends. With friends like them, who need enemies? When they were with Jacob, they were just wolves in sheep's clothing.

Unable to do anything to rescue the victim, Jacob only cried to the boys to stop beating the young man. Nobody would listen to his plea. They pulled the dead body on the side of the road near the restaurant. More passersby would come and pound the dead body with pieces of metal. Finally, the Evildoers called police to take the dead body away. Police came and loaded the body in their truck. They pretended that they took him to the hospital for treatment even though he was already dead.

The cops did not even bother to ask what happened. No investigation was conducted either. Parents would never know what happened to their child.

Jacob witnessed this kind of homicide several times. He was disheartened by this behavior. Atrocities of the kind happened on countless occasions. It was even dangerous to speak of human rights in that country. Under regimes of Evildoers, anyone who dared defend a victim of their bad acts could be assaulted and killed. It is within this context that Jacob decided to join other Human Rights activists. He started attending conferences and meetings of the Burundian League for Human Rights, ITEKA. It was through the meetings of the league that he became familiar with human rights activists such as Eugene Nindorera, Melchior Ndadaye, Jean Chrisostome Harahagazwe, Albert Mbonerane, and others. He enjoyed the pleasure of working with honest people. He knew that honest intellectuals, however few and powerless they were, had a heavy task to improve the situation of human rights in Burundi.

Thanks to ideas of the league, Jacob started preaching the respect of human rights. For that purpose, he organized a group of other university students to work with him. Their Project Proposal was approved. The team received a grant of US$20,000 from the American Government through USAID. In 1992, the group designed calendars with a picture illustrating the human rights abuses in Burundi and a message to Burundians to respect human rights. Underneath the picture, there was a translation of some articles of the Universal Declaration for Human Rights. The articles were translated into Kirundi so that the rural population could learn about their rights. In addition to the calendar, short plays were performed on the radio. Citizens could see the pictures and read articles of their rights. Those who could not read would at least hear about them on the radio. The activity that took several weeks to achieve contributed substantially to the understanding of human rights in Burundi.

The calendars were distributed free of charge throughout the country. One day, the team was returning to Bujumbura after a long day of work. At a military checkpoint, their vehicle was ordered to pull out. Soldiers searched the vehicle to take all the calendars, which were fortunately already distributed. They took the identity papers of all passengers and held them. Passengers were not allowed to continue on their way. John Engels, an American citizen and a member of the crew, informed the American Embassy, which immediately called the Minister of Home Affairs. Thus, if it weren't for the American citizen in the organization, the entire group would have been in big trouble. Ordinary Burundians had nothing to say to the soldiers in a towering rage. They would have to keep quiet and wait for whatever was to happen. Owing to the intervention by American Embassy, after almost half an hour, they were allowed to continue their journey, albeit without their photo identifications. The following morning, they were invited to one of a military camp pick up their identity papers. Not a single question was asked. The American embassy had put pressure on whoever was concerned to set them free. Jacob wondered what might have happened were they not with an American citizen in a vehicle owned by the American Embassy.

9. Change in Society Begins with Self-Change

At the university, Jacob found his acquaintances with Americans extremely helpful. He started organizing conferences in the Faculty of Arts and Social Sciences. Many a time, he invited the U.S. Ambassador to Burundi, Dr. Cynthia Sheppard Perry, who kindly responded to his invitations. In 1992, democracy was all the rage. As the topic was becoming more popular and fashionable, so was the number of politicians at loggerheads. Most professors and students were fighting it with all the devotion of a dog. In contrast, owing to his acquaintances with Melchior Ndadaye and Pontien Karibwami, Jacob had set his sights on democracy. As he could not dare speak about it, he invited Ambassador Perry to give a conference on the importance of democracy. However, her conference on Principles of Democracy did not attract large audience. Perry talked about a subject that the majority of hearers did not wish to hear. It was at the time of political upheaval when the opposition was emerging. As American diplomat with extensive experience with democracy, Ambassador Perry demonstrated the importance of democracy by offering supporting evidence. That was the first speech in support of democracy during the dictatorship of Evildoers. It became obvious that her speech was not well received as the majority of attendees were supporting dictatorship. Thus, as an organizer, Jacob found himself in disagreement with university authorities. Evildoers constituted the great majority of university students and personnel. They were supporting dictatorship and oppression. Jacob was introducing ideas of democracy in the hope that he would change the Evildoers who were stick on the dictatorship of Buyoya. They would never listen to him. Still, Jacob persisted. He soon invited Walter Theurer, director of the American Cultural Center of Bujumbura, to exchange views on topics of general interest. Jacob was determined to invite anybody who could share experiences with Burundians. It was also a way of opening himself to the outside world, an opportunity to air views in a country traumatized by the evil of oppression and segregation.

Eventually, Jacob realized that the head of department was unwilling to give him support he was hoping. Like the dean of the faculty of arts and social sciences, Dr. Gregoire Njejimana was a broken reed. He did not like Jacob's openness. Evildoers were too focused on their supremacy, and they would not dream of a democratic society. Jacob's enthusiasm about new ideas of democracy made him a bitter enemy in the eyes of Evildoers. They discouraged him in many ways, but he resisted. Gregoire gave him shit for inviting the ambassador without his approval. Jacob could not trust the Evildoer, knowing that he was supporting oppression. Thus, if Jacob required his authorization to organize conferences on democratic change, he would never get the approval of the university. Gregoire went too far to instigate other students to boycott Jacob, for he had reached too far and was already well-known in diplomatic spheres of Bujumbura. He could express his ideas through international channels. He was organizing other students to meet diplomats and express their desire for democratic change. In a few words, his voice could reach wherever he wanted.

Few months after the first conference, Jacob told Ambassador Perry that university students needed to discuss the political situation of Burundi with her and she agreed to visit the university again. Jacob informed the faculty that his club would receive a conference with Ambassador Perry. Rather than supporting the project, Gregoire tried to make organizing this visit more difficult. He claimed that the Ambassador would not be ready in less than three months as one had to invite her through the Ministry of Foreign Affairs, which was a long process. Jacob did not like the endless procedures. He just walked in the American Embassy and asked for an audience, and that was it. The Ambassador received him without any appointment and kindly accepted his invitation. Jacob was chairman of a club of university students with some civil servants of Bujumbura as its members. This position allowed him to invite anybody who could bring a contribution to the understanding of a democratic change in the country. He believed that any change in society had to begin with self-change. He needed leaders to pull the plug on discrimination and social injustice. University students were young people, the future leaders. They needed to be educated in order to contribute to the democratic change.

The club grew in popularity as it gave everyone involved. It was the only opportunity for Jacob to express himself on a variety of issues. At the time, members of Uprona party were fighting new ideas of democracy. They tried to convince the society that everything was perfect in Burundi as a proof that Burundians were not ready for a change. They did not make the same arguments during conversation with different people. To outsiders, they purported their belief in democracy while trying to convince Burundians that it was too early to claim democracy.

While this was happening, there was a political storm outside the campus with thousands of people claiming democracy. Ideas of democracy were all over the map when Uprona members were fighting any change in the rotten political system. As a university student, Jacob knew enough about his country. Like all pro-democracy activists, he was determined to speak the truth. He had to make sure that his opponents did not know that he was supporting the movement for change. One day, the American Embassy sent him a vehicle to meet an American delegation from the National Democratic Institute for International Affairs. The delegation had already met President Buyoya and Prime Minister Adrien Sibomana. They wanted to talk to more people, in particular those who had nothing to do with politics. In other words, they needed accurate information from ordinary and neutral individuals. Jacob was an obvious choice. They met a couple of times at the Novotel Hotel, downtown Bujumbura, during which time, the diplomats double-checked the information provided by the top leaders of the country. It seemed that they did not believe their speeches. Through the meetings with Jacob, it became apparent that he was more trustworthy than the president and the prime minister. As student, Jacob was neutral as he had no obligation to defend the position of the government. In their eyes, Jacob was an onlooker who only needed change.

As Burundians could not achieve their dream of democracy alone, they needed other countries' intervention. Military dictators were so stubborn that they would never hand power to civilians. Jacob revealed to the American diplomats the real political situation. They asked him questions on ethnic conflict. They wanted to know why Melchior Ndadaye and Nicolas Mayugi had opposing views when they were of the same ethnic background. Mayugi was chairman of the ruling party when Ndadaye was leading a campaign against the dictatorship of Uprona party. The situation was confusing. Power was held by a small minority of Evildoers. In the eyes of outsiders, the prime minister and the chairman of the ruling party were not Evildoers, and thus, Burundians were not oppressed. This line of discussion embarrassed Jacob somewhat. It required rather extensive explanation. Jacob had to give a lecture on the historical background of the country. He explained that Nicolas Mayugi and Adrien Sibomana were marionettes used as puppets. They subjected themselves to the caprice of the ruling party and the arbitrary government as their employer. They fell in line with their wishes no matter how bad they were. With this mission in mind, even if they were asked to betray the whole nation in order to keep their positions, they would do it without hesitation. There were such politicians who did not agree with the reliability of their consciences. By supporting a government that was threatening lives of their own people, they imprisoned their consciences. They placed materialistic interests above the will of the people. By so doing, they guaranteed themselves a safe income. Jacob concluded his talk that Ndadaye was one of the reliable politicians the country would count on.

The diplomats were satisfied with Jacob's explanation and unanimously agreed that Burundians needed their voice to be heard. It was happening amid a political upheaval when the country was heading to elections. It was obvious that the ruling party would be vanquished and people feared their reaction. They considered Uprona as a disaster waiting to happen. Whether they win or lose, they would do harm.

CHAPTER II

Jacob's Long Ordeals

1. Self-Confidence, Way to Success

In the fourth year of the university, Jacob was busy working on his thesis. At the end of the year, his classmates went abroad for a training session, in which, as it was not compulsory, Jacob did not participate. He had got a job offer with the World Health Organization that he considered as much more important than the training session. He was working with the national program for the fight against AIDS and other sexually transmitted diseases. Jacob liked his new job, which was also the first full-time employment in his life.

As he never did things at the last minute, he was far ahead in advance with his thesis. He really hated rushing things. The director of his thesis project, John Engels, had left Burundi, leaving a big gap in Jacob's project. For several months, Jacob had to work on his own as there was no one who could supervise the thesis. It meant working three or more times harder.

Aware that the topic of his thesis was not familiar to the majority of professors, Jacob was guaranteed success. He trusted himself and he was certain that he would not have trouble during the presentation. He did more research on the subject and decided to get through with it in no time. Three quarters of the work were already done when his supervisor left the country. Still, Jacob did not see a need to worry too much, especially since he trusted himself. Nonetheless, he still needed somebody to proofread and approve the final manuscript.

He approached Prof. Jacques Bacamurwanko and asked for his help. Though he kindly agreed to help him, he was too busy to devote much time to the thesis. He was running a private business and teaching at the university at the same time. Frodebu party had won elections, and Melchior Ndadaye was the new president. Jack was recently appointed Ambassador of Burundi to the United States of America. Thus, at the time, he was packing his belongings in preparation for his new position in Washington DC. He was so busy that he could not squeeze the thesis in his already booked-up schedule. Thus, finally, the young Jacob turned to a friend of his by name Methode Ndikumana, an employee of the USAID. Methode himself was appointed diplomat and was planned to go to the U.S. Still, he did everything to find time for

Jacob's work, which was finalized and promptly submitted to the department for presentation.

This final step was the source of most of Jack's headaches, for it seemed that neither the head department nor the dean of faculty cared about doing their job. They kept delaying the presentation. Finally, Jacob asked why he was being delayed to present his thesis. Dr. Njejimana pretended that he could not find enough professors for the panel of examiners. Jacob found this argument awkward. All professors were there, and they were supposed to be available. It was not time for vacation. How was it possible that none of them was available for several weeks? All other classmates were in Dar El Salaam for a training session, which meant more free time for the teaching staff. Surprisingly enough, professors could be seen playing cards in the facilities. In Jacob's opinion, they simply didn't want to partake in his final presentation. It had never been impossible to find a body of three professors to compose a panel, which could only mean that Jacob's ideas of democracy upset them too much. He had organized many conferences at the university. Now, democracy had won. Most members of the university staff were Evildoers who were opposed to democracy. Jacob had been telling them that it was no use following the darkness of oppression when the light of democracy was rising. They were his teachers, and he was their good student. He was always the best of the class. After class, he became their teacher of democracy, and they were always his bad students. He was a leader too. He had been organizing students' extracurricular activities. Now that they had lost elections, they wanted to show him that they were still in charge of his future. Jacob was working with the World Health Organization. They could see him riding a nice white SUV, Toyota Land Cruiser, with diplomatic number plates. He was always smartly dressed in white shirt with a black necktie. Owing to the diplomatic plates of the World Health Organization, the professors thought that he had a job in the new democratic government, especially that he was related to some people with high positions in the new government. They could see names of Karibwami, Ntaryamira, and others of the new figures who were changing things in the country.

The professors were vanquished in democratic elections, and they were losing their influence on the political system. The names of Pontien Karibwami and Cyprien Ntaryamira in Jacob's thesis brought them nuts. They kept asking why he was not in Dar El Salaam like his classmates. Jacob had to explain that he had a more worthwhile cause to devote his time to. This was happening during the time when many changes were taking place in most sectors of the administration, with Uprona members losing positions held for several decades. There was growing discontent with changes occurring at all levels of the administration. Uprona party had dominated the political and economic life of Burundi for four decades. Now, citizens who were denied their rights for centuries were taking over. Throughout the country, losers were uprising against winners. And Jacob was a winner.

By delaying Jacob's presentation, his teachers tried to prevent him from progressing further. On October 17, 1993, Jacob decided to take the matter to the chancellor of the university. For the first time in the history of the University of Burundi, the chancellor was a Democrat. Not an Evildoer. A Democrat. He was also a Hutu. As the news of Jacob's meeting with the chancellor spread and reached Dr. Njejimana, he immediately composed a panel of examiners. Jacob was sitting in the waiting room when he got informed that he was scheduled to present his thesis on October 20. He ran to the faculty of arts and social sciences to check his name on the notice board.

Although Jack wanted the presentation very badly, he found that three days were not enough to prepare an excellent presentation. Students were usually given a two-week notice to prepare the presentation. Jack was the first student to be scheduled with a three-day notice, and he still had a lot of work ahead. He needed to proofread the work and make an errata sheet. His suit was still at the Taylor, and it would not be ready in three days. His family lived in Gitega, and he could not make them come to Bujumbura in two days. He had not even invited anybody to support him. In short, he was ready and was unlikely that he could give a good presentation. Still, he could not tell the panel that he needed more time, especially after all the trouble he went through.

Jacob decided to take it easy and perform as well as he could. As he did not have his suit ready in time, he borrowed one from Honorable Pierre Barusasiyeko. As member of parliament, he had several smart suits. He lent him one of his brand-new suits. The problem of suit being solved, Jacob focused on organizing the presentation. He informed Pontien who signed him a big check. Sylvana Ntaryamira provided transportation and refreshments. On the eve of the presentation, everything was in good order as far as the presentation was concerned.

Jacob knew that his work was not perfect. On the other hand, the selected panel did not have enough time to go through the entire work. Jacob also believed that none of the members of the panel mastered the topic on the American Experience with Civil Disobedience and the Transcendentalist Movement. They were not given enough time to do research on the topic. Thus, he expected that they would be impressed with his findings.

The day finally arrived. During the presentation, Jacob was confident and emphasized on his strong points. In his view, he gave a wonderful presentation. He eloquently answered a series of questions and it was over. The president of the panel, Dr. Marius Rurahenye, stood up and proclaimed him "Bachelor of Arts" with distinction. All members of the panel shook his hand and congratulated him. Friends and relatives wholeheartedly congratulated him for the great achievement. Soon after the ceremony, Jacob and his visitors headed to the graduation party at SOS Children's Village in Nyakabiga III—an area of the capital city of Bujumbura, located at one block south of the university compound. The village was hosting numerous parties, including graduations. Jacob's guests included some Members of

Parliament who were his close friends, his relatives living in Bujumbura and many other university students.

That evening, a rumor started that the army was planning to operate a military coup against Pres. Melchior Ndadaye. The coup was known in the corridors of power. Since the election that took place in June of June 1993, rumors pertaining to a military coup had been circulating from person to person. They were passed from mouth to ear to such a point that, at a given time, they became an old chestnut and people did not pay any attention to them.

Ndadaye and his party had won elections and their authority was uncontested. Even the army seemed to fall in line with the will of the people. However, while losers of elections were armed with sophisticated weapons of all kinds, winners' power was resting in their pacifist organization. They counted on the support of the people.

On October 20, 1993, even the dogs on the street knew about the coup. Jack was too busy to have any ears on rumors. Like every Burundian, he knew that military coups were disasters waiting to happen. If soldiers had easily operated several coups against military dictators, they would not allow a civilian, a democrat at that, to stay as president. Soon after the function, Jack and his alter egos—namely Tharcisse Ntibarirarana and Bernard Ntahiraja—headed to the residence of Ambassador Emmanuel Gahungu in Mutanga north. They joined other friends who went to say their good-byes. Many dignitaries, including the vice president, members of parliament, and ministers were there. They went to bid farewell to the newly appointed ambassador, also a friend and companion in the struggle for democracy. Ambassador Emmanuel was preparing to leave for Moscow, Russia, the same week. Jack sat next to Cyprien Ntaryamira, then Minister of Agriculture. Everybody cheered on Jack and congratulated him for his performance at the graduation.

Although there were rumors of a military coup against democracy, it did not seem the dignitaries kept the eyes on the ball. They behaved as if there was nothing to worry about. Bernard, Tharcisse, and Jacob stayed there until midnight before they decided to go back to the campus. Jacob decided to spend that night in the campus so that he could pack his belongings and leave the university the next morning.

As Jacob got to bed, he heard detonations of heavy weapons downtown. He awakened Bernard and informed him of the detonations. As they were listening to the explosions, Tharcisse joined them. Nobody had an idea of what was going on the streets. After a while, they heard voices outside. They glanced through the window and saw groups of Evildoers gossiping about President Ndadaye. The trio of friends joined the Evildoers to hear what was going on.

One nation's loss is one group's gain. The detonations of heavy weapons at the Presidential Palace were like music to the Evildoers' ears. They were extremely happy to see that Jacob was worried. They discussed people they wished to be killed. All agreed that Pontien Karibwami should be removed. Jacob understood that the situation was not amusing at all. As he had no idea of what was happening, he stayed with them, listening to their comments. They knew that there was a military coup, and they kept abreast of things. Jacob and his friends seemed to be the only ones not to be informed of the developments. They stayed outside waiting for five o'clock to listen to the radio. In the morning, the radio did not broadcast as usual. They became more curious to know what was really happening. Later on, they turned on Radio Rwanda and heard that there was a military coup in Burundi. In the news bulletin, Radio Rwanda announced that the president was already in hands of assassins. The news came as a kick in the teeth. It confirmed that the nonviolent resistance movement was strongly quelled by the military junta. The army, which never believed in the miraculous power of the people, resorted to violence as a means of maintaining themselves on power. In the crack of dawn of October 21, 1993, Col. Jean Bikomagu commanded his troops to the Presidential Palace, determined to pull the plug on democracy. He took out his velvet glove and greeted President Ndadaye with his iron fist. Buyoya had to crack the whip to make sure the president was killed.

Soldiers danced to Bikomagu's tune. After several hours of humiliation, Bikomagu, with a face like thunder, betrayed his country and his conscience. He offered the president to an angry mob of Evildoers who mercilessly slaughtered him. Once again, they forced the country into the darkness. Ndadaye's efforts to lead the country to justice, peace, and development ended on that day. He was killed alongside with Pontien Karibwami, chairman of the parliament, and several members of the government.

More killings came on the heels of the military coup. Police and soldiers combed the country searching for Ministers, MPs, and other leaders to kill. A massacre of large scale took place soon after the assassination of democracy. All patriots who fought for democracy alongside President Ndadaye met a miserable and dramatic end. The Evildoers became too harsh to democrats. All politicians who did not run away were murdered. All high-ranking officers were coordinating military operations against democrats.

At the sunrise, the students gathered and started walking down the streets of Nyakabiga III to seek information and new developments of the military operations. Only Evildoers were kept informed on the coup. Streets were seething with people, but there was no traffic.

Later in the morning, a few private vehicles, mainly pickup trucks, combed through the city with soldiers on board. They went to residences of politicians, members of the ruling party. At that time, not a single democrat was still at home. Some were already killed. Others had run away. Only a few had so far found refuge in western embassies. At around ten in the morning, Radio Rwanda confirmed the death of the president and his cabinet.

In order to suppress opposition for good, the army slaughtered thousands of innocent civilians opposed to their misdeeds. To escape the killings, Jacob, like other survivors, ran off like a scalded cat. If the army managed to catch all intellectuals as scheduled, only a few would have survived. By killing ruthlessly, they were making sure that Evildoers could still oppress Burundians like before.

The situation left a bad taste in Jacob's mouth. He could neither eat nor drink anything for three days. In the meantime, he heard that the situation up country was worse than it was in Bujumbura. Governors of Karuzi and Gitega—namely Anglebert Sentambo, Tutsi, and Joachim Nurwakera, Hutu—were killed by Evildoers. Both of them were Jacob's friends. The army was destroying entire villages. There was no sign of life in many communes of the country. As all democrats became like cats on hot bricks, Jacob remained stuck in the university, not knowing where to go. He was not supposed to stay there after graduation. His presence there was illegal. In times of sorrows, the university was the worse place to be. Jacob was stuck in the wrong place at the wrong moment. If he waited longer, he might not survive another day. He had to get out of there as soon as possible.

The military coup opened a can of worms. Following this assassination of democracy, citizens battened the hatches. The reaction was of profound horror. Thousands of innocent civilians were killed amidst the bloodshed. Jacob started calling his friends and relatives, but no one was answering the phone. He was leaving the campus, but he got nowhere to go. Democrats were exposed to violence of all kinds. Jacob was stunned by the deaths Ndadaye, Karibwami, his brothers, and many other friends had suffered. Whenever he witnessed scenes of violence, he remembered members of his own family being stubbed with butcher knives and bayonets. He knew that something needed to be done to stop the killings. If students could kill people for no reason, could one expect a better treatment when horrible killings were happening elsewhere in the country?

Aware of the scale of violence, Jack decided to leave the university compound. He went down the streets of Nyakabiga to seek refuge. He met Salvator, his country fellow. Jacob never saw Salvator as a Tutsi; to him he was a friend and a neighbor, practically a brother. In Jack's reasoning, a friend is neither Hutu nor Tutsi, but a member of an ethnic group called friends. Salvator fed him and offered him refuge. Jack was comfortable to stay with Salvator. He was kind to him in spite of the sociopolitical situation that was turning citizens apart. Salvator was living with Evildoers. They started shadowing Jack. They did not tolerate the presence of a democrat amongst them. Finally, out of fear, Jacob decided to leave Salvator's house. He went to Camile, one of his cousins living in Bwiza. He too was living in close proximity with Evildoers, just as everyone else did. Still, Emile felt uncomfortable to accommodate his cousin. Still, even though he thought that he was on good terms with his neighbors, he feared that they might turn against him because he accommodated his cousin. When his neighbors started shadowing them, Emile thought it was because of Jack's presence. He feared his neighbors and told Jack to leave his apartment for the sake of his safety. Jack decided to flee to the mountains overlooking Bujumbura. There were few Evildoers there, and people were free from the foolishness of the army.

Once Jacob crossed Ntahangwa River, he heard soldiers shooting at runaways. He could neither continue his way nor return to Camile. Neither of the two alternatives was safe. He had to go somewhere all the same. The nearest place was Emmanuel Gahungu's house. Jacob was sure that the ambassador could not still be there. But he had to be out of the streets. Otherwise he was exposing himself. He had eaten nothing for several days, and he looked like death warmed up. He was so weak that one could knock him down with a feather. This time, he needed food. He couldn't go any farther with his stomach cramping. As he had no choice, he strode to Emmanuel's house. He did not expect to meet somebody there. He pushed on the buzzer. Alice Manirambona, Emmanuel's sister-in-law, opened the gate. As Jacob was walking to the balcony, he fainted and fell down. He tried to stand up, and he fell down again. Now he was unbalanced by hunger, not fear. He was not terrified that Evildoers might catch him there. Alice helped him with a cup of milk and food. As he ate, she explained that Emmanuel had found asylum in the German Embassy. Jacob had no idea of where else to go, and the sun was setting. He watched darkness thickening, and it congealed around him. He watched military trucks going back and forth and panic threatened him. Frightened as he was, he could not even sleep. He lived only for the moment. He spent an unforgettable ghastly night, one of the worst of his life.

In the meantime, proponents of the status quo were setting the country to chaos. Hundreds of thousands of civilians were killed. The country ran out of control. While Evildoers secured their families in military camps or places for displaced persons, democrats were wandering in disarray, trying to save their lives. Lucky ones could get the chance of crossing the border to seek asylum in neighboring countries. Soldiers killed so many people that there was not a single family that did not lose at least one of their beloved ones. Some families were completely destroyed. What was worse, the survivors could not organize funerals in the chaos and many dead bodies were simply left lying on the streets. Decaying corpses were scattered throughout the country. At Emmanuel's, he heard that more friends were assassinated. Tears and blood were dropping like trees shading their leaves in autumn.

The worst was still yet to come. In the beginning, soldiers were selecting their victims. Only eminent leaders and businesspeople were killed. It was a selective genocide as the Evildoers targeted a category of people. Jacob called it an Intellectual Genocide. From October 1993 onward, the world witnessed what might be called the annihilation of a human species. The mopping-up operations for the destruction of Frodebu forces was to follow. Not a single member of the Frodebu party remained at liberty. Few days later, civilians joined the army in the search for pro-democracy and human rights activists. They killed randomly. Even visitors from Tanzania and Congo were killed. They arrested a great number of civilians who were subsequently tortured and killed. At the same time, civilians were assaulting democrats throughout the country, stabbing them mercilessly. Villages were bombed, schools and churches demolished or set on fire, to make sure nobody was left behind to tell the story.

2. One Night, Eight Hours of Ordeal

In times of troubles, nights are more dangerous than days. Jacob had no choice but to spend the night in the ambassador's house. Yet he could not know how safe it was to be there. It was unsafe to stay in the house of a pro-democracy activist when the army was hunting them. He was on the list of people to kill. Night was approaching, and Jacob had to spend it somewhere. He did not have a choice as it was already curfew time. The sound of military trucks going back and forth scared the hell out of him. Military cars were passing every now and then. Jacob thought that soldiers were coming to kill Ambassador Emmanuel. They would not find him there, and they would kill Jacob instead. Thus, Jacob had to find ways of hiding himself.

Like everybody, Jacob feared death. It was even worse to wait for death to come. He found impossible to remain in the house. He could not go out of the household because of the curfew. Yet during the 7:00 p.m.-7:00 a.m. curfew, soldiers had the right to shoot anybody, anytime, and anywhere without any order. Jacob was forced to wait for whatever might happen. The army was breaking into people's residences to kill democrats. A great many of them were already executed. As Jacob was pondering on what to do, another military truck stopped over, this time, right at the gate of Emmanuel's house. Jacob thought that they would kill him. He jumped up in panic and trembled in wide-eyed terror. Some deep instinct told him to crawl on his hands and knees toward a small cabin built in the backyard. It was used in the manufacturing of soaps as the family's small business. To make sure that no one would see him, Jacob had to creep on his stomach through the fence.

The cabin was so narrow that Jacob had difficulty squeezing in it. It could not provide enough room for a fully grown person to hide in. Jacob tried to squeeze in it; but could only hide his head, arms, and chest. The rest of his body was left hanging outside.

The cabin did not even have a door. Even if it did, it could not close with Jacob's feet hanging outside. If soldiers were to come to the backyard, they would easily see Jacob's body hanging out of the small cabin.

Jacob stayed in the narrow cabin for half an hour, trembling all over. One minute there seemed like eternity. When the soldiers left, he got out of the cabin and entered the house.

The situation was repeated half a dozen of times. Jacob waited for the morning impatiently. It seemed that the night lasted longer than usual. One would say one thousand nights in one.

Finally, as the dawn broke, Jacob strode to the balcony. He watched military cars going back and forth. They transported people to kill. Jacob planned to leave the city at the sunrise. He needed somewhere to go. Bujumbura could not provide safety to democrats. Everybody was wanted. Jacob thought of leaving the city, but there was nowhere to go. He decided to go up the mountains overlooking the capital city. When he was planning the rescue, he remembered the shootings of the previous day.

By chance, he had the phone number of one of his teachers at the university, Jean Chrisostome Harahagazwe, affectionately called Chris. Chris was not living far from Emmanuel's place. Jacob thought of him as the only person who would throw him a lifeline. He was honest and prominent supporter of human rights. He was secretary of the Human Right League, ITEKA. Jacob trusted him for his wisdom and his love for humanity. During conversations, he had always appreciated his interventions on behalf of justice. Chris was opposed to any act debasing human dignity. Jacob found him an extraordinary man, very different from the majority of his kinsmen. He entrusted his life to him believing that he would be in safe hands.

Jacob called Chris and explained his desperate situation. He was wandering up and down in disarray. He described the ghastliness of that night and told him he needed someone to save his bacon. He had to leave the dangerous streets of Mutanga North as soon as possible, or he would not survive another hour. He had no one else to save him from the most dangerous situation in his life. If he stayed on the streets any longer, his life would be in jeopardy. Finally, he revealed his location to Chris.

Chris did not wait to steer Jacob out of trouble. He arrived in less than five minutes. Jacob entered the car and sat on the front passenger seat. Chris drove straight to his home and introduced him to his family. Jacob would stay there for a while, the time for the chaotic situation to cool down. They had to double up because there were other visitors. In this foster family, Jacob was treated as their own child. He was weeping for his brothers and relatives killed by the army. All the while, Chris's family was on his side, trying to calm him.

On the third day, Jacob's roommate was informed of the death of some of his family members killed by Evildoers. The boy started weeping too. This time, there were two young men of different ethnic groups weeping together, in a shared room. The boys could not control their emotion. Each had lost several members of their families. The cries brought too much noise in the family, and the chaotic situation was too confusing.

After a couple of days, Chris realized that the situation was worsening. He decided to find a safer place for Jacob. He called Eugene Nindorera and told him about the situation. In the evening, Eugene came to Chris's home. Chris informed Jacob that Eugene would try to find him a safer place. He invited him to get ready to go with him. Jacob trusted Chris and Eugene. He put his life in their hands, and he would go wherever they would take him.

Eugene and Jacob left Chris's house at 6:45 p.m. In those days, everybody had to be off the streets by curfew time except people with special passes. Eugene had it. In other words, Jacob was violating the curfew. They took the Boulevard du 28 Novembre. The time was just coming up to 7:00 p.m. when they crossed Ntahangwa River, near the university compound. Three soldiers ordered the vehicle to pull out of traffic. Eugene pulled over and parked on the side of the road. One soldier was so furious when he saw Jacob's face.

"What time is it?" he asked Eugene.

"Five to seven," replied Eugene.

"The curfew means nothing to you, right?" the soldier asked.

"I have a pass to work all night long," Eugene answered, handing his pass to the officer. The latter stared at Jacob and saw that he did not look like Evildoers.

"Who is this guy with you?" he asked angrily.

"His name is Jacob, my coworker," Eugene said

"Your identity, please," the soldier ordered.

Jacob reached for his wallet and pulled out his photo identity. The officer lit a torch light to check the identity. The second soldier pulled Jacob out of the car with a finger on the trigger. Jacob tried to resist, but the soldier pulled him violently. Jacob's body was shaking all over. He resisted as he expected Eugene to speak on his behalf. Eugene himself was not in control of the angry and mad soldiers. The one who was checking their identities came forth and asked Eugene.

"Are you Eugene Nindorera?"

"Yes, I am," Eugene confirmed.

The officer turned to his colleagues and said that he recognized Eugene.

"Juvenhack, I know Eugene. Let him go."

"Eugene can go, but this guy will stay here. Look at him. How can we let him go? We need to do our job, buddy," Juvenhack said while pulling Jacob by the right arm. Jacob tried in vain to resist. The other officer objected.

"Please, Juvenhack, don't kill him. Since he is with Eugene, he might be one of ours. Let him go."

Juvenhack was so furious that he did not want to hear anything. Finally, the soldier managed to convince Juvenhack to let Jacob go. The angry Evildoer waved his head and allowed Jacob to continue his way.

Jacob breathed a sigh of relief. At least he survived that moment. He did not know what was awaiting him next. The duo still had a long way to go. From Mutanga to Kinindo, there were several groups of Evildoers looking for people to kill. As Eugene and Jacob proceeded, Eugene made sure that the incident of the kind would not happen again. At any sight of Evildoers doing a night watch, he took the nearest exit to find an alternative route. He did all he could to keep Jacob away from harm.

Evildoers were everywhere. Eugene had to drive in zigzags to avoid them. The trip from Mutanga to Kinindo would normally take no more than fifteen minutes. It was now taking almost an hour. Eugene's wife and kids were impatient to see him back. Jacob stayed in his family for several days.

During Jacob's stay there, Eugene was rarely at home. As chairman of a Human Rights League in a country where people were killing one another, he was so busy that he could hardly see his family. One morning, he came and told Jacob that the situation was getting worse, and his home could not offer him full protection. He revealed to him that even his life was in danger given the nature of his work. He informed him that he was trying to find a safe place for him. Jacob remained in standby throughout morning.

Later in the evening, Eugene gave Jacob a bunch of essential items. They entered the vehicle and drove to the French Embassy. Jacob waited in the car outside the gate while Eugene negotiated a room for him. The embassy was full and could not allow any more refugees. After fifteen minutes, Eugene came back and drove downtown. He parked at the Avenue de la Mission. They got out and headed to a residence of a family of French citizens. Eugene introduced Jacob to the family, and they welcomed him. The family led Jacob to the second floor of their house. There was a large empty room with a queen-size bed. Jacob would be staying there until the situation reverted to normal. The new foster family took care of him for almost two weeks, ensuring him that he could stay there as long as he needed.

During his stay there, the French government announced their plan to evacuate European citizens from Burundi. The announcement did not take a weight off Jacob's mind. The situation became complicated and difficult. He wondered what would happen if the foster family had to be evacuated. They would leave him in a terrible mess. He wondered if Evildoers would let him go with them. If not, he would find himself in hot water. He did not even have a passport.

As the plot thickened, he decided to paddle his own canoe. He planned how to get out of the country. One afternoon, he called Bernard who informed him that people were marching to the city. They were claiming bodies of the president and other dignitaries assassinated by the army. Jacob packed his belongings and joined the march at the Boulevard de l' Uprona, two blocks away from his hiding place. As they were marching, he met many friends. They informed him that roads were open to the traffic. As the march reached downtown, Jacob hastened to go to the bank to cash the check that Pontien Karibwami had signed the eve of his assassination. Jacob had been hesitating to take it to the bank for fear that he would be killed. Friends convinced him that there should be no problem to cash it. Finally, he took it to the bank.

At the bank, a cashier took it to the supervisor, who, in turn, brought it to the manager. Eventually, the cashier came back and dispensed money. Jacob took a cab to the bus stop to check if there would be a bus going to Nyanza-Lac, near the south border between Burundi and Tanzania. Fortunately, there was one. To his great disappointment, when the bus arrived in Rumonge, the bus operator made a final stop. Passengers left except Jacob who expected to be taken to Nyanza-Lac as promised. The bus operator told Jacob that it was too late to go to Nyanza-Lac. He lied to him just to collect his fare. Jacob was obliged to exit the bus though he had nowhere to go. Not only it was his first visit to Rumonge, he didn't even know anybody out there. He wondered how to spend the night on a strange land. He had no idea of the political situation there. He thought that people were killing one another like in other parts of the country.

He entered an open shop and introduced himself to the shopkeeper. The shopkeeper confirmed that there would be no bus at that time of the day. It was at the sun set when the trip to Nyanza-Lac would take several hours. Jacob had to wait until the next morning. He could not spend the night in a hotel when he was hiding from the army and police. Justin, one of the customers, heard the story and felt sorry for Jacob.

"I wish I could help you, but I live a bit far from here. You can spend the night in my family if you don't mind. I don't wish to leave you here when you don't know anybody. You will catch the bus tomorrow morning."

Jacob did not know Justin but he had no choice. Any solution would do. He was comfortable to go with him. He needed anything that could save his life. Justin had a white pickup, a Toyota Stout. They boarded the pickup and rode to his home in Kizuka.

Justin was every inch a gentlemen. He made Jacob forget the troubles he had just gone through. The next morning, Jacob did not bother going to Nyanza-Lac as scheduled. The family treated him well and he felt at home. They invited him to stay with them until the situation comes back to normal. The province of Bururi was not affected by the killings that were taking place in other areas of the country. People knew that there was chaos, confusion, and trouble in Bujumbura. Still, although President Ndadaye was killed, not a single act of violence was reported in Bururi. Jacob saw no reason to rush to Tanzania anymore. He cooled down and relaxed with the new foster family.

3. Jacob's Odyssey on Tanganyika Lake

In the morning, Justin had to go to Bujumbura for business. Jacob had to stick around and wait for his return. Before departing, Justin introduced him to one of his friends who was running a small business on the main road. He invited him to take care of his visitor until his return.

The shop was on the road from Bujumbura to Rumonge, by the shore of Tanganyika Lake. There were many activities going on with fishermen dealing with their boats. There were a score of men chatting and playing some games. As Jacob expected a long stay, he introduced himself to the gentlemen. They were curious to know him. Jacob briefed them how all hell broke loose in Bujumbura. Everybody listened to him describing the ordeals he had gone through.

Something made Jacob uncomfortable though. Even though he had told them everything, they still wanted him to say more. Whenever he uttered something, they would interrupt their activities and listen carefully. No one else could speak again, which scared Jacob. It became obvious that they were mistrustful although Jacob could not understand why. As they were talking, he checked if there was any acquaintance in the neighborhood. He gave them names of some university students who lived in the region. The people knew them and told him that they had fled to Congo. Jacob wondered if he could go there too.

"How can one go to Congo from here?" he asked, eager to know an easy way to get out of hell. They kindly explained everything.

"Our boats sail across the lake. So far, we helped a bunch people to cross to safety. We charge a small amount of money, just enough to cover the cost of gas. Let us know whenever you are ready to go. We will be more than happy to take you there."

Jacob was excited to know a shorter route to asylum. He would not have to deal with Evildoers checking identity papers on the bus. Crossing the lake would be much safer.

The fishermen waited impatiently for Jacob to ask for the promised ride. Jacob was not ready to leave the country that day. He was waiting for Justin's return. Later in the afternoon, one of the fishermen kindly suggested that Jacob should take a ride in the boat. He explained how awesome the ride would be and noted that he would surely love it. Jacob found it an excellent idea, especially since he was planning to cross the lake to Congo. This ride would give him a first experience of being on water. He boarded the boat with four other gentlemen. There was no sign that this ride was a beginning of another ordeal.

There were several other boats on the lake. During the trip, the crew explained to Jacob everything about the lake. They tried to make the journey enjoyable. As they were proceeding, Jacob looked back and saw another boat sailing in the same direction as theirs. The crews could communicate by signing to each other.

Jacob found it a good new experience in his life. As they were sailing around two miles from the shore, one member of the crew asked Jacob.

"Do you know how to swim?"

"I have never swum before," he replied.

"Goodness gracious! A gentleman like you that can't swim! Didn't you learn any swimming at school? What did you study, then? Criminology?" Jacob looked surprised, and his lips tightened.

"Are you going to answer me?" the man asked.

"I am sorry I didn't catch the question. Can you repeat it?" he enquired.

"What did you learn in school? Swimology? Criminology? Or just Evildoing?" he asked.

Jacob could not understand why the mood changed all of a sudden. He tried to avoid arguing with strangers, especially that it was his first experience on water. He was helpless and under their control. Whether he liked it or not, his life would depend on the fishermen. If they decided, he would be found floating on the lake a few days later. He tried to avoid the stupid questions by changing the subject.

"How often do you cross the lake?" Jacob asked.

"Listen to that. This guy wants to swim from here to Congo. He is going to teach us how to swim across the lake in ten hours. Let's go, buddy. Teach us how to swim."

"I told you that I couldn't swim," Jacob said in a weak voice.

"Let's go. I am going to teach you," the man told him.

"I don't want to swim," he said.

"Come on, buddy! You can't just board on my boat when you can't swim. I need to train you now. This is not a car on the road, man. This is a boat. You need to swim. You don't need a degree to swim. All of us can swim. We didn't even finish elementary school," the man concluded staring at Jacob. He shook his head. Jacob looked surprised by the declaration.

"I told you that I didn't know how to swim, and you convinced me to ride with you. Didn't I tell you that I had never been on the water before? This is my first experience of being on a lake."

"This guy has an attitude. How dare you speak to me like that? You dare raise voice to me, eh!"

Jacob realized that something was not quite right. He was not in a position to discuss as he was under their thumb. He apologized for a mistake he did not make.

"I am awfully sorry. I didn't mean to disrespect you. Please, forgive me."

Jacob was not in control of anything. He knew he had to dance to their tune. They had him by the short hairs. They were in control of the situation and Jacob could not escape. As every word he said was causing him problems, he drew his lips tightly across his teeth inside his mouth.

The dialogue went on. The second boat came closer to theirs with four other crewmembers on board. The four men shut the engine down and jumped to the other boat that sailed away. Jacob found himself in an embarrassing situation. He was left alone in the boat floating miles away from the shore, slowly drifting away. Terrified by the waves, he cried for help.

"Where are you going? I want to come with you . . . I am scared. Please, come back and take me out of the water!" They were already too far to hear him. Jacob could not believe it.

"Jumping Judas! What the heck is going on here?" he said to himself as the second boat disappeared from his view. He had no idea of how long the empty boat would keep floating before sinking. He thought that the wind would drive it ashore, but instead, it kept floating up and down. Jacob feared that it might keel over. It had no seat belt to hold him either. He could see big rocks in the boat. He wondered if a boat needed the heavy rocks for counter balance. He thought the rocks were used to stabilize the boat in the event of strong waves. He did not know how to use them. He was not even certain if that was the purpose of the rocks. There was nobody to ask what to do.

Jacob wondered why he was left alone. He had his heart in the mouth with the whole body shaking. There was no communication whatsoever. Even if he had a cell phone, there was no one he could call for help. Jacob knew that, even if there were somebody willing to help, the country was controlled by angry soldiers killing civilians, and their intervention would only make the situation worse. If the army or police learned that there was somebody stranded there, they would certainly intervene. For Jacob, that would not mean a rescue but drowning in the lake.

Jacob feared the army and police more than he did anybody else. Even though he was stuck in the lake, his greatest fear was that a military boat might pass by. The Evildoers would see him and mark the end of discussion. Nineteen ninety-three was not a good year for Burundian democrats who were being killed by the army of Evildoers.

Jacob had no idea that the fishermen were Evildoers. Physically, they did not look like them. He still counted on them to rescue him from the water.

Violent waves started coming and Jacob left his seat to throw himself down. He leaned against the wall and held traverses tightly. He closed his eyes and remembered the ghastliness of the night in Ambassador Emmanuel's house. He thought of the incident when Juvenhack, the soldier, pulled him out of Eugene's car. He was in hands of Evildoers, but he did not die. He did not expect the worse to happen. If Juvenhack had killed him the other night, he would not be suffering on the water. As he was thinking of dying in the water, he thought of his brothers killed in Gitega two days earlier. They were killed with bayonets and Jacob was going to drown.

The rock beside him conjured up memories of his friend Denis Begenyeza, who was killed in Gitega a few days earlier. The archbishop of Gitega, Joachim Ruhuna, had convinced him to leave his hiding place. He wanted him to participate in the campaign for peace. Denis believed in peace and wanted the violence to end. He answered the Archbishop's appeal. When he went out, he was assaulted by an angry mob of Evildoers who stabbed him with butcher knives. Red Cross crew intervened to evacuate him. They were providing first aid when another Evildoer erupted with a heavy rock and pounded him on the head. Denis died a horrible death. Jacob opened his eyes and wiped tears. He had a look at the rock beside him and thought of Denis. Hundreds of his friends were killed in the same manner.

Jacob thought of how he was going to die a stupid death. No one of his family knew what he was going through. They themselves were struggling like rats in hot bricks. If any survived, they would never know what happened to him. He looked around to see nothing but water and steam. He started praying loud:

"Oh! My Lord, where are you? I need you to rescue me from this situation. You are the only one to see what I am going through. Don't let me die. I just finished my studies, and I hoped to help my country and my family. I have been dreaming of a happy family, and all I ever wished for was to take good care of my future children. Now I am dying a miserable death. God, oh God, protect me from this situation and lead me to safety. Teach me how to swim out of this water."

As he prayed, large tears welled up, streaming down his face. He sat on the rock and clutched at the cross bars to steady himself as waves bobbled over the boat. After an hour or so, Jacob saw another boat coming toward him with several men on board.

He hoped that they were soldiers as he was planning to tell them that he was an Evildoer like them. He would lie that he was with other Evildoers, killing Democrats, and he was arrested by Democrats, who threw him in the water. The soldiers would probably believe the lie and take him out of trouble. As he was planning the naive lie, the boat was approaching. He could see that the members of the crew were not soldiers. He did not know where they were coming from. It was no more possible to make a distinction between north and south, east or west. He was completely lost. His boat was going back and forth in all directions. The waves were so violent that they did not allow him to see clearly.

When the boat approached him, he wondered if it was the one that took the crew. The boat came closer. Six of the guys jumped into Jacob's boat and sat around him. He noticed that they carried ropes and a sledgehammer. One of them sat on Jacob's left side, two in front and two others behind him. They all faced him. The sixth started the engine and the boat started moving. Jacob could not dare meet their gaze. He hung his head and wiped tears with his fingers. He could not ask what they were doing to him. One of the men finally spoke.

"How are you doing, buddy?"

Jacob hesitated a while before he could answer.

"Just fine," he said.

"I have a question for you. Are you a Burundian or a Rwandese?" he asked him.

"I am a Burundian," he replied.

There was silence. One of the men in front, the one who offered him the ride, spoke next.

"Let me put the question this way. Tell us who you are and where you come from."

Jacob gave his name and birthplace.

"I come from Bujumbura where the army is killing people. I came here because I needed a quiet place far from the dangerous zone."

The man interrupted him with another question:

"Are you a Democrat or an Evildoer?"

It was the first time Jacob encountered that taboo question. Usually, Evildoers did not need to ask. By looking at people, they already know who is who. If the fishermen could not distinguish a democrat from an Evildoer, it meant that they were not experienced killers. Evildoers never asked questions. When in doubt, they just killed. Many Evildoers were taken for democrats and killed. Jacob hoped that a smart answer would save his life. He had to make sure that he did not betray himself. He looked at them and answered the question. He thought the smile was enough to show that he trusted them. Since they clearly had doubts about him, he understood that they were not Evildoers. They had spent many hours together, and Jacob did not expect any harm from them. The man persisted, "Are you going to answer? I asked you if you were a Democrat or an Evildoer."

"Can't you see me? Look at me, and you will know who I am." He remembered that Evildoers were killing Democrats. Things might be difficult if he missed the right answer. "I am a Democrat," he said.

"Are you sure?" they asked for proof.

Jacob knew there was no frolicking there. They needed a proof in order to believe him. He told them how the entire country was on fire.

"Several members of my family and relatives were assassinated by Evildoers. Survivals are wandering in disarray, trying to heal their lives. That is why I am here."

The fishermen listened carefully as he told them that it was a jungle out there.

"The situation is dangerous, and Evildoers are out of control. I am here with you because I trust you. I am trying to leave the country to avoid being killed."

When Jacob mentioned the name of Pontien Karibwami, they felt sorry for him.

"What a pity! We knew Karibwami well. He was honest, and we trusted him. He came to Rumonge few months ago, and everybody loved him." They apologized for what was happening and decided to sail ashore.

Jacob understood that they were not Evildoers. They had mistaken him for an Evildoer planning massacres of democrats in their village.

As they sailed back, they explained to him another reason for their interest in him. In fact, a few days earlier, Radio Burundi announced that assassins of Ndadaye and his entourage were trying to leave the country. The announcement invited citizens to keep an eye on them and catch them. Following the announcement, the fishermen had been looking out for the killers. They thus assumed that Jacob might be one of the killers trying to run away. They had to make sure that they were not dealing with one of the assassins of their democracy.

"We are awfully sorry. You democrats from other parts of the country look different from us. Looking at you, we cannot tell you apart."

Jacob was a young man in his twenties fresh, from university. He was dressed in brand-new jogging clothes. He really looked different from the fishermen.

"You are lucky because the guys in the second boat came to warn us that you might not be Evildoer. Though you looked and dressed like a young military officer, you appeared to be honest."

"I am not an Evildoer," Jacob said.

"We believe you," another man said. "The men in the other boat told us how you have been speaking evil of assassins of democracy. Since you sympathized with victims of the foolishness of the Evildoers, they believed you are not an Evildoer. They invited the first crew not to harm you. That is why we had to double-check with you."

They docked the boat and all of them went ashore. They welcomed Jacob in their village and invited him to feel at home. They introduced him to their families who prepared a nice dinner for him. In the evening, they drove him back to Kizuka, Justin's village. From that moment on, Jacob realized that every situation could constitute a hazard to one's safety.

Jacob stayed in Justin's family for an entire week. Still, after this ordeal, he never went out unaccompanied. He also knew that he could not stay in the rural area forever. On November 11, he thanked the family for their hospitality and expressed his desire to leave the country once for all. Justin accompanied him to catch a bus to Nyanza-Lac. From there, he took a boat to Kigoma. Yet he still retained the fond belief that he would return home soon. He could not imagine staying the rest of his life in a refugee camp. Little did he know that the trip to Tanzania would soon prove to be a fool's errand.

On the Tanzanian soil, Burundian refugees were welcomed as guests of honor. Tanzanians hated barbarous acts of the Burundian army. They believed that all bin Adams are brothers. Jacob followed other refugees who were familiar with the country. He spent the first night in Rose Corner, a Guest House in Mwanga, one of the suburbs of Kigoma town. The owner of the Guest House, Enoce Karabagega, had been a Burundian refugee since 1972. The next day, Karabagega sent him to his family in Mwandiga where he stayed for several days during which he was treated as their own son. After a week, Jacob decided to join other students in the Welcome Home in Mwanga Majengo. Like Eugene Nindorera, Karabagega gave him everything he could need in the shelter. He even accompanied him to make sure that he was given accommodation.

The Welcome Home was like a boarding school. The place was reserved to student refugees. There were hundreds of them. Most of them had come from schools of Ruyigi and Cankuzo. Jacob was the first university student to join them. The students were assisted by the United Nations High Commissioner for Refugees. In the shelter, Jacob learned that all days were not Sundays. There was neither water nor electricity there. The refugees began a new kind of lifestyle. They learned to sleep on the ground with neither mattress nor blankets. Like other student refugees, Jacob had to chop wood and cook his own food. Although he was used to a variety of meals, he had to rely solely on maize bread with cooked beans for nourishment. Once other refugees realized that Jacob did not know how to make maize bread, they invited him to join their group, where boys would chop wood and draw water while ladies cooked meals.

While Jacob was struggling with these new eating habits, six other university students were hosted in Mwanga Lodge. These people had a foot in both camps. While in Burundi, they were democrats. Like other survivals, they left the country for their safety. On Tanzanian soil, they changed completely. They pretended to be Evildoers. They told a certain Migembe, a UNHCR agent, that it was dangerous for them to stay with Democrats in refugee camps. They lied to Migembe because they knew that he was an Evildoer. He believed them. He accommodated them in Mwanga Lodge where they lived like kings. Jacob never understood how educated people could lie about their identity. There was nothing wrong with living in the Guest House. Still, Jacob was bothered by the declarations that democrats were dangerous to their safety when no one was hunting them. When they revealed to Jacob their declarations, he was taken aback.

"Why did you have to lie about your identity? There is nothing to fear here. Killings are happening in Burundi but not in Tanzania. Refugee camps are secured by police. No one is worried about anything. Even in Burundi, only soldiers and their death squads are killing people. Democrats never killed people."

"We lied in order to get better treatment. We wanted that Migembe to believe that we are Evildoers like him," the young refugees declared.

Still, Jacob did not support them. Whenever he went to see them, they never felt comfortable. They suggested visiting other refugees instead. Jacob understood that they did not want Migembe to see that they were in touch with other refugees as he might start mistrusting them and send them to stay with them in the camp. The situation in the refugee camp did not bother Jacob at all. He told his friends that he was happy to share his experiences with other students. Then he asked them.

"When you will return to Burundi, will you join the Evildoers?"

"No way. We will become democrats again. We are not involved in the Evildoers. Our opinions and ways of thinking remained the same," they said.

Still, they did not wish to be with him. And Jacob decided to leave them alone. He spent his spare time at Rose Corner Guest House, where he could meet other Burundian intellectuals on their way to Dar El Salaam. He met Daniel Bacinoni, who had helped him to obtain the job with the World Health Organization a few months earlier. Another day, he met Innocent Nimpagaritse, otherwise Usumbura, his former French teacher in Mugera Seminary. Both Daniel and Innocent gave him some money that helped him to purchase some commodities.

Other university students and intellectuals were scattered throughout the city. Some were living in families whilst others had rented places to stay while waiting for better times to return home. Isidore Minani returned to Makamba too early believing that he was needed to help rebuild the country. He was shot dead as he was parking his car after a long day of work. Many other new refugees decided to move to Dar El Salaam while others went much farther. Anicet Niyonkuru came and stayed in the Burundian Consulate General to Kigoma. He introduced Jacob to the family of Charles Ndorimana, then General Consul. Jacob would now spend most of his spare time with them. Unlike the other boys, Anicet always came to see Jacob in the camp. Sometimes, he even brought other people to see how refugees were living.

4. Jacob's New Exodus, Another Ordeal

Several months later, Cyprien Ntaryamira was elected the new president of Burundi. Jacob was still waiting for a moment of respite to return home. He needed his diploma and record cards from the university. He needed the proof of his education, just in case. He returned to Bujumbura and stayed with his friend Augustin Ngendakuriyo in Cyprien's house. However, as the president sent two soldiers to protect his house and relatives living in there, Jacob could not sleep in a house secured by soldiers. He found it hard to trust Evildoers who killed the former president and his ministers. Inside the country, they were still killing people in great numbers. If thousands of soldiers did not protect the president, could the two corporals protect simple citizens like Augustin and Jacob? Jacob hated having to be protected by killers. He knew that it was calm before the storm in a country where things could chop and change. He decided to stay away from Evildoers.

One morning, Jacob went to see Caritas Igirukwayo working in the American Cultural Center of Bujumbura. Caritas knew that Jacob had no safe place for residence or refuge. She supported him morally as well as financially. She offered him refuge in her family and reassured him that even though her husband was a soldier, he was a nice person. He would be happy to hide Jacob.

They talked about how their communities in Gitega were turned apart. In the confusion that followed the assassination of leaders of democracy, their brothers were killed. They felt sorry for what happened but were helpless to do anything about it. Both Jacob and Caritas believed that every human being was created in the image of God. Therefore, Hutus and Tutsis were brothers. When Jacob saw a human being, he only saw an image of God. Jacob and Caritas knew each other since childhood. Their families were in good terms. Salvator, her brother, had hidden him in Nyakabiga.

Although Caritas offered Jacob protection in her house, he was hesitant to accept it, knowing that he needed a safer place for concealment. Seeing how soldiers were terrorizing pro-democracy activists, Jacob doubted if it was a good idea to seek protection in a soldier's house. Many hundreds of thousands of citizens were already killed by the army. The same army had killed members of his family. They sought to kill him too. How could he throw himself in their hands? Even if Caritas's husband was a nice person, would he really accept to hide a democrat in his house? Even if he did, would Jacob trust him? What would other soldiers say if they saw him there? They would treat their colleague as a traitor. Jacob thought about it and decided to stay away from soldiers. If he had to die, he would die with other innocent civilians. He told Caritas that he would rather seek protection with a foreign army.

As Jacob could not stay in Bujumbura, he moved to Kivoga, where he could teach in high school. There were no militaries moving back and forth as in Bujumbura. He took a bicycle and rode through the coffee plantation, arriving in Kivoga late in the evening. To his great disappointment, the school was empty. Teachers and students were on the move. They were hiding in banana plantations on top of the mountain overlooking Kivoga. Jacob walked silently around the deserted school wondering where to go from there. He could neither stay in the empty school nor go back to Bujumbura. He did not know why the school was empty. He had only one choice—to follow the teachers and students up the hills.

Half a mile away, there was a group of people watching him. They observed his movements as he walked through the footpath leading to the mountains. Jacob saw them and walked toward them. As he was approaching them, they commanded him to halt. They ordered him to drop his luggage down and move on his knees with hands up. Jacob complied with the order. One of them opened the baggage and checked all items in the bag one by one, making sure that he had no weapons. As nothing dangerous was found in his possession, they let him introduce himself.

"Tell us who you are and what you are doing here," they ordered.

"I am new here. I was hired as teacher in Kivoga High School. I had been here before, and the school authorities were expecting me. When I got there, it was empty. I need to join the others." They assigned one boy to lead him to Matyazo where teachers and students were hiding.

In Matyazo, teachers and students were scattered in small groups. Jacob recognized most of the teachers. The majority of them were new hire fresh from the same university. They were sitting under banana trees, listening to detonations of grenades, and other heavy weapons in Bujumbura. All of them spent the night in the banana plantation of Matyazo.

As the army was firing rockets into Kamenge and Kinama, many more people were fleeing to the mountains. Shootings were also reported in Carama, just half a mile from Kivoga. Soldiers were following and shooting at runaway civilians. From Kamenge, they could shoot in villages surrounding the city.

In the morning, Jacob decided to go as far as he could. He wanted to leave the country once for all. He joined a group of other fugitives who seemed to know the area well. They bunched together and walked a long way to Musigati, miles away from Bujumbura. After a twelve-hour walk, they arrived in Musigati dead tired with perspiration streaming all over the body. The parish priest, Serapion Bambonanire, kindly offered them refuge in some of the parish buildings. Some of the students could not move any farther. Evelyn Maniragaba, the youngest student, was exhausted by the march through swampy valleys and mountains. She could not afford another five-day walk. After one night in Musigati, some fugitives informed the priest of their desire to move to Rwanda, upon which he showed them a map of the route. The road would be very long. The parish priest offered them a ride in his pickup truck. After driving for many miles, he dropped them and showed them the way to Cibitoke and he turned back.

The fugitives continued their exodus on foot. They made their way through forests, mountains, and valleys, trying to avoid military barracks. In order to cross the treeless land, they had to wait for nighttime as the darkness would help them cross incognito. They cut across the Kibira natural reserve and headed to Cibitoke. There were always people ready to help them by offering food and a place for rest. During the night, they placed them in concealment. In the morning, they showed them footpaths leading to neighboring forests, where other villagers would take over as their guides. They always assigned somebody known in the area to show them the way, just to make sure they would not fall in hands of assassins. The travelers were thus neither hungry nor thirsty as village people offered food as a sign of solidarity.

In Cibitoke, they had difficulty crossing the border to Rwanda. Rwandese people took them for rebels invading their country. They accused their conductor as helping enemies of Rwanda to enter their country and threatened to kill him if rebels attacked their country. The conductor himself did not know Jacob and the other fugitives. All he knew was that they were Burundians seeking refuge in Rwanda. At the time, Rwandese refugees too had been infiltrating Rwanda from neighboring countries, including Burundi. The Rwandese Patriotic Front was in war with Rwanda government since 1990 and had killed countless innocent people. If Jacob were arrested inside Rwanda and taken for member of the RPF, no one could predict what might happen.

Undertaking such a dangerous trip into Rwanda was hazardous. Thus, the refugees were moving in small groups of two or three. Jacob's conductor advised him to turn back so as not to get into more trouble. Thus, Jacob went back the way he had come. He crashed out at a friend's place in Mugina and waited the next day to continue his journey. His other travel companions were familiar with the region and joined their families. Others still decided to go to Rwanda because they knew how to get there without any problem. Jacob found himself lost in the wide mountains of Cibitoke, in the Northwest Territory, without any idea of what to do. Once he learned that there were no more shootings in Bujumbura, he decided to return there. However, all places he knew were deserted. Survivors of his friends and relatives had fled the country.

At that time, survivors of the holocaust were planning to resist the army. They would stop them from killing citizens. Citizens feared that the army would commit more crimes in order to annihilate democracy for good. Unable to protect citizens from the brutality of the army, young men took action to counteract the military activities that aimed at shedding more blood. By resisting the army, the freedom fighters defended democracy as their only hope for survival. At different occasions, they blocked Evildoers from wiping out villages.

Evildoers were more than determined to annihilate democrats once for all. They crossed the sword with resisters. These young patriots were not well trained to fight a powerful army. They could only organize self-defense. By resisting the rebellious army, these unorganized young boys created a new rebellion fighting for their survival. They started attacking military trucks. The army would retaliate with more violence by killing thousands of democrats. Jacob managed to escape from the danger. For several months, he sought asylum in areas controlled by resisters.

Although he was near the border between Burundi, Rwanda, and Congo, he never thought of going to Congo. Instead, he decided to cross the country from the Northwest Territory to the south and eventually managed to cross the border to Tanzania. The UNHCR, Kigoma branch, sent him to Mtabila Refugee Settlement in Kasulu District. Tens of thousands of Burundian refugees were already settled there.

They were given hoes, machetes, blankets, and plastic sheets. Refugees had to build their small grass huts and cover them with plastic sheets.

As a young gentleman, fresh from university, Jacob did not like to live in the savanna. He got a plot number and a plastic sheet to build his grass hut. But there were too many problems to solve. The plot was full of grass, and it would take a whole day to clear the path leading there. Jacob also needed wood to build his hut. There was not water around. He had to walk half a mile to fetch water and carry a bucket of twenty liters on his head. Then, he had to walk three miles to cut wood to build his hut. Again, he would carry it on his head. But how could he build his hut without nails? It would collapse. He was given a hoe to till the soil, but it had no handle. Jacob considered the extent of work awaiting him and decided not to do it at all. He would sleep on the grass and cover himself with the plastic sheet. He sat down and remembered Dickson closing his books as a way of showing him that schools were not built for children like him. Dickson's words echoed in his brain.

Go to the village. There are jobs that suit you. You are good at tilling the soil, cleaning latrines and chopping the wood.

In spite of the situation, Jacob refused to believe that Dickson was right. At least he had seen that people like him had won elections, and they could lead the country. That was the first victory. Even if they were killed, it would be an honor for his tribe. Although he was struggling for survival, he still hoped that things would change. He would not live in the savanna all his life. He would rather die than living that kind of life. He quit everything and joined other boys of his age. No one liked the kind of life they were destined to live. They started complaining about the situation. Jacob told them that he would never support it.

"If we stay here for an entire year, we will be done forever." Another boy supported him.

"I entirely agree with you. What can we do then? If we go back home, the Evildoers will kill us. Still, this is worse than death. What did we do to deserve this hell of life?"

The boys decided not to stay there. They sold all the items they received on arrival and went back to Kigoma town even though it was illegal for refugees to stay in town. Asylum seekers were bulldozed into living in refugee camps established in savannas and forests. Police could arrest any person suspected to be a refugee and lock them up. In Kigoma, Jacob lived like in Burundi. He had to hide from police. Knowing that he could not survive without any assistance, he reported to UNHCR as a new refugee. This time, they sent him to Kirwa, another refugee settlement in Tabora Province. Once in Kirwa, the game was over. Life was worse than in Mtabila. Refugees lived a real miserable existence. Jacob never believed that he could survive a year there. The living conditions were unbearable. Refugees were living the worst lifestyle one can imagine on any planet. Hundreds of people were dying of diseases every single day. Jacob looked at the refugees who had been living there since the genocide of 1972. They were living in desperate situation for over twenty years. Jacob could not understand that there could be human beings living that kind of life. He would rather die.

Life was also boring. There was not a single book to read. One could not even think of a newspaper. In 1994, those people had never heard about television. When Jacob spoke about it, they asked if it was an animal or a tree, for they knew of nothing else. Zebras and panthers were their neighbors. There were hundreds of animal species. Jacob spent days moping around as there was neither work nor entertainment. The only activity available was sitting down, watching the grass grow.

Jacob tried different ways to turn back to Kigoma but transport was hard to come by. Worse still, he did not have much to sell in order to pay for a bus ticket. Still, even with a ticket, leaving the camp without a pass would be another headache. That was not a big deal though. He was used to more trouble anyway. The only issue was to find the fare. He could not ride for free, especially given that he was a refugee without papers. He searched every nook and cranny only to find nothing. He knew that there was only one truck going to Tabora once a week. If one missed it on Wednesday, one would have to wait another week to try a second chance. Luckily, trucks in Tanzania were never full. Passengers could stand anywhere except on the tires.

Jacob explored all avenues to find a fare to Kigoma. Finally, he managed to sell the remains of his food and some other items. He collected some money, just enough to get to Kigoma. On April 6, 1994, he took the truck to Tabora. He squeezed among other passengers with bicycles, goats, cocks, and luggage. He did not care too much, for comfort was the least of his worries.

Tabora was more dangerous than Kigoma. In the town, everybody spoke Kiswahili, the national language unfamiliar to Jacob. Jacob could speak it with an accent. If police heard him speaking Kiswahili, they would notice that he was not a Tanzanian, and they would send him to jail. So he took precautions to remain silent. When somebody asked him a question, he would answer with gestures. He could not eat in restaurants as he would have to place orders. He tried to avoid public places. In the evening, he took a train to Kigoma. This time, he did not report to the UNHCR. He stayed with a family of a Tanzanian citizen, Kapata Ntaho.

Even though Jacob found accommodation, he could not find a job when he was living in hiding. After a few months, he saw no reason to stay there. Lifestyle was really different from what he was used to. He found life very hard. He would rather be struggling with life on his motherland. He decided to return home in spite of violence.

5. The Homecoming Nightmare

Jacob arrived in Kamenge late in the afternoon. There was no sign of life. The few people he met were on the move. Kamenge looked different from the suburb he had seen before. There were only ruins of what had once been a busy suburb. Jacob walked silently through the ruins, checking the address of his old friends, the ones

he was living with. Their house was burnt to the ground. He wondered if his friends
were burnt inside. He walked on the ashes to look for any signs of human remains.
He could see some ribs. He walked around to inquire about his friends. None of the
other houses was occupied as they were destroyed as well. Kamenge was eerily silent.
There was an old woman watching him through the ruins. Jacob wondered where she
lived when no house was still standing. He joined the woman and told her his story.

"I just arrive here, and I am very tired. I have nowhere to go. Do you know of a
place I can pad down tonight? I am really in a terrible mess."

"My son, you want to sleep here? Do you know how many people were killed
here? Soldiers come every day to kill people. If you stay here longer, you will be cut
to pieces. This country is rotten . . . It stinks. Look over there."

She pointed at a human body still bleeding. Jacob turned and walked away.
He could not go back to Tanzania at that time of the day. The border was too far
from Bujumbura. He took a bus to Gatumba, near the border between Burundi
and Congo. He did not know if he would be able to cross the border without a
passport. A passenger gave him a hint. He suggested buying a loaf of bread to give
to a Congolese soldier who would help him at the Custom Office. Jacob bought two
loaves of bread, one for himself, and another for a Congolese soldier or Immigration
Officer as advised.

At the Customs, an officer searched his pockets to see if he had money. Congolese
soldiers searched everybody's pockets. However, due to the ongoing crises, Jacob had
learnt how to hide money. Like other men, he kept it in his socks. With money in the
shoes, they could run as fast as they could without fear of losing it. Money hidden
inside one's shoes was safer than it would be anywhere else.

Women hid precious objects in their slips or in the brassieres. Napkins and
children's diapers provided more security than anything else did. All other places
were searched. Because towns had become no go places, people kept their money on
them, making sure to keep a small amount in their pockets. They knew that Customs
Officers would find it easily and most likely stop checking other hiding places. They
would then let the traveler cross the border without any traveling document. As Jacob
did not show any money, he bribed a Congolese soldier with a loaf of bread, and he
helped him to cross the border.

On the Congolese soil, he took a bus to Uvira. He knew nothing of Uvira though.
When he arrived there, Jacob did not even know that he was already in Uvira as he
expected a city as big as Bujumbura. When all passengers got out, he did not know
what to do. The bus driver noticed that he was bewildered. He asked him if he knew
where he was going. Jacob asked if there was a refugee camp anywhere around there.
The bus driver showed him a church and said that they might be able to help him.
Jacob went to the church and introduced himself. There was some kind of boarding
school, more like a seminary. He was welcomed to stay there. They gave him a bed
in the dormitory, and he spent the night there.

In the morning, Jacob went downtown Uvira, knowing that there were many Burundian refugees as was the case in Tanzania. They had rented places. Jacob walked down the streets, and was surprised to meet Nikita Chissocco whom he hadn't seen for ten years. She was a refugee there, and she welcomed him to stay in the apartment she was sharing with her boyfriend. Jacob found it awkward to stay with a couple in a one-bedroom apartment, especially since he did not know her boyfriend. He thus declined politely and asked her if she could direct him to any of their country fellows instead. She knew there were many refugees, but she did not know where they lived. She directed him to a place she used to see them playing cards. Jacob met some of his country fellows and stayed a few days with them. Life was very hard. He barely had anything to eat. Hunger became another enemy.

Few days later, Jacob learned that Kivoga Secondary School was reopening. He decided to return there. He was penniless, and he needed money to survive. As he could only afford a ticket from Uvira to Bujumbura, he took a bus without any idea as how to reach Kivoga. In Burundi, passengers did not have to pay before they boarded the bus and could wait until they reached the destination. Thus, Jacob planned to catch a bus from Bujumbura to Muzinda. Once in Muzinda, he would pretend that his money was stolen. The bus operator could do anything he wanted. At least Jacob would get where he wanted to be. He was not sure if the lie would save him. He knew that it might not be easy for him to lie. All the same, he decided to try it. If the lie worked, he would do the rest of the trip on foot.

Jacob arrived in Bujumbura and headed to the bus station. As he was rushing to catch the bus to Muzinda, he saw a white Toyota truck that looked like the one of Kivoga Secondary School. He checked if by chance it could be the one.

"Oh Lord!" He made a sign of cross. "What a coincidence! I cannot believe my eyes. This is a miracle!"

He approached the truck to make sure that he was not dreaming. He looked at the man sitting behind the wheel. It was Dr. Uzziel Habingabwa, headmaster of Kivoga Secondary School. He gave him a warm greeting.

"Good morning, sir," he offered his hand to shake.

"Good morning, Jacob. It is marvelous to see you again. Welcome back. We really missed you," Dr. Habingabwa said. He was happy to get one more teacher for his school. Others were still in hiding. Jacob was much happier to find a place to live. That was the only place he could go to. He boarded the truck to Kivoga where he stayed a year and half as high school teacher. At that time, Kivoga was quiet when heavy fighting between Evildoers and democracy fighters was reported elsewhere in Bujumbura and Bubanza Provinces. Though other provinces seemed to be calm, it was hazardous to move from one place to another.

Public transport was very dangerous. At military checkpoints, soldiers sorted out passengers according to their ethnic background. They ordered democrats out of the buses, and bus operators would leave without their passengers. The selected passengers were held for several hours. They were then herd onto military trucks that offered them the last ride of their lives. Others were ousted of the bus and executed right away, whereby military trucks would serve to evacuate dead bodies. Soldiers could bury the victims around the checkpoints. People killed away from the checkpoints could be left in the bush to decay. For this reason, citizens feared to use public transport.

Private transport could not offer full safety either. Vehicles were ordered to stop at every checkpoint. There were so many military barracks that not a single driver could avoid them. Soldiers checked passengers' documents and luggage. They could arrest and kill anybody they wanted to and many did so for no reason.

Few months later, rebels too started controlling traffic. They had their barracks not far from the Evildoers' checkpoints. Curiously enough, both groups respected each other. Like governmental troops, rebels ordered vehicles to pull out, and they checked passengers. Men suspected of being soldiers were taken out. Unlike the Evildoers, the rebels did not always select passengers for questioning. They needed money, food, clothes, and other items. After looting passengers' belongings, the rebels would let them proceed. Aware of the danger, Jacob did not venture to go anywhere else. He did not see his family for a year-and-a-half. Even small trips could be fatal.

On day, in March of 1995, Jacob had an afternoon off, and he needed to relax. His colleagues were busy, and he decided not to mooch about the whole afternoon. He saw a vehicle parked in front of the residence of the headmaster. Although he knew that the visitor was from Bujumbura, he did not know who he was or what he was doing in their school. It was none of his business anyway. All he needed was a ride from Kivoga to Bujumbura. He decided not to wait for the ride as he was not sure if the visitor would leave soon. Jacob needed enough time before he was due back in the evening. He decided to walk more than a mile through the coffee plantation to catch a bus. On his way to the road, a vehicle came from behind. The visitor was returning to Bujumbura. Jacob hitchhiked, and the man behind the wheel pushed the brake down. He rolled the window down to listen to Jacob. Jacob greeted him and asked if he could be kind enough to give him a ride. The man kindly agreed. As Jacob entered the car, he noticed a sudden change in the man's face. He asked Jacob if he had recognized him, to which Jacob replied in the negative. Thus, without any introduction, they proceeded to Bujumbura.

During the ride, neither one was comfortable. It looked as if they feared each other. Jacob felt unsafe. He wondered how, in March of 1995, an Evildoer dared to drive alone through the coffee plantation, an area controlled by democracy fighters. As this was not happening very often, Jacob thought that the man had to be somebody really important. A simple civilian could not dare undertake such a trip.

Jacob looked around, checking if the man had a gun. He did not see any. He looked at the backseat to check if there was any other military equipment. He could see a jacket. Jacob thought there might be a gun underneath the Jacket. He wondered if the man would let him out of the vehicle in Kinama. Kinama and Kamenge were the only places a democrat could visit. The rest of the city was dominated by Evildoers. Nobody who entered that land ever returned. Jacob did not stop wondering how he would get out of that hell of car. By now, he was certain that the Evildoer would not stop in Kinama to let him out. The place had become dangerous even for the assassins of democracy. There were always fighting between rebels and Evildoers.

Jacob feared that the man would drive straight to Evildoer-controlled zones while the officer probably feared that Jacob was a member of the armed groups fighting the army. Still, Jacob hesitated to tell him that he was going to Kamenge or Kinama. He regretted the ride. The information would raise more tensions. The revelation could be dangerous as the soldier would know that he was not an Evildoer like him. Soldiers were killing anybody from Kinama and Kamenge. They were accused of collaborating with democracy and freedom fighters.

Jacob planned what to do in case the soldier decided not to let him out of the vehicle in Kinama suburb. He swore not to let himself being taken to Evildoer controlled zones. Cibitoke and Ngagara were as dangerous as other areas dominated by Evildoers. There was a serious problem, yet none of them could talk about it.

Finally, Jacob came up with a decision. He would get off at the military barrack before entering Kinama. The vehicle would stop at the checkpoint, and Jacob would get out. It was far from the eyes of freedom fighters occupying Kinama. Then he would walk to Kinama without anybody suspecting that he was riding with their bitter enemy. At that time, soldiers were not killing people. They were only checking identities, and they could let passersby free to proceed. The road remained closed all the time. All vehicles and passengers had to be checked. Then, the soldiers could open for vehicles to proceed. In Jacob's reasoning, the car would stop at the checkpoint like others, and he would simply get out. As he was planning his rescue, the vehicle was already approaching the checkpoint. He had taken it for granted that every single vehicle must stop. He did not know yet how stupid his plan was.

As they approached the checkpoint, the man behind the wheel kept accelerating. Jacob wondered if he would go through the barricades. The place was so quiet that one could hear the sound of a car from three miles away. The soldiers saw the car and rushed to open the road. They stood along the road and greeted him in a military way. The man only responded with a nod and kept his foot on the accelerating pedal. Jacob looked in the mirror and saw the soldiers putting the barricades back. He understood that the man was not a simple soldier. He was an officer of high rank.

As his first plan failed, he had no other choice but to get out in Kinama. There, he would deal with his own people rather than being burnt or cut into pieces. He asked to be dropped off at a place commonly known as Main-d-oeuvre. All knew the place to be the stronghold for rebels fighting for democracy. If he passed that place, Jacob would find himself in Cibitoke or Ngagara, which would not be pleasant at all. He knew that the soldier might not stop, in which case he would pull the hand brake to force the vehicle to a complete halt. He was not even sure if it would work that way. The hand brake might not be in good condition when the vehicle itself looked very old. It was not certain that the park brake was still working.

Jacob wondered if he would be able to fight the officer if he refused to let him out of the car. Soldiers were trained for physical attack when Jacob had always been a peaceful person. He knew that soldiers had been killing people for forty years. They knew many techniques to put somebody out of harm. He had no military training whatsoever. He was not sure of how to defeat an armed military officer who had much bigger muscles than he did. He surely had a gun and a bayonet. If Jacob tried to force him to stop, the success would be unlikely. By the time he would be struggling with the hand brake and the wheel, they would have reached Cibitoke. In his paranoia, Jacob was thinking of fighting even though the soldier did nothing to hurt him. The problem was that he did not trust soldiers with their animosity. Finally, it dawned on him that, if the soldier were to harm him, he would have dropped him at the military checkpoint and handed him to the corporals to deal with him. Because he did not do it, Jacob hoped that he might not seek to hurt him after all. They reached the place Main-d-oeuvre place.

"Can you drop him off here?" Jacob implored. The man looked surprised.

"Here? . . . Why didn't you tell me that you were coming here?" he asked.

"Can you drop me off, please? This is my final destination," Jacob repeated.

The officer immediately put his foot on the brake pedal and made a complete stop.

"Thank you very much," Jacob waved him good-bye before exiting the vehicle. He crossed the road and walked away as the man accelerated hard to leave the dangerous spot.

Jacob knew another problem was awaiting him. At that place, there were always resisters watching soldiers. They had been fighting the army in Kamenge and Kinama. In Bujumbura of 1995, every single movement could constitute a hazard. The Freedom Fighters saw Jacob exiting the car, and soon three men were following him closely. After about a hundred meters, they commanded him to stop. He stopped and waited for them. They pulled him out for questioning.

"May I know who you are and where you are going, if you don't mind my asking?" one young man asked.

Jacob was feeling guilty for riding with an Evildoer. He knew that he would be treated as a collaborationist spying for their enemies. Usually, such people were considered as traitors, and they were treated accordingly. Knowing that the ride placed him in a terrible danger, Jacob gave a thorough explanation of the circumstances that led him to accept a ride from an enemy of their democracy.

"I am Jacob Barak. I work in Kivoga High School as teacher. I live here, and many of your friends know me. I just arrive from work."

Kivoga was not seen as a dangerous area. All knew that there was no enemy of democracy there.

"What about the man who dropped you here?" one of the combatants asked.

"Frankly speaking, I don't know him. I saw a vehicle coming from Kivoga, and I hitchhiked. I needed to get here." He paused.

"How come you accepted a ride with somebody you don't know in times of war? That Evildoer is a colonel in the army that is killing us. How did you dare ask him a ride?" another man asked. Jacob took a deep breath. He felt guilty and spoke apologetically.

"I really didn't know him. I only needed to get here as I had no other means of transport. I didn't know he was an Evildoer until I was in his car. Then it was too late."

"Didn't you fear that he could hurt you?"

"I was really scared. I got here with my heart in my mouth. To tell you the truth, I really panicked. I didn't know if he would let me out here."

"What would you do if he didn't stop?"

"Well . . ." He took another breath. "I had planned to fight him and force him to stop."

"You couldn't fight an armed soldier single handed."

"I was planning it, but I don't know how successful I would be."

As he was being interrogated, their commander joined the team with six other men. They did not ask questions. They stopped there and listened to Jacob explaining the whole story. They finally believed him. In order to prove that he was a resident of Kinama, he gave names and addresses of some Freedom Fighters living there. He lied that they had been sharing a drink the previous day. Jacob spoke about them as friends. He only knew them by names. They had arrested him once, and he paid a ransom to get released. That was the only relationship between them. When he gave their names as his friends, they understood that he was not a stranger. They let him go.

"What is your address?" the commander asked him.

"I live on 2123—6 Avenue, just five blocks from here."

The commander assigned two combatants to walk him home, allegedly to make sure that he arrived safely. In reality, he wanted to check if he was known at the address he provided. Jacob took them to a certain Evode Ndikumana, the only person he knew in Kinama. Nobody was there but his houseboy. He welcomed them in the living room and offered them drinks. From that moment, they trusted him. They started talking as friends. They exchanged their views on the situation. The boys explained that they were surprised to see him with a colonel of the army that had been killing their people. They could not imagine how somebody could cooperate with that army and yet dare come to their stronghold. They would never tolerate betrayals in their controlled zone. According to them, traitors were selling information to the enemy. Suspected ones were seriously punished.

After a couple of drinks, the boys explained to Jacob how dangerous his ride was. In fact, the situation was one of the most suspicious. They could hardly imagine how the soldier stopped in their stronghold and still left unharmed. They wanted the colonel very badly. They advised Jacob to stay away from the army if he wanted peace. They charged him two thousand francs for the mission to check his address. Once again, he learned that one simple decision could put one's life in jeopardy.

In the evening, Jacob decided to return to Kivoga. As soon as he took a ride from Kamenge, he met many people running away. Hundreds of soldiers were dispatched on the road. They arrested and terrorized any passerby. There were rumors that an officer of high rank was kidnapped by the democracy fighters. According to the news bulletin on radio Burundi, Col. Lucien Sakubu was reported missing. The news said that he was halted on the road at the place called main-d-oeuvre. Jacob thought of his ghastly trip and decided to take a circular route back to Kivoga. He arrived there with his heart in his mouth and thus decided not to go anywhere else unless it was very important.

6. Juvenhack Zim Anan and His Zero Tolerance

A few days later, Jacob went to Gitega for vacation for which he needed a pass. It was compulsory if one wanted to move from one area to another. He went to Bujumbura City Council to apply for it. On his way back to Kivoga, he took a cab. At the checkpoint of Kanka, a soldier ordered the cab to pull out. The driver made a complete stop behind barricades. Juvenhack Zim Anan pulled Jacob out of the cab. He ordered the taxi driver to leave the spot and placed Jacob under arrest. Jacob did not recognize the soldier. The soldier did not know him either. He took Jacob's identity card and started questioning him. Jacob recognized the voice as Juvenhack. He had never forgotten the day he forced him out of Eugene's vehicle. After a while, Juvenhack signaled to another soldier who was sitting in the shadow of a tree around fifty feet away. The soldier entered ruins of a house destroyed by military tanks some months earlier. He came out with four others, and all of them surrounded Jacob, who now found himself amid a group of six Evildoers questioning him. Juvenhack presented him as member of the Rwandese militia Interahamwe. Jacob denied it as he had nothing to do with the Rwandese people.

"I am not a Rwandese, and I have never been in Rwanda. I am a Burundian, and I have nothing to do with the Rwandese militia."

They had his identity, and yet they wanted him to introduce himself. They checked his accent to make sure that he was indeed Burundian. They asked who he was, where he was born, where he was going, and why he was going there. Jacob answered the questions in fluent Kirundi—their mother tongue. When he mentioned that he was visiting friends in Kivoga, they asked their names. He gave the name of William

Nikubwabo, then headmaster of Kivoga Secondary School. He answered all their questions with a smile as if he were familiar with them.

Naturally, in situations like this, Jacob spoke with a quiver in his voice. He knew that it would probably be the last of his days. He looked at two other civilians sitting on the ground with elbows on their knees, hands on the cheeks. They were waiting for their turn to be executed. Jacob feared that he would be sent to sit with them.

Bujumbura was more dangerous than ever before. From the officers of high rank to ordinary people, Evildoers were out of control. They used their power to kill anybody at anytime they wanted. They did not need orders to kill. They had a free hand to slaughter any democrat whenever they wanted. They were killing MPs and anybody who supported democracy. Everybody had to be on their guard. That time, Jacob did not quiver with fear. He kept his cool and answered their questions with a forced Duchenne smile. His smile was meant to indicate to the killers that he was honest and only desired to live his life in peace. He offered the olive branch to mean that there was no need to kill an innocent person. He was a human being like them and he had done nothing wrong to deserve death. As there was no reason to kill him, he counted on his positive valence to help him emerge from the dangerous situation. It seemed to have produced the desired effect as the soldiers were not threatening. Still, he knew that whenever they arrested somebody, the first question was about the victim's identity, whereby if one of the soldiers recognized the person, the victim had less chance to survive.

Of the six soldiers who surrounded Jacob, no one knew him, which was a sign of hope. They kept questioning him to learn about him. One of the soldiers was only staring at him without uttering a single word. Others seemed to value his opinion. They looked at him and asked, "Michel, what do you think?"

Michel simply shrugged. His name had a negative connotation in Jacob's mind. Jacob remembered a man by the name of Michel Micombero, who plunged the country into a terrible mess. Until then, Michel had a bad meaning in the country. It meant Hitler in Germany. The name of Michel was always associated with Micombero. Jacob wondered if this young Michel had anything to do with it. Michel's grimace frightened him. He thought he would be the one to stab him to death. Jacob found him a bit rude as he was only watching him from head to toes. He understood that his minutes were counted. He started shivering all over.

While Jacob was answering their questions, a minibus arrived and stopped at the checkpoint. One of the soldiers went to check the passengers. Every dog has its day. Jacob's day had not yet come. Michel, the guy who had been quiet during the interrogation, was a rough diamond. He spoke for the first time. Curiously, his intervention not only soothed but also saved Jacob. Jacob had found him rude, but he was good underneath it all. Michel turned to Jacob and asked, "Is your cab coming back?"

"I don't think so," Jacob said. He wondered how he could ask such a question when Juvenhack had ordered it out of the spot. Michel continued.

"How will you go from here without transport? Look, this bus is going to Muzinda. Why don't you catch it? It is the only chance to get out of here. If you miss this one, you may not get another one soon. You will be stuck here for a while."

As Michel was speaking, Jacob felt relief on his mind. He expected him to be as nice as a pie. He was surprisingly kind and friendly. Jacob thought that Juvenhack would oppose him; instead, he remained silent. Juvenhack showed nastiness, but he did not carry any weight. Michel was the one to call the tune. No one contradicted him. He was the one to decide whether to kill or liberate somebody. He would make it rain or shine. Jacob thought that he was dreaming. He could not believe it. He feared Michel would change his mind and order his assassination. He hastened to react to his words,

"Yes. That's a good idea. I will catch this bus." He stretched his hand to Juvenhack, who reluctantly handed his identity papers back.

The bus operator saw Michel pointing at the bus and waited. The other soldiers did not say a word. Until then, Jacob could not believe that Michel would be the one to set him free. He grabbed the identity card and waved good-bye as he ran to the bus. Another soldier opened the barricades to let the bus proceed. Still, Jacob did not believe that he was not dreaming.

Two blocks away, passengers who feared to pass to the military barrack were waiting for the bus. According to witnesses who were watching the scene from afar, Jacob was the first person to be released from hands of Juvenhack and Michel who usually had zero tolerance. Michel was notorious for his nastiness to civilians, especially democrats. He had arrested three men half an hour earlier. He himself took them to the ruins nearby and most likely executed them on the spot. People who were taken there would never return. A military truck was coming every night to load dead bodies. No one could understand how Jacob was released when others were killed.

Juvenhack Zim Anan could not blame his gun. It was said that he had a notebook in which he recorded the number of people he killed daily. He did not consider those killed by his team workers. He counted the ones he slaughtered with his own hands. At that time, he had a plan to kill two hundred people per month by himself. He would set new objectives once the first ones were reached. People feared him more than they did anybody else. He was always boasting about killing. Even in times of peace, when he checked his notepad and found that he did not kill enough in the week, he would catch up with more killings. He got mad and started shooting at every civilian around him. He could enter a full church and riddle the entire congregation with bullets. Like most Evildoers, he was loose cannon who displayed unpredictable aggression to democrats. The only difference was that Juvenhack was like a rabid dog. No one could control him. There were thousands of such Evildoers who took advantage of the chaotic situation to satisfy their desire to kill people. One could kill as it pleased them and make no bone about it. Jacob wondered if it was really the same Juvenhack who wanted to kill him in October of 1993. Most soldiers looked alike. They were so dark that one would think they were twins or brothers. Killings could comfort Evildoers in their miserable little lives.

From the day Jacob was released from the hands of Juvenhack, he decided not to pass near military checkpoints anymore. If anybody had recognized him, he probably would have undergone the same misfortune. His former classmate, Léonidas Ndikumagenge, was killed few days earlier just because an Evildoer recognized him as his neighbor. Dr. Marc Ndikumana, otherwise MAYE, and Dr. Gaspard Nzikobanyanka were arrested by Major Bizuru, their former classmate in Rutovu High School. If the Evildoer did not know them, they might not have been killed that day.

7. Dickson Rushatsihori, a Soldier as Ugly as a Sin

Jacob arrived in Kivoga and grabbed his baggage. With Lily, his coworker, he took a roundabout way to Bujumbura where he could catch a bus to Makamba. From there, they could connect to Rutana province. He went to visit Lily's family in Kayero. The situation was not bad in that part of Burundi. People there did not know what was happening in the west of the country. Friends welcomed Jacob and Lily on a balcony of a bar where they shared a drink. Jacob briefed them what he had just gone through. Eliphaz Singirankabo, education officer of Kayero Primary School, together with Philip Nderagakura, then communal administrator of Mpinga Kayove, reassured Jacob that there was nothing to worry about in Rutana insofar as security was concerned. To him, that was not reassuring news, as long as Rutana was part of Burundi. Another gentleman joined them and presented himself to Jacob as Gakiza. They went on sipping at the drink.

The conversation was quite serious when, all of a sudden, a military truck full of soldiers pulled to Kayero Center. It stopped at five meters from where Jacob and his friends were sitting. Jacob's body began to shake. In his mind, soldiers had become synonym of death. Their work was to kill democrats and Jacob was one. He wanted to run away, but Eliphaz and Philip tried to calm him. The Commander got out of the truck and moved toward them. After greeting them, he introduced himself to the communal administrator. Both men moved some steps away to talk in privacy. This coming of soldiers became another headache to Jacob. He started panicking. Eliphaz cooled him down promising that nothing would happen.

As the officer was talking to the administrator, one of the soldiers in the back of the truck recognized Jacob. Two soldiers as angry as bulls jumped down the truck and barged to the balcony. They were equipped with guns, bayonets, grenades, ropes, and hammers. They stood right in front of Jacob with their eyes wide open, glaring at him. They did not even introduce themselves. Jacob stood up to greet them, but they did not reply. He found himself in an unfortunate and uncomfortable situation. He was not prepared for that kind of visit, especially that he himself was a visitor. His whole body began to shake violently. He said to himself,

"Oh Lord! I have just arrived here and they come to kill me! How come Evildoers follow me everywhere?"

The soldiers glanced around and saw many people, Hutus, Tutsis, and Evildoers alike. There was a sudden deathly silence. They did not even apologize for badgering. After a short while, one of them asked Jacob rudely and brusquely, "What is your name?"

"My name is Jacob Barak," Jacob answered.

"I think I know you somewhere. Where are you from?" he asked, fixing him a look.

"I am from Gitega," Jacob said.

"Which area of Gitega do you come from?"

"Mwanzari," he replied.

"I say! How comes you are here now? You came to hide here, right?" he asked accusingly.

"No. I am not hiding. I just arrive here to visit relatives," Jacob responded with quiver in the voice.

"Do you have relatives living here?" the soldier looked surprised.

"Yes, I do. Some of these fellows here are my relatives."

Jacob presented Gakiza and other Evildoers chosen at random as his uncles, aunts, and cousins. The soldier gazed on the tall Evildoers presented. Obviously, they did not look like Jacob. On the contrary, they looked like the soldiers. All of them were very dark and tall, whereas Jacob was light skinned and athletic. The soldiers got confused. They did not seem to believe Jacob. Still, no one of the Evildoers introduced as his relatives contradicted Jacob although they did not know him. Gakiza himself seemed to confirm. They could not betray him in front of his in-laws to be, the communal administrator and the education officer. These gentlemen were key people in their community. Everybody respected them. More than that, there was a score of people watching the same scene. If Evildoers had offered Jacob to the soldiers, the incident would create tension in the community. The problem would make them catch hell, whether they were Hutus, Tutsis, whatever. Suddenly, their love for one another had grown stronger, and they decided to protect one another. In many areas of the country, some people who had been killing innocent civilians since 1972 were sent to the cemetery. One more time, Jacob witnessed an instant when Evildoers did not cooperate with their army to kill an innocent citizen.

Noncooperation with evil always saves lives. The soldiers waited for anybody to contradict Jacob. They looked at him and at the Evildoers around. They decided not to do anything at that moment.

Eliphaz was just sitting there helplessly, observing the scene like other onlookers. The soldier turned to Jacob and asked, "Are these your real uncles?"

Jacob gave a positive answer with more precision. This time, he pointed at the Evildoers and said who was who. They were more than twenty people, but he only presented Evildoers.

"This is my father's younger brother. This one is my aunt. These gentlemen are my cousins."

"How come they live here when your family is Gitega?"

"My parents grew up here. They moved when I was a baby."

Jacob knew they found him stupid to lie in public but he did not care. His life was so precious that he had to protect it, provided that he did not hurt anybody. He felt sorry for those who fell offended for being presented as brothers or sisters to his beloved parents. He cared about the well-being of people. He treated everybody who cared about the well-being of all people as a parent, a brother, and a sister. At the same time, he thanked the people for keeping the secret that saved his life.

As no one refuted the declarations, the soldiers took for granted that Jacob was one of theirs. They felt totally lost. The one who recognized him became like a fish out of water. He was the only one to know Jacob as a Democrat. The new revelations completely deluded him, especially that they seemed to be confirmed by the silence. He expected the Evildoers to refute Jacob's declarations. No one did. They feared that the confusing situation that would result from denying that Jacob was their nephew or cousin. Confirming that he was related to them meant that he was an Evildoer. The opposite answer would invite the soldiers to deal with him as they had been dealing with people like him. The assailant did not seem to fully believe Jacob. He knew his home place, and they had attended the same school. Jacob had never behaved like an Evildoer. In junior high school, he never attended any of the meetings of Evildoers. The soldiers wondered if they had been ill-treating one of theirs. In this case, they would have made a terrible mistake by killing his brothers. He started feeling guilty for having killed his fellow Evildoers.

A wave of confusion followed by bitterness swept over him. Yet he remained silent, not knowing what to do next. He became like a ball lost in the high weeds. When he came to Jacob, he was convinced that he was to be killed. He had negative attitude toward democrats and their families. He knew his birthplace and his family. He had also killed some people from his family. He knew that survivors were hidden somewhere in Rutana province. When he saw Jacob, he was so happy to put his hand on him. This would send a message to others who believed that they were free from Evildoers. Curiously, Evildoers were now introduced as Jacob's uncles, aunties, and cousins. His plans began to fade. He did not know what to do and how to do it.

Jacob noticed that the soldier was new to the area and didn't know anybody there. Thus, he could not check the information received. All he could do was to wonder whether to believe Jacob or not. Jacob lied on purpose. Sometimes, lies have their purpose; in this case, it was to save Jacob's life. Lying went against the grain, but he had no real choice. The lie seemed to be a magical solution to his problem. Still, Jacob checked if the false relatives would give the soldier some nonverbal sign. They remained silent, which was all he hoped for. If they had contradicted him, no one could predict what might have happened. After a long silence, the soldier asked another question.

"How far along did you come with your studies?"

By the question, Jacob understood that the soldier should be somebody who knew him well. He tried to trace his voice back to secondary school. He understood that recognizing the soldier would not help him in any way. He remembered that Evildoers hated educated citizens. As the majority of soldiers were corporals who could hardly read and write, they were jealous of civilians with degrees and often killed them shamelessly.

A little knowledge is a dangerous thing, thus uneducated soldiers were the most extreme. Jacob tried to hide his education to avoid more trouble. He gave superficial explanation, just for the record. Still, as he could not recognize his interlocutors, he wondered if it was a good idea to lie to somebody who might know him well. The soldier addressed him as somebody who really knew him.

Jacob had met many soldiers in his life. Some had seen him at the university while others saw him teaching in secondary school. There was also a military camp in Mwanzari, which made it difficult to guess where the man knew him. Finally, Jacob feigned confusion and answered, "You know . . . well . . . I am still at the university . . . Sometimes I . . . you know . . . work here and there . . ."

"Good for you," the soldier interjected. "As for me, I was not able to finish my studies," he added.

"Well, university is not the only place to gain education. What you are doing is very important to the country."

After that, Jacob ran out of conversation and asked some questions just to break the silence.

"Are you working here now? Since when have you been here?" he asked.

The soldier did not answer any of the questions. In silence, Jacob racked his brain, trying to remember him. The soldier asked again, "Do you have any news about Ronald Hakiza? He must be hiding somewhere in Bujumbura. Have you seen him recently?"

Jacob knew Ronald quite well. He was a nice person and he was a friend of his. They had been together downtown Bujumbura three days before when he introduced Nikita Chissocco as his fiancée. They were just engaged. At that time, Nikita was pregnant. Not wanting to implicate his friends, Jacob replied, "I have no idea at all. It is a long, *long* time since I last saw him."

"Do you think he is still alive?" He was curious to know.

"I haven't heard about him since war broke. I would be surprised if he is still alive." Jacob obviously knew that Ronald was still alive and working in the Finance Ministry. By telling the soldier that he might be dead, he was protecting him. The soldier would believe it and stop seeking to hurt him.

Because he asked about Ronald, Jacob understood that the guy must be somebody from the same area as him. He immediately recognized the tone of his voice. He remembered his broken tooth. In fact, he was Ronald's neighbor. He had been Jacob's classmate in primary, secondary, and high school. That was some years back, and they had not met ever since. Jacob had forgotten about him. He remembered his name,

Dickson Rushatsihori. He went by the name of Dickson. Dickson had failed high school and gone home. Jacob never knew that he had joined the army. In fact, he was not the kind of person to remember after several years. He saw him in military uniform, and he did not recognize him. Jacob only knew that his father had sent Captain Dismas Batamira with a helicopter to bomb their village. They killed almost everybody still remaining there.

Dickson and Jacob had something in common. Both of them were visitors in Rutana. When they were together in secondary school, they used to be taking the same long route on foot. There was always bad blood between them. Dickson was also considered an undisciplined and impolite student. He was nasty to everybody. Nobody liked him except hookers. There had been many conflicts between Jacob and Dickson as the latter was tough and Jacob did not tolerate him. As Dickson grew up in Mwanzari, Jacob's village, they considered themselves as friends, especially when they were still young and innocent. They traveled together with others such as Pascal Nzigirabarya, Philippe Sindayirwanya, Ambroise Cishahayo and Emmanuel Karikumutima. Philippe, too, had joined the army. Unlike Dickson, he was an officer of high rank. He met with Jacob a couple of times in streets of Bujumbura, but he never sought to hurt him. Jacob remembered how Dickson gave him hard time in high school. He would close his book to let him know that schools were not built for people like him. He usually made fun of him by saying that he would only be good at tilling the soil, cleaning latrines, and chopping wood. Dickson surely remembered everything. When he jumped from the truck, he wanted to kill Jacob because he knew him very well. Now that Dickson was lost in the confusion, he got bewildered, and he did not believe it was the same Jacob he used to treat badly.

After talking to Philip, the commander walked back to the truck. Dickson shook his head and invited his teammate to join their colleagues. He did not even wave good-bye. As he was walking away, Jacob thought that he was getting ready to shoot him. He remained standing, tongue-tied. He started counting seconds of his life, not minutes, seconds. He thought of ducking behind a pillar to hide there, but he could not find the courage for it. He leaned against it instead. His legs could not sustain him. He tried to duck out of sight, but there was nowhere to hide. He considered running away to avoid being shot, but he quickly dismissed the idea. He could not run fast enough to evade bullets. He wished the earth could open and swallow him. Without an alternative, he waited for death to come. His heart was beating fast in anticipation of the worst.

When Dickson did not shoot, Jacob assumed that he was going to request order to shoot. Instead, he went straight to the back of the truck. The truck started moving backward. As it finally pulled out of sight, Jacob heaved a deep sigh of relief and made the sign of the cross on his body. He did not accompany the sign with the Trinitarian formula. He was too frightened to speak.

Although the soldiers left the spot, Jacob was not comfortable to stay there any longer. He feared that they might get a change of heart and return there. Jacob decided to leave the place as soon as possible. He declined all offers for drink and brochettes. Dickson had spoiled his appetite, and he was feeling a bad taste in his stomach. Jacob apologized to his hosts and swore not to stay there another minute. They invited him to another location where he could feel more comfortable. He was welcomed in the living room of Blais's house. They talked about the incident, and everybody was shocked.

After two hours or so, Philip took Jacob to his family in Musotera, two miles away from Kayero center. As Jacob's mind was set on the soldiers, he asked Philip about them. He informed him that the assholes would stay in his commune for several weeks. The information left a heavy weight on Jacob's mind. As safe is always better than sorry, he took precaution not to return to Kayero center. He knew that Dickson would come back with more information on him. Jacob even feared that he would start looking for him in the host family. For safety reasons, he could not spend nights in the family. Thus, Philippe found him a place that no stranger could know.

Although Jacob tried to avoid public places, his ordeal with Dickson did not stop there. He spent the next day with Eliphaz in Kayero Primary School where he was introduced to the teaching staff including Generose, Lily's friend. After the visit, Jacob hung around with his new acquaintances. As it was getting dark, Jacob thought that it was not a bad idea to stop at Kayero center for a cup of coffee. He wanted to share a drink to his friends. He could not think that it could be dangerous to go there. He used to love skewers of grilled meat and a glass of Amstel Blonde, and he missed it. Knowing what had happened the day before, everybody reminded him of the incident and suggested that it was not a good idea to go there again. Still, Jacob really wanted to have a drink with his friends. He thought that he would be safe at that time of the day. He would only make sure the military truck was not there. As he was their guest of honor and he insisted, the friends agreed to share the drink with their host.

Just as they were about to get there, the soldiers started their truck to leave Kayero Center. Jacob saw the lights flashing in his direction. He immediately dashed off home closely followed by his friends. Fortunately, the soldiers did not see them. Had they waited a minute to turn on the ignition key, Jacob might not have seen day light again. The soldiers had the right to get rid of whomever they wanted. They did not even have to report the assassination. Everybody had to stay alert and remain on their guard.

The following day, Jacob woke up early in the morning to catch a bus back to Bujumbura. Eliezer, one of Blais's sons, heard that Jacob and Lily were waiting for transport at the bus stop. He feared that the soldiers would catch Jacob and hastened to warn him. As they talked, Eliezer informed Jacob that while he was gadding about in the school, the soldiers were looking for him. They stayed at Kayero Center all day long. The Evildoers he had presented as uncles, aunties, and other kinds of relation had eventually betrayed him. They met the soldiers and revealed that they were not related to him at all. They did not even know him. On hearing this, Dickson became angry like a bear with a sore foot.

Eliezer had a friend named Gakiza, who was a schoolteacher. He had confided to him that the soldiers wanted Jacob very badly. They were so angry and upset that they would beat him to death.

"The lies he told them yesterday drove Dickson round the bend. He was irritated more than anybody else. If he catches Jacob, only God knows what will happen," Eliezer said.

"You mean they will harm him?" Eliezer asked and Gakiza confirmed.

"Man . . . I tell you . . . if ever they put a hand on him, he is a dead man. Believe me. You won't see him again. You know what I'm saying?"

The conversation was reported to Jacob about 7:30 a.m., the time for students and teachers to go to school. Terrified by the revelations, Jacob and Lily left the bus stop and went to wait on the balcony of one of the shops, away from the road. They waited for a certain Roumanche who was supposed to be back by eight o'clock to give them a ride to Gitega. They sat there wondering if it was safe to use public transport, given that the soldiers were looking for Jacob. While they were thinking of the situation, a small boy dressed in the school uniform of khaki came running toward them. He handed a piece of paper to Lily and ran back to school. The note read:

> Dear Lily,
>
> The soldiers are looking for Jacob here at school. They are searching rooms nervously. Can you possibly keep him away from any danger? It is not a good idea to travel today as the soldiers control the traffic. I thus suggest that he cancel the trip and hide himself.
>
> Thanks for your cooperation.
>
> Generose

"Goodness gracious! Why are these Evildoers looking for me everywhere? What on earth do they want from me? They even know that I spent the day in the school. How come they know my schedule? This is ridiculous, man! What can I do now?" He sat down, pondering on what to do.

"Am I going to live all my life like this in this hell of a country? I have done nothing wrong. The soldiers want to kill me just because a stupid guy as ugly as a sin happened to be my class mate!" He fixed his look at the note. Then he shook his head.

As Jacob was pondering on the situation, he heard a truck coming to Kayero Center. He stood behind a pillar and watched it. It was the military truck. It stopped right where Jacob had been standing ten minutes earlier. If he did not leave the bus stop in time, the soldiers would have seen him. They jumped down and walked around looking in all directions, fingers on the trigger. Jacob watched them silently, his heart hammering inside his ribs. He whispered to Lily:

"Look, they already know that I was standing there. How did they know?"

"Somebody must have told them," she replied.

"Did you see Gakiza out there? I personally don't know him."

"The guy you presented as your cousin. Maybe he saw us there, and he didn't want us to see him. He probably took another path to avoid being seen," Lily whispered.

"I really don't understand this. I mean, I can't imagine why this is happening. How come they know my schedule? This is dangerous."

As the soldiers did not see Jacob, they must have thought that he was on another bus stop. They reversed to the other bus stop. From that moment on, Jacob understood that he was in serious danger. The soldiers could not see him, but they were certain that he was somewhere around there. Most likely, they would start searching the area around the bus stops. If they did, they could not miss him, and they would mark the end of the upsetting game. The truck took the exit to the center. Jacob ran to hide in the woods. He stayed there for a while to determine which direction to take.

Planning the trip from Kayero to Bujumbura on foot was unthinkable. He would go to Gitega, which was another long row to hoe. Still, to Jacob, it did not matter how long it would take to get there. He had walked from Bujumbura to Musigati before. He had crossed the provinces of Bubanza and Cibitoke on foot, having to climb steep mountains with thick forests. This time, it would only walk seventy miles to get to Gitega. Walking long distances was not an issue. The problem was finding safe footpaths. He had neither a map nor a compass to guide him. Consequently, he could not know if he was heading north, west, or south. It was his first visit in the region, and he had to avoid the road as much as he could. Soldiers controlled all the roads of the country. Still, he had to leave the province by whichever means.

The road was very long. Jean Prime Minani, Lily's brother, offered to give him a ride on a bicycle. He knew shortcuts to get to Musongati commune using muddy footpaths. They would ask other pedestrians how to get from one area to another.

The trip from Kayero to Gitega was far from pleasant due to soldiers being everywhere. Jacob met many military trucks. All of them looked alike. At the sound of any vehicle, he thought it was Dickson and his buddies chasing him. Jacob jumped from the bicycle and ran through the swamps to hide in the woods. Most of the time, he ran in muddy gardens having to cross creeks without bridges. When the vehicles passed, he turned back and proceeded on his way. He heard other vehicles coming toward him every now and then. He repeatedly erupted into residences or shops and ran away through backyards. People sitting in the yards saw him running and got scared. They ran away as well, not knowing why. From Kayero to Bukirasazi, Jacob had his heart in his mouth. He went like swimming upstream on a river.

Lily had taken a bus to Gitega to inquire about the situation. As their plans had fallen through, the soldiers followed Jacob in Gitega. Lily saw them at the bus terminal, checking every bus. She feared that Jacob might get there. Thus, she decided to turn back and wait for him in Bugumbasha, miles away from his hometown. Jacob arrived there dead tired. Lily was excited to see him coming out of the woods.

Jacob could not go to Gitega on the bicycle. There was no footpath leading there. Even if there was one, the trip would take a couple of days. He could not go to his village either. Survivors of his family were driven away from their homes. Thus, Jacob and Lily had to walk another three hours to spend the night in a remote village called Mwumba, several miles from Mwanzari.

They could not stay in that village forever. They were working in Kivoga, near Bujumbura, west of the country. They had to use public transport to get there. The route from Mwanzari to Bujumbura was short, but the most dangerous to Jacob's safety. It was controlled by soldiers of Gitega and Evildoers of Mwanzari many of whom knew him. They had killed his brothers, neighbors, and his old friends. Everybody feared to take that route.

To avoid more troubles, Jacob decided to take a circular route. The route was five times longer compared to the regular one. Like most people, Jacob had fake documents he could use to hide his real identity. He hid his identity papers in his shoes and used a fake document with different names and address. He traveled under the alias of Jean Paul Mugisha, a fisherman, not a teacher, a fisherman from Nyanza-Lac. This fake identity would make him a different person. It allowed him to catch the bus without fear of the soldiers looking for Jacob Barak. He presented the fake document on every military checkpoint, and no one bothered him. Thus, he could get to Bujumbura without any problems en route.

From the center of the country, he went to the west through the east. From Rutana, he connected to Makamba, then to Nyanza-Lac, the Deep South. When soldiers checked passengers' documents, Jean Paul was a resident of Nyanza-Lac returning home from Gitega. From there, he connected to Bujumbura. No one would bother him, as he was just a simple fisherman from Nyanza-Lac going to sell his fish in Bujumbura. When asked about the fish, he would lie that it was shipped on a truck, and he would pick it in Bujumbura. The roundabout trip consumed much more time and money, but it was safer. Traffic was controlled by soldiers operating in the south region. As Jacob was originally from Gitega, he guessed that no soldier of Bururi or Makamba would know him. That was the route he took whenever he had to go out of the city. As soon as he got to Bujumbura, he switched the identity papers and became Jacob Barak again.

Jacob hated that kind of life. The vicissitudes of life affected his dreams of childhood. The situation destroyed his self-esteem to such a point that he doubted if he was really still alive. He had no more confidence to move out and forward. He left aside his dreams of the past and set new goals to survive in spite of the chaos in the country.

Although Jacob was experiencing the hardest moments of his life, his situation was much better than that of others, most of whom were being tortured or killed. Medias were reporting a minimum of a hundred people killed daily. In secondary schools, headmasters, teachers, and students were being killed by student members of the death squads. At the university, Prof. Stanislas Ruzenza was shot dead. In the university campus of Mutanga, scores of students were killed by their schoolmates. Survivors were forced into leaving the institution without anywhere to go. They spent months panhandling on mountains overlooking Bujumbura. Few days later, they built self-confidence and assumed to be masters of their own destiny. They learned that God helped those who help themselves. Their courage and conviction to break away from the past drove them to the Kibira National Park, joining other democracy and freedom fighters.

8. Neither Dickson nor Juvenhack Was Cut Out for the Army

In secondary school, Dickson always told Jacob that Burundi was not his country, and schools were not built for people like him. He arrogantly suggested that he return to the village to till the soil. He could even destroy his books to prevent him from preparing his exams. Throughout the country, innocent people were victims of such attitude. In 1995, Evildoers were still forcing children to drop out of school. As they had nowhere else to go, they joined the fight for freedom. They would no more exchange words but bullets.

The brutality of the army called citizens to respond to violence with greater violence. In fact, physical force was the only language Evildoers could understand. This new struggle was approved as the best solution to the problems of Burundi. Citizens had to fight for their freedom in democracy. They proved to Evildoers that they were conceived and born to live and not to die. They refused to acknowledge that Evildoers had the inherent right to kill. Now that citizens were armed to fight the Evildoers, they had to do or die.

As Dickson was a son of a military officer, he was not sent to the battlefield. Juvenhak too was originally from Bururi. For that only reason, he could not go to the battlefield. Only soldiers from other provinces were sent to die on the front lines. The soldiers from Bururi were only commanding the war. As freedom fighters were determined to win the war for democracy, they attacked Evildoers in all their hiding places. They used attacks as not only the best form of self-defense but also as a way of collecting weapons. They decided to destroy the ancient political system to force Evildoers to abide with the will of the people.

Soon, governmental troops got cold feet about the war. The Evildoers, who had a false but strong belief that citizens were born to be killed, got disillusioned by the determination of youngsters fighting tooth and nail, barefoot and dressed in worn out clothing. At the battlefield, Dickson and Juvenhack were kind of chasing rainbows. They learned that the battlefield was far different from a merry-go-round. It was not a game. Their sophisticated and modern weapons and armored vehicles could not provide them with full protection. Using tanks and airplanes against civilians armed with stones, bows, and machetes, they agreed that the practice of "an eye for an eye, and a tooth for a tooth" would not only leave them toothless and blind but also deaf and handicapped. Heavy losses were reported. Dickson's father was killed while leading an assault against unarmed civilians. Many other officers died as well. The death of that Evildoer discouraged his son who had been boasting that his dad annihilated some human species in 1972. Now that the orphans of the genocide could hit back, Evildoers learned that orphans did not need heavy military equipment to defeat the enemy. Dickson remembered his statements that democrats could not run fast, that there were no boots that could fit them. He was facing peasants with no military uniform fighting barefoot and still inflicting the damage. They gave him plenty of trouble. Dickson's duty was to bury Evildoers who died in the war. When he buried his own father, he feared that his turn was coming soon. He found no reason to continue the war.

The more the movement of freedom fighters grew, the stronger they became. The army, which had a forty-year experience killing unarmed citizens, could not blame their guns. They had difficulty facing organized orphans of genocides. These inexperienced combatants recruited and trained on the battlefield were incredible. They enjoyed their baptism of fire. Within few hours of military training, they could manipulate heavy weapons taken from the enemy. They pushed the enemy away from their stronghold. These young patriots, who had almost nothing left to lose, proved to the Evildoers that they did not go to the battlefield to take a hair out of milk. They were trained to fight the enemy of peace and democracy and nothing on earth would stop them. Only the sky was the limit. Their hard-line attitude discouraged the enemy who were trained to shoot on unarmed civilians.

In addition to this commitment to the fight, another factor contributed to the extreme importance of the freedom fighters—their incredible morale. They were fighting for a cause they believed to be true—peace, justice, freedom, and democracy. If one fights for these values, nothing on earth can stop them. On the other hand, the prevailing morale of the army was terrible. Soldiers from different provinces of the country were dying for a cause they did not support. The majority of soldiers had joined the army just to earn a good living while killing civilians. The army had become a refuge for undisciplined young Evildoers who were not able to pursue their education. When fighting, they kept watching the time to go home and drink beer. It was as if they were paid by the hour. Even then, they would never accept to work over time. After heavy losses, they questioned the importance of that war.

Citizens were not afraid of war. Their obligation was not to give in but rather to defend themselves and their democracy. They were ready to die for this cause if need be. If they did not fight for their freedom, their fate would be the same as that their parents suffered. They resisted attacks and gave Evildoers plenty of trouble. Some Evildoers feared to die and quit the army. As Dickson's father was killed on the battlefield, Dickson pretended that he was sick and left the army to avoid meeting his father's fate. He soon teamed up with other troublemakers who called themselves the Sans Echecs, the biggest death squad that was terrorizing the city. He took part in terrorist activities.

Jacob heard from friends that Dickson was seen in Bujumbura training young Evildoers to terrorize citizens with weapons. Now that he was in there, Jacob feared that he might meet him, knowing that such meeting would mark the end of his life. He informed Ronald that Dickson would snap his head off if he ever saw him. It would not be difficult to put his hands on them now that he was in Bujumbura. In 1995, it was impossible to predict what might happen to anybody. Jacob advised Ronald to leave the country for his safety. He was planning to flee to Tanzania, when, all of a sudden, Nikita changed his mind. She advised him not to go anywhere. As if she was better informed than he was, she managed to convince him that the situation was improving. Ronald cancelled the plans to leave the country. He told Jacob that he was not coward to leave the country to Evildoers. Still, Ronald wanted to stay close to Nikita whom he adored, especially that she had his first boy. Jacob himself was getting ready for parenthood. He awaited the arrival of his first son with excitement. Jacob decided to send the future mother away from the city until the birth of the child. She returned a week after the birth. As soon as she arrived, Evildoers attacked their place with rockets and grenades. They had to leave and hide in banana plantations, which meant that Jacob could not see any of his friends.

A few weeks later, Ronald was shot dead. Many friends came to support Nikita in the mourning. A certain Schadrack Kubwa was among the mourners. After the funeral, Kubwa tried to comfort her. As Nikita was weeping, he held her by the shoulder and offered her a comforting hug. The magic hug gave rise to a comforting kiss. He took a handkerchief and dried tears from her eyes. They sat on a mat under a mango tree in the backyard. In the evening, as the visitors left, Nikita and Kubwa found themselves alone. Kubwa started caressing her hair mournfully, telling her comforting words. Feeling vulnerable, she let him touch her wherever he wanted. His hand reminded her of Ronald. She understood that she lost him as a human being. As a boyfriend, she would soon find somebody else. After all, Ronald was dead and she needed to move on with her life. She was only twenty-four, and she had feelings like any other young woman.

Kubwa comforted her when she was feeling desperate. She doubted that it might not be easy to find another man, given that she was widowed before marriage. Thus, Kubwa's advances were hard to refuse. Within one hour, he was stroking her private parts. He put his hand under her slip, and she stood up to allow him to roll it down. She sat naked on his lap. She felt guilty for what she was doing in the backyard during the mourning period. She feared that neighbors might come over and find them in the act.

"What will people say if they see me with another man in the mourning?" she asked. Kubwa, who was not thinking of lovemaking that day, understood Nikita's worry as an invitation to go farther. He reassured her.

"They don't have to see us. Besides, you remain the same beautiful girl in spite of Ronald's death. Your life must go on." Nikita let out a deep breath.

"I'd rather we didn't do anything in the yard. I don't feel comfortable here," she said.

"Let's go inside then," Kubwa held her hand and pulled her up. She led him to her bedroom.

After the act, Nikita looked at Kubwa and asked him, "Do you really love me?" Kubwa had never said that he loved her. Still, he could not say no when he was in her bed. Thus, he said the only thing he could, "Honey, of course I love you. That is why I am here with you."

"I love you too. Aren't you going to leave me?" she asked.

"Why should I leave you? Where else can I find such a charming woman? I will always be with you," he concluded reassuringly.

"I didn't know that I would find someone else so soon after Ronald's death. Most guys are superstitious, you know. They fear ladies whose boyfriends were killed. They think that they bring bad luck or misfortune."

"I am not superstitious. I love you and nothing will break our love," Kubwa said gently. Nikita kissed him, and they continued their lovemaking.

The new relationship grew strong and fast. Still, Nikita kept it in the dark as she would be ashamed if friends found out that she was sleeping with Kubwa that soon. Nikita and Kubwa met in special circumstances, and their love was upside down. Neither one had asked for a date. They made love, and they talked about love afterward. Even when Kubwa's passion was bursting and flooding her with his seeds, all he could do was to groan and tremble. He did not say that he loved her. He had what he wanted, and he was sure to have her as many times as he wanted.

Nikita was determined to do everything she could to ensure that he did not leave her. Thus, she decided to trick him. They went on with their affairs when she was certain that she would conceive. That strategy was used by most Burundian girls to put men in the trap. A lady could let a man impregnate her and wait several months before announcing to him that she was pregnant. If the man suspected that his partner was pregnant, she would deny it. She would only confirm when she was sure that everybody knew about it with no possibility of abortion. The father would, therefore, be obliged to marry her before the birth of the child. Burundian society did not approve of girls giving birth to children before marriage. Thus, the fathers that refused to marry them would face prison.

Parents and relatives were angry when they found out that Nikita was pregnant. She herself felt shameful, and she persuaded Kubwa to marry her. Kubwa was shocked that Ronald's death took only a few days to wear off. Nikita could not even remember that she was in mourning. Kubwa could not trust somebody that forgot her lover in one day. He reasoned that if she slept with him after the funeral of her lover she might not be a faithful woman. She could not love Ronald and still sleep with another man on the day of his funeral. Besides that, Kubwa had won her effortlessly. He had never planned to seduce her. He was only comforting her, and she allowed him to go as far as he could. He caressed her in the hope that she would jerk his hand away, in which case he would not go any farther. Instead, she encouraged him and invited him into her bed. They enjoyed as if Ronald had never existed. Kubwa was the only one to remember him. Thus, even though Nikita was pregnant, Kubwa refused to marry her. He feared the mystery surrounding Ronald's death. Finally, he decided to leave the country for his safety. Nikita followed him to Nairobi, Kenya.

9. An Unforgettable Week under Banana Leaves

Jacob and Lily spent an unforgettable week in the banana plantation of Nyabunyegeri. In June of 1995, shootings reached Muzinda, near Kivoga. Explosions of grenades were heard around the school. There was no way one could not be affected. If Jacob did not leave in time, he would be caught in a sandwich. His first son, Eddy Franklin, was two weeks old. Jacob had to keep him away from detonations of heavy weapons. He left Kivoga with his new family to seek asylum in the banana plantations of Nyabunyegeri. The road was controlled by soldiers shooting on runaway civilians. To avoid being hit by stray bullets, they followed a river bend and crossed the road from under the bridge. They joined several families hiding in the banana plantations. There were no roads leading there. If soldiers were to attack them, they would have to approach them on foot. Only women and children could sleep as men organized night watches. They could rotate every other day to allow themselves to sleep. Because Jacob had a newborn baby, he was allowed to stay with his new family. He declined the offer. It was not the time for sleep. He had to be on his guard, and he watched with others.

Eddy Franklin could not help crying. He cried days and nights. Other fugitives were not happy with Jacob whose child was crying all night long. They did not want noise in their hiding place, knowing that Evildoers would eventually hear him cry and discover the hiding place. No one wanted that to happen. During that period, people were living day by day. Nobody could make a plan for the next day.

Looking at the misery they were living in, Jacob named his first son Izodukiza, meaning *God will rescue us*. The name was not chosen at random. He hoped that the name would encourage Lily not to lose hope in times of trouble. The name was just a sign of encouragement. Jacob encouraged Lily to keep hope and not be in despair about the situation. Yet he knew that it was hard to survive the situation without the hand of God. As human beings, people were not strong enough to fight for their survival. The family left everything to God. Jacob needed to comfort his family terrified by detonations of heavy weapons. He reminded them that in a lifetime, all days are not Sundays. People would love to have only sunny days, but they have to cope with nights, clouds and rain. At least, nights allow people to rest and sleep. Clouds too are important. They give a shadow from the sun. The assassination of democracy and the killing of innocent civilians were bad lessons to the world. Jacob learned that there is nothing as dangerous to man as man himself. He still believed that God would save their lives.

Jacob had a portable radio. He carried it with him all the time. He could sit under power and phone lines and switch to Long Waves. Then, he could listen to communications between soldiers via their radios. They were communicating places to attack. One day, Jacob heard them saying that there were rebels in Kivoga coffee plantation. One officer was requesting armored vehicles to dislodge the rebels. In Burundi of that time, rebels meant democrats. The army pretended to pursue freedom fighters. On their way, they killed all they encountered. While fighting the so-called rebels, they killed expectant mothers, babies, and elders. Animals were killed as well, not to mention trees they cut down. Coffee and banana trees were destroyed. In a nutshell, they destroyed all living things.

Jacob knew that the situation would worsen. It was late in the evening, and he could not let the grass grow round his feet. He was quick on the trigger. He took action and dealt with the problem before it was too late. He had to vacate the dangerous zone. He ran to the hiding place and told Lily to get ready to leave the area in less than half an hour. As she was getting ready, Jacob went out to look for people who would escort them to Gatumba. He hired four bicycles to carry them. As soon as they left the plantation, bombs rained down on Nyabunyegeri. Several hundreds of people were killed.

Jacob and his family arrived in Gatumba after the sunset. They had to spend the night in a friend's house. As they were talking about the situation, they noticed an unusual movement of military trucks. They joined other groups of people to ask what was going on. Everybody was in the quiet before the storm. There were rumors that soldiers would attack Gatumba that night. The rumors spread throughout the town. Many people had been crossing the border to spend the night outside the country. It was too late for Jacob's family to go any farther. They were already tired of running with a baby on Lily's back and bags on Jacob's head. Jacob had used all his energy on securing his family in Kivoga and Nyabunyegeri, arriving to Gatumba without knowing that something else was horribly wrong there. He survived the killing in Nyabunyegeri to put himself into another mess.

Jacob was not coward to forget his responsibilities. Thus, he decided not to spend the night in the house. He had to continue the struggle for survival though he was exhausted. With the host family, they left home and went to hide far from Gatumba. They spent the night on the grassy land near Tanganyika Lake, close to the border. No one could sleep as mosquitoes were everywhere, all biting at the same time. They spent the night fighting the mosquitoes, scratching the bite marks all over their bodies. Apart from the mosquitoes, the night was quiet. No killings were reported as the city was deserted.

Early in the morning, Jacob swore not to spend another night exposing his family to such danger. He was hoping to move his family to Kenya, but flights were too expensive. Jacob could not afford a trip that would cost him an arm and a leg. Still, he had to move his family to safety even though there was no safe place in the country. As they could only move from one province to another, he decided to go to Gitega, his hometown. He left Gatumba like a thief at night. As usual, he took the circular route to get to the destination as Jean Paul Mugisha. Once in Gitega, he became Jacob again.

10. Good-bye, My Mom

Gitega seemed to be quiet. No more killings were being reported out there. In fact, after the assassination of most intellectuals and businessmen and women, survivors had relocated to the eastern part of the country. Others had left the country. The army controlled every inch of the province. Having lived in Burundi all his childhood, Jacob agreed with Baruch Spinoza that "peace is not an absence of war; it is a virtue, a state of mind, a disposition for benevolence, confidence, and justice." Even if Gitega seemed to be quiet, Evildoers had behaved as immoral beings. Yet Jacob would give trust a second chance.

He went to his home place, one mile from the Military Camp of Mwanzari. Only peasants, mostly old women, were returning from their hiding places. All houses were destroyed by the army and their militias. After several months living in ruins of a destroyed house, Jacob's mother had a new small house. Jacob had to make sure that there were no Evildoers around. Thus, whenever he went home to see his mother, he placed people on the road to look out for any suspicious movement. Even then, he did not feel safe to stay more than half an hour. His mom was concerned about his safety. Once again, Jacob was forced to spend days and nights far from his home place. He could spend a day in Makebuko, another one in Itaba, then in Bukirasazi or Kibuye. He could not stay two days in roll in one place.

One day, Jacob went to visit his sister in Kibuye. They decided to share a drink in the nearest lounge. There were four soldiers sitting at their chosen bar, quenching their thirst. Jacob was worried that they would notice him as he looked differently from Burundians. Besides, intellectuals and local village people were different not only physically but also in their attitude. Jacob and Lily were dressed to the nines, as usual, and all eyes were on them. They could not go unnoticed.

One of the soldiers approached them and addressed Jacob politely, which was rather unusual, given that Evildoers would typically just butt in on a conversation and never apologize for the disturbance.

"You are new here. Where are you from?" he asked Jacob.

"I am not new here. This is my home place," Jacob replied reassuringly.

"I don't think so. You are a stranger here. If you were from here, I would know you. This is the first time I see you. Can I know where you come from?" the Evildoer insisted.

"I am not a stranger, buddy. This is my birthplace. If it is the first time you see me, it is because you are the stranger, rather than me," Jacob said, not considering the implication of his words.

By ignoring the officer, it looked as if he added insult to injury. He was still mad with what had happened to him in Bujumbura and Gatumba a few days before. That is why he blurted out the words. The soldier returned to his group. Jacob started to worry, knowing that he had been rude. He wanted to apologize. He saw the officer reporting the conversation to his teammates. He remembered other troubles he had gone through and wanted to avoid yet another incident. He considered offering them beer as a sign of apology. He stood up, walked up to them, and offered a greeting,

"How are you doing? The weather is beautiful today." The corporals, however, showed no interest in talking to him. They did not even invite him to share a drink.

"We are here, just having fun," one of them replied. Rebuffed, Jacob went back to his seat.

After a while, Dominick, the bartender, went to check if the soldiers needed to order something. He came back and whispered something to Jacob's sister, to which she did not respond. Dominick asked her if she heard what she was told. She ignored him, and she kept gossiping with her sister-in-law. Soon, Jacob noticed a change of atmosphere in the bar. Everything became too quiet. Customers were leaving without finishing their drinks. Dominick kept going back and forth shaking his head. Jacob looked at him and noticed that there was something unusual. He came back and spoke to his sister again. This time, he raised his voice.

"Chantal, are you deaf? Why did you bring your brother here? Take him out of here now!"

After these words, Dominick exited the bar through the back door. Chantal did not pay any attention. Instead, she started to argue.

"Dominick, what are you talking about? Let me talk to my brother. I haven't seen him for almost two years."

Jacob understood that something was cooking there. He rushed out of the bar to ask what was going on. Dominick did not listen.

"This is no time to fool around, man. If you stay here any longer, you are dead meat. Get out of here, now," he ordered. He pushed him out of the yard through a hole in the fence. He showed him a footpath and ordered him to disappear as quickly as possible. Jacob found it awkward to squeeze in the hole. Rather than going through the hole, he jumped the fence and ran down the hill as fast as he could.

One minute later, the soldiers entered the bar and asked for Jacob.

"Where is the new guy? We need him, now. Where is he hiding?" They ordered Dominick to open the rooms, which they searched thoroughly. Chantal spoke to them.

"He buzzed off because he has a lot of work to do at home. Why do you need him so badly?" she asked.

"We want to share a drink with him," one of them answered.

"Why do you have to break things if you wanted to share a drink, then?" she asked.

"Madam, shut up!" he ordered.

They went to knock at the restroom.

"Are you there?" No answer. The soldier spoke louder. "Get the hell out of there." They knocked louder.

When they got no reply, they bumped the door with their boots. Two of them backed up to get ready to shoot. Two others stayed by the door of the restroom. They decided to break it. One of them started counting.

"One, two, three, go . . ." They pounded the door with a hummer and broke it. They pushed it violently, and one of them entered.

"He is not here! Fuck." He cursed.

The others checked if there was another place he could be hiding in. Jacob was nowhere to be seen. He was still running. The soldiers did not understand how he could disappear in just one minute. They thought he entered the nearby school compound. Jacob had already crossed Nyamuswaga creek at a mile from there. He remembered that he had left Lily and the baby behind. He feared that the soldiers might get mad and harm them. He sat down and wondered whether to go back. From where he was sitting, he saw them walking down the hill in his direction. The soldiers followed them half a mile and returned to the bar. Chantal and Lily joined him after an hour. With them, Jacob went home to wave his mother good-bye. He reported the incident, and his mother pleaded with him to leave the country for good.

"I have lost so many children. I do not want to lose you. Please, my son, I beg you. Leave this hell of a country and find a safe place?" She wiped tears from her eyes.

Jacob's brothers were killed in 1972, 1993, and 1994. His mother reminded him that other friends and neighbors had left the country. She begged him to join them in Tanzania. Jacob, too, was sick of the whole situation.

"That is what I am planning to do, Mom. I am tired of this." He gave her a last hug as she walked him down the street.

"Good-bye, my mom," he said as he waved his hand. They would never meet again.

Bujumbura had become a no-go area and so had the rest of the country. Although Jacob had had numerous problems in Bujumbura, Rumonge, Cibitoke, Rutana, and Gitega, he still wanted to work for his country. He remained in the country as he was promised a position as first secretary of embassy. He liked the new position, and he had to stay around waiting for his nomination.

However, because of political crises in Parliament and government, important decisions were delayed. While Jacob was waiting for the new position, people were killed. Jacob himself was escaping death every single day. He could not dare return to Bujumbura or Kivoga. Although he escaped death a dozen of times, he wondered if the position was more important than was his entire life. He had been waiting several months, and he was getting frustrated. Thus, he agreed with his mother that he should leave the country for good.

11. Kabonga, the Last Ordeal on Burundian Soil

The following morning, Jean Paul, *not Jacob*, took a bus to the border between Burundi and Tanzania. As misfortune never comes singly, the border was closed. He got no idea of what to do. He got a short-term accommodation in a hotel of a certain businessman from Kabonga. Sinzinkayo had met Jacob in Tanzania, and they had shared experiences as refugees. He had returned to Kabonga to take care of his business. His hotel was still under construction, and it had no phone line yet. As Jacob could not stay in the hotel forever, he rented a room from a man nicknamed Cinq Cents.

Kabonga was so peaceful that nobody expected problems there. Only small business owners and peasants lived there. Like everywhere else, there were soldiers and other Evildoers.

One day, there was a security meeting in Nyanza-Lac. The United Nations's new envoy to Burundi and many local authorities were there. Jean Paul attended the meeting and sat in the tribune. The speech of the bishop of the diocese of Bururi was of particular interest. Jean Paul was used to hearing speeches undermining democrats and thus expected Bishop Bernard Bududira to deliver the same speech of hatred. The bishop took the floor and condemned the army that killed the president of the republic. He stated,

"How can soldiers dare stand up with their horrifying weapons and put an end to the life of their president! Can we still believe that such soldiers are moral beings? Could normal people do that?"

Jean Paul was excited to hear these words from a very important person, especially that he was of the same ethnic group the killers were. Most bishops had been accomplices in the killing of members of their congregation. Jean Paul thought that Bishop Bududira was an Evildoer. The bishop pronounced the speech in front of hundreds of Evildoers who had been killing people. Jean Paul exclaimed while commenting the speech.

"The soldiers are foolish, so to speak!"

An Evildoer sitting next to him overheard him. He reported him to the commander of the military camp. Jean Paul was frightened when he saw Mukubajoro pointing a finger at him. He assigned one Evildoer to watch him until the end of the meeting. The soldier came over and sat beside him. Jean Paul assumed that there was a plan to kill him soon after the meeting. Without further ado, he got to his feet pretending to need some water. He asked the soldier watching him to keep an eye on his jacket and his seat until his return. He let him know that there was just a cell phone in his jacket and it was on vibrate. Then he motioned toward a water tab as the soldier waited for him to come back. The jacket was nothing but a cloth, and there was no cell phone at all. Jean Paul disappeared in the crowd of people. He strode to the back and vanished in cassava and palm trees. He did not need to catch a bus to Kabonga as he could make it on foot. He ran several miles through the cassava plantation. He swore not to appear in Nyanza-Lac anymore.

Jean Paul saw things through rose-intended glasses. In spite of the chaotic situation, he always saw life in a more positive light until Evildoers proved their inhumanity. The way he saw it, Evildoers of Kabonga seemed to be in good terms with the local people. They were not killing them. Jean Paul started trusting them. He enjoyed meeting with people and watching the day go by. He spent time playing cards with people regardless their tribes. It was the only way of killing the time as life there was more than boring. He seemed to forget that the soldiers were two faced. In times of peace, they behaved normally. They were sociable and interacted well with other people. Jean Paul was becoming more comfortable spending the day with them, especially as they were of similar age. Given that the majority of the people there were illiterate, being in the company of semiliterate soldiers was a nice change. Within a few weeks, all soldiers of Kabonga knew him by name. He was new there, an intellectual at that. Everybody paid attention to new faces.

One day, as Jean Paul was playing cards with the soldiers, Léopold Chissocco, a neighbor and childhood friend, had been hiding there too. He was amazed to see him there. He greeted him, "Hi, Jacob, how are you bearing up?"

"I am fine, buddy. I haven't seen you for a while. Where have you been?"

"I live here now."

They talked for a while during which time Léopold used the name of Jacob on several occasions. Jean Paul tried to avoid him as he was revealing his secret.

"Okay, Jacob. See you later."

Léopold noticed that Jean Paul was bothered by his presence, and he went away. He understood him. He himself was staying there incognito waiting for an opportunity to join the fight for democracy. After the talk with Léopold, the soldiers asked Jean Paul,

"Why does your buddy call you Jacob? Is your name Jacob or Jean Paul?"

"Well . . . my name is Jean Paul, but you can call me Jacob. Some of my childhood friends found my name too long, and they prefer to call me Jacob. Actually, only a few people still call me Jacob."

Jean Paul wanted to change the subject on his name, but the officers insisted.

"Can I see your identity papers?"

"Sure." He reached for his wallet, pulled his identity, and handed it to the officer. Jean Paul feared that the officer would discover that he was using a fake document. The document showed that he was born in Nyanza-Lac, and all knew that he was just a visitor. Fortunately, the officer did not bother reading the place of birth. He only checked the name. He was Jean Paul Mugisha. Then he apologized while handing the identity back to Jean Paul.

"I was curious to know how you go by two different names," the soldier muttered.

Jean Paul could not feel safe anymore. The next morning, he went to the government offices of Nyanza-Lac to report that his identity card was lost. Wilson Sayumwe, otherwise Desho, was the Communal Administrator. He gave him a new piece of identity with the same name of Jean Paul and Gitega as his place of birth. He could now live in Kabonga without fear of fake identity. As he was new there, everybody assumed that he was just passing through. Now that he had a new legal document with no confusion of places of birth, Jean Paul felt safer. From then on, everybody knew him as Jean Paul originally from Gitega. He had to hide the other identity papers.

Jean Paul started considering putting his roots down. He thought of buying a piece of land to grow cassava and peanuts. As he was walking through cassava gardens, he saw a man reading a book in front of a small and crude shelter. The hut was built of mud, palm leaves, and grasses. Jean Paul was surprised to see a man who looked like a genuine intellectual living in those hard conditions. He stopped over and greeted him. As they exchanged greetings, Jean Paul glanced at the book. It was not a Bible he expected it would be as most people out there could only read the Bible in their language. Jean Paul read the title of the book *Au Nom de Tous les Miens*. That was the French version of Martin Gray's book *For Those I Loved*. In Burundi, only intellectuals can read French novels. The two intellectuals were surprised at the meeting in remote and hidden valleys and gladly introduced themselves to each other. The man was an intellectual. He held a degree in Geography, and he had been working for the government. Before he entrenched himself in the woods behind the mountains, he was headmaster of a secondary school. He was hiding in the small grassy hut for several months. He would never show up in public places. He had never been at Kabonga Center for fear of the soldiers. He advised Jean Paul to stay away from them too. From that day on, Jean Paul stopped wandering in the streets of Kabonga. The man lent his novel to Jean Paul who read it for the first time. *For Those I Loved* portrays a picture of what was happening in Bujumbura. Treblinka was very much like Kamenge.

In the meantime, plans were underway to arrest Jean Paul. The soldiers knew that democrats were hiding from them. They understood that Jean Paul was one of the fugitives. They checked up on him every day. They also knew that he was planning to leave the country. They decided to arrest him before he could go anywhere. They would create a chaotic situation the aim of which would be to put their hands on him and accuse him of instigating rebellion, which would warrant a death sentence. When they were ready to act, they did not see him anymore. When Jean Paul did not show up for a week, the soldiers tried to locate him. They asked everybody about him, but their efforts were in vain. Jean Paul had kept his address secret.

Although the soldiers did not know where Jean Paul was living, he feared that he would soon be discovered. Thus, he started moving from one place to another, changing addresses every other day. He could spend days in Kabonga and nights in Gisenga, right at the border. He was getting tired of this kind of game and finally decided to leave the country for good. His new acquaintances there helped him to cross the border to Tanzania. Once in Tanzania, he was Jacob once again.

12. Welcome Back to Tanzania

Jacob's presence in Tanzania was illegal, but once inside, Tanzanians treated him well. There was no more fear of death. He had been there before, and he knew how to deal with serious difficulties. Local leaders wished him the best during his stay there. They invited him to feel at home and enjoy peace as a human being. Tanzania was a peaceful country, and people related to one another as moral beings. Even refugees were treated fairly. People were taught that all human beings were equal and should, therefore, be treated with equal respect. Jacob thanked Tanzanians for their welcome when his own country was treating him as a bitter enemy. He stayed in Kigoma for a while before he could decide whether to join a refugee camp or not.

According to the law, refugees were required to stay in camps. No one was allowed to work outside the camp. One could not leave the camp without a special pass from the Ministry of Home Affairs. As Jacob was not supposed to stay in town, he had to hide from police and immigration officers. Kapata Ntaho did his best to keep him safe. He managed to get him a fake document with Tanzanian names. The document allowed him and his family to stay in Mwanga-Majengo as Tanzanian nationals. Jacob Barak was now known as Richard Kindata.

After several months with the Kapatas, Mr. Kindata planned to leave the town. Kigoma was not the environment in which he could utilize his education in the French system. Not a single individual spoke French there. He struggled to learn Swahili as he needed to communicate with people. He memorized some Swahili speaking styles, but his French accent betrayed him. If he kept trying, he would be discovered. He remained Tanzanian by name and the fake identity paper. As his manners were different from Tanzanians, police arrested him several times to check if he was not a foreigner without papers. Each time, once he showed his new document and remained silent, he was released.

Richard could not even apply for a permit to start some business. He could not do anything as Tanzanian when he did not speak their language. His official documents were in French with a different name. He could not use them in Tanzania where no one spoke French. Eventually, it would be obvious that he was a foreigner with Tanzanian documents. Thus, he considered other alternatives. He had seen refugee camps before, and he did not wish to bring his family there. One day, he met old friends of his, Sophonie Batwenga and Désiré Hezumuryango. They came to Kigoma from the Kanembwa Refugee Settlement. They spent a night in the Rose Corner. In that guesthouse, customers informed them that they had seen another Burundian from Gitega. Désiré and Sophonie asked for his name. Some said that it was Jacob, others replied Jean Paul. Others still called him Richard Kindata. Yet all converged on the description. Désiré and Sophonie got the address and went to see him. It was their old friend, Jacob Barak. They told him about life in their refugee camp. They looked fine, and they were not complaining very much about their situation. They were doing well with their business. They invited Richard, aka Jacob, to visit the camp and see for himself how refugees were living.

Few days later, Richard took a bus and rode to the Kanembwa Refugee Settlement. He stayed for two weeks exploring the milieu. Life there was not too bad at all. At least there were no Evildoers killing people. The refugees lived in peace. That was the most important to Richard. Intellectuals had jobs that helped them to keep body and soul together. They worked with nongovernmental organizations operating in refugee camps including United Nations High Commissioner for Refugees, International Rescue Committee, Tanganyika Christian Refugee Service, Tanzania Red Cross Society, Care Canada, Christian Outreach, and so forth. Students were going to schools as usual. There was even a modern secondary school in construction. It was due to open in a couple of months. Elie Sabuwanka was working hard on the project. He told Jacob that the school would need qualified teachers like him to join their staff. He promised to offer him a position if he decided to stay in the camp.

Jacob found nothing wrong in living in the refugee camp. He needed a place to live in. There were many relatives and friends too. He went back to the office of UNHCR to request a transfer to the camp. As he was not registered in the UNHCR, it was not possible to get the transfer. He could not declare himself as a new refugee when the border was closed. So he lied to UNHCR that he had been hiding on the shoreline of Tanganyika Lake and that he wanted a camp. The protection officer did the paperwork and sent him to Kanembwa Refugee Settlement as a new refugee called Richard Mbonimpa. He was accommodated by Désiré for several weeks. The latter helped him to find a plot not far from him. Richard hired construction laborers to build his brick house. He still had some money to build a three-bedroom house. Unlike most refugees who lived in huts with plastic sheets, Richard could afford a house with brick walls. The next month, Richard and Lily sent résumés to John Nduna, project coordinator of Tanganyika Christian Refugee Service, Kibondo Branch. Many other candidates were selected for interviews. Now that Richard was in a refugee camp with his old friends, he vainly tried to lie on his identity. Everybody knew him as Jacob Barak. He was selected for interview. The interview panel called Jacob Barak, and they saw Richard Mbonimpa. He introduced himself as Jacob Barak, and he presented his official documents from university. He also had an identity card of Jacob Barak. He explained why he had to hide his name. Most refugees had done the same, thus the panel did not take that against him. Jacob was hired to work as teacher but he had to change his name in the Ministry of Home Affairs as well as in UNHCR. He could not work under a different name. Hence, he started the process of changing the name, and he became Jacob again. He worked for TCRS as teacher under his real name. However, as refugees assisted by UNHCR, they were not entitled to salaries. They only received some incentive that helped them to cover their basic expenses. Among other things, they were assisted in plastic sheets, food, clothing, school material for children, and medical care. They could only live modestly.

After several weeks under a tent with the logo of UNHCR, Jacob started organizing young refugees in different activities. He was elected deputy chairman of the Kanembwa Soccer Federation. With Sophonie Batwenga as chairman, they achieved a lot. They had a soccer team of Burundian refugees, mostly young students of Kanembwa Secondary School. The team competed with other teams and won most matches. One day, after winning a friendly match in one of the villages of Kibondo District, the coach of the Tanzanian team handed two hens and two hens to Jacob and Sophonie. He was impressed by their zeal and courage to organize the young refugees to take part in the soccer tournaments. He wanted the hens to produce eggs so that their young children could eat better.

When Jacob's hen produced eggs, Jacob hesitated to break any as they could produce more chickens. He waited until he got twelve eggs and broke six of them for the family to eat omelet. He fed his family, and he would still have six more cocks to come, which was better than nothing. Within a week, the hen had laid another half dozen of eggs. The family could eat omelet more often. It seemed the hen was decided to replace every single egg taken. In the end, the hen produced twelve young cocks. Within two years, the family could eat omelet at breakfast and chicken meat for dinner. That was a bonus for a refugee who had no chance in life.

As Jacob had decided not to return home in the near future, he planned to grow fruit and vegetables. He got a land to cultivate. In his spare time, he traveled several miles to hoe and harvest the crops. Tilling the soil in his bare feet became one of his hobbies. Finally, Dickson was right. With his coworkers such as Sylvere Sindakira, Onesphore Ndayizeye, Anaclet Bampema, and others, they crossed villages looking for better land to dig. Peasants got surprised to see intellectuals, teachers at that, with university degrees, tilling the soil in their bare feet, sometimes under heavy sun or rain. They would dig wet areas with composing organic materials. Peasants thought that it was their duty to do the odd jobs on the marshland. Jacob was encouraged by Sophonie, Désiré, and many other intellectuals who were already harvesting tons of crops. They worked hard to maintain a moderate lifestyle. There was no way one could survive without digging the soil and harvesting crops as otherwise they would have to buy everything, for which their income was insufficient. They planted cassava, potatoes, beans, corn, and many kinds of vegetables. They also planted dozens of tree fruits such as oranges, guavas, avocadoes, and papayas. The crops helped them greatly in coping with life in the refugee camp. Within a few months, they did not need to rely solely on humanitarian assistance. They even had enough crops to sell, which meant that they could buy clothes for their families and afford other necessities.

In 1997, God blessed Jacob's family with a second beautiful child. She was christened Eunice Scheilla. She was born when Jacob seemed to have forgotten the terrors of the Evildoers. Lily did not have to suffer as she did when Eddy Franklin was born. It was marvelous to have the second child on a peaceful land that treated them as its own people. The birth of Eunice Scheilla reminded Jacob of the warm welcome received in a foreign country as a refugee. In recognition of their hospitality, he called his beautiful daughter Kaze. She was named after the warm welcome received. In Tanzania, every guest is welcomed with a smile. Tanzanians say *karibu* at least ten times a day. *Karibu* is a Swahili translation of "welcome." The Kirundi translation would be *kaze*. Even if one waves them good-bye, Tanzanians reply with *karibu tena*, i.e., welcome again. "We will be more than happy to welcome you anytime." If Jacob were not welcomed to Tanzania, it is not certain that Eunice Scheilla would have been born. Jacob would never have seen the beautiful smile on the face of that charming creature coming to the world. Eunice turned out to be a fine-looking girl, more intelligent than her parents could imagine. At six months, she was speaking like a three-year-old child. When she began school, her reports were always excellent. She came top of class in all subjects. She won many competitions in drawing, singing, writing poetry, and sports. She enjoys cheerleading very much. She was doing so well that Jacob had to add more expenses on her talents. Her parents are happy for their successful children who demonstrate talents in an egalitarian society that recognize and value people's achievements. Jacob hopes that his children will not live in nightmares like their parents and grandparents on the land of the dead. As the only girl in the family, Eunice Scheilla seemed to be the favorite child. Her Oedipus complex is so strong that she always imitates her father's talents in drawing pictures and writing poetry and short stories. Like her brother, Eddy Franklin, Eunice forgot that she crawled on hot dusty or muddy ground in the refugee camp. No refugee ever had a stroller. They did not even know that it existed. Jacob himself had never seen it. In 1999, another boy was born. Lionel Joe's birth was uneventful. The family was already settled as refugees, and they were applying to resettle to Canada. Now that Jacob would find a safe place for his children, he decided to give his family name to the newborn.

Since 1997, the African great region was on fire. There were threats that Tanzania too would be attacked. Jacob decided to move his family away from the danger.

Eventually, he took a flight to Nairobi to prepare a place for his family. He met Nikita Chissocco, who was now living with a new man. As they greeted, she hastened to tell him that Ronald died eight months earlier. She did not elaborate. Jacob had to ask her how he died. She told him that he was shot dead by members of the Sans Echecs Brigade. Jacob looked surprised to see her pregnant with another man with Ronald's boy on her back. If Ronald was killed eight months back, it meant that she conceived a few days after his death and probably right after the funeral. As she noticed that Jacob was bewildered, she presented him Schadrack Kubwa as the new man in her life. They were expecting a baby in three weeks. Jacob was busy trying to locate his friends who would introduce him to the Canadian Embassy in Nairobi. He waved Nikita good-bye and went his way.

13. From the Land of the Dead to the Land of Free Blue Skies

Jacob spent a desperate life in his home country. Burundi was a land of his birth but not the land of his dream. He did not want it to be the land of his death either. People suffered horrible deaths; their bodies were left to decay on the ground. Jacob had three kids, and they needed a better place to grow up. After five years in the refugee camps, he became curious to learn what democracy and freedom were all about. He had his heart set on living on a peaceful land, a country where peace and justice were not fatal dreams as on the Land of the Dead. He dreamed of a country with no painful memories around every corner. The refugee camp was not his home. He did not wish his kids to go through the misery he had gone through all his childhood. His curiosity led him to cross creeks, rivers, lakes, and countries as he searched for a land of freedom. He did not find it and finally realized that he would have to cross oceans and continents. He wanted to explore the world, allowing airplanes to take his family wherever they could.

The decision to immigrate to Canada was not welcomed by other refugees though. Pessimistic people saw the process of resettlement as a new form of slavery. They accused Jacob of abandoning his motherland to the Evildoers. Jacob, however, believed that the life of a slave in America was much better than the life he lived in Burundi. He would rather try his luck in Canada than living a dog's life on his own land. He had nothing to lose anyway.

Others saw his decision as a betrayal of a man who had negative attitude toward his country. Whilst condemning him, they knew that they were not able to return home. Their families had that stayed behind were terrorized or killed. Jacob believed that life in any country in the world was far better than the life he was living in the refugee camp of Tanzania. Actually, refugees were not living. They were attempting to survive. There was too much distress out there. Refugees could not return home when their country was worse than hell. No one was really missing that kind of country.

Jacob needed a better place for his children. He had read about slavery. He knew the story of Malcolm X since he was young. He decided to leave the refugee camp, not because he hated his country but because it did not want him. If he stayed in Burundi, he would be dead. If he hated his country, he would hate his roots. Only Evildoers hated their country. They could not love it and still kill its people. Good citizens can only hate the social evils, but never the Evildoers. Those who hated Evildoers still loved their country. A country is just a physical territory, which has nothing to do with man's immorality.

When Jacob arrived in Canada, his first question was to know if he would be able to get enough food for his three little kids. Not only did he get eggs and milk, he also got honey. He visited many Canadian and American stores. They were selling almost everything. He was surprised to find that most customers included eggs and chicken on their shopping lists. Then he wondered why people keep breaking eggs when they could eat anything for lunch. In the refugee camp, Jacob broke eggs because he did not have enough food to feed his lovely kids. Here, people broke eggs because they loved eating them. It sounded strange.

After two years in Canada, Ryan Malcolm B was born, not as a slave but as a free person. He was named after Malcolm Little, the African-American human rights activist of the twentieth century. He called himself Malcolm X to signify his lost tribal name. He considered his name Little to have originated with white slaveholders. He wanted to assert his identity as African but he did not know his tribe. The little Ryan was born in Canada from an African family of the Baraks. The parents were proud to give him their family name. He went by Malcolm B in recognition of the fact that Canadians of African descent were free to pursue their happiness in the western hemisphere. In fact, they lived much happier life than they could ever hope to experience in their country of origin.

While in Tanzania, refugees were not even allowed free movement from one camp to another. They were controlled day and night, 365 days a year. Everybody's freedom was limited to their plots of twenty square meters. Any refugee caught outside the camp was treated as suspicious for months. The Baraks found Canada to be a country of hope. They explored the arctic and the land of midnight sun. They discovered a friendly and nice people in the wild rose country and the land of living skies. Their four little children could enjoy life on Canada's ocean playground. They agreed with their parents that Canada was really the place to be. They found it as a country of insurance. They had seen nothing in Burundi and refugee camps but pure misery.

As Canada is a melting pot of different nationalities, Jacob got the chance of meeting people from all over the world. They discussed the sociopolitical situations of their countries of origin. To Jacob's great disappointment, only a few knew about Burundian Evildoers with their greed and inhumanity. Jacob rarely met people who really knew the truth on Burundi.

In Canada, as in United States, he even had difficulty explaining the location of Burundi on the world map. He could hardly find a world map that clearly showed Burundi and its boundaries. On all maps, the word Burundi is far bigger than the country it refers to. Even pointing to the country on the map was difficult as the fingernail would hide it. Jacob had to use a thinner object, such as the edge of a pin. Even then, his students could only see a small dot made by the pin. They saw Tanzania and Congo but nothing in between except the Tanganyika Lake.

The situation reminded Jacob of a childhood joke. Before the coming of democracy, the Twas were considered as the lowest class of the society. They were so ignored that they knew nothing of development. They could not go to school either. Obviously, very few, if any, had been at the airport. In other words, no one of that community had seen a plane. They were more neglected than democrats were. Governments did not care about them in the least.

There was a joke undermining that group of people. It said that, when members of that community are shown an airplane flying, rather than looking at the plane in the air, they looked at the finger pointing it. In other words, they had no idea of what an airplane was.

As young children, people were telling the joke not knowing its reel meaning. The joke tickled Jacob's ribs. He remembered this joke when he used his finger to show the location of Burundi on the world map. He understood why only a few people knew about the misery of Burundians for centuries. The country is so tiny that people do not pay too much attention on a banana republic like Burundi. They seem to be more interested in big and rich countries like Congo, eighty-four times bigger and far richer than they were in Burundi.

Finally, Jacob found a way of describing Burundi. The neighboring Land of a Thousand Hills became a good reference. Though the country is smaller than Burundi, it still contributes much to a good understanding of the history of Burundi. If one mentions that Burundi is located south of Rwanda, people will get a rough idea of the sociopolitical situation of the country. At least they will know of the composition of that country. Therefore, the best way to describe the Heart of Africa is to state that it is a brother to the Land of a Thousand Hills. Whenever this name is mentioned, five other expressions come forth—Hutus, Tutsis, Twas, Evildoers, and Genocide. The five words are always associated with the country. Thus, people often want to know if Burundi, too, is composed of these five elements. Yet more precision is required when talking about Jacob's homeland. If Rwanda had crimes of genocide once in their history, Burundi suffered much more tragic destiny. More horrible killings took place but very few seemed to care. Those who did care, have, for some reason, preferred to hide the truth. It was bothering Jacob to see thousands of innocent civilians killed and not a single person condemned it. His friends and relatives, presidents, ministers, parliamentarians, and others were cut into pieces. Assassinations were carried on thanks to some powerful countries that provided funding, training, weapons and intelligence to the Evildoers.

PART TWO

THE GAME IS OVER

1. The Beauty of Life with Nature

Flowers make nature more beautiful and colorful. Some flowers live with animals in nature while others live with humans in their homes. People love lowers that are full of life. When their beauty vanishes, however, they are disposed off and placed in garbage bins. Like beauty found elsewhere, flowers do not last long. They are fragile and vulnerable. When the beauty dies, sometimes love dies with it. All people love positive experiences. Negative ones usually bring hatred.

In all societies, people adore children as they make life enjoyable. They are loved and cherished not because they are fragile but because they are innocent. By providing good education to children, governments, and parents build a better future for their nations.

Everyone rejoices at the birth of a child, awaiting it with excitement. Witness the tradition of baby showers in some cultures. Moms, relatives, and friends organize a baby shower as a way of celebrating the new arrival to the world. New mothers are showered with gifts and attention. However, the biggest value of a baby shower is in friendship and love it demonstrates. People are excited for the new little one joining the community of friends and relations. It is also a way of supporting and encouraging the new parents. Through baby showers, friends prove their solidarity in times of joy. Adolf Hitler, just as Dickson Rushatsihori, Juvenhack Zim Anan, Geram Murara, and anyone else in this world, was born naked and wet. His parents needed support. Because he was an innocent baby, even Jewish people participated in his baby shower. Today, the entire world hates him for his evildoing as an adult.

Society corrupts and transforms people. Young kids can grow up and turn into dangerous terrorists. The friends that showered them with gifts can thus become their bitter enemies. Not only do they fear them, they also fight and prosecute them. That is to say, people love beautiful things when they are still good and hate them when they turn bad.

Like most people, Jacob loves living things including plants. He sees flowers as symbols of love, happiness, beauty, and innocence, which are loved and desired by all. When people gaze upon flowers, though, they meet with butterflies and bees enjoying them too. Bees do not grow flowers and still seem to hold the torch for them more than we folks do. They do not allow everybody to access their flowers in their own gardens. People fear their stingers. They try to stay away from them as much as they can. In order to get close to their flowers, they have to wait until the bees finish their job. By putting flowers in their houses, they attract bees and butterflies. These undesired guests are thus in open competition with humans. People know that the bees will not steal the flower as they are only interested in the pollen. Still, people defend their flowers against anything that may harm their beauty.

Like other men, Jacob loved a flower. In his heart, there was room reserved for love. It was vacated by a Lilium that had died a few months earlier. Since January of 2007, he was aching from being forced to live away from Eddy Franklin, Eunice Scheilla, Lionel Joe, and Ryan-Malcolm B. The father in him was grieving. Days without his kids were agonizing. Nothing else could give him the happiness they provided. He genuinely adored his four little kids and missed their smiles terribly. He missed reading them stories, taking them to parks, daycare, kindergarten, school, and other ordinary activities most parents take for granted.

The first Christmas without his kids caused him much pain and sorrow. Not only did he miss the joy of parenthood; he feared that loneliness and boredom would kill him. He missed taking them to get Christmas presents from Santa Claus in the Fleur de Lys Mall, Quebec City. He could not spend time with them in Les Galeries de la Capitale, the biggest shopping mall in the city with everything children can enjoy.

Jacob would do everything on Earth to recover the lost happiness. It looked as if the sky had fallen on him. He played with toys, remembering beautiful times he had with his beloved children. His heart was broken and it needed to be fixed. He needed to spend the rest of his days with someone with a heart of gold, somebody whose smile would light his days. It did not have to be a human being as it is not always easy to find the right person at the right time. He knew that all too well, remembering those who betrayed him and their consciences by seeking to kill him. Evildoers had threatened his life for four decades. Others just destroyed human lives purely and simply. Things worsened with the separation with Lily. With his kids far from him, he slowly underwent total transformation.

As he was heartbroken, he stopped hoping to find a perfect match among humans. According to him, pets and plants were more trustworthy than were human beings. They neither hate nor hurt. Besides, they are honest and faithful. For this reason, Jacob decided that his heart should be filled with a flower, *not a human being, a rose*. He needed to replace the dead lily with a living rose. He had been hoping against hope to get a flower stronger than the lily was, one that would make him forget the terrorism of the Evildoers. He had to get it from a place where winter was not as harsh as in Northern Alberta.

Flowers in the Evergreen State had all to envy. They had rain twelve months a year with flies buzzing all around. Jacob became remotely attracted by a rose in Shelton, Olympia, in one of Auntie Sammie's gardens in Washington State. Auntie Sammie was a big supplier of flowers. One had to purchase her flowers in the Home Depot or

RONA stores. As Jacob was talking to his friend Ram Dee about his need to replace the dead lily, Ram Dee thought that Nikita might be of good help. She had immigrated to North America and she was working in the Home Depot of Lacey, Olympia. She was a florist and thus knew all about flowers. She had an extensive experience selling flowers to tourists. She had sold them in many places such as Bujumbura, Nairobi, Lome, Bamako, Cotonou, Seattle, and Olympia. She had been asking about Jacob's phone number. She was speaking very highly of him, and she appeared to care about him deeply. Ram Dee told him how she was insisting on having his number. She was asking about him every single day.

"If you could get hold of her, she might help you with her flower. She is very nice and kind with extensive experience helping customers. Just give her a call, and she will serve you."

"What if she doesn't? I haven't spoken to her for a long time. I almost forgot about her. How is she doing anyway?" Jacob asked.

"She is fine. She asks about you every time we meet. I only needed your permission to give your number. She tells everybody that you grew up together and that you are a nice person. I don't think she can say no to you," Ram Dee reassured him.

"I guess she is still with Kubwa, isn't she?"

"Not at all. She is single at the moment."

"I don't think she can be alone for long. I always saw her with men. Anyway, this is none of my business."

As Jacob remembered Nikita of his childhood, he allowed Ram Dee to give her his number. He himself needed love and caring. He had last seen her in Nairobi eleven years back. He had no news of her ever since. He could not even think of meeting her someday as there was no reason for that. As soon as she got his number, she immediately called him to let him know how much she missed him. Jacob was surprised to hear that as she had presented him Kubwa as her boyfriend. He wondered if she was thinking of a relationship with him. They talked for a while, and she never mentioned Kubwa. They only spoke about their childhood adventures and exchanged other stories from their past. They avidly talked about the games they played together and their fondness for each other. In the meantime, many things had changed. She was a single mother with three kids from three different fathers. They were no more familiar to each other as they were back in the village. Twenty-two years had slipped by since they played hide-and-seek in the villa of Jacob's uncle. Since then, they only met three times.

Now that they were adults and free, they spoke as mature people. They did not always talk about old stories of childhood. They spoke like man and woman who really knew what they wanted and were eager to help each other given that they had the same needs. Both knew the meaning of a relationship between a man and a woman. Jacob could feel her happy smile. As they talked, he told her about the lily.

"Nikita, my flower died last year. I am considering a new relationship."

By telling her that the lily was dead, he was expecting sympathy. She sounded giddy with happiness instead. Jacob noticed that he hit the nail squarely on the nail. She spoke with a note of happiness in her voice, and she encouraged him to forget about the lily. She clearly intended to fling herself on him. She started seducing him on the phone, promising him the best.

"Don't worry, my honey. You needn't go all the way to Bujumbura for a flower you don't know. I am here to help you. I have a very nice and beautiful rose, the best you can imagine in the world, *not in Bujumbura, in the world.* I have been saving her for you since the death of the lily. By the way, I knew your lily was going to die eventually. She had no stamina. You didn't need that kind of flower. You needed something much better like mine. You will have her any time you want. You know, a bird in hand is worth two in the bush."

"I don't have a bird handy," Jacob interrupted her.

"Honey, my rose is your rose. When will you come to pick her up?"

Jacob was surprised by the promise. He thought about Schadrack Kubwa, but he did not ask about him. He did not want to intrude in her privacy. He thought about the proposal for a while and spoke to himself.

"If she promises to offer me her rose, it means that Kubwa is no longer in her life. What happened is none of my business. Besides, I didn't know Kubwa. I only saw him once, and I know nothing about him. I would hesitate only if Ronald was still alive. Now that he is in heaven, I can take care of his charming flower, his beloved boy, and of course, Kubwa's toddler and the unknown boy."

Jacob still thought of Kubwa even though Nikita had forgotten him a long time ago. After him, she had affairs with a married man who left her pregnant, and she later had another boy. To avoid problems with his wife, the man paid her flight to Western Africa. She stayed there several years before immigrating to America. Jacob never knew about this story.

Jacob had met Nikita three times with different boyfriends. She was pregnant each time he saw her. He never knew that they would sit down and talk about facts of life. Since childhood, they had been relating to each other as brother and sister. Now that they were grown-ups and romantic, their philia developed into Eros. They had to speak a new language, the romantic one. Jacob asked more about the treasure.

"Nikita, I am serious. I want your rose very badly." She interrupted him and reassured.

"I cannot deny you something I have. From now on, she is our flower, not my flower."

"So she won't be my rose but our rose! You mean you will give me a half of her, and you will keep the other half for yourself! I want my own flower. She will live in my house. She will be part of me."

"We will share. Don't you want to share with me?" she winked.

"How can we share her when we are in different countries?"

"Come on, Jacob, don't set boundaries on love. My flower is limitless. She has been all over the world. Everybody knows her. Just come here and pick her. She will be yours forever."

"Deal?"

"Deal."

"Okey-dokey. Where is she then? I want to come and see her."

"She is in Auntie Sammie's garden. She has been there for a while. Now that you will take her, I will bring her closer, and I will keep her in the store. I have many clients in Shelton. I wanted them to see her regularly. Now that you will buy her, I will take good care of her. Just come anytime. I promise you, she is ours."

"What do you mean by 'ours'? I thought I will own her as my own treasure."

"Definitely. I will need to help you taking care of her. I will be feeding her in your house. I want to make sure that she makes our lives enjoyable."

"Nikita, we need to sit down and talk seriously," Jacob interjected, knowing that she was the only woman he could trust. He knew nobody else. They knew each other since a long time, and they liked each other very much. They would be happy to meet and talk about their flower.

"I know you, but I never saw her. I need to see her with my own eyes. However, as we said, I don't see how I would treat her well without your help. Will you be accompanying her?" Jacob wanted to know how serious she was.

"My honey, I already told you. As you say, we have known each other since young age. It is true that you didn't know my flower. We were too young to know about treating flowers. Now is the time to think about it and enjoy what we have been saving for each other for twenty-two years. I have every reason to believe that you will love her. You won't be disappointed. As you see, in the meantime I met bad men who ruined my life. I know that I will be comfortable with you."

Jacob took good care of her when she was thirteen. He was then fifteen. They still remembered everything as if they were never turned apart.

"Once you love my rose, I will make your life happier. We will take it from great to excellent. Just come here, and we will plan everything together." Nikita tried to get him interested in her so that they could start their romance. She wanted an opportunity to ambush him with her flower. Jacob could not wait to meet her. Thanks to her reassuring sweet words, he would buy her flower and enjoy her beauty.

Nikita appeared to want Jacob very badly. She committed her interest and all her energy to him. She would do everything possible to win his love. As he was far from her, she feared that he might have somebody else. Still, even if that were the case, she would do everything to make sure she won him.

Jacob was at loss of words. He was happy to know that there was somebody interested in him. She was hunting him for several months, and he needed to know what she was bringing to his life. Now that she promised to support him all his life, the hunter became the hunted. Jacob could not decline somebody that was offering everything he needed. She was promising milk and honey when he was hungry and thirsty.

Before going to meet her though, Jacob wanted to make sure that he was not barking up the wrong tree. He wanted something that would resist the hot summer as well as the cold winter. He knew that Nikita's flower knew only of heat. Jacob was not sure if it was tenacious and strong enough to support four seasons. Nikita, more determined to sell her product, guaranteed that nothing would disturb her rose. She pushed him to hit the iron when it is still hot. However, Jacob was still doubtful.

"Nikita, are you sure that a rose has more stamina than a lily? When I sow a seed, I don't seek something that will later ruin my life. I have to make sure I buy the right flower for the type of soil I have. If anything happens, I will be the one to get the rough end of the stick. You know what I am saying? I am looking for the strongest flower, the best blooms, and a great growing habit. In other words, I need a genuine and continuing relationship with nature."

Nikita reassured him that the rose was an excellent flower.

"Honey, I like you so much that I cannot lie to you. Your happiness will be my happiness. As far as I know, my rose resisted strong tornados, hurricanes, cyclones, tsunamis, and twisters. Thus, I am confident that she will resist winter."

Jacob wondered why such a wonderful flower was not sold yet. He could never understand why she was selling her to him when there were many tourists buying flowers every day. They saw her beauty, yet no one bought her. It meant that no one liked her. Even Kubwa had left her. He asked himself many questions about the rose. The way she was described, she would not stay one minute in the shop. Everybody would want to buy her. Then Nikita said that she had been saving her for him. Jacob understood that she was well kept in her room, and no one touched her. She would be his heavenly gift. He believed in true love and desperately wanted to trust her. He really needed her. He had been praying hard to have something to fill his heart. He heard Nikita's words as his prayers being answered. Then he remembered that she was in Auntie Sammie's garden and that Nikita would bring her to the store. Jacob was embarrassed. He asked more about her.

"Why do you keep your flower in someone else's garden and in the store when she is supposed to live in your room?"

"Honey, she is so beautiful that everybody wants to smell her scent. If I kept her home, my privacy with my kids would be disturbed. I prefer to keep her outside. That way, my kids won't know what is going on. Trust me. No one who saw my flower was disappointed."

Jacob clung on those words and trusted her. Without asking how deep the roots were, he believed Nikita. He knew that the flower had lived on hot lands with hot bees. She would now live on a cold place with one owner, *not many hot men,* just one cool gentleman, Jacob Barak. If she resisted tornados, it was not obvious that she would resist winter season. Jacob could not even think about it. He had already lost a lily in the tornados of February 2007 as the flower, imported from a tropical country, could not survive the change. Now he wants a new flower with new roots, new leaves, new branches, new sepals, and a new petal. He ignored that Nikita's flower would only be new to him but not to the world. Everybody else knew her. She herself told him that the rose resisted tornados, hurricanes, cyclones, tsunamis, and the like. She had been in all those situations. If Jacob had been smart, he would have thought of the aftermath of the disasters. He did not even ask if the passage of storms leave plants stronger or weaker. Could the flower still be good with stronger and newer sepals, petals, and leaves? That was a question he chose to ignore, yet the answer to it would change things later on. As they were calling each other at least three times a day, they sort of fell in love on the phone. They even started missing each other. In reality, they were the ones who wanted each other.

The more Jacob loved the rose the blinder he became. One would even say the more stupid. Nikita's description of the flower was too good to be true. Yet he never questioned her word. Instead, he looked at it with a blind eye,

"Well, regarding your flower . . . I don't disagree with you, but seeing is believing. You claim that she will resist all seasons and nothing will disturb her! That is the flower I need! I really want her in my life."

Jacob informed his uncle about his new relationship. He advised him to be more careful as he did not know the flower.

"We have been good friends since childhood. She reassured me that she is a nice one," he insisted.

"Are you sure she is telling you the full truth? How do you know a flower that lives in the garden? Well, make sure she doesn't screw your life. I saw Nikita in many cities. That lady has strong customer service and selling skills. Don't trust everything she says."

Jacob only wanted them to encourage him. He did not want anybody telling him the negative side of her.

"Nikita is working in the flower shop. She is a florist, and I love nature. I am going to see her soon."

"Seeing her and knowing her are two different things. Women are like flowers. You will see leaves and petals, but you won't see the sap. You will see the branches and stalk but not the roots. But please, beware. Still waters run deep."

"Still waters run deep? What do you mean?"

"Nikita is beautiful, but all that glitters is not gold."

"I still don't get your point here. What do you mean?"

"It's up to you to decide. I support you, and I wish you success with her. By the way, did you speak to your family about her?"

"Not yet. I will tell them soon."

"They know the Chissoccos more than you do."

Jacob only wanted to listen to Nikita as his own heart. He never wanted anybody to question the truthfulness of her words. Because of hesitations from his uncle, he decided to see the flower with his own eyes. He knew that natural beauty was part of the American dream. He learned from books that everything was shining out there. He thought that an American flower smelled much better than any other flower in the world. For this reason, he booked a flight to the country of Uncle Sam to see the rose with his own eyes. It was April and nature was amazingly beautiful—bright sun, blue skies, crisp air, green grasses, and blue lakes. Everywhere he turned he saw black, yellow, Hispanic, and white people. Everything was shiny indeed. In a few words, it was a rainbow coalition. Two of Jacob's friends waited for him at the airport with a nice Toyota, a Camry. Al Diego, affectionately called Ram Dee since secondary school, was one of Jacob's old friends. He was with his sister, Crystal Muna. Nikita was busy taking care of the flower in the store.

As they left the airport, Jacob requested a stop at 9303 Orion Drive Northeast, Lacey. There was a Home Depot store. It was late in the afternoon, and he wanted to see what the rose looked like before sunset. He would see her again at sunrise and then at noon. Ram Dee drove to the store. He called Nikita to let her know that he was arriving soon. She took her lunch break and waited for her visitor. She informed another associate that she had a new and important client coming for the rose. She requested Agnes to take care of him and praise the flower for her beauty.

Ram Dee parked in front of the main entrance. Jacob got out of the car and hastened to the counter to ask for Nikita. Nikita recognized him immediately even though they hadn't met in many years. Jacob's gloomy appearance cheered her up. She took him by the hand and directed him to the backyard. She warmly hugged him, and they exchanged many kisses. Jacob really loved her welcoming smile. They looked at each other and hugged again. It seemed they were checking if they were still the same. Jacob was only checking if she was not pregnant as usual and was relieved to find that she was not.

Now that Jacob and Nikita were reunited by love, they had to observe each other at close range. They had many things in common. Both had grown up and had experienced the same deception in love. They had been comforting each other, and now they had to console themselves with each other.

Although both of them had completely changed, Nikita was practically a different person. Her shyness had disappeared. Jacob knew her as a tall country girl living in the village when her legs were as skinny as a stick with bony hips. Her breasts were just beginning to sag. She was now such a zestful woman that he could not believe it. Though she had gained some pounds, she was such a pretty woman with big legs, large and perfect breasts, and wide hips and thighs. She was exactly the way Jacob wanted her to be, the prototype of African beauty. In a word, she was seriously attractive.

Getting together again after more than twenty years, their bond of friendship had become stronger than before. They did not hug each other like brother and sister as before. At first, Jacob saw Nikita not as a friend but as his real sister. In fact, Nikita bore some resemblances to his sisters with distinctive features of the Baraks. When she was with Chantal Barak, very few would believe that they were not twins. These resemblances were enough for Jacob to feel her in his heart. One thing disturbed him though. She had completely changed. She had nothing left of the African values. She was a city girl with manners of a lady who grew up in western cities. Jacob found her too westernized when he was conservative and had kept his African identity. He was gradually acquiring western values, selecting only those he considered worthy and good. Nikita had lost her African values in a couple of years. She only had a few reminders of Africa; the color of her skin and the Kirundi language she still spoke with difficulty. Even then, she would not ascertain her African identity. Jacob understood the sudden change as a compensation for her lack of education. He himself had been in big cities, such as Quebec City, Montreal, Toronto, Calgary, and Edmonton; and he had learned a lot there. Thus, he had remained the same African with Burundian values. He still cherished his Burundian identity. He still spoke his mother tongue fluently and respected Burundian standards. Nikita's native language, however, was far to be understood as her mother tongue. It was a mixture of Kirundi, French, Kiswahili, and English. That is the consequence of speaking many languages. When Jacob told her that she was now speaking pidgin, she did not like the comment and decided to communicate in English.

After three minutes of warm hugs and kisses, Nikita led her guest through the main aisle to the garden center. There were hundreds of flowers of all kinds. Wild flowers were being sold to tourists from all over the world. They walked to the section of roses. Agnes came forward and greeted Jacob with a smile, "Good morning sir. Are you looking for a particular flower? We have plenty of roses here. What is your favorite color?"

"Good morning," Jacob answered the greeting. "I need a nice, *nice* rose." He pointed at a rose believed to be the one he was looking for. "That one seems to be a nice one. What do you think?"

"You betcha! This is a cute flower, the nicest we have in the store. Everybody loves her. She performs well in garden beds, in mass plantings, and in large patio pot. She is easy to grow and to care for. Other important attributes that add to her glory are her tolerance for heat, cold, and her heavy flowering. You have every reason to fall in love with a rose that blooms twelve months a year," Agnes reassured him. Yet she said nothing about the thorns on the stem though she knew her better than Jacob did. Somehow, she found the detail not worth mentioning.

"I will let you gaze on her. Let me know once you're decided. I will be right back," she went to help other customers.

Nikita wanted Jacob to hear the comments from somebody else. She looked excited.

"I told you, honey. Everybody knows that there is no flower superior to a rose." Jacob looked at her and smiled. She smiled back and kissed him.

"Don't question what I tell you, honey," she teased him.

"I will always trust you, dear. That is why I am here today." She kissed him again.

The flower was beautiful indeed. After a minute gazing on each other's face in admiration, they smiled and nodded in agreement. Jacob succumbed to her beauty and her smile. Nikita was confident that her flower was always desired by every man. Jacob was a man of five senses like others; he would not make an exception. She invited him to a secluded place where they could talk in privacy. With Jacob's right hand holding the flower and the left arm wrapped around Nikita's shoulders, they had a walk around. With an attractive smile, she offered him the rose as her lavish present.

"Honey, this is the lovely flower you have been dreaming about. You had never seen her, and I hope you were waiting for the right time. This is the perfect time. From now on, she is yours, *not ours*, yours and forever."

Jacob answered with a kiss before proceeding with his compliments. He fixed his hopes on her never disappointing him. No woman had ever tempted him like her. He fell into the trap.

"Hmmm! I can't find words to thank you. If this rose is mine, I am the happiest man in the world. I cried for the lily not knowing that the best was still to come. Thank you, God!" He hugged her.

"She is marvelously attractive . . . and she has unrivaled beauty. She will match the colors of my beautiful bedroom. With you in my life, my house will be a rainbow of beauty."

He walked around the flower, ran a hand along the round vase and lifted her. He gently touched the leaves with his nose. They sent a little note of joy. He kissed the petal and held her close to his nose. He let the leaves touch his cheeks as he moved them up and down, humming. With his heart beating against his ribs, Jacob gave the flower a sharp shake. The admiring look gratified her. She sent fluff that went in all directions. Jacob nodded sweetly and whispered to Nikita:

"What a wonderful flower! Look! The flower seems to smile to me. I will enjoy the air she breathes. She will give me odorous at sunrise. She will bring my lost smile back to my face. Uh! She represents the seductiveness of life."

It seemed that Nikita would change Jacob's life. She only smiled. Her smile was like a deadly weapon that could kill any man in need of love.

Jacob and Nikita stayed in the room longer than they were supposed to. They did not care about Ram Dee and Crystal still sitting in the waiting room. Within only a short time, the liking became love. For the second time in his life, Jacob pronounced the magic words, "I love you, Je t'aime." He was talking to the flower, and Nikita understood that the message was addressed to her. She had been expecting the declaration for several weeks. She did not hesitate to reciprocate, "I love you too, my honey." She held his cheeks and kissed him. "I have been yearning for you."

She could not believe that Jacob was speaking to the flower, especially that she had been preparing him to make that declaration of love. If he did not say it, she was the one to declare her love for him. She wanted him, but she would not say it first. She would only show it and let him make the declaration.

Although Jacob was less interested in love affairs with human beings, he saw Nikita as a different person. Her sweet words, "I love you too, my honey," echoed in his heart. He had not been close to her in twenty-two years. He got confused in the dilemma of loving the flower and being loved by Nikita. He found himself wanting to kill two birds with one stone. As he did not wish to hurt her feelings, he decided to couple her with the flower. He raised the flower, kissed her, and handed her to Nikita.

"I love you," he said.

"Je t'aime moi aussi," Nikita replied.

Jacob felt that she had a lot of love to give him. He needed it to fill the gap in his heart. As both of them took the declaration seriously, the desire for each other grew stronger.

Jacob had been restraining from uttering these strong and beautiful words before meeting Nikita in person. They were easy to say in the language of William Shakespeare. Jacob preferred the language he mastered. If flowers could talk, he would ask if she loved him too. She would surely say, "Moi aussi." She spoke through Nikita. The flower could smile though. As the relation between Jacob and Nikita turned into love, Jacob asked her if she would be kind enough to help him take care of the flower.

"Will you help me to take care of her in my house?"

"My honey, I will never deny you anything in my life. I am ready to come with her."

Jacob found her so nice with a soothing voice and the happiest smile he had never seen except from his beloved children. Thus, the two old friends decided to embark on their love adventure. They picked up the threads of a friendship of childhood that was developing into an adult relationship. The reunion after two decades of friendship convinced them that they were perfect match to each other. Nikita became Jacob's dream come true. They agreed to share happiness and misfortune. Nikita was confident that Jacob was the right man she wished to spend the rest of her life with. He was every inch a gentleman. Jacob too believed that living with Nikita would be like living in heaven. He believed—given that he knew her already—that she was a perfect human being. He also believed that she would be a jolly woman in his house.

Jacob felt the kind of mad passionate love he had never experienced before. He met Nikita who had the biggest lust for him, and he knew that they were attracted to each other. Their feelings took them into another world, a world of their dreams. In Jacob's mind, Nikita was the symbol of real love. She would no more sleep with any other man in her life. She had found the man she had been dreaming of. After an hour-and-a-half, they returned to the store.

Ram Dee and Crystal joined them in the flower center. Ram Dee spoke first though both of them wanted to know Jacob's impressions on the flower.

"What's up, buddy? You got the flower. You surely love her, don't you?"

Jacob could not find words to describe her. "Certainly," he said. He was not ready to elaborate. Still, one could read the sweet smile on the face.

"Will you buy her?" Ram Dee asked.

"Absolutely," Crystie replied instead of Jacob.

"How do you know, Crystie?"

"One can tell from his face," Crystie said.

Ram Dee wanted to confirm with Jacob himself. "You gotta buy her, I guess."

Jacob glanced at Ram Dee's and Crystie's faces and smiled. Nikita answered the question.

"If he doesn't take this charming creature, where in the world will he find something better? She is all he needs."

Both Crystal and Ram Dee gave him hugs and burst into joyful laughter. Jacob felt supported.

"Give me five. You're the man." They gave him five. This time, Jacob spoke more poetically.

"I have found the flower. I call her Rosie. I cannot wait to see her on the headstock of my queen-size empty bed, which will soon be full of love. I will collect her when the time is right."

Jacob grabbed Ram Dee by the hand, and they walked around through Hanging Baskets. There were many varieties of roses and geraniums.

"It is no use looking at other flowers. I already got the one I wanted. There is no need to waste my time on others. I will take Nikita's flower."

"You mean you are not taking her right now? Why? Others might buy her," Ram Dee said, wanting the flower to go as quickly as possible. Jacob was not in a rush.

"They did not buy her before. Now it is too late. They will buy others. I still need time for preparation, y' know."

Ram Dee looked surprised and tried to convince him.

"I'd rather you didn't leave her in the store. Take her with you, man. Why do you have to wait, bro? Pick the fruit when it's ripe. Bees may pick her pollen while you are away."

"No need to hurry, buddy. I will have to fix something before I make a final decision. I don't want her for just one week end, you know . . . I mean . . . I . . . I . . . I need her for life. I will prepare her to handle the stress of winter. Y'know what I mean, bro?"

"You are kidding. Are you saying that you already hooked up with that woman? I thought it was only for part-time," Ram Dee said in surprise.

"We love each other, and we feel attracted to each other. She is my princess, I mean, my angel."

"What are you talking about? Just pick the pollen and forget."

"What are you talking about? I am not after the pollen. You know me for many years. I am not a bee."

"Okay! That sounds good," Ram Dee said in resignation. "And you are getting one hell of a deal. You could have had her long ago if you knew. She really needed somebody like you, y'know. You don't have to pay for her flower. You just pick and go."

"What would I say if they caught me shoplifting! Come on, Ram Dee, be serious. Money isn't an issue. I will pay no matter the price. By the way, what happened with Kubwa, the guy I saw with her in Nairobi? She presented him as her new boyfriend."

"Kubwa is a stupid asshole. He dumped her with a child."

"Don't say that. He is a nice person. If he didn't drop her, how would I get such charming creature! Still, you might be right. How could a man leave somebody like Nikita! Anyway, now she is mine and forever."

"Good luck. If I were you, I wouldn't pay a dime for that flower. I would just pick it and forget like others. Shoplifting is okay once in a while."

"Why do you say that? She is burying the past to build a bright future."

"Okay. You may be right, but I don't think so."

"No kidding," he pulled Ram Dee by the hand and joined the ladies. They moved to the cashier. Jacob reached for his wallet and pulled out a twenty-dollar note. He promised to come back for the final payment on July 4, 2008. He pocketed his change and stayed a while gazing on the rose. Nikita put the flower aside with a new rose label marked in black bold **SOLD**.

Jacob was sincere in his determination to never let any disturbance in the course of his life. Nikita, too, took the same vow. However, in purchasing her flower, Jacob never knew that he was entering a serious competition. He and Ram Dee exited the store as Crystal assisted Nikita in wrapping the flower as she wanted to talk to Nikita in privacy.

"Congratulations. He is incredible in his yuppie way. He is a virile man with nice ways. He sounds sweet and honest. Don't disappoint him like the others. He is really interesting . . . chivalrous. And he is romantic."

"Well, he's really my type. He has always been cool. He has incredible eyes. I really love him. But please, don't reveal my agenda to him. I won't deviate from it. And please, don't tell Thomas and John about him. I don't want them to know it now." They exchanged knowing smiles.

"I am not saying anything at all. It's none of my business." With that, Crystal waved good-bye and joined the guys.

The group headed to Lacey for a luncheon with other friends. Later at night, Nikita not only presented Rosie to Jacob once again, but she also served him.

The next day, there was a welcome party in Jacob's honor. Friends were milling around to congratulate their host from Canada. Ram Dee took the floor on behalf of the community and presented Jacob to the guests. He officially presented Nikita as his precious gift from Olympia.

The impromptu party was wonderful. Guests ate all kinds of food, drank, and danced. Nikita was excited. She had had innumerable romances none of which had given fruitful results. She had been so nice that she accepted every man who wanted to crowd into her life, provided that they would cooperate. Jacob was only adding fresh romance to her long romantic history. In essence, she needed romance, rather than imprisonment of a family. Jacob, too, was a romantic person. However, he would only limit his romance to Nikita, hoping to build a family life with her. He had been living in a family, and he loved that kind of life. Nikita, who only knew of romances, had never thought of an organized family. She had had her ups and downs. Now that she was aging, she finally decided to bite the bullet. She thought it was high time she settled down with one man who would shoulder her load. She found Jacob as a very nice bet. Jacob's arrival brightened her life like sunrise. His smile reached deep in her heart. She felt relieved.

There was a huge problem though. She did not know duties and responsibilities of a husband and wife. She did not bother asking her conscience if she was ready for responsibilities. She found Jacob so charming, caring, and devoted to her. She would soon be wrapped in his arms all night long, and she would be secure with somebody she grew up with. Without thinking, she promised to respect and take care for him. Guests applauded.

All faces were alight with joy except one man who appeared to be nervous. This gentleman, by name Thomas Something, was like a *bee* that had been sucking the pollen until the day before. Now that Jacob was there, Thomas was taken aback. He watched Jacob kissing Nikita on the mouth and giving her an engagement ring. He did not believe what he saw as he was not aware of the new relationship. Until that day, he had been taking control of the flower's vase, polishing it as he enjoyed the flower's scent. Nikita was his everything. Now that she would be taken away, he was heartbroken. Yet he tried not to show emotions in public. He moved around, going back and forth. Jacob noticed that Thomas did not seem to share the joy of the party. He had no idea of his being with Nikita. Jacob invited him to dance. Thomas apologized and promised to dance later. He shot to his feet and exited the house. He stood at the balcony and smoked cigarettes one after another. Jacob joined him and held out his hands to him. After shaking hands, he put his hand on his shoulder:

"Brother, we're enjoying ourselves inside and you are all alone out here! Come'n hav'a drink with us. Dis is a very great day, y'know what I'm saying. I am the happiest man in the world. Come and share the joy of our engagement."

Thomas took a deep breath and sighed. He turned his head down and promised to join the others shortly. He did not want anybody to see the tears welling up in his eyes. The others knew about his affairs with Nikita. They had been a couple since Nikita's children kicked Kevin out a year before. They kept quiet to let Nikita enjoy the happiest event of her life. They believed that it was worth it if it meant that she was finally with a man who would go beyond just picking the pollen. Jacob, the new flesh from Canada, had no clue about what was going on. Even Ram Dee and Crystal kept the affair top secret. They had seen Nikita and Thomas locked in each other's arms, cheek against cheek, and lips on lips. Yet they told Jacob that Nikita was the best woman for him. Thomas watched Jacob lifting an engagement ring with a diamond cluster as big as a watch face. He twisted it around and around Nikita's finger. Friends acclaimed. Thomas turned his eyes down and cried hopeless tears.

Jacob left Olympia with a promise to come back for his treasure. Since that day, they missed each other so much that they had to meet every other month. The story of Thomas lusting after Nikita was revealed to Jacob about three months later. According to Ram Dee, Nikita found Jacob to be the right person for her. She looked down her nose at Thomas in favor of Jacob. From that moment on, Jacob doubted that she might not be serious. She had never told him that he was in competition with Thomas. Even though he won the competition, breaking up with Thomas was not reassuring news as long as they were still living in the same city. Jacob worried that there might be others around. She might break up with Thomas and flirt with others. He felt insecure. He thought that Nikita was so fragile and vulnerable that she needed a lot of attention. He decided to bring her closer to him as soon as possible. Once they were together, she would be free from other suitors.

2. Jacob Was Forewarned What Nikita was Forearmed

Jacob and Nikita did not allow themselves to miss each other. Jacob loved her more than he could love any other woman. With his red Porsche, he cruised to Olympia every other month to double-check if he was not on the wrong side of love. Nikita was a talkative person, and Jacob was a good listener. He loved to listen to her stories. When she started talking, she was like a radio with new batteries. The only difference was that radios do not broadcast everything. Journalists screen their news and broadcast what they want their listeners to hear. Nikita would neither control her language nor count her words. One day, she joyfully reported an incident that Jacob would never forget. The thing happened in a nightclub when a man tried to woo her.

"The guy approached me in a friendly way, and I thought he knew me somewhere. Then he started pampering me, 'you are so cute.' I told him to go to hell."

"Why did you send him to hell? He did nothing wrong. He told you what every man could tell you. I personally could have told you the same if I were there," Jacob commented.

"It was the first time he saw me and I did not like him," Nikita replied.

"You did not like him but he liked you," Jacob said.

"He insisted talking to me and he pissed me off. You know what I did?"

"Don't say that you assaulted him."

"I gathered a lot of saliva in my mouth and spat in his eyes."

"Are you kidding me?"

"He immediately ran to rinse his face and shirt with water. He hid in the washroom for a while because his shirt was wet with my saliva. He could not joke with me again," she concluded her story as somebody who did a brave act. Jacob thought that it was only a joke. He did not believe that she could react like that. Needing to check if she was really serious, he asked,

"Did you really spit saliva in somebody's eyes?"

Nikita confirmed with obvious satisfaction.

"Of course I did. He had pissed me off and I didn't really like him," she concluded.

Jacob heard the story as a stupid reaction. He could not imagine that she could do a stupid thing like that. It was a terrible thing to boast about. He looked at her in the eyes to check if she felt any remorse for the terrible reaction.

"That is not a proper way to treat somebody who shows interest in her," Jacob said.

"I hated him."

"You could just say "thank you" and turn away," he said, finding it rather odd to spit saliva at somebody who gave a positive comment.

If Nikita rewarded him by spitting in his eyes for admiring her, then Jacob deserved worse than that. He had said the same thing hundreds of times.

"I don't know the man but I feel sorry for him. Did you apologize afterward?" he asked.

"Why should I?" Nikita said, not feeling guilty for the mistreatment of the poor boy.

"I think you should say sorry," Jacob said. He feared that she might not be a nice person.

"If the event was reported by somebody else, I would reject it as a lie."

Even though the stupid thing was told by Nikita herself, Jacob chose not to take it seriously. It was too bad to be true. He did everything to forget it, but it never left his mind.

A few months later, Earl, a friend of Jacob, who believed to know Nikita really well, forewarned Jacob that he was clinging on something that did not have any substance at all. He had seen her many a time in different circumstances. He advised him not to lose his time and money on someone like her.

"Nikita is a disaster waiting to happen. She was an easy prey for men. She is now burned out . . . I guarantee you that it will never work out. She will bitch up your life. If she did it to others, she will do it to you too. Please, Jacob, believe me. It is not going to work," he concluded pleading with him to break his engagement with her.

"How do you know her when you live in London? How dare you assert that it's not going to work? I love her and she loves me. That's all I need," Jacob replied with reassurance.

"Everybody knows that mouse of girl. Anyway, that is not the issue. What I am concerned about is her past. She grew up all over, and her life is full of mysteries. She is too big a flirt. She had terrible romances and experiences with numerous men. No one dared marry her. They feared infidelities as she never respects herself. Loving her has never been rewarding to anybody. If it works with you, I bet you will be a special man. Of course, she will pretend to love you. As far as I know, she will never be satisfied. She keeps changing men like underwear. You won't handle her, man. She is beautiful but difficult. Men flung themselves at her just because of her perfect body. I wouldn't recommend you to her."

All knew only too well that Nikita had never been hesitant about lovemaking. The only thing she had been hesitant about was committing for life. She was not sure if she would make it with one man. If she wanted Jacob that much, she needed to be relaxed in her body as well as in her mind. She had been with so many men that she was trying to educate herself with one man though she was not too sure about one man being enough for her. Earl thought that Jacob would be disillusioned and agree to leave her aside.

"Obviously, you don't know her. If you did, you would never have thought of dragging her with you. So you need to know her before you make your decision."

"What do I need to know about her?" Jacob asked Earl.

"A good example of her dishonesty is that she is not telling you the truth. She knows of her customers' dissatisfaction. At first, they believed like you that she was a wonderful person. In the end, her flower turned to be a dangerously reactive material. Customers had to return her to the gardens or the stores. Since then, she moves from garden to garden, from one store to another. Now that she is worn out, she needs somebody that doesn't know her black history."

"I know her since childhood. There is no other person I know more than her."

"In the meantime, she changed. You mean, none of your friends told you about her stories?" Earl asked Jacob who shook his head. "Maybe somebody told you and you forgot, or you simply chose to ignore them. Anyway, it is a good idea to bring the matter to your attention. I know you since childhood and I would not like her to spoil your life as she did to Ronald, Kubwa, Kevin, Thomas, Shawn, John, and others. I tell you, man, the lane you are driving on leads to a ditch. Your buddies should not be indifferent to the value of your life. I hate to reveal Nikita's personal life, but I think it is important to know the product before deciding to take it." Earl did not even mention the storms. Jacob laughed to hide his embarrassment.

"She did silly things when she was still young. Men took advantage of her weaknesses and lied to her. Now that she is with three kids hanging all over her, no male faces will turn her way again. I am confident that she would have the heart to reject them."

"This is wishful thinking on your part, my friend. If it was not hard to say no to a man, will she learn to respect herself in your house? She did everything with her kids clinging on her. She learned how to deal with the situation. She trained them to stay home unattended all night long when she was enjoying herself with men. She did not care what might happen to them. Basically, her kids never saw her on weekends. Don't you see that they are only one year apart?"

"I know what you are saying, man. Somebody else told me something like that. Like you are saying, those kids seem to have educated themselves. I don't know why Ram Dee did not tell me anything at all. He only advised me not to take her."

"That was a big piece of advice. It is no use asking Ram Dee about her. What he told you explains everything. I am sure he knows all about her. He must have seen something. He surely doesn't want her to bitch your life. I am telling you what everybody else knows. By the way, does your family accept your engagement with her?"

"I told them about her. Frankly speaking, no one wants the Chissoccos in our family. They have a bad history. Most people in our neighborhood hate them. They say that they are unreliable and untrustworthy. They even put pressure on me to abandon my commitment with a lady they consider worthless."

"What did you say?"

"I tried to explain that I love her, that's it. Our love has nothing to do with her family having a damaged reputation."

"Did you convince them?"

"They still retain a deep distrust of the Chissoccos. They feel a shock about their son loving a lady from that family."

"What does her mother say about Nikita's being in the Baraks?" Earl asked, unable to hide his curiosity.

"Actually, to my surprise, I realized that Nikita is trying to keep this relationship a secret. She does not even want to involve her mother in her affairs. She claims that her mom is spying on her, wanting to intrude in her privacy. Therefore, she doesn't want her to know about her life. I have been trying to change her mind, but she never wants me to meet her family. I don't know why she should hide our relationship. It looks weird. Can you imagine that I was the one to introduce myself to her mom?"

"How did you do that?" Earl asked.

"I insisted on having her number. Nikita finally gave it to me. She had been reluctant to let me talk to her. I started calling her to say hi. She hadn't seen me in twenty-two years, and she was not expecting my call. At first, she thought that I was calling to ask about Nikita, and she wanted to give me her number. Finally, I was the one to give her news. When she learned that we were in touch, she was so happy. I also let her know that we were planning to fly to see her together. That is the time she understood that there was something between us."

"Have you met her then?"

"How could I meet her when Nikita doesn't want me to? She convinced me that it was not necessary. She did not even inform her of her engagement. She said she is mature enough to take her own decisions. I did not insist."

"If Nikita doesn't want her own mother to know about her life, then there is something suspicious. She must be hiding something. You need to pay more attention, man! Her refusal to inform her family of her engagement is not only due to the permanent estrangement between them but also result of her doubt in her own decision. She is not sure if she can handle a family life," Earl explained.

Forbidden fruit is the sweetest. Earl was telling Jacob every truth about Nikita when their relationship was just firing up. In Jacob's mind, she was the only woman in the universe that he could think of. In fact, he knew very few women. In the meantime, an image of Jacob holding his kids with her was already formed in his mind. He was working on the dream days and nights. He was so obsessed with the dream that he never wanted to hear anything negative about Nikita. He was out-of-control in love. Rather than doing him good, Earl's revelations shocked and intrigued him. Jacob had his heart set on being with Nikita no matter what. Changing the plan was out of question. He only looked on the bright side. Whenever it came to her negative points, he closed his ears. He had already made up his mind, and he decided to take that risk. She was the only female he knew, and she had promised to take care of his life. Jacob did not want to live without love. He was determined not to break her heart.

"You needn't tell me about her negative points. It is too late to change anything now. I do not wish to disappoint her and she promised the same."

Jacob was as proud as a punch that his childhood friend was his future. He defended her to the hilt. Earl insisted and revealed her bad past history. Jacob closed his ears. Instead, he talked himself hoarse defending her.

"Well, Earl, I'd rather you didn't rain on my parade," he concluded, only wanting to listen to his heart.

"She said she has found the proper man, and she is proud of me. Besides, I do not dwell on the past. Now that she belongs to me, the years of dirt have been wiped away. This is an opportunity for her to enjoy what she really missed all that time. The future is bright, and it is all that matters now. After all, everybody has their own stories."

"This is the downside of true love. You have always been a man of positive thinking. You rarely look at things in the negative side but don't compare Nikita to the sun shining in your yard."

"What do you mean?"

"When the sun shines, no one tell you that the light smells good or bad. A human being is different."

"Earl, Nikita may have done terrible things in the past. Now she is promising a brighter future, she will correct her mistakes to build a sustainable relationship with the man of her dreams."

"I say, the more you love, the blinder you become," Earl said, confirming what everybody knew, including Jacob himself. "She has been acting odd to other men, and she had been boasting about it. You are a man like the others though much younger. If she did not show respect to men twelve years older than she was, why would she respect you? Do you think that her abusive language will be over now that she has found the proper man and she promised to treat you with respect?

"I don't believe that she will still act irresponsibly at her age."

Jacob wanted his heart full of love. Nikita was the only one he wanted to fill the gap in his heart. He only looked at the good side of this charming creature, listening to what he wanted to hear, adoring the physical beauty. Her love would make him complete. In his eyes, she was an angel. She was as clean as drinking water. Although Earl proved that all that glitters was not gold, Jacob defended her instead.

"There are no saints in this world," he said later. "Besides, I am not seeking perfection," he concluded.

Jacob knew that Earl was right. However, he did not want to break Nikita's heart. He met her in his greatest moment of need for caring. At that time, he was still in shock grieving the loss of his lily with all the gossip surrounding it. Emotions were still seesawing. He needed comfort, and Nikita was the first to support him. She had promised to be on his side no matter what. Earl badmouthed her during the year of torment and struggle when Jacob was trying to pull himself together. Nikita was the only one to give him strength and happiness. She became his present and future. Rosie was the only flower whose scent attracted his sense of smell while Nikita attracted all of his five senses. Jacob had never known special moments in his life. His life had been marked by political crises with Evildoers seeking to kill him. This was the first time he felt real love with no Evildoers shooting all around and he wanted to treasure it.

As he was not rushing, he took time to think about his new adventure. As Nikita had been living with different boyfriends for many years, Jacob started wondering if she was really serious about her engagement. He asked her if she was really looking for a genuine and long lasting relationship. She swore that she was determined to build a lifelong relationship with him. Jacob agreed that she was the best woman for his life. He expected more than just happiness. He hoped that their loyalty to each other would be absolute.

Nikita did not wait to get to Canada to show her true colors. More than once, she reacted violently, exposed her flower to the extreme heat. She moved from club to club and from bar to bar, exposing the flower in public places where bees picked the pollen. The flower remained like public property as she let everybody play with her. Jacob saw her turning white, then violet, then blue, green, or red depending on circumstances. By changing colors like a chameleon, she revealed her true face, and their relationship began to disintegrate. He wondered why she allowed this to happen when she vowed to protect his flower. He even considered betraying his promise to love her all his life.

The worse was still yet to come. Nikita's children were so jealous that they would never accept any man as their stepfather, less Jacob. More than once, they opened valves of his vehicle to let all the air out. Jacob never believed that a twelve-year-old child could do that. Another time, he broke Jacob's laptop computer and threw it in the garbage bin. Nikita was mad at them. She spent days and days explaining to the kids that she needed Jacob to help her take care of them. The boys were so jealous that they hated to see their mom with men, especially Jacob, who was trying to discipline them. One day, Jacob took them to their favorite Vietnamese restaurant. The boys hastened to ask for a table for five. Jacob informed them that they would need a table for six sometime soon.

"We are just five. Why would we need a table for six?" the oldest boy exclaimed. Jacob let them know that the family would have a new member in a couple of months.

"What! You mean my mom is pregnant?" he screamed, looking somewhat shocked.

"I thought you knew it. You are expecting a sister soon."

The boys got crazy and started breaking things in the restaurant. Nikita tried to cool them down.

"What is wrong with you, boys? Don't you want a young sister?"

"We would love to have a sister but not from him. We hate him," one of the boys answered pointing a finger at Jacob.

"He was only teasing you." Nikita tried to calm them down. Jacob looked disappointed by Nikita's reaction.

"Come along, Nikita, you ought to tell them the good news. There is no reason you should hide it from your children. It seems that you are not happy about it either."

"I am just trying to calm them down because their nerves are on edge. I will tell them when they will be quiet."

"My deepest fear is that you yourself don't seem to be happy with it. You ought to have told them already. They would not have created disorder in the restaurant," Jacob concluded.

Nikita feared to lose Jacob as he had lost Kevin. She tried to convince her kids that they really needed a father in their lives. Her efforts were in vain. The relations between Jacob and Nikita's children remained strained until they left the restaurant. A flat tire united them. Nikita was driving home and ran over a piece of metal. The metal punctured the tire, and it deflated rapidly. It was late in the evening, and there was heavy traffic. Nikita had never experienced a flat tire. She panicked and lost control of the vehicle. She did not know that it was a flat tire. Jacob knew that it was not something terrible. All eyes were on him to tell them what to do. Jacob advised Nikita to slow gradually and pull out of traffic so he could figure out what to do. He informed the boys that it was a small issue that he could fix himself. He asked Nikita if she had a jack and a spare tire. She did not know anything about car maintenance. Jacob opened the trunk of her vehicle, pulled out a jack and started lifting the car. He took out the flat tire and replaced it with a spare one. He scooted behind the wheel and drove to Olympia. Nikita explained to her children that it should be obvious that they could not exist without a man in their lives. They would be in terrible mess if Jacob had not been there. In spite of that, Nikita's children never treated Jacob with respect. They never agreed with their mother when she claimed that a man was really important in their lives. Gradually, the relation improved. However, Nikita became another problem.

Jacob was a great admirer of arts. He planned to visit some museums the next time he went to see her. He told her of his desire to visit the Seattle Art Museum. She promised to take him there. When it was time for the visit, Nikita was reluctant to go. As Jacob insisted, she took him to the Washington State History Museum in Olympia. Jacob liked the visit hoping that it did not mean that his visit to Seattle was cancelled.

"Are we going to see the Seattle Art Museum?"

"I hate driving in Seattle. There is more traffic than I am used to," she said, not wanting to go there.

"Don't worry. I will do all the driving. I have driven in Seattle many times and didn't mind the traffic," Jacob replied.

"All the streets are busy there."

"It doesn't matter. I can drive in any city in the world." Given that he drove for several years in Montreal and Toronto, he did not fear to drive in any city in the world. He insisted that he would not leave without visiting the Seattle Art Museum.

"Honey, I don't know Seattle well, and I don't have a GPS," she persisted.

"Come on, Nikita. I drove from Edmonton to Olympia, eighteen hours without a GPS. I trust my brain. All I need is a good map," he tried to reassure her.

"This guy is pushing me to go to Seattle. I don't want to go there," she changed her mood.

"Never mind. I planned to visit the museum, and you promised to take me there. It is only an hour from here. If you did not promise to drive me there, I would have stopped over there before coming here. That is not a big issue anyway. I will go there tomorrow while you are at work." Nikita did not want him to go by himself. She told her boys to get ready, and the whole family went to Seattle with Jacob.

They got to the museum, but there was no parking at the first avenue. Jacob drove around the block looking for a parking space. He went around another block, and there was no parking available. There were stop signs at each intersection. At every stop sign, the car rolled back down hill. Jacob had to press hard on the gas pedal to avoid rolling back. All vehicles were rolling back on the hill. Nikita started yelling.

"Why did you bring me here? I told you that I feared driving here. Now, look at what is happening!"

"There is nothing wrong here. Driving up hill is always like this."

"I didn't want to come here, and you insisted. You never listen to me. We shouldn't be driving here. I hate driving uphill."

"Honey, I am not asking you to drive. I am doing all the driving. Can you let me find a parking?" he looked disappointed by her attitude.

"Look at those vehicles rolling back. I am scared. Take me out of here!" she yelled louder.

Jacob was shocked by the strange behavior. He could not go to the museum with somebody screaming and yelling on him. He decided to get out of there. There were still other stop signs at the fourth and fifth avenues. Nikita ordered him not to respect the stop signs that were making her crazy. He did not respect the order.

"Why do you stop again? I told you not to stop at the stop sign. Are you deaf?" Jacob did not say a word. "Why don't you park there?"

"Honey, I can't park in a No Parking Zone."

"What about the other empty space?"

"That is a tow-away zone. I can park there if you have enough money to pay a stupid contravention."

"That is not a tow-away zone. There are other vehicles parked there."

"Can't you see that sign?"

The situation was so tense that there was no more communication between them. He hit the fifth avenue and took a left turn. He immediately pulled out and took a deep breath. He told Nikita that he was not fit to drive. They changed seats, and Nikita drove to one of her friends in Shoreline. She reported to Crystal what happened.

"This guy took me to Seattle, and I did not like it. The car was rolling back, and I felt dizzy."

Jacob listened to her and wondered why she behaved like that. He found her as a too domineering person. It was either her way or nothing. He decided not to go any further in their relationship. When they arrived in Olympia, he rebooked the flight and left Olympia the next morning.

Jacob arrived in Edmonton and decided to move on without Nikita. He feared that she might not be the right person. Three weeks passed without any communication as he would not return her calls. Nikita ached to see him. She decided to ambush him. She had met him at the right time in her life, and she did not want to let him go. She kept calling him, and he did not pick up the phone. When he finally did, he advised her to move on with her own life or find somebody else. The next day, Jacob arrived home from work. He checked his phone and found eleven missed calls of a same number 360-491-9480. Although he recognized the area code as he had been calling Olympia ten times a day for several months, he did not recognize that number. He returned the calls. He asked the receptionist about who had called him, but she had no idea. Finally, when Jacob checked his messages, he realized that the calls were made from Providence St. Peter Hospital. A message from Dr. Lloyd informed him that Nikita felt down and depressed. She was admitted in the Providence St. Peter Hospital, at 413 Lilly Road Northeast, Olympia, for treatment. Dr. Lloyd left a number to call as soon as he got the message. Other messages were left by Ram Dee informing him that Nikita was heartbroken. She was in a bad state, and she might end up suffering prolonged depression if he did not intervene in time. All she needed was his special care. He insisted that he stay close to her as he was the only one to cheer her up. Jacob was the only one she needed as a cure. Nothing else was working.

Jacob called the hospital to comfort her. The receptionist transferred his call to the emergency room. A nurse picked the phone and held it on Nikita's ear. She felt comforted as she listened to what she wanted to hear.

"My darling, you are the only one that gives me happiness. You are my heart's true love, the only being I dream about. I need you beside me, now and forever, listening to the beautiful words of caring. I miss your magic kisses that light my days and your sweet laughter that warms the cold nights. Your smile reaches deep in my heart. A day without your smile is a lost day. You are so precious to me, my dear heart. I can't wait to share life's beautiful adventures with you. I will do whatever possible to see you today, my sweetheart."

Thanks to Jacob's apologies and caring words, Nikita started feeling better and better. She needed this sweet talk of missing her. She needed the comfort of a man she was used to. Among other things, she missed enjoying fresh air under a tree, listening to bird songs. She needed to bliss out with him, lying on the beach of the Capitol Lake and talking softly. She missed having fun and feeling the beauty of things under the stars on a moonless night with lightings painting the horizon. Missing Jacob was tantamount to missing the peace of the mind, so to speak.

Jacob managed to squeeze a trip in his already booked schedule. He drove to the airport and asked for the first nonstop flight to Olympia. That evening, there was only a connecting flight with a stopover in Seattle. There was only one executive seat left. In three hours, Jacob was already in the Providence St. Peter Hospital where Nikita was waiting for him anxiously. He told the nurses about her, and they let him go straight to the emergency room. Jacob sat on the edge of the bed. He touched her cheek and she opened her eyes. She rolled the blanked down and reached for his hand. She started feeling warmth turning inside her. She pulled him toward her and he gave her a hasty kiss. She put his hand on her chest under her nightdress. He helped her to get up so she could rest against his shoulder. Shy as he was, he felt uncomfortable to caress her large breasts on a hospital bed. She was now speaking normally. Two hours later, a nurse came and saw that she was doing fine. Nikita wanted to go home. She had to wait for her doctor. Dr. Lloyd came and discharged her. Jacob hooked his arm through hers and helped her walk to Ram Dee's Infiniti waiting outside. Nikita was teary with happiness. Jacob wiped her tears. She gave him a glorious smile. He opened the back door of the SUV, and he helped her to the backseat. After fastening her seatbelt, he rounded the vehicle to sit beside her. Ram Dee drove through Yashiro Japanese Garden to Nikita's favorite Chinese restaurant. After the dinner, they took E Bay Drive NE and headed down Fourth Avenue, where Nikita lived. She did not look as somebody who spent a night in an emergency room. It was as if nothing had happened at all. She had the same look, but Jacob saw her as more beautiful than she was ever before. They arrived home, and she wanted a dance. "Let's have a dance." She put "The Power of Love" by Celine Dion—the music they had been playing every time they met.

Absence makes the heart grow fonder. Jacob didn't know that Nikita loved him so much that his absence would break her heart. He understood that her love was a genuine one, what he doubted before. Now that it was confirmed, she was the sweetest woman in the world. She was levelheaded and showed enthusiasm to be in a lifelong relationship. She saw how much Jacob cared for her. She would do everything to please him. After a score of kisses from head to toe, she whispered sweet words, "You are my dream, the embodiment of love, care and strength. I will always love you."

Jacob loved the flowery speech. He was too busy to utter any word. He was saying much more with his protective hand wandering around her smooth body. She enjoyed more when the hand reached downtown. Their desire for each other grew stronger. They spent an unforgettable night together. They were so enthusiastic to meet again and share some of the pleasures of life. Nikita's words encouraged Jacob. She was more than determined to live with him, uttering words that no honest person would betray.

"Honey, we would have an excellent life together now if we had got married twenty years ago. We really loved each other, and I knew that we would be together some day. At the age of fifteen, I wanted to be wrapped in your arms, but you did not care. You knew nothing about love. I understand that you were too young."

"You were younger than I was," Jacob objected.

"I was younger, but I was a girl. In love matters, girls are more mature than boys. One day, we were in one of our hideaways. I gave you many hugs and kisses in the hope that we would understand what I meant. I pressed my chest on yours, and I forced your hand on my breasts. Do you remember what you did?" she asked him.

Jacob remembered the day, but he pretended he did not. "Don't say we did it, did we?"

"Of course not. You did not even kiss me. You looked away. I was really shocked. After that, I tried several times, and it never worked. Anyway, our time had not yet come."

"I knew nothing about it. That is why I went to study in church schools. I remained virgin until I finished university. My mother was worried about me. She never saw me with any girl until two years after university. She was so happy to finally see me with a lady."

"Our moment has finally arrived. You are no longer the timid boy."

"And you are not the country girl I used to hang around with twenty years ago either."

"At least we know what we are doing," she concluded. They continued their romance, and they were wild in their enjoyment.

After the wonderful night, Jacob invited her to improve what had been going wrong. Without any apology, Nikita smiled and promised to work on it. They agreed to stay closer and closer to each other so as not to be missing the moments that had been haunting them. They decided that they should not stay far from each other.

Although Nikita's mother, brothers, and sisters lived not far from her, no one knew that she was planning to move to Canada. After visiting Jacob in Edmonton, she returned to Olympia to pack her personal belongings. She did not even inform her family that she was now engaged. Without waving them good-bye, she planned to move to Canada. Jacob wanted closeness with Nikita's family. After several weeks, he called his mother-in-law to let her know that her daughter was now with him. Nikita did not like it though.

3. The Great Union of Lovers and Evildoers

After a year or so, Jacob was reading a book in his empty queen-size bed. He opened a window and saw Dickson Rushatsihori behind the wheel of a black Honda CRV. He was astounded to see him in Canada. He asked other friends how the killer happened to be in Canada. He could not be a refugee when he was one of the

Evildoers who forced millions of citizens to death and exile. When survivors were down and out in refugee camps, Dickson and other Evildoers had deep pockets as they were enjoying their full rights. Only a few of them could sympathize with their fellow citizens. It was unbelievable that the terrorist was now enjoying life in Canada.

Jacob's informers confirmed that Dickson had become a refugee. After leaving the army, he joined the death squad. They killed people and looted their personal belongings. Although they had to share all the spoils, Dickson screwed them on stolen vehicles. He sold the vehicles, and he did not want to share the money with other gang members. He started hiding. As the gangsters got mad at him, Dickson was in big trouble. They were armed with guns, grenades and bayonets. Dickson feared being killed, and he ran away with the money. He kept hiding in different places. Finally, he left the country and stayed in Kenya where he did the business of stealing vehicles and selling them abroad. He targeted new SUV of humanitarian organizations operating in Nairobi. He met with Nikita Chissocco and they started secret romances.

Schadrack Kubwa knew that Dickson was involved in the assassination of Ronald. He tried to avoid him. Each time he changed his address, Dickson would know his new address. As Dickson was always updated on his whereabouts, Schadrack feared that he was after him. Then he found out that there was something going on between Dickson and Nikita. He immediately broke up with Nikita.

Dickson got a job with the International Rescue Committee, an organization that helped him to resettle in Canada. In order to be accepted in Canada, he had to lie that he was persecuted by political authority. He never revealed that he was the one to threaten lives of innocent citizens. In other words, his victims became the accused. Jacob did not fear him in Canada. He knew that he could not do evil acts anymore. They met and shared a drink. They exchanged views on the situation of Burundi as if nothing happened between them. They were in Canada, a country of law and order. As Burundians, they had to relate to each other as country fellows. Dickson introduced him to one of his friends.

"Zim Anan, this is Jacob Barak, my old friend and classmate. Jacob, this is my best friend Juvenhack Zim Anan." Juvenhack and Jacob shook hands.

"How do you do, Juvenhack?"

"How do you do? Nice to meet you."

"It's nice meeting you, too. I think I know you somewhere. Is it the first time you see me?" Jacob asked. Juvenhack could not recognize him.

"I am thinking about where I saw you. You look familiar to me. What was your job in Burundi?"

"I was a teacher. And you?'

"I was a soldier in Muzinda Military Camp."

Teachers and soldiers had nothing in common. No one was sure about where they first met. Jacob knew that Juvenhack was somebody he used to know. He kept wondering where he knew him from, considering that soldiers wanted to kill him.

"You look very familiar to me, but I can't remember exactly where we met. Have you been in Kivoga High School?"

"Not quite often. I know Kivoga because I was working in Muzinda Military Camp. Most of the time, I was controlling traffic near Kivoga, on the road from Bujumbura to Muzinda. I might have seen you there."

Jacob finally recognized him. He was the one who arrested him at Kanka checkpoint. He even remembered the name of Juvenhack Zim Anan who pulled him from Eugene's vehicle. He was not quite sure if it was the same soldier though. As they talked, Jacob checked if he was the same Evildoer.

"I was at the university in 1993. Did you see me there?"

"I don't think I saw you there. Most the time, I was checking passengers on the road. I met many university students, but I don't think I would have met you," Juvenhack said, wondering how he would have seen him and let him live.

Jacob knew that Evildoers killed many students. Juvenhack's statement meant that if he had seen him he would have killed him. Jacob discovered that he was the soldier who pulled him out of the vehicle in October 1993. Juvenhack could not remember the incident. He was involved in so many killings that he could not remember small incidents. Jacob pretended that he did not recognize him. He still needed other occasions to make sure he was the man who tried to kill him. One day, as they were talking about the situation in Burundi, Juvenhack spoke about his experience in the army. Jacob noted places and dates of events. It became obvious that Juvenhack was the same guy that tried to kill him on two occasions.

As Jacob had befriended Dickson, he told him about his engagement with nature and how he met Nikita Chissocco after twenty-two years. As if to cover for the terrible things he did in the past, Dickson offered to support him in everything. He was excited to hear that Nikita was coming closer to him. Jacob had no clue that there had been something between them. With Ronald killed by Dickson's gang, Jacob could not imagine that Nikita would allow Dickson in her family.

Dickson helped Jacob to strip the walls, scrap the window, sand and varnish the floor. They painted the house with the rainbow of colors. They decorated it, embellished it, and made it more beautiful than ever before. They repapered the bathroom with rose wallpaper with summer butterflies, bees, and flowers. The house was immaculate. With pictures of Jacob's children on the walls, the house looked spectacular. Yet Jacob was not satisfied. Something was still missing. He thought that Nikita would bring new air in his room and light his days. He longed for a hug, a kiss, and a smile. Nikita kept telling him sweet words. And Jacob believed that nothing was more powerful than his love for her.

Jacob arranged a spot on the window of his room. When he was all set, he called the store in Olympia to check if they could do home delivery. The front desk confirmed that they would only deliver the flower to Kelowna, British Columbia, where Jacob would meet her halfway. He gave an address, and she was delivered the second week of September. The shop confirmed that she was still good for at least another year. This was not a warrantee though.

Nikita would come and become all his, not anybody else's. She would change Jacob's life. Loneliness without the smile of his beloved children was unbearable. He was feeling unsettled, alone, and bored. Technically, he was alone. He had no one to talk to or share meals with. Things become difficult when a lovely parent is separated from his beloved children. Nikita would make up for the loneliness of life. She would make his life happy once more. Jacob would now feel less lonely. He would fill his life with her. She would wipe tears from his eyes and revive him from two years of sufferance. He would have a marvelous time with her and that would give him a surge of new energy. He would not have to beg for the love he wanted nor dream of a flower in the store. They would share the joy of being together. In sum, they would be one body and their life together would be glamorous.

Nikita's friends of Goldcrest, Shoreline, Des Moines, and Castlewood believed the opposite. In their view, Nikita would not last that long. Chances for a flower to survive more than two months were slim. Jacob did not bother asking how they knew her life expectancy. Actually, they knew her better than anybody else did. They could describe the flower's strength and weaknesses. They knew how deep and long her roots were. She was already eighteen months old when the life expectancy of a perennial plant is only twenty-four months. She might not even make it, given the cold weather she was to live in. Even the thorns had been growing tall and strong. Jacob might not support them.

Jacob wondered what to do to be better than Schadrack Kubwa, Kevin, Thomas, John, and others. None of them managed to keep Nikita more than a year. They men like him. He hesitated a while and finally said, "She may longer, who knows? My room is warmer than outside. I will keep the flower away from the cold of winter. If the rose is to die soon, at least she will leave some seeds. The offspring will easily get accustomed to the new environment."

Nikita moved to Canada, and she did not inform either her mother or her siblings. They only learned it from friends who learned about the news as rumors. They wanted to check with her family, to make sure the news was not a rumor. No one would confirm the news of her moving to Canada.

In Kelowna, Jacob received Nikita with great expectations. He drove her home, and the dream came true. She was not public as she used to be in Olympia. She came, and Jacob felt something peaceful. She was the embodiment of happiness that Jacob needed then. Thanks to her, he had all the pride and respect in the world. At night, Jacob put Rosie on a nightstand. He could smell her scent and hold her vase all night long. He had set up a desk lamp to provide enough light so that he could see the flower whenever he needed to. In the morning, he would put her on the windowsill to catch energy from the sun. During the day, she stayed in the living room to embellish the house.

4. The Love War over Nikita's Flower

Jacob set his hopes too high. Nikita was part of him, and she became his source of strength and courage. Nevertheless, she never felt him as part of hers. She had lived with many men, and Jacob was just a man, no different from the others. Unlike the others, Jacob loved her so much that he wanted her in his life. The others were only interested in relieving their needs. Jacob went much further to make her part of him. However, he did not see the love he had been expecting. Nikita's affection decreased dramatically.

Nikita did not seem to know that there is a difference between a man and a lover. She came with unwomanly habits she developed in Kenya, West Africa, and Olympia. She did not even know that she had to avoid her old habits of flowing with every flow. Even the wedding ring on her finger did not remind her that she was somebody's treasure and not just a friend. Her marital status only changed on paper, not in her heart. Even though she was living with Jacob, she considered him like the other men she had been living with.

Jacob considered life in his house as sacrosanct. Only he and Nikita were supposed to enjoy the privacy of their bedroom. Nevertheless, Nikita did not look quite right about her behavior. For several months, Jacob shut his eyes to the tall and ugly human bees loitering around the window of his bedroom. The bees found Rosie inscrutably beautiful. Dickson was the first to be introduced Nikita.

"Dickson, this is Nikita. I told you about her." Dickson shook her hand.

"Still beautiful, eh! How do you do? Hmmm!"

"How do you do," she answered with a smile.

"My name is Dickson Rushatsihori."

"I am Nikita Chissocco. Nice to meet you, Dickson," Dickson looked at her amorously.

"Nice to meet you, too, Ni-ki-ta Ci-so-ko. Wow! What a wonderful name! Oh! I really love your beautiful name. It is as beautiful as you are, the embodiment of beauty."

"My name is Chissocco, not Cisoko," she reminded him.

"Hmmm. A wonderful name indeed."

"Can I just call you Dick? It is shorter and easier."

"Well, everybody calls me Dick. They prefer it to Dickson."

Dickson saw her as extremely beautiful. He had been missing her since she left him in Nairobi. He looked at her in a way that presaged desires for her. He was also attracted to the cunning look she fixed on him. The familiar look itself seduced him. The smile pleased him a lot. He had missed it for several years. Jacob noticed strange grimaces on their faces.

"Did you guys know each other?" he asked.

"The face looks familiar to me, but I am not too sure," Dickson said.

"It is my first time to see you," Nikita said.

Dickson was the kind of man who would not hesitate ogling a married woman in front of her husband. Jacob found the smile disappointing, especially that he knew Dickson's weaknesses. He would surely try to find a way to Nikita. In fact, he already desired her. Nikita too seemed responsive; the more the folks idolized her, the better she felt.

Hearing that she was very beautiful made her a thousand times happier. In Olympia, no one was telling her these words anymore. She had lived there ten years, and men had had enough time to ogle her. Now that she was in a new country, meeting new people, sweet words refreshed her life. They reminded her that she was still attractive.

The idolization made her too big for her boots, thus, too beautiful for Jacob. At first, Jacob did not make a big deal out of it. He believed that Nikita had sense enough to know how to respond to men who admired her. If Dickson desired her, that was not a big issue. There would be an issue if Nikita did not disapprove of attempts to ogle her. She had gone through a wide experience with men who loved her and quit her afterward. Jacob thought that no one could impress her anymore. Besides, Rosie was no more for sale or hire. Jacob found no need to worry about Geram Murara and Juvenhack Zim Anan. As they were his *good* friends, they knew that Nikita was his. Only the smoky long-legged boy bothered him. Since young age, Dickson had never respected him.

Nikita did not seem to be bothered in the least. She was still an easygoing woman and she wanted to treat other men better than she was supposed to treat Jacob. Jacob always caught Dickson staring at her in admiration. To his astonishment, she responded with a sweet smile and a wink. The smile meant many things to Dickson. He read her mind and saw that she did not change. He could still have her. He lit up one cigarette after another, waiting for an opportunity to seduce her. Jacob did not know that many more clouds were gathering and thickening in front of him. He closed his eyes as he did not want to hurt Nikita's feelings. Besides, it was too early to mistrust her though she was one of the women the mere sight of whom would make unfaithful men melt. Nikita was flattered to see that Dickson was still interested in her. She remembered their old romances, and her mind started to focus on him. They shared their first private talk in Dickson's house. Nikita had formed the habit of having breakfast with him. She pretended that she went to see his wife when, in fact, she knew that Dada was at work. She only went there during work hours. Dickson reminded her that she was still beautiful, the same way he attracted her in Nairobi. She loved being idolized. Dickson went on,

"It is wonderful to see you again. I was wondering how to meet you alone. I have been thinking about you."

"Are you serious? Are you still thinking about me?" she asked smiley.

"I think about you since the very first day Jacob told me you were coming. I was so excited, and I encouraged him to bring you sooner."

"I knew that you still loved me. One could tell by the way you smiled to me even in front of Jacob. I feared that he might find out that there was something between us."

"I could not believe Jacob could have such a beautiful woman. I feel jealous."

"Why didn't you marry me in Kenya? You only wanted to play and that was it."

"How could I marry you when you were with another man?"

"I could have left him."

"How could you leave him when you were pregnant of him?"

"Miscarriage occurred."

"Is that true? I thought it was that small boy."

"That was a year later."

"I loved you so much, and I still want you."

"Well, I am happy to hear that."

"I tell you, I dream about you every night. I don't know what you think, but I am still crazy about you. You may say that I am crazy to love you now, but I am powerless to resist you."

"It is normal. There is nothing wrong with that. It is human nature, you know."

"But Jacob will get mad when he finds out."

"I am mature enough to have my freedom."

"I want you so much. When will you have time?"

"I am here."

The conversation went beyond words. They planned to go out the same day.

Although Nikita did not seem trustworthy, Jacob could not believe that she would allow a man to seduce her when she was fresh in a relationship and expecting a baby. He got disillusioned when, one day, he found himself watching an undesirable scene. Nikita was walking to the street. Jacob was about to join her in the park. He opened the window to see how far ahead she was. He watched her giving her hips a seductive wiggle. Jacob wondered why she was wiggling her hips on the street. She waved Dickson standing on his balcony. He glanced at her flirtatiously. He came bouncing up to meet her. He was wearing an undershirt and shorts. He would break his neck to seduce her, telling her sweet words. After kissing her, he tapped her buttocks playfully. Jacob got enraged watching him touching her breasts and her behind in a friendly way. He watched Dickson holding and rubbing Nikita's hand. He expected her to do something to avoid him and refuse the provocation. As reaction, she giggled and smiled. Jacob saw complicity in the smile. When Dickson put his arm on her shoulder, she seemed happy. Jacob wondered if she was not mature enough to understand the meaning of the act. She allowed Dickson to approach her so close that they did not leave an inch between them. She did not flinch or did she draw away. Jacob could not believe that a woman her age could let a man touch her breasts on the street. After a while, she drew away, probably because they were on the street, and she feared being watched. Jacob began to have some inkling of something going on between them. If she waited a whole minute to withdraw from Dickson's arms, one would wonder how long she would have waited if they were behind closed doors or in the darkness. Nikita tended to forget that Jacob was currently in her life. She had signed her life with him it was too early to get used to one man. She was not used to avoiding her admirers.

Jacob had been hoping that nothing would happen since he had taken her away from the others of Olympia. The new acts with Dickson shocked him. Dickson would certainly coax her into sleeping with him. Until then, Jacob had no clue that they had been together several weeks. He found it odd for Nikita to be treated as Dickson's mistress. To avoid seeing what he was seeing, he decided to join them on the street in spite of disappointment. At least his presence would stop the upsetting scene.

That meeting with Dickson brought a gap in Jacob and Nikita. The gap widened each time Jacob discovered other signs of infidelities. Jacob acknowledged having made a terrible mistake by introducing Nikita to Dickson, but loving Nikita was the worst mistake of his life. He also regretted allowing Dickson in his house. He knew that he would not trust him, but he did not expect that kind of situation. By allowing Dickson in his house, he compounded the biggest mistake he had made by not listening to Ram Dee, Earl, and others. The love for Nikita would only spoil his dream of living a happy life on a land of freedom.

Although Jacob's dream came true, Nikita transformed the dream into a nightmare. Her beauty caused her to sin too much. She never saw her affairs as immoral acts. In her mind, adultery was not a bad thing. Within one month, she was head over heels in love with Dickson. After another couple of months, Dickson hooked her to Juvenhack. Jacob did not have the faintest idea that there was already an affair going on with his other friends. He only suspected Dickson, but there were corroborated murmurs about other affairs. Jacob tried to be fair. He thought that they might be innocent, as he had no clear evidence of the affairs. Folks spoke about it, but nobody had seen a thing with their own eyes. Even though people had seen something, Jacob had no evidence that it was true. He trusted Nikita and felt that he did not need to control her. She was a mature person supposed to know that she was Jacob's treasure. She deserved his respect. However, because Dickson was notorious for his affairs with multiple partners, Jacob felt unsettled. No one could trust him around a female. Jacob had also heard a lot about Nikita's past behavior. Hence, he worried that her contacts with Dickson might revive her past desires. Jacob did not wish her old acts to happen again. It became obvious that many people were seducing her. Jacob saw nothing wrong with her as long as they did not go too far. Still, too many suspicious contacts made him nervous.

Jacob really appreciated the beauty that Nikita and the perfumed Rosie brought into his house. They gave him unbelievable energy. Rosie's smell and her colors produced a marvelous rainbow. She occupied a great place in his heart. He tried to make her proud of him whenever the situation allowed it. Everything loved the pretty rose, especially when she bloomed at sunrise. Some loved the smell and the colors. Others loved the delicate form and the fragrance. Like bees, Dickson, Juvenhack, and Geram loved the pollen. Jacob could never let anyone forget that he truly loved his dear rose. The flower did not belong to the shop anymore as he did not belong to himself either. Jacob and Nikita belonged together and to each other. Jacob loved Nikita as a part of his own body.

As Nikita was being idolized by everybody, she started showing disinterest in Jacob. She let him know that Rosie was not used to staying with one customer. The flower was so beautiful that she needed to be seen by other clients too. She introduced her to other men who took good care of her.

Jacob was working a double shift. When he worked night shift, Dickson would drop in on Nikita anytime. He entered the house without knocking at the door. Nikita would yank the door wide open so he could not have to knock, which would alert the sleeping children. He could go straight to Jacob's bedroom.

Jacob wanted to hear Nikita's voice very often. He regularly called home to check if she was doing fine. Nikita would never pick up the phone. Either the calls went to the voice mail or the phone was turned off. Nikita never apologized for missing his calls. What shocked Jacob the most was that he could see her checking missed calls to select which ones to call back. One day, Jacob wanted to find out what was going on in his house.

"Honey, you didn't pick up my calls last night. Where were you?"

"I slept early because I was tired. What time did you call?"

"You were not sleeping. I called many times from eight o'clock to ten o'clock. No one picked up the phone. When I called at eleven, the line was busy for at least half an hour."

"Yes, I remember now. I was bored, and I went to the mall to do some window-shopping. I stayed there until ten. When I came back I went straight to bed."

"The mall closed at six. How did you do window-shopping when all shops are closed? Did you break the doors?"

"Remember the last time we went there? We left at nine, and it was still open."

"It was on Friday. The mall closes at six on Tuesdays. What day was yesterday? Tuesday, I guess."

"After the mall, we wound up at Grandma's place. I arrived home at ten."

"There you go. Who were you with?"

"Just me and Grandma."

"Grandma is blind. Were you in the closed mall with her because she cannot see?"

"We just went to see her after the mall was closed."

"You and who?"

"Just me."

"Why do you refer to yourself in plural then?"

"What do you mean?"

"You said 'we.' Anyway, I am worried because you never answer my calls nowadays."

"I was surely sleeping when you called around ten."

"Honey, I called two times after eleven, and the line was busy. You could not even put the person on hold to take the second line. With the caller ID display, you could see that I was the one that called you. You did not even call back. When I called again, the phone was off. I never understood. There must be something wrong here."

"Honey, I did not hear the phone ring. I usually turn the volume down when I sleep."

"You never turn the phone off when I am here. You could even pick it at three in the morning. Now that I am out for work, you turn it off. Don't you want me to call home?" There was a moment of silence.

"So what are you thinking about?"

"Why do I have to think about something? I only wanted to know what you were doing."

Jacob watched her obvious disinterest in him. He got to his feet and walked around. He wondered what kind of a human being would be doing window-shopping until ten in the evening when the mall closed at six. When he left home for work, the mall was already closed. It was after six, and Nikita had no plans to go anywhere. Anyway, she went to the mall with a blind person. She did not even see that the mall was closed. At the same time, she wound up at Grandma until ten when Grandma always sleeps at seven due to her disability. After doing all this, she allegedly fell asleep because she was tired. She was not even working. While she was in deep sleep, the phone was so busy that she forgot how to take a second line. She even forgot Jacob's work phone to call back. At seven in the morning, the bedsheets that were freshly spread in the evening were in the dryer. If Nikita was so tired that she could not even answer the phone around midnight, how could she change the bedding and wash the sheets at five in the morning. There were too many dirty clothes that needed washing. She rarely had time for them. Jacob wondered where she got the habit of changing bedsheets in the middle of the night if she was the only one to sleep on them. He always arrived home in the morning and found her in new sheets. To make sure that he was not mistaken, he changed sheets at night before going to work. Sometimes he left her sleeping already. In the morning, the sheets he put on were either in the washer or in the dryer. Curiously, she never changed sheets when he was there. Jacob got lost in the confusion.

Jacob was worried that he might be walking on eggshells around Nikita. He might not be the happiest man as he thought he would be. He was going to be the most miserable man betrayed in his own house. He thought something needed to be done to strengthen the agonizing relationship. He decided to work on their closeness. He learned to repeat the same magic words at least five times a day. Whenever he said "Je t'aime beaucoup, ma chérie," Nikita stared at him and replied with "thank you." As days went by, she said "thank you" without even bothering to look at him. Finally, the "thank you" disappeared. Jacob told her that he loved her, and she did not even seem to hear him. She remained silent. Jacob thought she might be developing hearing impairment. Did the silence mean "moi aussi, mon trésor" as before? That was the question. He repeated the declaration of love louder.

"I love you, my honey."

"Do you think I am deaf? Why do you have to shout?" she asked.

Jacob understood she did not suffer hearing loss. She simply did not seem to care. Few days later, he told her how much he loved her. There was silence. In the end, she replied, "Moi non plus."

"Tabarnak!" Jacob exclaimed. "Where in the hell did you learn this expression? Is there somebody that teaches you bad language, my little darling?"

The answer left him breathless. He spoke in languages that he believed she understood better. He said in his mother tongue

"Ndagukunda cane."

Then he said it in Kiswakili, "Nakupenda sana."

It produced the same silence. Jacob added, "Te quiero mucho." He knew that Nikita understood Spanish. She pretended that she didn't. Then, Jacob decided to say it in English again.

According to him, English was easier than French. He had read the French poet Richard de Ronsard and Petrarch's love sonnets. He could not tell if they were less romantic than Geoffrey Chaucer, the father of the English literature. That was not a problem. He could easily say, "Honey, I love you very much. And I will love you all my life."

The unexpected answer shocked him, "I hate you."

He did not believe his ears. As he was not expecting such declaration, it seemed unreal to him. He thought that he had been daydreaming.

"No, you don't. I know that you love me."

Jacob replied thoughtfully still thinking that he was dreaming. He still saw Nikita as a nicer person than she actually was. She could even tell him that she hated him in public places. As she would insult him in presence of Juvenhack, Jacob saw her as an impolite person that did not respect anybody. He never knew that she was proving to outsiders that she had power over him. The message was that Jacob was under her control. Therefore, they were welcomed to tell her whenever they wanted. When it happened again and again, Jacob understood that there was no kidding. It was really serious. Then he said, "I will always love you."

Nikita repeated the sentence by replacing the verb with its opposite. Yet Jacob went on loving her as promised. He had learnt to be patient. His infinite patience would allow him to harvest Nikita's fruits. He loved her so much that he longed for harvest day to enjoy fruits of their love, at least his love for her.

Jacob believed in fatherhood as ennobling. Holding children was giving him great pleasure. He was born and raised in a traditional family that believed that children brought happiness and joy to the family. He was still close to parenthood that he loved to be with kids. He was also missing holding Ryan Malcolm in his arms with Lionel Joe and Eunice Scheilla clinging to his legs. His life without kids playing around was meaningless. It was a lost life. He had been preparing himself for fatherhood since early age. He looked forward to a day when his arms would be holding his kids with Nikita. He prayed for it every day. But would that day ever come? Only God knew and time could tell. Rosie herself was worn out. The stigma was still fine and able to receive the pollen during fertilization. He counted on Nikita to give him children. He was more than happy when, one day, she informed him that she was not in the nightclub but in the pudding club. He looked forward to seeing her in the family way since day one. She had also informed her mother that a child was on his way into the world. Her mother started counting months. After ten months without any news of a newborn, Nikita's mother called her daughter to ask what was going on.

"Nikita, it is now ten months since you informed me that you were expecting. You never spoke about it ever since. I just call you to ask what is going on with you."

Nikita hesitated at first and finally replied, "Mom, didn't you know that I lost a child? A miscarriage occurred."

Her mother understood that she willingly aborted. If there had been a miscarriage, Nikita would have told her. She asked to speak Jacob. She asked him the same question. Jacob, too, had been waiting for the seeds that never came out. Now that the mother was mad at him, he understood that something awful happened. He sighed and then turned to Nikita.

"Isn't there something wrong with you? I heard you telling your mother about a miscarriage. What happened?" he asked.

"That has nothing to do with you. I just avoid her questions," she said.

"You must have done something. What did you do, Nikita? Did you dare abort my child? Why did you do that?"

Jacob could tell that something was cooking there. In fact, whenever they tackled the subject of facts of life, she lost her temper.

"Why do you want to know about my life? Mind your own business," she spoke with her anger flaring anew.

"Beg your pardon. Honey, we are quarreling about love every single day. This is ridiculous. When are we going to enjoy life together? Why did you keep it secret?"

"I don't want you to question about my fucking life. What do you think you are? I didn't want you to know it, that's all."

"Can I remind you that you are my lover?" Jacob asked.

"So what?"

"We need to work together whether in moments of joy or in times of sorrows."

"You want a child so much that the miscarriage would have given you a lot of trouble. I didn't want you to suffer. Is that clear?" she concluded.

She hit him exactly where it hurt. Jacob buried his face in his hands. He took a deep breath before continuing.

"Nikita, am I dreaming or what? Are you honest with yourself?" He paused a while and continued. "Honey, you had a miscarriage and you did not bother telling me! I am spending sleepless nights with nightmares. I fear being ambushed by your lovers as they did to our families in Burundi and Rwanda. Now you are aborting my children. Two abortions are unbearable. Even if they happened by accident, I would be the first one to know. You had been luring me that it never happened. Now I learn about it from your mother. No one had ever aborted in my family history. Why is this happening to me? What will people say when they find out?" His voice was strained with emotion.

People knew it anyway. The news was spreading that she was aborting without Jacob's knowledge. Jacob learned last when the abortions were already on everybody's lips. Others even knew that they were not his children and they knew the fathers. They kept the secret of their friends. There was no reason to inform Jacob when they did not inform him that Nikita had affairs with Dickson, Juvenhack, Geram, and others.

Nikita had been pregnant many times out of wedlock. All her three children were born out of wedlock. Now that she had a man in her life, she got pregnant and she aborted. Jacob did not understand why she should abort when she knew that Jacob adored children. In fact, she was not sure of the babies' fathers. She could not even pinpoint the week she conceived. She had been with Jacob steadily for several months. The month she missed her period, she had slept with three other men, not to mention the ones who used protection. She feared that Jacob would crack up if he discovered that the child was not his, especially that he was suspecting her affairs with Dickson. If the child were born, he would surely require a DNA test for paternity. As Dickson was married and did not want a baby with her, she was sure that he would help to get an abortion. It would also save his family. In addition, the cheating couple benefited from the abortions as the pregnancy would restrict their moments of pleasure.

Jacob never realized that there were always plans to get rid of any of his seeds. Nikita's partners persuaded her to have two abortions. As they were experienced in the matter, they knew places and the proper doctors to do the job. They took care of everything, and Jacob never knew about it.

Jacob started discussing the issue with Nikita. He negotiated chances for seeds to grow. He did not want her to disappear forever. Besides, his job was not limited to just taking care of her. His arms longed to hold children. Nikita, however, raised the voice. She did not want any more children with any man. She was right. If she had to have a child with every man she slept with and the nature allowed it, she would have ten kids every year. Jacob believed in parenthood when motherhood was the last of her concerns. He was committed to a lifelong relationship, what Nikita saw as a prison. In her life, a whole year with one man was too long. She knew that every man would love her. Generous as she was, she hated jealous and selfish people who did not want her to satisfy her friends in need of her body.

Jacob thought that a baby might make a huge difference in her behavior. He was even dreaming of twins. He hoped that with a baby to look after, Nikita would stop wandering around. Her lovers would give her a break and her family would see her more often. At the same time, she would be learning how to live with one man in her life. By the time the child would go to daycare, Nikita would be mature and wise, hence more respectful of Jacob. For the first time in her life, she would bring up a child with his or her father. Jacob thought of pregnancy as the only card left on the table. Everything else had failed.

As he insisted on having a child with her, she got mad and ensured him that she would never let any man impregnate her.

"Why do you want to intrude in my private life? You don't have to know about my ovaries! I can't have a child with every man I fuck with. I am not a goat."

"I am not asking for a child with every man. I am the only man in your life. Is there anything wrong wanting a child, a gift from God? Our relationship needs blessings from the Lord. I think I have something to do with your ovaries. If they were yours alone, your egg would not need my ovule. By the way, I did not love just some parts of you. I loved the whole of you. And I want fruits of our love."

"Okay. Since you insist, I will give you one when the time is right. Are you happy now?" she said, trying to calm him.

"You will give me one!" Jacob exclaimed. "I didn't say I want a child for myself. It will be yours too."

"Whatever. Didn't you say you want a child?"

"Yes, I did."

"So wait."

While waiting, Jacob remembered the words that came through Nikita's mouth.

"I cannot have a child with every man I fuck with."

The message was so clear that it did not require further explanation. He had to wait for the day Dickson decided to let her bear a child.

Before Jacob could get the feedback, Nikita reported to Dickson and Juvenhack about the talk she had with Jacob.

"The stupid asshole wants a child. He said that if I did not give him a child, we would break up or something. I don't know why he wants a child so badly. He says he wants fruits of our love."

"What did you tell him? I hope you won't let that fucking Democrat impregnate you. Never default on your decision. We don't need a child. If you want one, he will be mine, not anyone else's," Dickson told her.

"I only listened to him. He thinks I love him. I will never bear a child with that stupid asshole," she said with a categorical refusal.

"Please, don't. If he makes you pregnant again, we will do the same thing," Dickson reassured her.

"No way. I don't want to abort again. I am getting too old for that. I can no longer withstand another violent shock like the last time."

"I know what you are saying. You lost too much blood."

The discussion with Nikita took place behind closed doors. Everything was off the record. Frankly speaking, outsiders had nothing to do with it. Curiously, by the time Jacob was waiting for the response, Dickson was the one to answer through other people. Within a few hours, he and Juvenhack were going around asserting that they would never allow Nikita to have a child with Jacob.

Jacob was bothered that his privacy was disturbed. Not only would Dickson come and go as if Jacob's room were his own, he also intruded in his private life. Nikita disclosed every piece of information she had on Jacob. Jacob found it ridiculous spreading personal information about his privacy especially that the information was revealed to Evildoers who would bite his head off. Dickson could now make fool of Jacob in public. He wanted to prove that he was not as important as Nikita thought. He started treating him the same way he did in secondary school. He over generalized by stating that democrats were bad people who did not deserve any respect. Juvenhack went too far to state that democrats were not actually full human beings.

Whenever Nikita was with them, they only criticized Jacob angrily. What was worse, Nikita was the one to start a conversation undermining Jacob. Others felt encouraged and followed her lead to destroy his dignity. Dickson told her that she made a terrible mistake by following a democrat. He once told her that if he had met her sooner, he would have divorced his wife to marry her. Now that it was no longer possible, he would rather see her with another man who would not be jealous of her being with him. She reassured him that her being with Jacob had nothing to do with her freedom as she would not allow anything or anybody to restrict her and bind her free spirit.

"I needed a man that has sense enough to give me freedom. Jacob is not that kind of man. He is an old-fashioned African, too conservative. After years in North America, he still behaves like a pure African," she complained.

One day, there was a group discussion in Dickson's house. Jacob and Nikita, who were passing by, decided to join the friends sitting in Dickson's living room. As Dickson saw Jacob, he veered the discussion toward politics. He started picking on him, showing to Nikita that Jacob was a worthless person. Whatever he said was rejected as wrong. Jacob could not accept being treated the way the Evildoers treated him all his childhood. He took the floor and told the gangsters that things had changed thanks to courageous patriots smitten by peace and democracy.

"The freedom fighters are doing an extraordinary amount of work without which Burundians would be held in the bondage of Evildoers forever. It was owing to them that honest people ate gaining the upper hand. Thanks to them, people will act toward one another in a spirit of brotherhood. The oppressed are gaining their right to life, liberty, and security of their persons. Even refugees, driven away by four decades of dictatorship and oppression, have returned home to enjoy their full rights as members of the human family."

Jacob was right. As a matter of fact, the democratic government inherited from the struggle for freedom was determined to promote social progress and better standards of life for all citizens. The new leaders were working hard to maintain basic security and public order.

Jacob reminded the Evildoers how their governments were more concerned with terrorizing the governed rather than improving their conditions of living. Under previous regimes, citizens never found happiness. Whenever they saw governmental troops and police, they had to hide to preserve their lives. One could even question the importance of government at the time.

Jacob invited Dickson and his friends to follow the tracks of the democratic government and help Burundians to reconcile and forget the terrors of the past. Jacob used himself as an example. He stated how he had forgiven Dickson and Juvenhack who tried to kill him on several occasions. He still respected them as human beings, and Nikita would invite them for dinners in his house.

Dickson, however, did not want to hear anything positive about the new democratic government. They only hang out with Jacob because they loved Nikita. They filled his house not because they liked him, but because they wanted to be close to her. When they took control of her, they only spoke disparagingly of democrats. Jacob could not support their bad language. He expressed his support for democracy.

"Democracy is the only hope to the problems of Burundi. By killing Pres. Melchior Ndadaye, you, Evildoers, thought that you assassinated democracy for good. As human being, Ndadaye was only a messenger. You killed the messenger but you will never kill the message he delivered. Ndadaye's message will never die. You killed millions of messengers, yet the message of peace and justice is still spreading and the light of hope is shining. The wind and water carry the message farther and faster than we humans do. Even if you kill everybody and burn them to ashes, the smoke will convey the message that you are evildoers. It will take away your inhumanity and all your negative forces that are harmful to human species. It will purify the country and lead it to democracy. By killing the pro-democracy activists, you sent more ammunition to the freedom fighters. In other words, you were digging your own graves."

The Evildoers were not even remorseful about the terrible things they did against innocent citizens. The only thing they were remorseful about was that they could neither kill everybody nor win the war. Consequently, they lost power. If they managed to kill all honest citizens, they would have never had to worry about losing power. They were still willing to do worse were they given an opportunity to do so. They boasted about killing Ronald, Léopold, and Nikita's father; and now they were relieving their needs with Nikita. Rather than feeling ashamed of flirting with Evildoers, Nikita felt relieved. The Evildoers understood that her behavior was an acceptance of what they had done as well as a sign of encouragement to hurt Jacob. They started planning to get rid of him. When Nikita was in their company, she never complained that they victimized her family. She became an Evildoer purely and simply. She supported all their evil acts. By betraying her lover, parent, and siblings, she became more dangerous than the other Evildoers.

Jacob did not let himself be dragged like a wet rag in front of Nikita especially that her brother, Léopold Chissocco, died a noble cause. Léopold was a smart boy. He would not let anybody ill-treat him because of his ethnic background. He would blow himself up in order to destroy the power of Evildoers. He joined the movement of freedom fighters, the Forces for the Defense of Democracy and he died for that noble mission. Ronald too had fought for democracy alongside with President Ndadaye. Even in difficult moments, he would tell the troublemakers that citizens would never resign the fight for democracy. By asserting the greatness of the freedom and democracy fighters, Jacob believed that he was comforting Nikita whose first boyfriend, parent, and brother had sacrificed their lives for the values she used to believe in. She had been supporting democracy until the day she met Dickson. Dickson managed to brainwash her, and she became like him. Rather than supporting Jacob's constructive ideas, she remained silent. In other words, she did not want to betray Dickson. She would rather sacrifice Jacob.

By attacking the new democratic government, Dickson was targeting Jacob. He knew that Jacob had defended ideas of democracy since young age. In secondary school, Jacob was always opposed to Dickson's bad behavior. Dickson could never forget that he revealed to him how his dad killed people from 1972 onward. When he grew up, he knew that he made a terrible mistake. He thought Jacob would never forget it. Jacob was supporting the new ideas with a government that was improving the sociopolitical situation.

As Dickson had gained support inside Jacob's house, he continuously committed an ad hominem circumstantial attack against Jacob's personality. His purpose was to discredit him in front of Nikita by showing her that she was not with the right person. At the same time, he invited her to discount his ideas. At first, Jacob thought Nikita was on his side since she was victim of oppression. Her family was threatened by the Evildoers that forced them to exile. Nikita had had many lovers who impregnated her and abandoned her afterward. She had informed each one of her sons that their father was killed by the Evildoers. The children grew up knowing that Evildoers were very bad people. Now that their mother had become one of them, she felt remorse for telling them the story of their fathers.

Nikita's children were never told that they had different fathers. For the first time in her life, Nikita had a caring man who cherished her in spite of her infatuation with the enemy. He loved her and her three children who never knew their fathers. He thought that she was a quiet woman with who he would share the joy of life. Yet whenever he was verbally attacked by Dickson and the other troublemakers, she only smiled in support of the enemy. The guys felt encouraged to move forward.

Nikita knew that Jacob was a nice person. She would love him if he were not jealous about her. She wanted more freedom to enjoy what she called extra good love, which, according to her, was better than normal love.

Nikita also knew that Jacob was a good forgiver. Even if she did wrong, he loved her so much that he could not help but forgive her. So she felt free to do everything she wanted, knowing that she would always be forgiven. In fact, Jacob had forgiven her many times. She told Dickson, "Dick, don't worry about Jacob. He knows about my affairs, but there is nothing he can do. If he raises a voice, I threaten to leave him and he cools down. He knows that he can't find another beautiful woman like me."

Nikita knew that Jacob loved her so much that he wouldn't wish to lose her. She took advantage of him, taking his kindness for stupidity. She even made fun of him.

"If I leave him, he will hang himself. Still, even if he does kill himself for me, I am fine with that as long as I am not the one to be blamed for it."

With these convictions in mind, the affairs went on for several months. When Jacob spoke about them, Nikita promised to stop them, but she never did. She only changed strategies.

Dickson and her other lovers took advantage of her weaknesses to win her weak heart. She had never been able to resist men who suggested kissing her. She knew that many men wanted her badly. Whenever they called her, she already knew what they wanted. She told them to call when Jacob was not at home. They could then meet at Dickson's. They turned the situation upside down by placing the burden of truth the wrong side. They badmouthed Jacob in order to win Nikita. The insults comforted her. Rather than defending him, she would insult him even more. She continuously criticized and belittled him as she did most of the talking.

One day, Mzee Chief Maneno asked her about Jacob.

"How is Jacob doing? I didn't see him for a while."

"The hell with him! He wants to treat my sons as his own children when they hate him," she replied cheerfully.

Nobody saw anything wrong in treating them like his own children. Still, if they wanted her, they had to support her and encourage her to say more. They listened to her stories cheerfully.

"Jacob is too demanding. He wants the house clean and neat all the time. He told my boys to clean the mess in their rooms. There was a stock of plates, spoons, forks, glasses, and stuff. My kids always eat in their rooms, and they keep used dishes underneath their bed. Today, there were no more dishes available for use. All dishes were scattered in the rooms, unwashed. Jacob ordered the boys to collect them and put them in the sink so that he could wash them."

"Did they do it?" Dickson interrupted.

"Hell no. They never do what he asks them to do. He had nothing to do with their mess. They ordered him out of their room. The stubborn guy insisted as usual."

"I am curious to know what happened next," Juvenhack encouraged her to say more.

"You know what happened? My ten-year-old boy slapped him and violently kicked his ass out of their room." All of them jiggled as a way of supporting her.

"Good boys! I like them. They should break his head. He deserved it," Juvenhack said encouragingly.

Nikita felt enthusiastic to be supported. Then she could continue. "As the asshole did not want to go, the boys got to their feet and squeezed him in the door to force him out."

"Brave boys!" Dickson exclaimed as Nikita continued.

"The stupid ass always wants quarrels. He did not listen." Dickson interrupted,

"He never listens. I know the guy. He is a stubborn. Go on, Nikita. Go to the point."

"My boys slapped him and cracked him solidly on the door jamb."

"That is what he was looking for. He deserved much more than that," Juvenhack said.

"Did he go out then?" Dickson asked.

"Not at all. He still refused to get out of their room."

"So you see? The guy is a stupid asshole. I tell you. Why didn't he go out? He had nothing to do with their room," Juvenhack said.

"They slammed the door on him, and he came bleeding to complain to me," she concluded.

Everybody laughed with her.

"Shake my hand. You have good boys," Dickson exclaimed, and everybody gave her high five.

"I like my boys. They are like me. They don't let anybody give them shit," she said enthusiastically.

"He is not even their father. Why does he treat them like his children? Does he think that they are stupid?" Dickson said angrily.

"The guy is saying that I did not give them good education. It made me angry that I congratulated my sons and I encouraged them to hit him even harder next time."

As she was talking, the guys pretended to support her. Some fell uncharacteristically silent. They could not imagine that a parent should encourage her kids to behave that way. The others kept laughing with her as a way of encouraging her to say more. They were not interested in the message but rather in the messenger. They knew that she supported anybody who would bullshit about Jacob. If they had nothing bad to say about him, they would just support her bullshitting him. When she spoke, they only looked at her white teeth, her lips, and smile. They smiled with her. They found the message itself awkward. After all, they were good parents, and they would not wish their children to behave like hers.

After the report, the guys looked at each other and laughed. They agreed with her that Jacob deserved more than just slaps. Nikita gave them a happy smile.

"My boys got mad and started pounding on the walls with whatever object they could find. When he went to stop them from pounding the walls, they grabbed empty bottles and threw them at him," she concluded laughing.

"Let them teach him a lesson. He will stop treating them like his own children," Dickson said encouragingly.

"The stupid asshole returned to their room to take out the bottles they used to pound the walls."

"Again! He is foolish. I must say that the guy is crazy," Dickson said.

"I told you. Did they let him take them?" Juvenhack asked.

"As they were mad at him, they bumped their heads, fists, and feet against the walls and they broke them." All laughed in unison.

"If they broke the walls, you will have to pay a lot of money to fix them," Mzee Chief Maneno remarked.

"Who cares? I don't give a fuck how much money it will cost. Jacob will pay, not me," Nikita answered.

"How can't you care? Your kids should not break the walls. The maintenance guy charges fifty dollars an hour not to mention the materials used. It will cost you a fortune," he concluded. Everybody ignored him and encouraged Nikita.

"I like my younger boy. He is like me. He is the one to kick Kevin out," she added.

"Who is Kevin?" Dickson asked.

"Kevin was my boyfriend, but he wanted to treat my kids as Jacob does. They kicked his ass out."

"You have serious boys, eh!" Juvenhack concluded.

"They are brave boys. Imagine a young boy kicking a man out of the house at the age of ten. But sometimes they are tough on me too." She looked at them and waited for comments.

"I remember the day you called police on them," Dickson noted.

"They were crazy that day."

Mzee Chief Maneno was the only person to dislike the conversation.

"Jacob wants his stepchildren to grow up with good manners like other kids. I cannot imagine children insulting their parents. I had never heard about children squeezing their parent in the door and slamming them," he said in disbelief.

The guys listened to him with disdain. They did not let him continue as he was raining on their parade. They only wanted him to support Nikita.

"Those children lack education because they are bastards," Chief Maneno continued. "They need caring parents like Jacob. Jacob is trying his best to educate them. He cannot influence them if he has no support from their mother. Children like them need to be treated with a firm hand."

Dickson and Juvenhack did not like his comment. They did not want him to annoy Nikita who was entertaining them on Jacob. They feared that he might break their secrets with her.

"What are you talking about?" Dickson screamed to Mzee Chief Maneno. "By the way, who invited you here? Get out of here now. I don't want to see you," he ordered.

The others fixed him a long suffering look. Mzee Chief Maneno shot to his feet and exited the apartment. The men could then deal with Nikita without any disturbance.

Another man had been following the conversation without making any comment. He learned that Nikita loved men who don't call the dogs off Jacob. He stood up and followed Mzee.

"I had never seen a conversation like this. I didn't know people were like this," he told Mzee Maneno as they walked away.

"Those Evildoers use her to destroy Jacob," Mzee Maneno said.

"Why do they do that?"

"It is the easy way to win her. Whoever needs her have to show that they hate Jacob."

"But they are his friends," Valery objected.

"What kind of friends are they? With friends like those ones, who need enemies?"

"My goodness! They speak unfavorably about Jacob and they win Nikita. One has to attack his character or his reputation, and they overcame her effortlessly. I had never seen a person like that."

"At the same time, they have all the secrets of Jacob's private life. They go on demeaning him in order to raise themselves above him. They cannot help degrading him in order to keep her."

"I say, the world is upside down. Why are people like that?" Valery wondered.

"As they insult him, Nikita feels uplifted. She is satisfied to be surrounded by men who do the dirty job she instructs them to do," Maneno said.

"And they do it perfectly," Valery supports.

"As she is easygoing, scads of men flung themselves on her. She turned everybody against Jacob, and she is confident that she cut him from the roots. She can now blackmail him without fear of anything."

"She is always trying to find out bad things to say about Jacob. And she feels supported by the Evildoers who are glued to her. I don't understand why she has such a weakness for men."

"Before she came, those people liked Jacob. But since she is eager to serve them, they had no choice but to betray him. They told me that they need her more than they need Jacob. She offers them what Jacob cannot give."

"Does Jacob know about this?" Valery asked.

"Not everything. If he says something, he is the one to be blamed, the jealous motherfucker who denied Nikita's freedom to be with her friends."

"I went to Jacob's, and I did not notice that she had a strange behavior. Everything looked fine."

"Nikita has softness and sensitivity at home when she wants freedom to enjoy other men's hardness. In her mind, having affairs is neither adultery nor infidelity.

She calls it extra love. She has desires that will never be satisfied by one man. Jacob, on the other hand, believes that people should not have extra marital relations."

"Extra love had nothing to do with freedom. It is adultery purely and simply," Valery said.

"Nikita sees adultery as freedom."

"If adultery is what she calls freedom, then, either I am a hundred years behind the times, or she is a hundred years ahead of the times."

"Freedom and respect for one's engagement are two different things. Jacob has been doing everything necessary to treat her with dignity. Let me give him a call."

Nikita left the place, and the guys discussed her life. Dickson was the one to introduce the subject. As Mzee Chief Maneno was no longer present, the guys felt free to say everything about her.

"This woman likes men. I had never seen a woman as hot as Nikita. The time I stick my big thing to her, she goes crazy and she starts coming. Juve, she is a way better than Josiana." Juvenhack seemed to disagree with him.

"I am surprised to hear you say that. I spend hours on her like an animal, and she never comes! I even crush my body to go deep in her womb hoping that she would eventually come. After an hour-and-half, I feel exhausted, and she still looks like nothing happened," Juvenhack reported.

"It is different with me. Sometimes, she even starts coming the minute she sees it. And the more you give the more she wants. She does not even want me to come before an hour. She is never satisfied."

"I prefer Josiana to her. What do you do to make her come?" Juvenhack asked, wanting to learn new strategies for her.

"She had to show me what to do. Even in the grip of her ecstasy, she would not let me come. She would cry, 'Don't come now, don't come.' And I have to push hard another half an hour before she would allow me to come."

"Dickson, tell me. What did you give her? I am spending a lot of money on her, but she shows no more interest in me. She wants me to do everything in rush. Even in the Empire Studio 16, there is much privacy but she still rushes me."

"Well . . . just work smart and never allow yourself to come before she tells you to. Of course, you need a cock like a horse's. Otherwise, she will feel nothing."

"Maybe I need a crooked cock," Juvenhack said as a joke.

"Then it will take two hours to satisfy her."

"But she forces me to come in the first minute, then three minutes. I come five times in two hours. And the more rounds I do, the more money I pay. If I don't come in three minutes she would yell on me, 'Why don't you come? What are you still waiting for? You paid for sex, not for love.' Then I have to give more money."

The conversation went on for several hours. Still, none of that was reported to Jacob.

Jacob and Nikita had opposing views about freedom. Jacob sensed a kind of conspiracy in his life. He was betrayed from inside to outside his house. He could not understand how outsiders could thwart his plans with Nikita. They were not even supposed to know anything about their privacy. Jacob sensed that all his plans with Nikita were water under the bridge. Nikita seemed to love Dickson more than she loved Jacob. Actually, she did not love him at all. She was doing everything needed to blackmail him. Since Dickson did not kill Jacob in Rutana, he hated him to death. As he could not kill him physically in Canada, he would use Nikita to kill him mentally. One day, Dickson asked her, "What are you still doing in his house? Do you really love that man? He is not the right man for you. You deserve someone much better that that son of a bitch. Look at yourself. How do you feel with him? I myself feel ashamed to see a beautiful woman like you in his house. We need to do something."

Nikita apologized and tried to explain herself. "To be honest, I never loved him, and I don't think I will ever love him. I came to him for my personal reasons. Now that you are here to help me, I don't need him anymore. He is an asshole, an old-fashioned man. Just show me what to do, and I will do it."

"Juvenhack and I are working on your case. Still, we have to be careful because he already knows that we are having an affair. That makes things complicated. He is controlling you now. I am scared."

"The asshole doesn't realize that there are times I need to be alone with my boyfriends. I will never let him control me. He will try but he will not succeed. I have always been an independent woman, and he knows it. From now on, if he raises his voice again, I will teach him a lesson that he will never forget. So don't worry about him."

"The problem is that you don't seem to keep the secret. If you had been discreet, he would never find out about our affairs. Now, he knows everything and even talks about it. I wanted it secret like Juvenhack. He does not know anything about him. That is why he still allows him to come to your house. I personally can't see you every day like before. We have to meet outside."

"I tell you Dick. Jacob is so obsessed to me that he can't do anything. He will support everything I do."

"If that is the case, we are lucky."

"How about yourself? I hope Dada is not jealous like Jacob. Won't she be mad at me when she finds out about our affairs?"

"No. She doesn't care. You just turn her into your friend and everything else will be fine. I know her well enough. Just try to hang up with her sometimes."

"I will be calling her regularly and will invite her for a coffee."

As they were gossiping about Jacob, Nikita told Dickson that she saw his name in Jacob's computer. Jacob had once told her that he was thinking of writing a book on all events that ruined his life. As she knew that Dickson was one of the Evildoers that tried to kill him, she knew that Jacob would write about him. Dickson asked her to delete all files from the computer and empty the recycle bin. Nikita was not computer literate. She could hardly open her electronic mail address. The only thing she could do on a computer was to write, read, and delete email messages. She could not delete Jacob's files when she did not know the meaning of a file or a folder. She invited Dickson to come home and delete the files himself. Dickson was not better than she was. Thus, when Jacob came to the computer, he noticed that some programs were disturbed. He knew that Nikita would do anything to annoy him, but he never suspected that Dickson had been on his computer. He knew it was something that might eventually happen. From that day on, he decided to protect important documents with a password. As Dickson knew that Jacob might be writing about his life, he informed Juvenhack about it. He knew that Juvenhack was involved in so many incidents that his name would surely be in the book. Both Evildoers started treating Jacob with open hostility.

Jacob was blind in love. He still believed that Nikita would improve over time. Now that he could not control her, he implored her to protect the flower at least. He did not want to lose two things at once. Nikita had been so vulnerable that she needed a lot of care. She appeared to be aloof. Because of her errands, her strength seemed to have vanished. Jacob thought that it could be due to the new weather conditions, but was not sure. She never seemed to belong to him in any way. There was always a part of Olympia that she kept to herself. She never understood that she was not a hooker. She belonged to Jacob, and she was thus part of his life. She seemed not to know it. She grew less and less familiar to Jacob, always wanting more and more pampering. She offered herself to whoever wanted to touch her. She really had strong customer service skills, and she focused on client satisfaction. Her public relations were excellent. Everybody was satisfied except Jacob who kept fetching true love. As days went on, she grew more and more distant from him. Jacob repeatedly told her that his bedroom was her room, a world of their own. It seemed that Nikita knew beforehand that life in a family house would be different from life in the store or in the garden. Human beings don't fly like birds. Only butterflies and bees jump from one flower to another. Jacob wanted Nikita to know that he was the only man supposed to be in her life. This is what Nikita and Dickson called jealousy and selfishness.

5. Flowing with Whichever Flow is Flowing

As days went by, Jacob got obliged to abide by Nikita's will. He could leave the window open to allow fresh air to blow into the room. He knew that plants, like human beings, needed air for respiration. Among other things, the rose needed light energy from the sun. When he worked night shift, Nikita needed much more air, and she took out the screen. She let the window wide open. Butterflies and bees took advantage of the open window to spoil her flower. Nikita did absolutely nothing to protect Jacob's treasure. She served it instead. Rather than putting their dirty legs on the petal, the bees and butterflies stood elegantly on the anther and the stigma. The filaments and style were not strong enough to uphold the weight of multiple butterflies and bees sucking the pollen with their dirty proboscis, long legs, and tall abdomens. The flower received more energy than she could release. Consequently, the bees and butterflies blocked oxygen and caused fermentation. The same thing was happening with Nikita. She ignored Jacob in a way that suggested that she was having affairs with others.

Jacob knew that Nikita had fallen in love with Dickson, and they were having an affair. He also discovered that she was hanging around with others of Dickson's friends. Because there was no explanation for her disappearance, Jacob feared that she might be kidnapped, raped, or even murdered. She was new in the country, and she did not know which places were dangerous and should thus be avoided. Her boyfriends were the kind of men who would not fear to go to dangerous places where they could get their throats cut off. Now that they were hanging around with Nikita, if anything were to happen, they would die with her. Jacob could not go with them nor could he know where they were going every day. He hopelessly watched Nikita trudging across the street to Dickson's apartment where she met other men. Jacob tried to develop her awareness about the danger of hanging around with the bad people. He reminded her of their evil acts. He noticed that if they were bad in his mind, they were nice with her. Whatever the situation, he could not support her infidelities. Now that she was offering herself, there was no fear of kidnap or rape. They had all they wanted. AIDS was his worst fear now. If she was having affairs with multiple partners, it was not certain that she was protecting herself against AIDS and other sexually transmitted diseases. One cannot always trust a naked woman in another man's legs, especially Dickson and Juvenhack. Jacob could not tell her to use protection when she was denying the affairs. Besides, he would be encouraging her to do it when he wanted the affairs to end. He planned to bring the subject for discussion. He let Nikita understand that he was not happy with what was happening behind his back. He joined her in the room and gently asked, "Honey, why are you doing all this to me? You are torturing me. Have you so easily forgotten the promise?"

She looked surprised and exclaimed. "Which promise?"

He reminded her of the promises she made in Olympia.

"You promised to be all mine and forever. Now I am living like a priest without a church. It is not the same as a husband without a wife. It is more like a parent without a child." He paused a while and sighed. Then he continued, this time, he spoke his thoughts aloud, "This situation reminds me of the Nigerian writer, T. M. Aluko. He entitled his first novel *One Man, One Wife*. I don't know why he didn't think of the other way round too. There should be a reason for the omission. Then he wrote *One Man, One Matchet*. Is there a relation between a wife and a matchet?" A wife is a human being, man's partner. In the African tradition, a matchet was man's partner too. It is a weapon, a large heavy knife with a broad blade. Man used it to protect himself. Like a wife, a man needs only one matchet. I like T. M. Aluko. He is a wise man. I have never seen a man with more than one matchet. And every man I know has only one wife."

After the short monologue, Jacob turned to Nikita.

"What do you think?"

As if he was talking nonsense, she turned her back and moved away.

Jacob insisted. "Are you going to answer me?"

She turned her head. "You did not ask me a question. You just made a statement. If you had asked a question I would have answered you."

"I did ask a question."

"About what?"

"About the relation between a wife and a matchet."

"What are you saying?"

"I am talking about T. M. Aluko's two novels."

"Who is T. M. Aluko?"

"The author of *One Wife, One Man* and *One Man, One Matchet*." By insisting on this subject, Jacob opened a can of worms.

"One wife one man? What do you mean?" she fixed him with a stern look with eyes wide open.

"Sorry, it is *One Man, One Wife*."

"This guy is crazy. I advise you to seek treatment. You are sick. You really need counseling. You had better do it before it is too late. I personally can't do anything to help you." She waved her head and left the room. Jacob followed her, begging her attention.

"Please, honey, listen to me. You are my honey, my everything. You are the only one to make me happy. You don't know how much I love you. Please, honey, come back."

He tried to kiss her, and she turned away. She was not making him happy anymore. Jacob insisted so that he could get the lost happiness. Unfortunately, everything Nikita said brought more sadness than happiness. Jacob seemed apologetic.

"I am your honey, so what? I can still do what I want. I am not your prisoner," she noted in dismay.

"You are right, my dear. I entirely agree with you. But can you do me a favor?"

"What?"

Jacob had been trying to avoid it, but he thought the time was right. He just wanted her to know that he was aware of the affair with Dickson and the other bees that sucked Rosie's pollen. There had come a time when Nikita could hide the intimate relation with Dickson no longer. She could spend tens of hours talking about Dickson. She always sounded excited when talking to him and rushed when talking to Jacob. She was more interested in hanging around with Dickson than spending her time with her children. All knew that there was chemistry between them. Many a time, Jacob saw signs of infidelity. He was bothered by the smell of cigarette on his pillow when neither Jacob nor Nikita smoked. The situation upset Jacob too much. However, nothing of it was spoken about. It remained top secret. Jacob did not want to ruin their relationship. When he tried to talk to her, she became more aggressive with strange behavior. She yelled gibberish at him. She could even hide the flower for weeks. Jacob had to speak sweet words in order to win her love again. Occasionally, she would report some of the private conversations she had with Dickson. If he was bored listening about her former boyfriends, her new ones made him practically crazy.

Nikita was curious to know what favor Jacob was asking for. She knew he was suspecting her affairs but she did not know that he would ever talk about it. She insisted,

"What favor do you want from me, then?" Jacob had waited weeks to bring up her affairs. Suddenly, he had a change of heart.

"Don't worry about it."

"No. Tell me. I want to know."

He did not want to see her with Dickson. Jacob feared that even if Nikita was not intended to do anything, many contacts with Dickson might make her love him, in which case it would be too late to mend. Jacob spoke hesitantly as her reaction was unpredictable.

"Well, I hate to say it, but I know that there is an affair going on between you and Dickson. I do not want to hear about you with your Dick anymore. I don't need that man in my house either. I am not always at home but I know what is going on. I am tired of the situation. He has been pampering you, showing excessive kindness even in my presence. I understand that you need pampering, but there are limits. I don't know where you got this business of wanting pampering every now and then. I mean . . . I never expected this to happen to you. You are here because you chose to be with me and not with Dickson."

Jacob was not happy with her, but he could not prevent her from wanting what her heart wanted. She shot him a bemused look and turned her back.

"Nikita, you change nothing by looking at me like that. Look into your heart instead. I am serious," Jacob insisted.

"It always hurts my feelings when you keep speaking very high of somebody who doesn't stop blackmailing me. He even knows how I snore at night when I have never slept in his apartment. I don't see why you should report this to him. Does he really need to know how I sleep? I never need to know how he sleeps with Dada either. By the way, how does he how everything that happens in this house? Anyway, I want my place in my house. You are not just my mistress. You are much more than that. Why should you want to sleep with everybody? This situation must change. I will never let Dickson keep preying on my beloved one. You are my lover, not his. You are my everything. Most of all, I love you." Jacob wrapped his arms around her.

Nikita did not seem to pay attention at all. Jacob thought she would be surprised to hear that he was aware of her indiscretions. Jacob wanted her to leave Dickson at the time when their romance was flourishing. He was jealous because Dickson was taking precedence over him. Nikita's face remained expressionless. Jacob was the one to feel like a real stupid asshole as Nikita did not deny the affair. Instead, she tried to make him feel ridiculous.

It was not Nikita's habit to give up easily. In forty years of her life, she had never lived a cooperative life. She had been bringing homeless men in her bed. They lived under her control as they needed somewhere to live. They had no power to impose order, for they had no engagement with her. Thomas had lived in fear of being kicked out. Nikita was not prepared to change her attitude. She believed it was still her right to flow with whichever flow was flowing. Now, Jacob was leading her to the right path. She shrugged before speaking arrogantly,

"There is nothing between Dick and me. We are just friends. Don't listen to people's gossip," she said evasively.

Jacob felt a twinge of doubt about what she declared. He took the explanation with a pinch of salt because nothing but her ego knew exactly what was going on. Jacob did not accept the claim as incredulity in his voice was audible.

"You are just friends! Are you kidding? You flirt with somebody who would bite me head off! And he plays with my flower, my treasure as his own property! Every time you take her away, she comes back damaged. My room smells of cigarettes now, and so does my pillow. Since when do you smoke?"

Jacob was ached when she compared other men favorably against him. Dickson's name was recurring in every conversation. Jacob felt a clutch at the sound of that name.

"I am sick of hearing you speaking admiringly of that goddamned son-of-a-bitch. Why don't you just leave him alone? You are not lonely. People won't say anything if they don't see you together. Anyway, you are part of my life and not his. You can't have a foot in my house and another in his apartment. You need to keep your feet together and choose between Dickson and me, period."

Jacob thought these remarks would be of some help. He did not want anything to break them apart. He was determined to keep the distressing relationship in the hope that it would improve. He did not even accuse her of infidelities. He only noted that he was aware of her affairs. He was not even mad about it. He only wanted to increase their closeness.

Her reaction could not reassure him though. He was expecting her to fall in line with his suggestion. Her answer, however, did not take the weight off his mind. She went into paroxysm of rage.

"You don't want me to have any friends. You are too controlling. I need my freedom. Why are you so jealous? You're nut . . . corny as hell!" She stared at him with hatred before she continued assaulting him,

"I dated a lot of men, but I had never known an old-fashioned man like you. You are a horrible man, always acting stupid. Fuck you, son of a bitch!" She exited the house.

Jacob realized that there was too much at stake. He followed her shouting,

"Nikita, you are flirting with a goddamned Evildoer. Why shouldn't I speak about it?" He shut up because she was getting too far to be able to hear him. If he spoke louder, he would be telling the neighborhood and not Nikita. His neighbors next door were already listening. At the same time, they watched Nikita going to Dickson. She took a time off in Dickson's house where she reported everything to whoever could listen to her. Dickson called Juvenhack to join the conversation. Nikita started her narration.

"The asshole doesn't want me to be with you. He hates you so much that he doesn't even want to see you."

"What did he do?" Dickson asked.

"He is telling me nonsense as usual," she said.

"And what did you tell him?" he asked.

"I told him to fuck off. I am an independent person. Why does he want to control me? I never allowed anybody to control me. Even if I am in his house, my body is still mine, and I have full control of it. I hate jealous men."

"I told you. He was an asshole. Don't worry. We will deal with him."

"I have to stay with him until I get papers."

"That is easy. Just push him to do it fast."

"He is delaying things as he wants me to stay with him. It may take long before I can get everything done."

"It is very simple. I will take care of it. Call me when he is not at work. I have friends who can help you."

Nikita stayed with Dickson for four hours talking about Jacob with whoever came in.

For many years, Nikita had contempt for Evildoers. She had sworn not to forgive them for destroying her country and killing members of her family. Jacob remembered her declaration when she was still a child.

"If I had power, I would hang the goddamned Evildoers on trees. I would cut their tongues hanging out of their throats and throw them in the dumpster."

Twenty-five years later, Nikita could not remember that she pronounced the words. Even before coming to Jacob, she could not share a drink with an Evildoer. When she saw Evildoers passing by, she would spit to show her excessive hate for them. Jacob had to give her civic lessons. He told her that Evildoers were part of her people. He encouraged her to respect them as human beings. They had lost power to do immoral acts. When she arrived in Jacob's house, she changed sides. She made a 180-degree turn and she became an Evildoer like the others.

Jacob was watching television when she entered the house. He thought that she was not trying to hurt him deliberately and felt sorry for accusing her earlier. He stood up and apologized for the talk. She stared at him and said bitterly, "Leave me alone, please. I don't want to hear anything from you."

"I am worried about you. I understand that you are getting into the swing of things, but you should know right from wrong. You were not born yesterday. It is high time you put your roots down. I am not too controlling. I am just an attentive and caring person. It is gratifying when one lives a happy life. You know what I am saying?"

She did not pay any more attention to him. Jacob never knew that he was beating a dead horse. He thought Nikita needed time to think about what he said. He let her cool down a while to think of the situation. He moved to his desk and turned the computer on. He pretended to read the news, but he was thinking of how he was being treated as a hayseed. He was always making time for her, but she rarely had time for him. Even when she was there, she was always absentminded. Jacob thought of ways of improving the situation. Suddenly, he spoke out, "Why is it so difficult to talk to you? The name of Dickson keeps popping up. Can't you think of anything else? How many times shall I repeat it to you? Aren't you the one who told me that Ronald was killed by those Sans Echecs! Dickson was member of that death squad. He himself could have killed Ronald. Have you so easily forgotten how many people were killed by members of that brigade?"

"So what? They died. Are you going to resuscitate them?" she asked.

"So you treat their killers as your boyfriends so that the dead can be resurrected. Is that right? Nikita, you are too much. Think of the grief the death of your lover, your father, your siblings, and relatives caused you if it caused you any. Think of the nice times you had with them, at least what I witnessed when I saw you with Ronald. Think of your own family they forced to leave their properties to seek asylum abroad. How can you accept their killers as your lovers? That is a shame! How do you even dare say that you loved your family? You could not love them and still flirt with their killers. You are lying. You never loved anybody. You only love attention you get from roving eyes. By betraying everybody, you betray your heart as well. You are doing exactly the same thing to me." Silence ensues, only broken by Nikita's occasional sighs.

"I could foresee that you would betray me. I never doubted about that. You do it every single day. I don't see where I am going with you." Suddenly, he changed the voice and spoke more slowly.

"Nikita, you changed completely. You are not the Nikita Chissocco I treated as my sister many years ago. I should learn to look before I leap." As he waited for her reply, silence took over once more.

Jacob saw no need to continue the conversation. Nikita knew that the Sans Echecs would have killed Jacob if he did not stay away from them. They would have killed her too. She knew that Dickson sought to kill Jacob in Rutana. He had also reported to her how badly he treated him in secondary school. But when her inside was burning, all she needed was a man. She did not care about his history, just a man would do. She even ignored that she was dealing with a lover dedicated to love her all his life. She motioned to the living room and sank in the sofa. She watched the *American Idol* as if nothing was wrong. Jacob remained seated in the bedroom thinking things over.

As Nikita seemed unaware of her deeds, Jacob considered dealing with her more softly. He knew how hard it was to transform a grown-up dishonest person into an honest one. In their language, there is an adage saying that a bent tree is straightened when it is still young. The adage applies to human behavior. The best way to change a grown-up's behavior is to do it smartly and smoothly. Jacob went to watch the *American Idol* with Nikita. He sat on a couch. Nikita stood up and moved to him. She sat on his lab and wrapped him with her arms. She gave him many noisy kisses, and he told her how much he loved her. The wheel of love turned again as if nothing had happened. Problems occurred because Jacob thought that life was more than just enjoying sweet things. If he limited himself there, life was but a rose. She was ready to love him as before on condition that he allowed her freedom to enjoy herself with whoever she wanted. Now that communication was improving, Jacob wondered what to do to love her better. He thought of things the other men could not offer her. He paid her trips to discover the best places of Canada. All the efforts were in vain. They gave more pain than happiness.

As he did not know how to love her much better than his competitors did, Jacob asked Nikita what else she needed in her life. He would do anything she wanted in order to improve their relationship. He had made a point of never making her unhappy. As she seemed to look unhappy, he showed his willingness to compromise with her. He would compensate her if she quit flirting with other men. He thought there might be something she needed in which case he would make efforts to provide it. He wanted them to put their heads together and solve the problem once for all.

"Honey, you know that I love you. We have many years of life together. We cannot go on living like this. We need to enjoy our time and live a happier life. We need to have a little fun. I have been thinking of what to do to improve the situation. I may be doing something wrong unknowingly. I beg your help to make things work better. Is there anything I should do to improve the situation? I may not know my weak points. You see me more clearly than I can see myself. You are my eyes. You know me more than I know myself. Can you, please, tell me about things you would like me to change? I promise to change everything you want me to change."

By admitting unknown mistakes, he thought she would cooperate to improve things. However, trying to change her was tantamount to trying to corner a bobcat. There was nothing he could do to compensate for her affairs. Her desire for many men was overruling her. When she looked for Jacob, it was his turn. He had to enjoy his time and then go away. Nikita did not care how nice and caring a man was. There were few nicer men and more caring than Jacob was. The only problem was that he did not really want to share with others or give her more freedom with Dickson and others. Jacob wanted to be glued on her. He seemed to ignore that the only reason he got her was that others had left her. After two years with Jacob, it was time for her to find new romances. The only way to make her happy was, therefore, to leave the house and never follow what she did there. She would be free to flow with whatever flow was flowing. She could still find part-time for Jacob, not as a lover but as a man.

As long as Jacob wanted her full time, she would never be satisfied. With twenty-two years of adulteries, one could not expect her to become a faithful person overnight.

Jacob was determined to get over the situation. He insisted on solving the problem. Yet Nikita was straightforward. As always, she called a spade a spade. She innocently spoke about Jacob's major weakness and even made a suggestion on how to fix it.

"There is only one problem with you. But it is a big one, and you need to work on it seriously."

Jacob was relieved that he would soon know the cause of the disagreement.

"If it is only one problem, why did it take too long to tell me? You should have told me earlier, and this upsetting game would be over."

"It is never too late to change. If you change now, things will be fine," Nikita promised.

Now that there was promise to improve the situation for good, Jacob wondered if it was something he could achieve. He thought of two possibilities.

"Does she want me to pack my stuff and leave the house? Does she want me to move to Olympia with her?" Jacob wondered. He cooled down and listened.

"You are dreadfully jealous. You ought to do something to overcome jealousy and get rid of it once for all," Nikita said.

"Is this the only problem?" he asked, expecting a big one.

"You are too jealous about my being with Dickson. You take every opportunity to be rude to him. You don't even allow him in our house. You need to work on jealousy. Jealousy is my worse pet peeve," she said accusingly.

Jacob scratched his head for while. He had promised to do whatever she asked him. Now he knew the problem. If he fixed it as he had promised, things would work better. After a long silence, he explained apologetically that Nikita was too demanding.

"I cannot help being jealous when I feel neglected in my relationship," he said.

He wondered how to cope with jealousy. It only ate him alive. He thought of what else to do to satisfy her. But her requirement was clear. She would only be happy if he willingly greed to support her and not only love Dickson but also accept whoever she wanted.

If jealousy was her pet peeve, her adultery was Jacob's. He hesitated to state that he disliked Dickson. If he really wanted Nikita, he had to accept Dickson. There had come a time when whoever wanted her had to pass by Dickson. Dickson was a kind of bridge between Nikita and anybody who wanted to relieve their needs with her. Only a few did not pass by him.

By inviting him to work on his jealousy, she touched his nerve. He had to love Dickson. That was not too big an issue. The problem was that he could not accept him in his life. He was there anyway. Jacob buried his face in his hands and sighed. He spoke slowly and hesitantly.

"I liked Dickson before, but . . . since he is more and more involved with you, I feel insecure. Besides, he is not the kind of friend I should keep. I might like him if he stops interfering in our privacy." Then, he spoke a bit louder but uncomfortably.

"Do you want me to tolerate and spread a red carpet on people who are destroying my life?"

"They are not destroying your life," she reassured him.

For the first time, Jacob raised his voice and spoke defensively.

"Madam, stop badgering me to love Dickson. Nothing irks me more than the mention of his goddamned name. I am badgering myself to improve the situation, and you don't seem to live in this house. You plead for that rodent as if you belonged to him! Now you want me to spread a carpet to welcome him! I cut him off because he got my secrets, and he is using them against me. I will never ever allow him in my house again."

The fact that he cut Dickson off let Nikita feelings wretched. She decided to be following him in his house, especially that Jacob would not go there. Nikita tried to convince.

"You don't have to worry too much about me. I am a grown-up," she said.

"Why shouldn't I care when I was expecting to be the only one in your life? I don't agree with your wild theories of jealousy. Jealousy is common sense."

Nikita did not speak again.

"I don't see what is wrong in loving you and wanting you entirely for me. I am jealous because I don't want anybody interfering in our relationship." He paused and waited for Nikita's reaction. Silence.

"I cannot help being jealous when I think of you with my bitter enemies. No one can trust Dickson around his woman. You do absolutely nothing to secure my heart. On the contrary, you show me that you want him around. He is a person to be avoided."

Nikita had a reckless look in her eyes. By inviting Jacob to work on his jealousy, she made a bald statement that confirmed her affairs. Jacob understood the declaration as a request for authorization to sleep with whomever she wanted. He had promised to do whatever she would ask him. He defaulted on the promise in less than a minute. If Jacob had known that he would be asked to share, he would never have thought of her in his life. To him, it was clear from the beginning that they would be faithful to each other. The issue of sharing was never discussed. Jacob started explaining himself, trying to convince her of his strong love.

"Don't tell me you want Dickson in your life. I am jealous because you treat him much better than you treat me. No one else loves you more than I do. Why do I have to compete with others? I am bitter in rivalry with others. The situation is causing me a lot of pain, embarrassment and humiliation. I feel insecure and threatened in my life. I don't want to lose you. I also fear HIV. Hon, can we argue with the logic of jealousy and selfishness? I like my life. I don't want to lose it because of HIV and other STDs."

"You fear HIV! Do you think I am stupid not to protect myself? I, too, love my life."

"I am not accusing you, but . . . you wouldn't like me to have affairs, would you?"

"No. You are a man, and I am a woman."

"Okay."

Jacob did not want to go any further. He noticed that she was not ready to understand the meaning of love. Still, he had promised cooperation in order to improve the situation. He vowed to respect everything she asked him to do. Now that she required him to fight jealousy, cooperation with her was puzzling him. He only wanted her to get rid of the filthy habits of seducing everybody.

The next day, Jacob confided to Geram that there was chemistry between Dickson and Nikita. He told him how rumors were being confirmed by Nikita herself who accused him of being jealous about their affair. He needed to know what to do in such situations. Jacob was confiding to Geram when the latter was already making plans to have her. Now that Geram was informed that Dickson and Zim Anan had already won her, he would not lose any more time. He started expressing excessive kindness to the couple. He visited them three times a day with a bottle of wine for Nikita. He suggested different kinds of wine, and Nikita had to choose the best wine, the price notwithstanding. Geram did everything needed to attract her. He was always there for supper, trying to get more familiar to her.

Nikita was the kind of woman who was ready to flow with whatever flow was flowing. She started seducing Geram. She knew that he would resist her. She planned to ambush him with her body; after all, it was the only weapon at her disposal she could always count on. One day, she called Geram to ask how he was doing. In her sweet voice, she asked him if he would be kind enough to give her ride to the grocery store. Geram longed for such an opportunity to be with her. He had to go to work but he called in sick. Not only was he happy to take her to Superstore, he also offered to pay for her groceries.

After the grocery shopping, Geram, more determined than ever, invited her for a dinner in a restaurant. They asked for a table for two, and they sat facing each other. Nikita could not stop moving her body. As she had not put a brassiere, her blouse exposed her breasts with every motion she made. Geram could see her large breasts through her unbuttoned blouse. As reaction to the provocation, he impressed her by ordering the most expensive meals. He told her to eat and drink anything she wanted.

"Don't worry about the cost. Money is there," he told her reassuringly. Nikita was experienced in dealing with men. She was not learning anything new.

During their conversation, Nikita appeared to be desperate about money. She complained that Jacob was not giving her enough money. Geram felt sorry for her and betrayed his friend.

"Why doesn't he give you money? That is not kind. A good man should give enough money to his woman," he told her sympathetically.

"He only gives me money for groceries. He even checks the receipts," she complained.

"That is stupid. A man should trust his lover," he said.

"If I take money from the bank account, he needs to know what I used it for. The guy controls me financially. Now, for example, I don't have any cash on me. On the other hand, he transfers hundreds of dollars to his kids every other week. He ignores that I need that money."

"What a pity! I am really disappointed. I thought that he was a nice person. A beautiful woman like you deserves special treatment," he said, still admiring her breasts.

"Exactly. But he doesn't care about me."

Nikita knew that Geram was admiring her breasts, and she exposed them even more.

"Geram, you seem to like my breasts. I didn't put on a brassiere because it is hot," she said encouragingly. She did not even button her blouse to hide them. Geram met her gaze. He coughed.

"I am not looking at your breasts. I am only listening to you," he said.

"I look ugly with my big tits," she said, stroking them. Geram kept looking at them and nodding. He coughed again.

"You look marvelous with your large breasts. I like large breasts with big nipples. Jacob must adore them."

"These tits will fall down to my stomach in a couple of years. I will look awful, and no one will like me anymore. You guys like young ladies' breasts, eh!"

"To me, your breasts are perfect. I haven't seen better breasts than yours. I wish I were Jacob," he said jokingly.

"Why? My body is mine and not his." Geram inhaled deeply.

"He is your—" Nikita interrupted him and veered the conversation to her breasts.

"I must have a problem with my nipples. One is more sensitive than the other."

Geram let out another deep breath. Nikita noticed that she had ambushed him with her breasts. Geram was already erect, and she decided to take advantage of his weakness.

"Geram, as I was saying, I am in need of some money. If—" Geram interrupted.

"You find me crazy, eh!"

"Why?"

"Because of what I said."

"What did you say?"

"I said that I would be happy to enjoy your breasts."

"That is normal. As a man, you have feelings and desires. This is human nature."

"What do you think about adoring somebody's woman?" he asked.

"Somebody's woman is still a woman," she said.

Geram took another deep breath. He decided to shift the gear and move to the point. He knew he would only win her with money.

"I am sorry I interrupted you. You were saying something about money," he reminded her.

"As I was saying, if you could lend me some money, I would be able to give it back in two weeks."

"Well, it is not easy for me to lend money to you when Jacob doesn't know."

"Don't worry about him. It is between us. There are still ways to show gratitude. I am not the kind of women who don't show gratitude," she said reassuringly with a note of satisfaction in her sweet voice.

"Really? How will you show me gratitude?"

"Whichever way you want me to."

"Stop killing me. Do you want your lover to kill me? He once said that if he caught a man playing with you, he would kill him. So I don't want to die."

"He always says that. Let him say whatever he wants. At any rate, he doesn't have to know it."

"How much money do you need now?"

"Well, two hundred dollars would be enough for now," she said while adjusting her blouse so that he could see her breasts better. Geram reached for his wallet and dispensed her some bills.

"I only need two hundred, honey," she said while pocketing the double of the amount she had asked for.

"It is okay. Money is nothing. Friendship is much more important than money."

"Like I told you I will pay you in two weeks."

"I did not lend you that money. I just want to help you, given that your lover does care about you. You don't have to pay me back."

"Thank you so much, my dear."

"You are welcome. By the way, don't hesitate to call me anytime you need money. I am not selfish like Jacob."

Nikita praised him as the kindest person in the world. She got to her feet and kissed him on the lips. She gave him such an enigmatic smile that he understood that she was ready for gratitude. They looked at each other with open admiration. They sipped their wine.

"You really attract me. I could not say it before, but you are killing me," Geram said.

"Really? You should have told me before."

"Now is the time to tell you. You attracted me from the beginning, and I am sure you knew how I felt about you."

"I could tell by the way you always looked at me. I was only wondering why you could not tell me anything until I make the first step."

Geram thought that the time might not come again. He decided to hit the iron when it was hot.

"How and when will you show me gratitude, then?"

"Never mind. We have all the time ahead. Let's get out of here. These people may be spying on us."

She picked up her glass half-full and drained it in one gulp. Geram sipped his and paid the bill.

As his erection was still pressing against his trousers, he did not stand up until he felt comfortable to walk.

"Wait a moment."

Nikita understood that he wanted to stay with her longer. She kissed him and held his hand.

"Let's go, honey. We still have time together."

Nikita never realized that she was worsening the situation. Geram could not stand up when everybody would see the big thing pressing his trousers.

"Give me one minute to make a phone call. Don't speak, please. I am calling Jacob to ask him what time he will finish work."

"He will finish work late in the evening," Nikita replied.

"I just want to confirm, one never knows."

"Don't say that we are together."

"Of course not."

"Okey-dokey.

The call lasted one minute, and Geram's excitement cooled down.

"Let's go now," Nikita ordered. They exited the restaurant.

On their way, Nikita reminded Geram that she would find a way to express gratitude for his kindness. By this promise, the deal was concluded. As they were approaching home, Nikita started bugging him.

"Geram, you never show me where you live. Maybe your girlfriend is there, and you don't want her to see me," she said.

"If I had a girlfriend, you would have seen her. I cannot invite a woman like you to my small room. Jacob knows where I live. But I can show you my place now if you have time."

"I have done all I had to do. Is it far from here?"

"It is just a few blocks from Marlborough Mall."

He immediately gunned the car to the left lane and drove to his place. He would not miss such an opportunity. He bought a bottle of wine that they would drink in his room.

"With all the money I spent on her, I hope she will be grateful," Geram thought.

There was nothing Geram wanted more than her at that moment. He had heard about Dickson and Juvenhack, and he felt that it was his turn.

Geram had always been like Dickson and Zim Anan. He ran after his friends' girlfriends or wives. He and Nikita got to his room, and he welcomed her on his bed. As they had been together for four hours already, they did not lose more time. They had had enough time to say all they needed to say. Geram needed her while she needed his money. She would sleep with him as a sign of gratitude. In other words, it was a matter of business. They were in the right place at the right time. The moment she sat on his bed, she asked him if he had a condom. Geram confirmed. He started stroking her breasts.

"You are a nice woman. I wish I had a beautiful wife like you."

"Geram, you have been too nice to me. I will always remember it."

"Will you be too nice to me too?"

"I am always grateful to people who show me kindness like you." She spoke while taking her blouse off, then her jeans. She lied down on the bed and relaxed in her underwear. Geram took off all his clothes and joined her in the bed.

Nikita behaved weirdly. Although she had repeatedly promised gratitude, when the time came to show it, she seemed not to think of Geram as a privileged customer that needed satisfaction. She just lied in the bed and spread her legs. Whatever Geram did, she appeared to be absent. She let Geram relieve his needs while she was watching television. With a remote control in her hands, she kept changing channels, looking for the *American Idol*. She did not even seem to feel Geram crushing his body on hers. Geram turned her, and she faced the wall. She could no longer see the television.

"Let me watch my favorite show," she yelled on him, turning back.

Few minutes later, she started speaking gibberish about Jacob. As Geram was not listening to her monologue, she grabbed his photo album and started turning the pages.

"Oh! You have a beautiful wife too. Why don't you bring her to Canada?" she asked him when he was busy moving himself into her.

Geram was sweating. The sweat combined with his odor. The mixture produced an awful smell that Nikita could not stomach. Soon, she felt nausea. She pretended that he was taking too long.

"Come now. What are you waiting for? I am tired. Come!" she spoke loud.

As Geram was taking his time, she jerked him away from her and she stood up. Without dressing, she ran through the corridor connecting the room and the washroom. She stumbled against a stool and fell down. She hastened to get up and reached for the washroom doorknob. She turned it, but she did not push to open the door. She did not know that other tenants were sitting in the living room watching her. They saw her trying to open the washroom's door. One of the tenants came to open the door for her. She felt ashamed of being completely naked in front of strangers.

Inside the washroom, the nausea was over. She did not even vomit. She sat on the toilet seat doing nothing but wondering how to return to the room when she would be watched. She got stuck there and counted on Geram to drop in. She let the door open so he could get in.

Geram himself was frustrated. He joined her in the washroom, holding his erect organ with his right hand. He did not know that the other tenants were nearby. In the washroom, he negotiated Nikita to allow him another few minutes so he could come. Nikita refused to do anything in the washroom while people were sipping coffee in the living room next door. She worried that they might need to use the washroom. She asked Geram to go back and bring her clothes.

Geram remembered that his neighbors saw him naked, and his erection began to shrink. He returned to the room hiding it with both hands. By now, one hand was enough to cover it. It was only two-inch long. He grabbed a towel and wrapped himself in it. He returned to the washroom with Nikita's clothes. She quickly dressed and returned to the room. She buried her face in her hands and started crying. Geram grabbed Kleenex and dried the tears welling from her eyes.

"Why did you do this? You made me drunk so you could fuck me. You took me for a hooker, eh!"

"I didn't rape you," he said apologetically.

"Why did you bring me here? Get me the hell out of here!" Nikita ordered.

"I just wanted to show you my place. I did not force you to come. You insisted to see where I live."

"Why didn't you tell me that there were people sitting in the living room?"

"They were not there when we came. Besides, you didn't have to run out of the room naked. Why did you do that?"

"Next time, you need to find a hotel room. I am not coming back here."

"Hotels are very expensive in this city."

"There are cheap hotels in North East. They have hourly rates. You can pay for just one hour if you want. A hotel room is very safe and comfortable."

"I don't know of cheap hotels."

"I will show you. Do these people know Jacob?" she asked.

"They know him, but they don't know you," Geram reassured her.

"I am scared. They may see me with him someday, and they will tell him what they saw," she looked worried.

"They never talk to him. They only see him with me," he said reassuringly.

"Jacob will eventually know it. I will never come back here. Drive me home now."

Geram inched her closer and wrapped his arms around her.

"Not right now. We are not done yet. You promised me gratitude. I still want you, please, be grateful."

She thought of the groceries he paid for and the money she pocketed. She remembered that she would need more money. Slowly, she unzipped her pants and spread her legs apart to allow her pants to fall on the floor. Geram jumped on her like an animal and buried himself inside her. This time, he worked hard to make sure that he came within three minutes. After one minute, he started coming. He flooded her with his sperm gushing from him like water out of a garden hose.

"Get the hell out of me, I am tired!" she yelled. She did not let him finish. She pulled out from him when he was groaning and trembling. She immediately got to her feet and started dressing. She did not even sit on the bed as before.

"I hope that you enjoyed it," she said.

Geram pulled a towel and covered his thing that was still spitting semen in his hand.

"I spent eight hundred dollars on a stupid whore like this. I should have spent a tenth of that money on a hooker, and she would serve me better," he complained inwardly. He was trying to catch his breath when Nikita pulled him up.

"Drive me home. I don't want Jacob to know it."

"Give me a little more time."

"What are you waiting for?"

"Let's wait for the guys to leave."

"I don't care. Let's go."

As she was insisting on going home, Geram told her to wait a few more minutes. He rushed to the bank and withdrew some banknotes. He came back with another bottle of wine that he handed to her. He also gave her several banknotes and thanked her for her kindness. The bills disappeared in her pockets. She opened the wine and swirled it in their glasses. They lifted their glasses. After clinking them, they sipped. Nikita met his gaze for a while before throwing her arms around him. She held him tight and started kissing him. He unzipped her trousers and pushed them down over the hips. He played with her buttocks, pressing them against his body. As the trousers fell on the floor, she stepped out of them and threw herself to the bed. She slept on her back with her knees wide open while undoing the buttons of her blouse.

In the meantime, Geram switched off the modem of his cable so she could not watch television. He did it in a way that she did not notice it. She did not need it anyway. With the bills she pocketed, she forgot about the *American Idol*. This time, she was no longer in a rush to get home. She allowed him as much time as he wanted, and she was the one to do most of the work. Geram sweated even more, but she did not seem to notice. Actually, he was now perfumed with the smell of the banknotes she pocketed.

After a few hours, Geram drove her home. Jacob was already there, worried. He was thinking that she was with Dickson. As Jacob trusted Geram, he thanked him for giving her the ride. He did not suspect anything. He considered Geram so ugly that Nikita would never allow him on her body.

The next day, Geram took the family to the nicest restaurant in the city. Jacob wondered how he could afford it when Jacob himself was struggling to make both ends meet. Geram would spend hundreds of dollars on Nikita and her kids and Jacob found him the most generous person. Jacob eventually doubted his excessive kindness. Nikita, however, did not seem to see Geram as being too nice to her. She always had negative comment about him even though he was nothing but nice to her. Jacob was the one to thank him for being too nice when Nikita did not seem to care.

Nikita was seen in Geram's room many times. She finally agreed that they had more privacy than in the hotel. Besides that, she did not want Geram to pay her and the hotel at the same time. She did not want to share his money with the hotel. She did not even want people to see her in the hotel with different men, especially that she had become familiar to people. She would only go there with Dickson to avoid Dada, his wife. Juvenhack had another place they used to hide from his roommate. Basically, there were fewer eyes to worry about in Geram's room.

One day, Nikita complained about life being as boring as hell. She suggested going out for the night. Jacob was not particularly interested in nightclubs. He had no idea of what clubs looked like. He had the habit of taking weekends as family time when Nikita needed them for fun. As clubs were her biggest hobby, Jacob negotiated a friend to take them to a nightclub. Almami Diatta was more than happy to take them to Tropicana, one of the clubs of the city.

Diatta was different from Jacob. He knew all the clubs. Jacob went reluctantly, just to satisfy Nikita's needs, hoping that she would come back home with a smile. Jacob sat on a high chair and watched Nikita enjoying the beats with Geram. He found the music too loud. Nikita was extremely happy. She danced, smiled, and laughed. Jacob wanted her to enjoy herself, but he could not go there very often. There were other social activities and events they could attend together. There were beautiful places to discover. Jacob suggested trips to Lake Louise, Banff, and Canmore; but Nikita showed no interest. Clubs were more attractive than visiting the nicest places in the world.

6. The Pain and Misery of Loving Nikita

One day, Jacob had some work to do downtown Edmonton, and he needed Nikita's company.

"Honey, I have to go downtown, and I will need your helping hand. It will take no more than five minutes."

Nikita stubbornly refused to take him company. She argued that she did not feel like going out that day.

"You go by yourself. Why do you want me to go with you? I don't want to go anywhere today."

As Jacob needed her to help him, he explained how important her company would be.

"Can you do me that big favor, please?"

"Why are you pushing me to do what I don't want to do? I told you that I don't feel like going anywhere. Don't you have ears?"

Jacob was thus obliged to cancel the appointment and wait for another time. After an hour or so, the phone rang. Nikita picked it up and went to the room. She slammed the door firmly behind her, and she locked it. She spoke on the phone for half an hour. Jacob found himself eavesdropping on the conversation. He overheard some words, not because he was interested to listen to the conversation but because she talked loudly.

"Yes, honey . . . okay . . . No problem. I will . . . No, he is here . . . Okey-dokey . . . I love you too . . . See you soon."

As he heard her talking about him, he guessed the caller was one of his friends. But why should she say "I love you too"? Anyway, Nikita hung up the phone and said nothing to Jacob. She only dressed up and put her makeup. Jacob waited impatiently to hear about the phone call. Nikita slipped into her jacket and winter boots. After rolling a scarf around her neck, she picked up her purse. She did everything in a couple of minutes, still avoiding telling him who had called or where she was going, let alone when she would return home.

Jacob was surprised by her expedience. Usually, when she had to go somewhere with Jacob, she was never in a hurry to get up. Jacob had to remind her the time every now and then. She took an awful lot of time dressing and putting the makeup on. Jacob had learned to be patient. He had to help her with the selection of clothes and makeup to wear. She could even ask him which earrings, necklace, and bracelets she would put. Jacob was even the one to polish her shoes and press her clothes. Otherwise, she would take forever, and they would miss all appointments. However, when Dickson, Juvenhack, or Geram invited her to go out, one minute was enough to get ready.

Jacob watched her getting ready to go out without saying a goddamned word. He spoke to himself,

"How come they talk about me and she tells me nothing!" Turning to Nikita, he demanded, "Where are you going, if you don't mind me asking?"

By asking the question, Jacob was opening the Pandora's box one more time. Nikita looked at him in a strange way and twisted her mouth. Jacob repeated, "May I know where you are going?"

She looked at him wryly and shook her head. As he insisted, she replied.

"I am going to the West Edmonton Mall," she answered as she adjusted the scarf around her neck.

"The West Edmonton Mall is a huge Shopping Center," Jacob remarked. Nikita shrugged.

"Why do you shrug every time I speak to you? You should give me a proper answer, rather than just shrugging. When I ask you a question, I expect an answer, not a shrug."

Jacob had been dealing with her with positive attitude and expected the same in return. Instead, she turned and fixated him a long look.

"Why are you checking up on me? You don't need to know everything about me." With that, she exited the house. Jacob followed her.

"Where are you going like that?" Nikita became mad as hell. She shot him a long-suffering look before adding, "Where I am going is strictly my fucking business and not yours. You don't need to check on me, okay? Kiss my ass, you bungling idiot." She said that boisterously with a flash of bitterness as she stormed out of the house.

Jacob watched her whipping away. By the time he was going to reply, she had already gone. She ignored him and continued her way. By insulting him, she compounded the mistake that shook Jacob from head to toe. If he insisted, not only would she raise the voice, she would also raise the hands. Jacob turned back without saying a goddamned word. He shuffled around nervously wondering if he was dreaming.

His phone had a caller ID. When he checked the last number dialed, he recognized Dickson's cell phone number. Instantly, he understood that she went out with Dickson as usual. Jacob decided to track them. He crept across the parking lot and looked out at Dickson's house. He saw his black CRV parked on the road. He drove his car and passed Dickson's vehicle to check if they were sitting there. There was no one in the vehicle. He assumed that they were in the house. Jacob called Dickson's phone. Dickson himself picked the phone and told him that Nikita was not there. Jacob was confused. He walked around Dickson's house several times to check any sign of Nikita. He saw Dickson smoking a cigarette on the balcony. He thought that he would not invite her in the apartment and be out smoking. He refused to believe that she was having an affair with another man inside Dickson's house. They might have gone out. Jacob had no idea who the person she went away with was.

Nikita returned after several hours. When she came, she tried to keep Jacob away from her. They could not sleep together, and he would not ask any question. The same situation was repeated many times. Worries and puzzles piled up as there was nothing Jacob could do to change her. She had to satisfy three men that wanted her very badly. She had to make time for each one. She could not leave them when she had their money, and she needed more. At that time, Jacob was not working. Nikita found her freedom limited. She could not use her free time as she wanted when Jacob was around. As she was losing income, she became nervous and looked grave.

Jacob still hoped for the better. He was optimistic that the situation would improve. He never knew that it was the money, rather than men, that Nikita needed so much. He only saw infidelities as result of her infatuation. As the situation was not improving, Jacob got increasingly upset about her infidelities.

Jacob had nothing against Nikita's errands. He was only worried for her life given her vulnerability. He had no intention to tail her, but he needed to know her whereabouts, just in case. This is common sense when somebody cares for his loved ones. Jacob feared that his enemies might kidnap her in which case things would be complicated. As she was always on the go, they would kidnap her effortlessly. One phone call was enough, and she would take herself to the kidnapper. She returned home, and she did not bother to appear apologetic. Jacob felt like a piece of dirt. The crisis went on for several days. Jacob felt embarrassed to ask any question for fear that the answer might be unpleasant. Whenever she returned home late, she complained in a voice full of contempt.

"The weather is too cold outside. Why did you bring me in this cold country? You know that I can't handle the fucking cold. By the way, Juvenhack and Dickson told me that you were a very bad person—" Jacob interrupted her.

"Stop this nonsense. Why in hell do you go around gossiping about me? I don't like this abusive behavior in my house. I really hate you going around and coming back speaking with all the panoply of street people. They tell you what you want to hear. Why don't you talk to my best friends if you really want to know me! I hate to take the blame for the stupid things your lovers tell you. I am tired of this nonsense!"

He tried to avoid it, but the mention of Dickson's name struck a chord each time. It drove him crazy.

"Do you want me to spend another hell of a week like the last one? I don't really deserve this treatment as a punishment for loving somebody. I did not love you just for your look. If you tell people how you eat, they will ask you where you sleep. And if you show them where you sleep, they will want you to show them how you sleep. They will prove to you that extra sleep is a way better than your regular sleep. They will surely do their best to prove to you that I am an asshole. The way I see you, you will certainly like it, and I will never see you again. If this situation hasn't already happened, it is likely to happen soon." He buried his forehead into his hands and spoke to himself.

"When I carried a torch for a human rose, I was so desperately in need of caring love. I was longing for peace, happiness, comfort, caring, warmth, sympathy, affection, softheartedness, familiarity, encouragement, hope, respect, compassion, and tenderness. Her arrival ended my dreams. She came with fierce competition, unhappiness, embarrassment, anxiety, worry, discomfort, concern, sorrows, troubles, dejection, tears, stress, and depression. My hopes were screwed up." Then he talks to Nikita.

"I am living a lonely life. The house looks empty even when you are here. Your mind has moved away from me. Only thoughts of your boyfriends are running through your head. You keep doing things behind my back. I was not aware of your sluttishness. You keep me in the dark as if I were stupid." Jacob folded his hands and stared at the ceiling. He continued, "This situation makes me feel useless. It eats me up. Chissocco, when will you stop acting as a damper on my spirits?" He moved to the edge of the bed and sat with his hands holding his head, elbows on the knees. He begrudged on the money he kept spending on her. Nikita sighed as she moved to the living room. Jacob could hear her uttering the same idiot phrases and various four-letter words. She sank in the sofa and flipped on television. She grabbed a remote control and went through channels. In the end, she put a DVD of a Nigerian movie *End of Discussion*. After a while, Jacob asked her if he could watch news on CNN.

"Don't you see that I am watching a movie, you fuckhead?" She abused him with darts of bitterness.

Nikita had a sort of recipe for abusive language. She spoke with all the panoply of street people's expressions. The abusive expressions—hell knows where she learned the street language—seemed to circulate in her veins. All abusive words she collected from streets of Burundi, Kenya, Togo, Benin, Olympia, etc., would pop out of her brain. They were like an ingredient to her speech. Whatever the situation, they were on the tip of her tongue. They were used in four languages—Kirundi, Kiswahili, French, and English. Every language she spoke had dirty words she favored. They were worse when used in her mother tongue. In Africa, bad language runs against customs and traditions. As a case in point, the translation of "fuck you" has a deeper meaning than in English. In the African culture, abusive words are not accepted no matter the situation. If a woman ever pronounced them, which rarely happens, she would be treated as a slut. Basically, Nikita's abusive language was socially unacceptable. It was a language of sluts purely and simply.

Jacob repeatedly tried to teach her how to control her language especially in front of her growing children. Although he would not erase the abusive language from her brain and heart, at least the bad words would no longer be coming through her mouth. Immoral acts are an expression of an unclean heart. If the heart is not clean, the holder cannot be clean. An unclean heart is harmful. It spreads venom in a relationship. By teaching good manners, one tries to clean the body and not the heart. Trying to correct Nikita's language was like trying to corner a bobcat. One would imprison her tongue in her mouth. In fact, the abusive language was her only medium of communication. When she abused people, she became like a snake talking to her venom.

Jacob still believed in good communication as the best medicine to cure the dying love. As victim of domestic abuse, he still believed in love as the only remedy to heal his psychological injury caused by the endless headaches. He tried to lovingly address the issues in their relationship.

"Honey, would you be kind enough to stop betraying our love? Can't you feel my love? If it is cold outside, what is wrong with it? That snow is not a mountain of blankets. It is part of nature. There is time for cold weather and time for warm seasons. We have to cope with weather changes. I am here for you, should you need any help. I will give you warmth whenever you need it. You don't need anybody else to give you what you already have."

She stared at him and cleared her throat. She sighed.

Jacob had so much love to give, but the abusive speech took away all the warmth, the hope and the pleasure of life. The desire for a better life eclipsed his anger and embarrassment. He was ready to forgive everything; otherwise, he would never enjoy life. He invited her to sit close to him so that they could talk in intimacy.

"What do you want?" she asked dryly, staring at him.

Jacob could not stand being unhappy. He was desperate to find happiness. He put his arms around her and gave her inkling of his intentions.

"Don't you know what I want? Can't you tell from the way I hug you? I want to feel your love," he replied. He wanted her to think of the common ground they were supposed to have. She withdrew from him, screaming, pushing him away. "Go to hell!" she screamed.

Bewildered, Jacob sat at the edge of the bed again and buried his face in his hands. He kept quiet for a while and tried to cool down. After a while, he stood up again and looped his arms around her.

"Honey, your bad attitude is sending bad messages to your growing children. I have never seen somebody treating her beloved one the way you treat me. Do you think I like you treating me like this? Remember that I love you, and I will always love you," he said, hoping to get her out of her rollicking mood. At that time, Jacob was feeling real love. He felt deep curling warmth. He gave her a pleading look, drew her into a close and bolstering hug. He held her tightly with his hands stroking her all over. He went on complimenting her, telling her how wonderful it was to have her.

"My darling, *je t'aime beaucoup*. I can't live without you. Every time you smile, you add a day to my life." He paused to give her a chance to respond. She remained silent. He implored again, "Honey?"

"What?" she replied.

"Can I tell you something?"

"I am listening."

"I love you."

"I know." Jacob felt aggrieved that she did not care about his love.

"And I will always love you body and soul, babe."

"You repeat the same shit every time. Don't you have anything else to say?"

"My darling, I will always tell you how much I love you. It makes me happy to say it even if you don't reciprocate."

She sighed a kind of sigh that Jacob hated—to him it was a sign of disdain. Jacob breathed high and unevenly, humming louder. He started feeling her warmth. Nikita turned abruptly and exited the room.

"Okay. I am going to prepare dinner." She noticed a pained look on his face and said, "Sorry about that." She stepped away to the kitchen.

Jacob was bereft of speech. A storm of emotions hit him. The pain of an unsatisfied desire would break him apart. He knew that her energy and emotion were invested somewhere else. He felt stung and cheapened for living an incomplete life, wasting time and money on somebody like her.

Freedom and gender issues were popular and compelling themes in the western democracy. One could powerlessly watch his wife locked into another man. One has to close one's eyes and pretend to see nothing. That is the kind of freedom Nikita wants. Jacob was beaten at his own game. He took a steadying breath. He sank in the bed, buried his face in his pillow, and threw on a blanket. His heart was thudding against his ribs. As his nose was stuck on the pillow, he sensed a cigarette smell and threw the smoky pillow away. He took the second pillow. It stunk even worse than the first one did. He threw it away in a violent, brisk move, knowing that a heavy smoker's head had been resting on it. He got up and took a deep relaxing breath. He turned the radio on and listened to his favorite song by Dolly Parton, "The Pain of Loving You."

> Oh, the pain of loving you
> Oh, the misery I go through
> Never knowing what to do
> Oh, the pain of loving you

You just can't stand to see me happy
Seems you hurt me all you can
Still, I go on loving you
But I never understand

To love and hate at the same time
The line between the two is fine
The two have bound me, heart and soul
So strong that I can't let you go

Jacob had heard the song first fifteen years back when he was still in secondary school. As an adolescent, he did not understand that loving somebody could be painful. Now that he was a grown-up, he understood the meaning of love and the misery true lovers go through. He stared despairingly at the ceiling thinking of how his feelings were being betrayed. Every part of him loved Nikita. He ached to be loved body and soul. Instead, she treated him as a wet rag. She wasn't much of a companion. Jacob was at his wits end trying to deal with the situation. He didn't know which saint to turn to as most of his close friends were involved with Nikita. She was spending good time with Dickson, Juvenhack, Geram, and others, when Jacob's insides were jangling. She grew lackadaisical about things that had been haunting Jacob for days. The desire, the heat, and all the sweetness of life with a beloved human being were put down.

Rosie disappointed Jacob. Jacob saw a different flower, not the rose he bought from the Home Depot store of Lacey, Olympia. He called the store to check if they did not deliver a different product. The customer service checked the code bar and confirmed that it was the right rose. The shop reminded him the day he visited the shop.

"You came to the store and asked for a beautiful rose, not a loving rose. Stores don't sell love. By buying the rose, he paid for beauty and not for love. Love and beauty are two different things. Not making that distinction is the mistake you made since day one. You equated beauty with love."

Jacob got lost in this confusion. He found himself trying to match beauty and love. The combination produced a new product whose eyes roved from one person to another.

"I find myself dealing with a rover and not a lover," he complained.

Some say that love is the cheapest thing in the world. Everybody can have it. Even the poorest person in the world can easily find love when some rich people may not find it. The bottom-line is everybody can find love. Others think it very expensive.

"Love is something no amount of money can buy. If it vanishes, the beauty is not even worth a cup of coffee," the shop concluded.

Disappearance of love gives rise to hatred. On the other hand, if love is strong, it can remove mountains. A combination of a positive and a negative value always produce a negative outcome. Jacob wondered why Nikita decided to water his flower with poisoned hot water. He asked himself too many questions none of which could be answered. He constantly thought about them, but there were no answers in sight. He was emotionally bruised remembering the time when they were like two peas in a pod. He expected to be in each other's limelight forever. Now that they were like fire and water, their future together remained an enigma.

Jacob cursed the impulse that pushed him to Nikita. Loving her was the greatest wrong he ever did. He committed a big sin like other Evildoers. He trusted the untrustworthy person. Her agenda had nothing to do with the promises she made to him. She was willing to deviate from her mission, which Jacob learned too late. He kept focusing on building a strong relationship with somebody who highly prized fidelity. However, he was not strong enough to change something that resisted tsunamis, tornados, hurricanes, cyclones, and other disasters.

Jacob could not compete with suckers that had glued to his flower. He was not prepared for such a battle. His duty was to protect the *rover* from all foes. It was his responsibility number one. As Nikita did not seem to have any eye on the problem, Jacob was the only one to care about the issue. Nikita and Dickson kept calling him a jealous and selfish assmonkey. They were right. Still other men would just do the business and forget. That is why she was having affairs with married men. They would not stick on her every single day. Nikita convinced him to accept Dickson, that he would always have his part. Jacob, however, was too overprotective of her. He wanted her to be quiet when she needed wings to fly. She got wings and she flew too high. When Jacob spoke of what he saw, he was accused of being too controlling, wanting Nikita around all the time. He expected too much from his childhood girlfriend. He believed her to be perfect, and he was immensely proud of her.

Jacob never assumed that their being together would be seen as selfishness. There was no way in hell one could let rovers destroy his love. Even if the others found Nikita vulnerable and fragile, she was still Jacob's treasure. His love was so precious that he would not wish to be disturbed by whomsoever. He wanted Nikita to adjust to the new environment and love one man in her life. Unfortunately, she would not accept one man hanging on her all her life when she was used to many people. She needed more freedom to seduce her admirers. She understood her beauty as rays of light. She was not used to hiding the light. As Jacob became tough about her infidelities, she decided to seduce her admirers in their own houses. In this democratic society, one cannot force somebody to behave in a way that they don't want.

Although Jacob respected values of individual freedom, he was not prepared for the kind of freedom that allowed somebody to bring her lovers to her marital bed. That was treachery or adultery. If Jacob had known, he would never have allowed this kind of freedom in his life. The "Nikita freedom" would lead to chaos. In order to fix the problem, he forced love as the only way to deal with the issue. He repeated it tons of times.

"Nikita, I love you very much."

"So you equate love with slavery! I say! Is your love for me a warrant to put me under house arrest? You are nothing but garbage among human beings, bastard. I need to establish my independence. Birds have wings to fly." She stared at him and shook her head. Jacob hung his head and tapped his forehead. He was not ready to share, and still he never wanted to let her go. He wanted to keep her when her heart and soul were away. She did not love the men though. She only accepted them in order to get money from them. They would pay for her services as a way of keeping her away from Jacob. She found no problem to hang around with him when Jacob was at work. They could then have the services any time they wanted.

Jacob showed her excessive love when her heart was not with him. He had to live with a body without a soul. Worse still, Jacob did not like being called selfish and jealous, which he actually was. If he were not jealous and selfish, he would cooperate with Dickson et al. and accept the unacceptable in this modern society. He would have to agree with Nikita going out with whoever she wanted and whenever she needed it, and return home if she wanted. Jacob was not the kind of person to accept such behavior. He had learnt from society that flowers were biologically monogamous. This image was imprinted in his heart. In his views, Nikita's behavior was a defiance of nature. Would Jacob resign his beliefs in one day? He would rather be dead.

Jacob also considered himself as descendant of a well-respected family. He lived with people worthy of respect. His uncles, cousins, and friends had occupied high positions in the democratic governments. They had been presidents, ministers, members of parliaments or chairmen of the parliament, governors and held many other respected positions. All of them were killed by parents, relatives, and friends of Dickson and Juvenhack. Nikita was not even ashamed of being pampered by killers of her own father and siblings, and Ronald, father of her child. It was an honor for the Chissoccos to be with the Baraks. Jacob expected her to behave accordingly and remain clean. He told her repeatedly,

"I want you to project the good image people expect from us. No one will respect you when they see you hanging around with freeloaders like Dickson and stuff. Everybody is now aware of your affairs. You need to change."

Nikita would never listen. She would rebuke with vehemence instead. In spite of everything, he tried to treat her with infinite warmth and kindness.

During the year 2008, Jacob was busy struggling to cope with the recession. He had been working around the clock for several days in row. Since Nikita's arrival, everything started going downhill. As misfortune never comes alone, Jacob was laid off his job when there were bills to pay. One could not live without utilities and other essential commodities. Money was really tight. Although he struggled financially, he had to make sure his flower still got enough winter and spring fertilizer. He worked his tail off so that Nikita and her three kids could live comfortably. He knew consequences of financial difficulties. Either they bring lovers together or they drive them apart. Jacob assumed the former though the latter was likely to happen. Finding the wherewithal to survive the economic downturn was essential to keep life with Nikita livable. He wanted her to continue blooming in spite of the unpleasant situation. Nikita was never satisfied. She kept hunting greener grasses the other side of the fence and sweeter things next door. She wanted Jacob away from home as that would give her the freedom she wanted. On Jacob's days off, Nikita was not happy. She accused him of being on her back controlling her.

Being with Jacob all day really bothered her. She had to stay with him and perform family activities together. That was not the kind of life she was used to. She wanted him away all the time.

"Why don't you go to work? Something is wrong with you," she told him. Jacob would reply,

"What else do you want me to do? Business has been slowing down since July of 2008. Companies are shutting down because of this recession. We are just waiting for things to pick up. If you read newspapers or listened to the news, you would understand what I am talking about."

"But I watch television every day."

"I know you do. The Nigerian Movies and the *American Idol* do not deal with economic issues. You need to watch news if you want to know what is going on in the world."

"Whatever . . . Anyway, you will do what you want."

Jacob expected Nikita to understand but it seemed she did not care at all.

During busy days, Jacob's schedule would not allow him time to fight with butterflies and bees in spring bloom. Even if he had the time, he would not wish a war with the bees. He was allergic to venom. He had assisted a bee sting victim before. He removed the bee stingers, but the victim continued to suffer for another two weeks. From that day on, Jacob knew that the likes of Dickson were harmful. He escaped them many times in Burundi when he could not venture a battle with them. Now that they were introduced into his life inside his own house, it was absolutely impossible to win such stupid war. The only option was to turn Nikita into a loving and caring person. As it was not possible to transform her, he folded his arms about himself and waited for whatever might happen.

7. The Worst Is Still Yet to Come

Once upon a time, Jacob had a talk with Nikita about her work schedule. She had a contract to clean five halls in the Empire Studio 16. She was scheduled to clean the cinema from one to five o'clock in the morning. Normally, she finished her shift at five as scheduled and she was at home by five-thirty. Now that she had where to spend the night, she got more freedom to be with whoever she wanted without fear of being watched. She informed Dickson about her job, and she gave him her schedule. Dickson received the news with great excitement. He was happy to have a place where they could meet and enjoy themselves freely.

"Now that you work in the Empire Studio 16 at night, we can be together all night long," Dickson told her.

"Not the whole night. I have to finish my work first. One or two hours are enough. I will tell Jacob that I had more work," she answered.

"That is wonderful. What time do you usually finish?"

"Come sometime around two o' clock."

"That sounds good. I will tell Dada that I have to work over night, so she doesn't have to worry about me. How will I see you, then?"

"I will tell my coworker that my husband is coming to help me. She will inform me when you arrive and I will come to meet you at the main entrance."

"Make sure that Jacob doesn't come to see you there."

"Don't worry about him. I will never let him go there. He won't suspect anything as nobody knows him there."

Things went as planned, and Jacob was happy that Nikita was busy as that meant that she would have less time to flirt with his enemies.

As a rule of thumb, speed comes with experience. Jacob was expecting Nikita to become more efficient and be home early. Curiously, the more experience she gained the more time she spent at work. She started coming home at seven and sometimes around eight. When she got home, she had to complain that she had a lot of work that took long time to complete. Jacob found the argument unconvincing. If she could get the work done in time when she started, it should not take her as much time now that she gained experience. Anyway, he encouraged her to work faster and finish on time as usual. He found unacceptable to work seven hours when she was paid for only four. Otherwise, she would have to renegotiate the contract. Nikita, however, did not think of any of the propositions. All the same, Jacob encouraged her and even offered to help her.

"I have an idea. Since the work is taking you too much time, I will be coming to help you on my days off. I will show you how to do it fast, and you will be done in less than four hours. We will finish the work in two hours instead of seven. Then we will have more time together at home."

Nikita did not welcome the proposition. She fought it instead. She explained that it was impossible for an outsider to enter the Empire Studio 16.

"No visitor is allowed in the facilities especially at night time."

Jacob could not understand why she gave him a sharp negative answer. She did not even want to check with management. As Jacob was upset about her tardiness, he insisted on helping her.

"Look, it is very simple. You are a contract worker. You just give them my name as your helper. It is as simple as that. The manager already knows me. Why would she say no if I would do the work better than you do! We will do the work faster and you won't have to worry about working four extra hours every day for no pay. You know what I am saying."

Nikita seemed bothered by the proposition. Rather than checking with the management, she was the one to refuse.

"Why are you insisting? I told you that it was impossible. Get the idea out of your head. You are not allowed there. Don't worry about me. I will keep doing my work the way I have been doing it thus far."

Jacob told her not to keep complaining to him if she did not want any help.

"Honey, let's meet the manager together and explain the situation. We will hear what she will say. She can't refuse the proposition if it means that the job will be completed on time. Do you see any reason she should say no?"

Jacob expected Nikita to be happy with the offer. He was expecting a smile and a kiss for the kind support. Instead, she changed her mood and forced him to stop thinking about it.

"I told you that I am able to do the job by myself. I don't need any help."

Because Jacob was insisting, she showed that the job was not as hard as she was pretending. Jacob got confused. She had been complaining about the job. Now that he offered to help her, she claimed that it was not that hard, that she could do it by herself. Still, she kept arriving home late.

Few weeks later, as they were driving on Deerfoot Trail, Nikita complained about her job again. She wanted Jacob to understand that she would continue to get home late because of her job. As Jacob did not seem to understand her, she got mad.

"Jacob, understanding and caring are the two things a woman expects from her lover. I tell you about my work and you don't want to listen. You don't even care. I don't know why you want to treat me like that."

"I understand you. Just hang in there until you achieve the necessary speed."

Nikita was a stubborn person too. She wanted him to say yes to everything she said. Even if he had to say no, she would still do what she wanted. Jacob's opinion did not matter at all. And Jacob, who had always lost all discussions with her, believed that he would finally win the argument. In fact, there was no reason to keep pretending that Jacob was not allowed at her workplace as he was most of the time dropping her there. She did not even bother to ask the management if it was possible for Jacob to help her. Any time he insisted on something she did not want, the arguments resulted in quarrels. Jacob insisted all the same. If he could not see her in daytime due to his work schedule and her outings, he wanted to see her at night at least.

"You are right, my dear. Understanding and caring are very important. However, one should not forget that one of the chief duties of a mother is to be close to her beloved children and lover. These duties apply to men and fathers as well. There are many more constraints imposed on human beings. They can't behave like beasts just for the sake of freedom." Nikita did not respond.

Jacob continued bugging her about her prolonged absence in hope that she would finally change. It seemed she did not live in his house. He spoke accusingly that she did not want him at her workplace. He insisted on helping her because he was missing her. Her friends had won her away from him, and he wanted her back. In fact, he missed the pillow whispers that he loved so much in the morning after sleep. They talked about their life without a lot of stress. The pillow talks were like a brainstorming session. Thanks to Jacob's warm and tender voice, Nikita started heading for somewhere she had never been before. She could forget herself and reveal her hidden secrets. Now that Jacob was staying alone, there were no more opportunities to learn about her infidelities. As he kept insisting to help her, suddenly, the atmosphere changed. She lost her nerve and flailed about.

"There is no need to get mad at me when you know what you are doing there. Do you think that I am sitting on my brain and really believe that there is no business interest going on there? I am not as dumb as you think," Jacob told her.

Nikita's face grew angrier, and she started breathing like a beast. She unbuckled her seat belt, threw herself at him, scratching his face, hitting him with her fists and pulse.

Jacob was driving in treacherous conditions. The road was snowy with poor visibility. He was cruising in the left lane between thirty-eight-wheelers speeding in both lanes of Deerfoot Trail. He struggled to protect his face with one hand. With the left hand holding the wheel, he used the right hand to keep her away from his face. Then she scratched his right hand and arm. At the same time, Jacob had to keep eyes on the road to maintain the vehicle in the middle of the lane with the same speed. He had to focus on driving as his main concern was avoiding a collision with the trucks, which would be more dangerous than the assault.

Nikita ignored that the trucks could run over their small Porsche. She did not even give a damn about her three little children who would end up in foster families or orphanage if she died. No one of their fathers would raise them. If they claimed their children, each father would claim his own child, and the children would be separated. Moreover, it would be a shock for the children who believed that they shared a same father called Ronald Hakiza. They would see three gentlemen declaring their paternity to each one of them individually. The number of fathers could even be higher than the number of children claimed. In fact, whenever she was pregnant, she gave the paternity to every man she slept with. As they did not know one another, everybody believed that he was the father. Each child would, therefore, see three or more gentlemen claiming their paternity to him. Other ex-lovers might drop in too, not knowing that their children were aborted. Whatever the case, the kids would at least discover that they were not orphans as they were led to believe. They would not see their mom to ask why she lied to them. At least they would not be orphaned by the crash. They would lose a mother to gain biological fathers. As immigration papers showed that their father was dead, any father who would claim a child would have to get DNA testing for paternity.

The worse scenario might happen if only Nikita were to die in the accident. Her children were not trained to respect anybody. They treated Jacob exactly the same way their mother treated him. Yet Jacob would have to raise them in the event of Nikita's death. He would probably try to find their fathers for help. He would be the one to introduce them to the bastards who knew that they were fatherless. They might not accept their biological fathers as their real parents.

Fortunately, Jacob avoided the danger. He was an experienced driver, thus he could still keep attention to the road ahead and the traffic behind and beside him. He drove all types of vehicles, heavy and light alike. He drove big and small vehicles with exceptional dexterity. Nikita, however, feared driving especially on a highway. Her driving skills were so poor that she didn't know that one could drive a vehicle with manual transmission and still be able to protect oneself against an assault. She thought that the only time she would teach him good lessons would be when he would be driving the standard Porsche, not the automatic Toyota. She ignored that, on a highway, a vehicle equipped with standard transmission would still run like an automatic as there would be no need to change gears frequently.

Still, Nikita's assault was so violent that Jacob could not concentrate on driving when his body and mind were struggling for protection. In a daring maneuver, he attempted an unsafe lane change in order to avoid the danger. As he was struggling to keep control of the vehicle while securing his face and arms from scratches, he slowed the traffic and forced the driver of a thirty-eight-wheeler behind him to push hard on the brake. Rather than putting the pedal on the metal, Jacob swung into the right lane without a shoulder check. He knew that it was unsafe, but he needed to avoid exposing his face to Nikita, who was violently scratching him with her long fingernails. In the right lane, they met with the thirty-eight-wheeler trying to pass them. The truck driver honked twice, and Jacob immediately swung back into the left lane. The trucker stuck his head out of the window and glared at the red Porsche driving in zigzag in two lanes and snarling up the traffic. He watched Nikita scratching Jacob. He slowed down and tapped the horn several times to alert other drivers massing behind the Porsche. Nikita rolled down the window and extended her arm to show him her middle finger.

"Why are you honking so hard, motherfucker?" she yelled.

The truck driver honked with a 139 DB Chrome Trumpet Air Horn. Other drivers saw Nikita showing the finger and yelling to the trucker. They honked and yelled back. As she whipped her arm out of the window to give the drivers a finger, Jacob managed to complete the maneuver. He downshifted the gears and pulled over. He found a safe place to park and then tried to calm her down.

They were out of traffic but the quarrel was not over. Jacob tried to calm the situation down. Yet everything he said only brought more threats. He rolled down the windows and turned off the ignition key to let nature solve the problem. The weather outside was very cold. It was minus thirty-two degrees Celsius. With the windshield, it was minus forty. With the engine off, Nikita understood that there was no more danger of being run over by trucks. She could now hit him without mercy.

Jacob, however, had both hands free to protect himself. Nikita noticed that she was not strong enough to hit him seriously with her bare hands. She looked around to check if there was any object she could use. There was nothing in the car. She put on her gloves and got out of the car. She gathered snow and compressed it into big pieces that she violently chucked to Jacob still sitting behind the wheel. Jacob tried to block them with his hands. The compressed snow broke and splashed all over the place. Nikita thought that she could not compress the snow better with her gloves on.

As Jacob was busy fighting to avoid the compressed snow hitting him, he took his foot out of the brake pedal. He forgot that he had not engaged the park brake on a manual transmission up hill. The car started rolling backward toward the highway. Fortunately, he noticed it in time and managed to stop it. He applied the hand brake, and he put it in a gear. Jacob invited Nikita to cool down and stop assaulting him. He was freezing because of the snow hitting his face and splashing all over his clothes. He needed to get out of there, but he could not leave her on the road.

Nikita, who had never touched snow before, took her gloves off and started gathering and compressing snow with bare hands in minus forty. Soon, she started complaining that she was freezing. She resigned the fight and entered the car. With windows rolled down, the interior of the car was as cold as outside. As she could not assault him any longer, she threw herself in her seat and asked him to heat the car. She leaned against him crying.

"I am freezing."

"Why did you do that? Didn't you know that the snow would be cold?" Jacob asked her.

She kept crying. Jacob started the engine, rolled the windows up, and turned the heat on. He helped Nikita with his jacket and gloves. She screamed again.

"I am sitting on snow. Can you remove it? I am freezing everywhere now," she complained, trembling.

"Come on, Nikita, you are the one to put it there. So you sit on it."

"How can I sit on snow? It is too cold. You need to remove it. You don't care about me. Do you want me to sit on snow?"

Removing the snow would mean leaving the car doors open for another couple of minutes when they were already freezing. Nikita decided to sit on the backseat. Jacob, however, found it dangerous to let her sit behind him when he was driving a vehicle with manual transmission. If she assaulted him from behind, he would not be able to protect himself while driving.

As they were discussing removing the snow from their seats, Nikita started freezing from her buttocks and legs. Jacob felt sorry for her.

"I will let her sit in the backseat on condition that you keep quiet," Jacob said.

"I will keep peace," Nikita promised.

She was not able to disturb it anyway. She was shivering all over, and she needed to get home as quickly as possible. She understood that her physical strength was not enough to win the fight with winter.

"Nature is more powerful than human beings," Jacob said, confident that it worked on his side. He looked at Nikita and saw that she was not able to do him any harm. Then he put the pedal in the gear, disengaged the park brake, and stepped on the gas. As his mind was not quiet, he did not feel that he could drive safely. He drove anyway.

When Nikita was hitting him with her fists and pulse, she twisted the rearview mirror. Jacob had to readjust it so he could keep constant vigilance in case she assaulted him again. She noticed that the aim of the mirror adjustment was to keep his eyes on her. She moved to her left side, right behind Jacob.

"Stay where you were. I don't want you behind me," Jacob ordered angrily.

"I don't want you to watch me in the mirror," she screamed.

"I need to keep you in sight. I don't trust you," he said balefully. He made another decision to pull out of the traffic and made a complete stop.

"Why did you pull over? Let's go home, I am cold," she insisted.

"I can't drive while you are sitting where I cannot see you. I have to make sure you do not assault me from behind. If you don't want to listen to me, I will leave you here and take a cab."

Nikita feared that he would really do that, given that he was really angry. She moved back to the right side. They proceeded home and not a single word was said. Eventually, the car warmed up and the snow on Nikita began to melt, making her wet. When they approached home, Jacob told her.

"You see! I will always love nature. It is more trustworthy than humans. It solved my problems. What else could save me from you? God is great. I was helpless, and he saved me."

Nikita remained quiet. They arrived home and Jacob parked on the street, thus they had to walk home. The wet clothes began to freeze on Nikita, and she walked to the house like a wet puppy. Jacob grabbed her hand and helped her to get inside the house as quickly as possible.

Once inside, he feared that she would assault him again. He needed a mediator to calm the situation down. He knew that the only person who could coax her from her folly was her faithful and most enthusiastic boyfriend, Dickson. That day, Jacob had no choice. He was forced to learn how to deal with jealousy and to cooperate with his bitter rival. For the last time in his life, he went to Dickson's house to seek his mediation. He explained to him the whole situation, and he told him that he was the only one to help. He implored him.

"Please, Dickson, can you call Nikita and tell her to cool down?"

"I will talk to her later," Dickson said.

"Just call her. She is at home."

"I need to see her first and make sure you didn't hurt her."

By turning to Dickson, Jacob officially recognized that the Evildoer was the boss of his house. Dickson was happy about the opportunity to be with her again. Rather than meeting both parties together to solve the problem, he decided to meet Nikita alone and in privacy. He invited her in his house. Now that there was an official meeting between them, Jacob believed that nothing would happen that day. They would not do anything knowing that Jacob was aware of the meeting. Nikita was not even in the mood for butt-fucking that day. Dickson's wife was there too and so was her mother. The meeting became an occasion for Dickson to congratulate Nikita.

"Don't allow him to tell you stupid things. Hit him more. He will never respond, you know. He will be obliged to respect you."

Jacob was never told what they discussed together. After meeting with Dickson, Nikita returned home with more rage than before. Jacob called Dickson to ask if his mediation was to add fuel to fire. Dickson started accusing him.

"Why do for force her to do odd jobs when she doesn't want? Do you think it easy to clean five amphitheaters in four hours?" Dickson asked accusingly.

"Which amphitheaters?" Jacob asked.

"The ones in the Empire Studio 16. It is too much work for her."

"How big are they?"

"Dickson, I am not offering jobs. Most companies and universities are hiring professors, engineers, managers, and technicians. Why doesn't she send her resume? She cannot complain about jobs when she has no educational background to offer. She is like you. You have no qualifications whatsoever, and you want to act as her lawyer. That's weird. With lawyers like you, who needs degrees?"

In Dickson's eyes, Jacob was the problem, not Nikita. As they were arguing, Nikita's anger grew again. She changed her clothes, threw on shorts and a T-shirt, and started yelling loud. Jacob was now fighting two wars, one with Dickson at the line and the other with Nikita in the house. The latter was more threatening. If he could win Dickson's war as one man to another, it would be hard to win an assault with a female. Jacob hung up the phone to focus on the immediate danger. Nikita jumped on him and started hitting him. Not knowing what to do, Jacob called police for help. Rather than coming immediately, the police kept asking him questions. He hangs up the phone and called again. This time, he imitated a female voice crying. Then police officers were dispatched in no time, and Nikita finally cooled down.

The cops arrived. Rather than listening to the victim of violence who called for help, the cops only checked if Nikita was hurt. They saw tracks of dried blood on the floor, and they asked if it was hers. Jacob was still bleeding. He showed them bruises on his face and his arms. The upper lip was swollen, and the right eye was red. They did not care too much. They only checked if he needed medical attention and concluded that not even first aid was necessary. To the officers, it was not a problem as long as it was a man who was hurt. They double-checked with Nikita to confirm that Jacob did not respond. She confirmed that he did not even touch her. As if the safety of a man mattered little, they told Jacob to spend the night at a friend's place to let Nikita cool down. When Jacob left the house to spend the night in Geram's room, the officers stalled out.

The next day, Jacob returned home with Geram. He wanted him around, just in case. He thought that Nikita might be mad at Geram, but she treated him nicely, as usual. Later in the evening, Geram had invited them for a dinner. She swore that she would never go to his place.

"Geram is your friend and not mine," she said.

In Jacob's mind, Nikita hated Geram because he accommodated Jacob in his room. Jacob never knew that she feared that Geram's neighbors would recognize her, and she would not feel comfortable. They might even reveal to Jacob that they saw her naked. She would never go to Geram with Jacob. She suggested going to a restaurant instead.

Jacob respected the environment. He learned how to handle jealousy and selfishness once for all. As Nikita had become uncontrollable, he wondered if the flower would last another two months. Not only did she live longer, she also grew in two months. Her glamour lasted for a few more precious months, but within the first days of winter, she began to faint. She faded in a fortnight and lost her original smell and color. Jacob tried to save her to no avail. Toward the end of winter, she had nothing left of the original flower.

Before the arrival of the rose, the bees and butterflies were quiet. The neighborhood could enjoy fresh air under the trees. But when a rose turns grey, she really smells awful. Her presence disrupted everything. The bad smell bothered neighbors who feared that there might be H2S in their environment. Rosie became a source of hazard that needed to be controlled. Neighbors kept complaining about her. They took the matter to environmentalists. The latter came to Jacob's home and asked him to get rid of the rotten flower as quickly as possible. That way, he would have less trouble with bees.

Jacob hesitated a while and asked what to do to save her. He cared about the environment and thus about Rosie who was a part of it. He did not want to destroy her. He insisted to know what to do and how to do it. The officers were not eager to cooperate in the matter.

"Our job is to take care of the environment and not to deal with your mess. It is your imperative duty to keep environment clean and safe. Garbage bins are provided for this purpose. You need to make use of them, man!" one of the officers muttered, adding that Jacob should understand that safety was number one priority.

"The place of a rotten rose is in the garbage and not in the house. You should consider getting rid of the dreadful burden immediately," the officer concluded.

Jacob did not want to be deprived of something he very much wanted to keep in spite of the headaches she caused him. He tried to negotiate a second chance.

"Sorry, Officer, I just brought her from Olympia a few months ago, and I do not desire to return there. Can you possibly take her with you, Officer? I am powerless to do anything. I am fed up of the situation, and I need to breathe fresh air. I have been there many a time, and I hoped to relax once she would be here. Now that she betrayed me, I have neither courage nor strength to ride another twenty hours back to Olympia."

The officer sympathized with him and suggested other solutions. Jacob promised to do as he was told first thing in the morning.

When the officers stole out to the door, Jacob stood in total awe feeling a twinge of regret for having to lose somebody he loved with his heart and soul, not with his body. He knew the importance of a love in man's life. Although Nikita was not good at all, Jacob was still fully committed to her. The beauty she had to give to his life disappeared. Still, considering losing her seemed as a betrayal of love. He gathered his strength and vowed that she would not go away. Yet he could do little to transform her into a good person. Her fate remained in her hands. Jacob asked himself how much time she needed to overcome her vulnerability. He thought that she was weakened by her flower, but he was wrong. Nikita had gone through everything in life, and the load was now falling on Jacob. He was worried about her for no reason.

When Jacob was carrying a torch in Olympia, he did so for something so dear and precious. He had no idea of the quality of the flower he was running after. She strived on being in gardens with bees buzzing about. Likewise, her owner was more comfortable when she was surrounded by her admirers. Jacob kept wondering what fascinated her in all those other guys when he was capable of giving her enough honey and money. She was used to a wild life to such a point that pampering occupied more room in her heart. Life without bees buzzing around would only be meaningless to her.

Taking care of Nikita was not for the fainthearted. In fact, it was a long row to hoe. Jacob loved somebody that loathed him. She gave him new names, sonofabitch, asshole, and the like. Whenever she called him by these names, her eyes would grow wider by the second. As reaction, Jacob would put his hand on her shoulder to give her a sweet smile.

"Oh! Sweet honey, it's okay. I love you, little darling."

After the sweet words, he hugged her closely and kissed her. She withdrew from him and stumbled to the door yelling.

"Don't touch me! I say, don't touch me. I am not in the mood today," she said in a disgusted voice as her eyes grew wider and wilder.

"Please, please, I love you," he insisted. He kissed her hand again and held it to his nose, then to his cheek. He begged her smile, to make him happy. He did everything guaranteed to clear the air. He pleaded, desperate for some kind of happiness in their life.

Pleasing Nikita was crucial. It could put her momentarily at ease. Like that, it would lengthen her life expectancy. To achieve this goal, Jacob learned to be more tolerant than ever before though he was sometimes forced into arguments. Still, he never knew that Nikita was burned out. Whatever he would do, she would never change. She came to him because she needed a young flesh, not a cold bitch, as she described him. Although she called him names, he did not say a world. He became like just a troubleshooter, trying to right things gone wrong.

8. Nikita's Revelations

Jacob was a man of his word. He kept the promise to love Nikita despite all she was doing against him. He decided to give her a last chance. He waited a few days to see if she had any feeling of love left for him. If not, their relationship would be doomed once for all. After a couple of days, Dickson's mother-in-law, Beatta, complained to Jacob about Nikita. She revealed the acts she witnessed with her own eyes and ears.

"Jacob, I was so happy the day you introduced Nikita to me and I congratulated you. I thought she was a nice person. I really liked her. However, what I witnessed since then is beyond words. She is Dickson's mistress. They do ridiculous things that no mother was supposed to see. They take advantage of my daughter's absence to do stupid things. They don't even respect me at my age. My daughter works night shift, and Nikita is the one to take her place in her own bed." She paused.

Jacob buried his face in his hands and listened. He believed she was telling him something new. He did not want to hear stories that would break his heart. He tried to avoid Beatta's report, but she was determined to say everything she had kept secret for several months. He knew that there was an affair going on anyway.

"Nikita usually arrives home and sits on the loveseat with Dickson. A few minutes later, I would hear them kissing. Then they watch pornography together, with Dickson's thing sticking out of his shorts and Nikita holding it in her hand. Then, Dickson would sneak her in his bedroom. Soon, I would hear jiggle sounds of the bed."

Jacob knew that Beatta was aware of the affair, but he did not expect her to denounce her own son-in-law. Beatta confirmed what he already knew without clear evidence. Even though everybody spoke about it, it was still considered as rumor.

"I knew things were happening on my back. Go ahead," he said. Beatta continued.

"They think I am deaf and blind not to hear or see what is going on. More likely, they don't really care whether I hear or see what they do. Jacob, I feel sorry for my daughter and for you."

Jacob sighed. He fixed his eyes on an imaginary dot on the ground to avoid eye contact. He did not interrupt her.

"What is worse, Nikita entertains people by talking about you. When she is with your rivals, she does all the talking."

"My rivals? Do I have rivals?" he interrupted her.

"Jacob, I see you like my son. The Evildoers turned her against you. She says that you are garbage among human beings when she is unfaithful to you. Now that they know how much she hates you, everybody is after her. Whenever she is with my son-in-law, you are their center of attention. They treat you as a piece of junk. They don't even care about people listening. Are you still with me?"

"Go ahead, ma'am. I am still listening." He pretended to keep eye contact, but he fixed his eyes above her shoulders.

"Dickson is doing with Nikita exactly what he has been doing with Josiana Mushatsihori and Laura for several years. He never respects his friends." She cried for the man betrayed by the one he loved body and soul.

"You need to take necessary measures that will prevent the worse from happening," she begged him. She was especially worried for her daughter.

"That apartment serves as Nikita's love lair as Dickson shares her with Juvenhack, just as they share Josiana and Laura. Nikita meets Juvenhack in Dickson's apartment, and they go out. After several hours, Juvenhack drives her back and drops her at the same place. While this is happening, they treat you as an asshole."

Jacob took a deep breath and sighed. The talk was now bothering him. He did not want Beatta to continue. It was already too much for him to support. He interrupted her.

"Thank you, Beatta. Thank you for telling me. I know what to do."

"You need to do something before it is too late."

Jacob scratched his head. "These games with devils must end," he concluded and waved good-bye.

Few days later, another wise man, by name Mzee Chief Maneno, invited Jacob for a drink. They had never been together for a private talk. After sipping his first glass, Chief Mzee Maneno confided to Jacob.

"I wanted to talk to you as one man to another. I can see that you are miserable."

"Do I look miserable?" Jacob asked, feeling shocked by the comment.

"Yah. I look at you and feel pity."

"You did not invite me here to make me feel stupid in front of you. You know that I respect you."

"Young man, living with Nikita is living miserably. Whenever I see you, I think of what is going on with that mouse of woman and I feel sorry for you. It seems you don't know the person you love. I see you smiling as if everything were fine." Jacob interrupts.

"Go to the point, Mzee. To the point. What is going on? I am curious to know."

"It is widely known that Nikita cheats on you. Even birds in trees know it. I myself witnessed it ten times at least."

"Now you are talking. Please, go on," Jacob encouraged him.

"I have been thinking of how to tell it, but it was not easy. I feel ashamed of keeping these things in me when I see you as a nice and innocent person. I think it is a good idea to inform you of what I have been witnessing for several months, not weeks, months."

"What is happening with her?"

"Terrible things are happening behind your back. You are betrayed from your own house. Everybody knows about Nikita's affairs with Dickson, Juvenhack, Geram, and many others."

"What!" Jacob stood up. He was surprised by the mention of Juvenhack and Geram. He had been doubtful about them. He already knew that Mzee Chief Maneno had seen quite a few things.

"She is making a lot of money with her body," Mzee Chief Maneno revealed. He gave him several names of people involved with Nikita.

Jacob could not believe that his friends would betray him. He always suspected them with no evidence. Now that he knew, he wanted more details.

"Are you sure that Juvenhack and Geram are having affairs with Nikita or it is just Dickson?"

"Man! Nikita is sort of a hooker. Actually, she is a hooker purely and simply. You kept accusing Dickson alone, but Juvenhack and Geram own her.

"Listen. Let's talk like men here. Are you confirming that Juvenhack had affairs with Nikita?" Jacob asked.

"Listen to this. Hundreds of times. Not just tens. I myself witnessed it more than forty times."

"Where?"

"In the parking lot."

"You saw them talking in the parking lot?"

"Talking? What are you talking about? More than that."

"Are you kidding?" Jacob exclaimed.

"Listen to me. I will tell you everything. That is why I invited you here. I wanted a one-on-one talk so you can know the games they are playing on you."

"Go ahead, please."

"At night, Nikita usually leaves Dickson's apartment to join Juvenhack, who is waiting in the car in the parking lot. As it happens many times, I went out to check. I could see the car shaking violently. They do not even care about neighbors who may see the car shaking. I don't know what they think about me. They don't even hide it from me. That goddamn Sentra had become their boudoir."

Jacob takes a breath.

"Is that true?" he asked.

"I am telling you everything."

"Go ahead, please."

"During the day, they meet at Dickson's and go away. You are the only one who does not know what is going on. They are aware that I know everything, but they don't seem to care. That is why Nikita keeps calling me to tell me that you are a very bad person. She fears that I would reveal the secret to you, and she tries to turn you against me. She tries everything to befriend with me."

As Jacob was informed of the situation, he was determined to learn more. Still, he could not imagine how she could behave that way.

As Nikita's boyfriends living in close proximity to Jacob's house, it became very difficult, even impossible to contain the situation. They knew his schedule, and they could track him day and night. Moreover, they had a spy who would inform them that Jacob was in or out of the house. The Gishubi boy could just go to the window nook and check if Jacob's vehicle was there. He could then inform Dickson or Juvenhack that Jacob was not there. Once they were sure that Jacob was out, they would call Nikita to invite her to Dickson's apartment where they planned everything.

The affairs scared Jacob out of his wits. They undid him to the point that he lost all strength and courage to keep working on his future with Nikita. The outcome of the relationship would certainly be a disaster. As a matter of fact, all clouds were gathering and thickening around him. He could not see where he was going with her. He could not even stand still as the clouds were moving in his direction. Rather, he had to back up and think things over. He thought of moving far away from Dickson and Juvenhack in hope that the move would solve the problem. He would only move away from Dickson but not from the likes of Dickson. If moving were the solution, then he would have to move every other month. He decided to move out anyway.

Jacob spoke to Nikita about moving to another city. She agreed on one condition—they had to go to Vancouver in British Columbia. Nikita's suggestion was a terrible trap. Vancouver was only a few miles from her old boyfriends in Seattle and Olympia. Jacob knew them. If he agreed with her idea to move to Vancouver, not only would he be taking the fish to the river, he would also be putting himself into more trouble. It was like digging one's own grave. He was already in the grave anyway. Changing the grave would not revive him. He would die twice or thrice, depending on how many times he would have to move. If he did not win the war with three Evildoers on his territory, he could not win the fight with soldiers ten times more numerous on their own territory.

Jacob thought of choosing between two evils. Neither one was a viable solution as he could neither move to Vancouver nor stay close to Dickson and his buddies. Other possibilities were open to him. He could find another city far from Edmonton, Seattle, and Olympia. Still, he knew that Nikita would not go anywhere. Even if they moved, not much would change between them as Jacob had lost all confidence in her. The only place in which he could trust her was heaven. Then it would be too late. As long as they were living with devils, he would not trust her. In the meantime, he decided to end the discussion by fighting the devils once for all. "These games must end now," he decided.

While waiting for the final assault, Jacob covered his face with his hands feeling ashamed of eating on the same plate with devils. They were not really Nikita's type. They looked so ugly that they could not attract a nice woman. They had faces that only their mothers could love. In order to win her, they had to invest money in her. All she knew that she was for hire. One call was enough, and she was in their bed.

As the community kept complaining, Jacob decided to get rid of the demons in his house. The easiest solution was to deal with Nikita, rather than fighting with every devil involved with her. He would just send her back to Olympia to allow the affairs to be conducted away from his view. He felt sorry for what he had loved with body and soul, but there was no way in hell he could keep her in his life.

Truth is the first casualty of any war. Nikita was the one to reveal her own infidelities. Surprisingly enough, whenever Jacob condemned her behavior, she got mad and assaulted him. He was required to listen to her and never give a negative comment. As he was not allowed to talk about it with her, he complained to some of his friends. They could not believe him. Rather than checking the truthfulness of the information, they kept defending Nikita, assuming that Jacob's accusations were just a figment of his imagination.

"There is no truth in what you are claiming. Nikita is a nice person."

"I am telling you the honest truth, the whole truth, and nothing but the truth. Why don't you believe the truth? I know that many things happened in front of your eyes. You never told me anything. Now that I know it, you are supporting her. Come on, guys, be serious."

Jacob did not want to accuse them, but he knew a lot about them. What disheartened him was he was aware that they knew all about the truth and he expected them to support him. For some reason, they preferred to hide the truth and convinced him to believe the opposite. Rather than supporting their friend, they went around calling him names. They supported other devils in spreading gossip against him. At the same time, they praised Nikita as the best woman in the world. Jacob could never understand why his friends betrayed him so much. As no one seemed to believe the truth, Jacob wondered if he was wrong. However, he had plenty of evidence to convince him otherwise.

One day, as Nikita arrived from her shift at nine o'clock in the morning, Jacob told her that she should have caught up speed by then. He rarely saw her at night, and he became very flustered and upset about it. He did not even like to see her complaining again and again.

"Darling, you have been doing the same work for several weeks. How come it is still taking you so much time when you were fast the first week! You were supposed to be faster now."

"How many times do I have to explain to you that the job is difficult? You don't care about me. My job is very hard, and it takes me a lot of time to get it done."

"But you are not paid for the extra hours you are working. You don't even want me to help you. Many hands make light work."

"I already told you. Only their employees are allowed in the buildings."

"If others put four hours to complete the task, why should just you put seven or eight hours? Something needs to be done to improve the productivity. Others learn from experience. You need to think of your family too."

"Who can do that job in four hours? I am not a robot. The work is too hard and too demanding. I cannot finish it before eight."

Nikita wasn't smart to hide her infidelities. Without any touch of remorse, she brought back the taboo name,

"I told you it is impossible. Can't you get in your ears? If you don't believe me, ask Dickson," she said flatly. "He knows the place very well, and he will tell you how big it is and the amount of time needed to get the work done. Then you will understand what I am saying," she said in a dull voice as if nothing awful happened at that very moment.

Jacob was puzzled. He looked at her questioningly. He turned round and let out his breath. By revealing Dickson's presence with her in the dark amphitheaters after midnight, she created a terrible mess that she could never rectify. Dickson knew the rooms she was working in after midnight. She herself confirmed the rumors of their affairs.

Jacob was thunderstruck. He retreated into an aloof silence for a while. He felt great weight in his heart. He became angry, annoyed, and upset by the revelation. He was also embarrassed by what he heard. He wondered if she found him so stupid as not to be able to read between the lines. Dickson was not working in the Empire Studio 16. Therefore, there was no way in hell he could access the interior of the halls if Nikita did not allow him there. If Nikita was the only one allowed to the facilities at that time of the day, how did Dickson get to know the inside of the buildings in all their details!

Jacob made a remarkable discovery. By revealing that Dickson knew well about where she spent nights working, things became clear. The truth was confirmed. There was no more doubt about their affairs. Poor Jacob was informed that when Nikita declared him persona non grata to the Empire Studio 16, Dickson knew it like his bedroom. He was the one to describe the amphitheaters to Jacob.

The truth was revealed when they had been quarreling about the situation for several weeks. Nikita had never told him that only Dickson was allowed there. Jacob could not understand why she herself decided to break the secret. Cheating people rarely reveal their love affairs to their spouses. All her life, Nikita was involved in too many love affairs that she saw it as a normal activity. Thus, it was not necessary to hide. She was used to total freedom. Now that she was committed to one person, she had to learn how to keep a secret. She could keep it only a few days though. The information shook Jacob up and made him determined to learn more about it.

Jacob had been giving her the benefit of the doubt since there was no clear evidence of what was being reported to him. Doors were locked, and Nikita held the key. Dickson had to come on appointments. Jacob had no clue of the mystery surrounding Nikita's job. The mystery about her nights with Dickson in the dark halls of the Empire Studio 16 always crossed his mind. The discovery was beyond words. It created more complications in the long-suffering relationship. It gave to Jacob more headaches, stomachaches, and stress. It really hurt his feelings. He wondered if Nikita revealed the secret in order to confide and confess the abominable things she did. If this was her way of informing him, then she would tell him about Juvenhack, Geram, and others. She knew that Jacob had only been suspecting the affair with Dickson. Jacob could not understand why she decided to tell him the secret. Once again, he felt cheapened and betrayed. He remained tongue-tied for a day, the time to let her cool down and possibly tell him more. He waited three days to ask for more clarification. When none was given, Jacob took the initiative.

"Honey, did you say what I heard? I mean, does Dickson know where you work?" he asked in wonderment.

"Yes, he does," Nikita confirmed.

Jacob's voice was incredulous. "So you send me to ask him about you!"

"Because you don't listen to me. You don't care about me, and you keep discussing the same issues over and over again."

"So you found somebody who cares about you?"

"Whatever."

"There is no whatever here. This is an important issue, and we need to talk about it. How does he know about your work after midnight, given that no one but employees is allowed access?"

She showed him that she was in the right way, and she tried to convince him.

"He came to see what kind of job I was doing."

"What is he in your life to be concerned about the kind of work you are doing? He cares too much about you, eh! By the way, how was he allowed inside? Does he have a key of the building?"

"Well, we went together because he wanted to know how the work was done so that he could start the same kind of business."

"When was that?"

"Why are you asking all these questions? Don't you trust me?"

"It has nothing to do with trust. You told me that no outsiders were allowed on the premises. You did not even allow me to help you to do the work so that you could get home early. How come you don't want me there and you take Dickson in there at night? Does it sound logical to you? Besides, you always leave the house alone and you never tell me that you are going together. Anyway, the damage is done, the secret is finally revealed. Our ancestors said that it is never too late to mend, but I believe they were *wrong*," he concluded.

Nikita felt guilty and remained silent. The damage was done. Jacob did not need an explanation to understand what he heard from Nikita's own mouth. He did not know how to treat somebody betraying him with people who would tear his head off. Jacob was bewildered. All he could say was, "Okey-dokey. I heard what you said. Thank you for telling me." Surprised by his own outburst, he tried to hide his embarrassment.

Although the revelation struck him as ridiculous, Jacob thought it was his duty to repair it. He was obsessed with Nikita and would never dream of losing her. It was a matter of his beliefs and traditions. He thought in terms of his community. He feared what people would say if he failed with her when everybody had discouraged that love. For this only reason, any breach to his customs was forgiven. He even accepted a behavior society never tolerated. Nikita knew that Jacob had sworn to love her all his life. She learned how to take advantage of that kind of blind love. She never understood that her mistakes were forgiven but never forgotten. They remained etched on his mind. Jacob took off on a flanking movement. He stood on the balcony and took a deep breath. He stretched his muscles. Nikita joined him there.

"Are you warming up to beat me?" she asked.

"Why should I beat you? Have I ever beaten you?"

"You are training for a fight."

"Did you do anything that would warrant a fight?"

"I don't know, you tell me."

Jacob did not dare look in her face any longer. He invited her for a dinner in a restaurant. After the dinner, they would be moseying along to the park. The activities would relieve him from stress.

Two weeks passed. As if the revelation was not enough, Nikita reported a disturbing communication she had with Dickson. She was very sympathetic and supportive of him, and she wanted Jacob to sympathize too.

"You know what, Dick's wife is crazy. She hasn't made love with her husband since last week," she told him confidently. Jacob supported her argument.

"Really? Can she refuse to her own husband?"

"Imagine, a whole week. That's stupid, man."

"May be he did something wrong, and she wants to punish him."

"No. She is always like that," Nikita said sympathetically.

"Are you sure? Did she tell you that? I hope she doesn't teach you bad manners."

"Dickson told me about it. I don't talk to that bitch. She has an attitude."

"How is that possible when they sleep under the same blanket?" he asked to learn more.

"They don't sleep together. Dickson sleeps on a small mattress on the floor while Dada sleeps on the bed," Nikita said, feeling pity for Dickson.

Jacob hated to hear anything about Dickson, but this time he listened. Dickson's name kept coming up in their conversation. Nikita could even slip up and confused the name of Jacob with Dickson. Since she kept reporting conversations she had with Dickson, Jacob listened to her in total awe.

The more he heard about Dickson the more jealous he became. Bothered by the revelations, he hastened to change the topic. He wanted her to know that he never wanted to hear anything about Dickson. The more secrets she revealed, the more headaches she gave him. Yet Nikita expected him to listen to her carefully. Sometimes, he pretended to enjoy the conversation. The problem was the feedback. Jacob rarely responded enthusiastically. He did not know what to say in such situations. He did not even ask why she had to discuss such topics with somebody else's husband. She could easily describe Dickson's room and the mattress on the floor. Dickson's wife never knew that Nikita knew her bedroom. Jacob wondered in which circumstances such topics were discussed.

By reporting Dickson's problem with Dada, she conveyed a confusing message. Jacob wondered if the information was a request for authorization to help Dickson. He could see Nikita was disturbed by the situation. She was so sympathetic that she showed excessive willingness to help. How could she solve a man's love problem with his own wife, especially that Dada never knew that she was concerned about it? Why was she so sympathetic of him to the point that she tried to convince Jacob to understand Dickson's situation? No one could answer Jacob's questions. Jacob sensed a kind of explanation of her affairs with Dickson. In other words, she was officially informing him that the aim of their affair was to help Dickson.

Jacob understood that they discussed their own private lives. They could not jump on a topic like that without a proper context at the right mood. In fact, it is a topic of high intimacy and privacy. It is not a subject a man and woman would discuss at random. There must be affection between them and enough closeness. Nikita and Dickson talked about the problem because they trusted and loved each other. The news shocked Jacob who understood that there was still some work to do to Nikita. He read her mind and saw that she was ready to salve Dickson's problem.

Nikita was revealing her personal secrets of adultery, yet she still thought that she was cleverer than Jacob was. Even though she was treating him as a stupid asshole, Jacob was not stupid. Now that she was revealing her own secrets, he gave her more opportunities to express herself. Still he could not understand how she decided to unravel her own secrets. In fact, she cheated on him so much that she felt sorry for him.

Nikita had always things to say about other people's privacy. After describing Dickson's small mattress on the floor, she complained about Geram's poor hygiene. She described his dirty legs and his smelly, untidy room.

"Geram really needs odor protection. Can you show him how to use deodorants? His hygiene is poor," she told Jacob.

Jacob could not understand why Nikita was the one to be more concerned about it than anybody else was.

"How do Geram's dirty legs upset her?" Jacob wondered. "She has nothing to do with his poor hygiene."

He could not ask her how she saw his legs when he was always wearing a pair of trousers. If he happened to roll his trousers up and she saw his legs, it was not enough time to see all his shortcomings. If she saw them, it was in his room and nowhere else.

"She is pissed off as if he were her husband."

Finally, Jacob believed Mzee Chief Maneno. Nikita might have been with Geram, and she was upset with his poor hygiene. She decided to bring the issue to Jacob to help Geram work on his hygiene. She could obviously not tell him herself as she feared that Geram would feel offended and leave her when she needed his money.

She wanted to be with him in a more beautiful and comfortable room, free of smell. Jacob thought about the situation, and he was bereft with speech. He was determined to learn more about the affair between Nikita and Geram.

Another suspicious report bothered Jacob. Nikita had spent some hours with Dickson as usual. Whenever she was with Dickson, Geram, or Juvenhack, she drank strong liquor and wine when her system was not familiar with alcohol. Thus, she often arrived home drunk and could not control her language. She started revealing private conversation she had with people. She could even forget that she was with Jacob, and she called him Dickson. The more Jacob listened to her the weirder she appeared. One day, she returned home with Geram somewhat drunk. Jacob had become very provocative. When he suspected something, he would only introduce the subject and Nikita would reveal everything. When Geram left, Jacob engaged Nikita into a conversation about him. Without any effort, he discovered about the affair.

Jacob evoked Geram who behaved like single when he was married back home. As always, Nikita dominated the conversation. She did not wait to listen. She always hastened to say something.

"Geram is not serious at all. What a slug of man! He goes wooing every woman. I hate people who cheat on their spouses."

Jacob encouraged her to say more. He defended Geram even though he knew Nikita was right. If he agreed with her from the beginning, he would not get the rest of the information. He tried to defend him.

"I don't think Geram cheats on his wife. I have never seen him courting any woman."

Nikita replied by revealing a hidden truth.

"What? You don't know Geram. He goes with everybody, and he does not even protect himself."

"What do you mean?" Jacob asked with surprise with a look of disapproval.

"How do you know that? You don't even know him enough to jump on such a conclusion. You never saw him with any woman. Why do you assume that he sleeps with many women when you have never seen him with a woman?"

Nikita tried to convince him. "What are you talking about? I know what I am saying," she insisted.

"Come on! You only see him in here. He never comes with any woman. Even if he were to have affairs, at least he would protect himself."

"That's the problem with him. He has many partners, and he doesn't protect himself."

"I don't think he can do that. Nowadays, one cannot play with life like that. It is dangerous to have unprotected affair," Jacob responded.

"Geram doesn't use protection at all. He wants *yango na yango*." She used an expression in Lingala that meant having unprotected love.

"I don't agree with you. He is not stupid to do that."

"What are you discussing? I am telling you that he is a player, and he doesn't protect himself."

"No. You can't be so negative about him. He is not coward to go with everybody with no protection. Nowadays, many people are infected with HIV. There are many other Sexually Transmitted Diseases. People have to be careful and avoid them."

Jacob took advantage of the discussion to tell her about dangers caused by unprotected affairs. He had once told Nikita that he feared HIV when Nikita was accusing him of jealousy. She had invited him to work on it and accept sharing with others. By condemning Geram, she told Jacob not to worry about HIV anymore as she was protecting herself.

"That is why he tests blood for the AIDS virus every six months. Why would he do that if he protected himself?" Nikita added.

Jacob was speechless for a while, just listening carefully. Even though Nikita saw him stiffening, she continued her story. He looked at her little skeptically and added.

"Hmmm! Why do you think he does blood test every six months? He is not a hooker."

"If you don't know about something, better ask rather than discussing. I know what I am saying."

"Really? If he does blood tests every six months, then it means something."

"That is what I am saying," Nikita confirmed.

"Still, I don't see any reason to have AIDS test so regularly," Jacob continued, wanting to learn more.

"Because of unprotected relations with many partners, he checks to make sure he did not get HIV. It helps him to stop worrying and take steps to stay HIV-free," she innocently concluded as if Jacob understood nothing.

"Okay. Then, he is a smart guy. He cares about his life," Jacob said in resignation, filing the piece of information in his heart. "But prevention is better than cure. Rather than checking that he did not get the virus, he should better avoid it. If he gets it, it will be too late," he commented.

Although Jacob noticed something awkward in the information, he did not give it further thought. He pretended not to make a big deal out of it. He could not accuse her when she was the one to inform him. If she had kept the information, he would never have known it. Jacob wondered if she willingly revealed her infidelities when she knew the consequences of adultery in couples.

Jacob was only surprised to know that Nikita knew everything about Geram's private life. He asked himself in which circumstances Geram told her that he enjoyed unprotected relation. He even revealed to her about his HIV testing. The answer remained a mystery. If Jacob himself never knew that his friend did regular blood test, he could not understand how Nikita was the one to know it. He never knew that they were so familiar to discuss such topics. Jacob wondered for what purpose Geram informed Nikita about his private life. The information reassured Jacob that at least she would not bring diseases. She had also confirmed to Jacob that she would always protect herself. But she had three kids. How could she protect herself and still have children? She had also aborted many times. Jacob concluded that she was a liar. If Geram confided to her that he did not like protection and he was HIV-free, it might be the result of the bargain?

As if nothing was revealed, Jacob remained silent. He understood that maybe Geram tempted her, and she refused. In this case, things would have stopped there. They would not go that far to talk about unprotected relations. Allowing this communication meant that they were in intimacy, and Nikita was insisting on protection. Geram convinced her that there was nothing to worry about. He had to prove that he was HIV-free. Whether they used protection or not, one thing was obvious—they had an affair. Jacob wondered why Nikita reported her infidelity one more time. He thought it might be a way of informing him that his friend had been bothering her, and she wanted Jacob to take measures. If it was the case, then she would speak of the others too.

Whatever was happening, Nikita was too involved in men's affairs. She had private information about sexual lives of people when Jacob himself was not privy to such information. Nikita was reporting stuff that his friends would not tell him. One cannot use this kind of talk to somebody they are not familiar with. It would facilitate them to know about Nikita's weaknesses and strategies to win her. Nikita was too talkative with men when they seemed to be only interested in things pertaining to sexual matters.

There were always remarkable discoveries of suspicious contacts and conversations between Nikita and other men. If the case of Dickson was obvious, it was just one tragedy in hundreds. Dickson behaved as the primary operator. He could not hide his desire for her. He even wanted her when she was with Jacob. The secondary operators were more discreet than Dickson. They never showed it to Jacob. They were only revealed by people, Nikita herself, spills and other imprints left in the house.

Jacob decided to deal with Dickson as he could not deal with every man involved with Nikita. He already had trouble with people who had made a coalition with Nikita. If Jacob opened many fronts, the enemies would unite and defeat him. Nikita had conquered everybody around her. With the source of trouble inside Jacob's house, Nikita would plot with them, and the game would be over. She longed for the kind of life she was used to, and she would not get it so long as she was with Jacob. Her friends would have to defeat Jacob in order to keep her.

9. The Medicine for Nikita

Jacob suffered a lot for being betrayed from inside his own house. Being betrayed by his friends was something normal. Things complicated when his own lover was the one to sell his secrets to the enemy when she and her three kids were living on his paychecks. He was like backing his own rebellion. Nikita would not even feel pity to betray somebody who loved her like his own body. There was nothing he could do to make her happier. He made many sacrifices none of which was appreciated. Rather than thanking him for his endless love, she would only tell Dickson that Jacob would die for her.

Jacob eventually believed that such person should be psychoanalyzed to see which therapy would work with her. He had studied Psychology and Psychoanalysis in high school and university. He read Nikita's mind, and he did his own analysis. However, he would not dare talk about it. Confused, he wondered if he was not the one that needed to be psychoanalyzed.

He loved a person who continuously cheated on him and she inflicted her infidelities on him. To make matters worse, she treated him as an asshole. To avoid more problems, Jacob learned to cope with her abusive behavior. The only thing he never agreed with is the infidelity. He did not agree with it, but he was obliged to support it and he lived in it. He remained glued to her as the only woman in the world. He was accused of not wanting to share, but in reality, he had been sharing. There was no point calling him selfish. In the end, he understood that he might be the one that needed psychoanalysis.

In his theory, he loved the person and not her acts. He did not even hate Dickson that wanted his head off. He always hated the evil and never the Evildoer. Nikita did evil things, but Jacob hated her evil acts rather than her. As human being, she was his old friend and a lover. One cannot hate one's lover when they yearn for life full of love. However, Jacob needed something more than just psychoanalysis. Some therapy would be required as well. Psychoanalysis would probably improve Nikita's abusive language, but it would not stop her from having affairs with others. That was Jacob's greatest enemy. Those evils combined and stressed him. As he did not want Nikita out, he had to live with evils all his life with Nikita. As a Christian, he psychoanalyzed himself, and he adopted a Christian attitude about infidelities and abusive language.

Jacob had hard time dealing with Nikita and her sons. He withdrew to the church to meditate about his future. He went to church twice a week to pay his respect to God. Prayers would provide him with strength and courage to resist abusive behavior. At the same time, they would help him to manage the stress.

The situation was beyond control. Jacob needed to chase the devils that had entered into Nikita. He wanted the bad spirits to be removed from her once for all. He even invited Jehovah witnesses and pastors to help. Jacob believed in prayers as the only weapon to fight the ghost and evil spirits. As individual, he was powerless to chase the demons. He took refuge in the church in the hope that his spirituality would transform Nikita's heart.

One Sunday morning, Jacob heard the doorbell ring and opened the door to find the ugly tall face that just breezed in. Jacob reminded him that Sunday morning was not the time for visits. He was preparing to go to the mass. Dickson did not want Nikita to go with Jacob. Nikita herself showed no interest in going to the church. Jacob found it awkward to leave her and Dickson alone in his house. He insisted that

Nikita go to church, the only place to turn to. Everything else had failed. The time was running out, and Nikita was showing no signs of improvement. Jacob reminded her that the mass was scheduled for ten o'clock in the morning.

"Come on, Nikita, be quick. Otherwise we will be late."

Dickson, however, tried to convince them not to go to church. Jacob was adamant, "No one has the power to stop me from believing what I believe. I believe in one God, and I want him to light my way. I need God to transform our lives and remove the ghost and other evil spirits from this house. I am praying for a long lasting relationship." He gave Nikita a choice.

"You can go to church only if you believe in Lord Jesus as your Savior. Personally, I listen to my heart and not to Dickson."

Nikita listened carefully and got ready to follow Jacob. Would going to church reluctantly be of any help? There was no choice. At least it was Jacob's refuge. Everything else had fallen apart.

Jacob likes the church, especially when it is empty. The silence itself inspires him. He can stay on his knees for hours, praying the Almighty to help him overcome bad situations. In Canada, silent churches are closed. Most churches only open on hours of service. Jacob was taught that God is one and that there is only one heaven. Every religion preaches to do the right thing. Hence, he visited a protestant church named Cross Pointe Fellowship. He was impressed by the teachings of Pastor Elijah Diallo. He decided to take Nikita there every week. They could share the good news and in the hope that it would change her behavior. One day, Pastor Elijah hit the nail on the head. He said everything needed to heal the agonizing relationship. He provided pieces of advice needed to keep unity and love in families. Jacob was happy that Nikita was there. He invited her to listen carefully. After the service, Jacob shook the pastor's hand and said,

"Thank you, Pastor. I liked your preaching." The pastor himself was happy to see him there.

"Thank you for being with us today. We hope to see you again."

Jacob turned to Nikita. "Pastor Elijah's preaching soothes me. I hope that it will improve our life together. Don't you think they will be of some help?"

Nikita shrugged her shoulders and asked. "Is it the first time you hear this kind of preaching? I had heard all that before."

The answer left a bad taste in Jacob's stomach. If the church was not the last hope to revive the situation, then Jacob needed something stronger than himself. As a man of his standing with his human weaknesses, he believed there was work to be done. That work could not be achieved by mankind. Jacob was feeling hopeless and helpless. He recognized his mistake number one to have judged a book by its cover. Yet he still believed that there was room for improvement. He kept hoping for the better. Unfortunately, nothing seemed to improve. Even when he told Nikita to stop looking for sweet things, he was met with a refusal. The stubborn refusal would surely put the agonizing relationship down the drain. With this kind of person in his life, Jacob would not achieve any of the things he had hoped to achieve with her.

Jacob decided to play the last card. As Nikita was getting mad, he invited her for a prayer. He took a Bible and opened it. He had underlined some verses about the meaning of a marriage. As he read about responsibilities of everyone to make a happy family, Nikita's anger grew. With the violence of a beast, she pulled the Bible from Jacob's hands and violently tore the pages. With the rage of a dog, she threw the remains of the Bible in the garbage bin. Jacob was taken aback. He could not imagine a Christian tearing the Holly Bible and throwing it in the garbage bin. He wondered if she was the same Nikita he watched growing, the one he spent his childhood with. Because of that daring act, Jacob's fear grew horribly. He understood that she might have a heart of a beast. A Christian who dares tear the Holly Bible could do any harm in the world. Jacob went to the garbage to collect the remains of the Bible and stuffed them in his bag. Once again, he understood that he had been playing with fire.

After seven penurious and hellish months, the cast was done for the sake of safety and environment. One Friday night, as they returned from church, Nikita wanted to see Dickson as usual. It was after 10:00 p.m., and it was dark. Jacob insisted that she go home, to no avail. She was so preoccupied as if she was missing a very important appointment. She insisted on meeting him. As Jacob did not agree with her, she looked angry and fierce in a strange way. They were coming from the church, and Jacob hoped that she had changed. He wanted her closer to him. He suggested going with her.

"Wait for me so we can go together."

"We don't need to go together. I will be right back."

She left the house and went to Dickson's. Jacob flopped on the bed and watched television while waiting for her. He expected her to be back in no time as promised. One hour passed, then a second one. Around midnight, Jacob started growing desperate. He stayed lying in bed awake wishing that she were there. He felt bitterly jealous. He started calling Dickson to let her go home. Nikita kept promising to return home in no time. Jacob waited with increasing discouragement. He wondered what his beloved one was doing with a man who treated him as his bitter enemy. Every half an hour, he glanced at the nightstand to see nothing. The rose was not on the headstock either. He checked on the window, and the rose was not there. He could not sleep when his precious treasure was away from him. He kept thinking about what she was still doing with his enemy in the middle of the night. He got out of bed to check if Dickson's house was still lit. Then he returned to bed.

Nikita did not return until the next morning. Jacob was still awake, his thoughts wandering aimlessly. She entered the house in a rage. Jacob kindly reminded her that a respectful mother should not behave like that.

"You should respect your family by being home at night at least. I am not responsible for what may happen to you in other men's houses, especially my enemies.

Next time you do it, I won't be able to let you in my house. I will have to tell you to return there."

Nikita responded with a violent fury, her rage growing. She turned things upside down to prove that Jacob was the wrong party, not her.

"I didn't know there was a curfew here. Next time, let me know in time so I won't have to disturb you. By the way, I am fed up with this discipline. You control me as if I were your child. I am tired of this. You know what? I have never allowed anybody to control me. I have always been an independent person. Stop treating me like a baby, you cocksucker!"

"What did you say?" Jacob retorted.

Nikita pointed a finger in Jacob's eyes and threatened.

"If you touch me, you will see what you didn't see in Burundi. You don't know me, man. Soon and very soon, you will know who I am. I will achieve what Dickson and Juvenhack failed to achieve in Burundi. I will show you what Evildoers didn't show you. You won't even have time to know me. Your days are counted, if you know what I am saying. I will make your head swim. Then you will know what people call Nikita Chissocco. You will regret messing with the Chissoccos."

Jacob looked up her face that now looked like death warmed over. He began to shiver. He had been living in fear that his archrivals would assault him. Now that Nikita warned him that his days were counted, his fear became more real.

"My goodness! My days are counted? What do you mean?"

He remembered being told that Ronald died a suspicious death. Nikita once told him that his days were counted. One day later, he was killed by the members of the Sans Echecs, Dickson's death squad. Jacob feared meeting the same fate. Nikita was spending nights with the same gang members, and she returned home threatening that his days were counted. The same thing had happened to Manassé, her brother-in-law, killed by unidentified assailants somewhere in Mozambique. He was treated worse than Jacob was. A certain Shawn was wandering in disarray in the streets of Kansas City. Nikita's father himself had disappeared mysteriously. Nikita was making fun of him in the same way she was treating Jacob. He remembered how Nikita made jokes about her late father whose death was being laughed at. When dead people are spoken about with respect, Nikita spoke of her late father as an asshole who did not deserve any respect. She flung out disgustedly against her mother and other siblings. She disliked her father so much that she did not even go to his funeral. She would never say anything positive about any of the Chissoccos. Then she turned against her mother to state that she was a tough woman who controlled her freedom too much. Jacob wondered if Nikita would ever respect him, given that she never respected her own parents. By badmouthing her own parents and siblings, she confirmed what everybody said about the Chissoccos.

Jacob knew that no one who married in that family was still alive, except an American who was being dragged as a wet rag like Jacob and ended up on the street. The situation became too much to bear. He understood that corrective measures were needed, and the sooner the better. He could not keep pleasing somebody that would never be pleased. He had understood that truth and honesty would not always triumph. He knew how easy it would be to kill somebody especially when his lover was involved. A spouse is like somebody's doctor. A doctor has full control over his patient's life. In post independent Burundi, doctors and nurses would kill their patients simply because they were of different ethnic background. During the genocides, not a single patient survived. People feared going to hospitals because all doctors and nurses were Evildoers. Nikita was supposed to take care of Jacob as his personal doctor. Now that she was relating to him as his bitter enemy, trusting her would put his life at jeopardy. Jacob was dealing with threats from outside as well as from inside his own bedroom. He had escaped death a dozen of times in Burundi because he kept running away and hiding from the enemy. Now, how could he run away from his beloved one? He feared that Nikita would allow her friends to hurt him at night. From that day on, he could no longer sleep in his own house, certain that a tsunami would hit soon or later.

Jacob decided to learn more about Rosie's ingredients. He unfolded the supply label and read it. It showed that the hazardous product was a dangerously reactive material causing immediate toxic effects. Now that he was forewarned of a disaster waiting to hit him, he decided to be on his guard. He returned the flower to one of the Home Depot stores of Edmonton with the original receipt. A customer service representative told him that their shop could not take returns from other countries. She advised him to return it to the original store. Jacob called the store in Lacey. He spoke to the florist who confirmed that there was no warrantee on the flower.

"Flowers are not like hardware. Your flower had to die eventually," she said.

"But you had guaranteed it for another year," he replied.

"She would live even longer had you placed her in an environment free of bees," she replied and apologized for the loss.

Jacob asked if he could leave her in the Edmonton store.

"I am sorry, but I cannot let you leave your garbage here. She would contaminate our plants. You wouldn't like it either, would you?" the customer service representative said.

"No, I wouldn't. I will return her to Olympia then."

Because of the bad smell, she did not even let him stay there longer. As he insisted on having Rosie returned, the florist felt sorry for him and suggested another solution, "Why don't you check with different flower shops to purchase a good one? You didn't have to go all the way to Olympia just for a devil you didn't know. You need to pay more attention and choose something with more stamina."

"But this rose was supposed to be strong," Jacob noted.

"This kind of rose is a summer flower. There are spring flowers, summer flowers, and autumn flowers. The rose even survived winter! She is an extraordinary flower.

You should be proud of her. In her normal conditions, you should not expect her to live more than two months."

"Are you serious?"

"You were lucky to keep her that long. You must remember that beautiful flowers are not necessarily strong. In winter, fragile roses are infected with germs that attack the ovary. I advise you to consider a different type of flower. There are really nice flowers. You need to look before you leap."

"That is a great idea. I will do that. Thank you for your advice."

"It was a pleasure," she replied as she walked away.

If the church did not transform Nikita, there was nobody else in the world Jacob could turn to. Nikita had never been on good terms with other members of her family. They had even warned Jacob that taking care of Nikita was not an easy task. Paul Chissocco's remark remained etched in Jacob's memory. As he was always in disagreement with his sister, he called Jacob to tell him that his sister was a femme fatale, tough as leather.

"Why did you consider my sister as your lover? Did you ask somebody's opinion before making such a daring decision? Be careful with my sister. She is dangerous . . . horrible."

Jacob was surprised to hear from her own family that she was a horrible person. He spoke to her about it and handed her the phone.

"Your brother wants to talk to you."

As she picked the phone, they started quarrelling and yelling to each other straight away and Nikita hung up the phone. When Jacob asked why she was arguing with her brother, the answer was the same, "Paul is foolish."

Jacob could not accept that everybody in her family was foolish, and she was the only one in the right.

"Remember the first day we met, you told me that your father was foolish, alcoholic and an asshole. Then it was your mother's turn to be crazy, foolish and too controlling. Now it is your brother's turn. I don't talk about myself. So who is next? Your kids? Do you mean that everybody is foolish in your world? I think you should learn how to treat people with respect."

For the first time, she did not answer back. Whenever she described her parents and siblings, she never said anything positive about them. If no one of them was normal, she could not be different from them when she had their genes. She herself was doing too many foolish things that no one of her family would do.

10. Jacob's Liberation from the Heavy Burden

Like most people, Jacob wished to live a happy life. He needed to liberate his heart from the heavy load of misery. To achieve this dream, he needed to understand that although nature was beautiful, it was not always nice to humans. Still, human beings are more precious than anything else found in nature. If the lily died a natural death, the rose would be killed by loads of heavy bees sucking her pollen with a hearty appetite in her own room, in their hives, in the car, and in the Empire Studio 16. Rosie proved that plants were more vulnerable than humans. Very few resist four seasons.

Jacob was disappointed by life with Nikita, who changed colors like a chameleon. Human beauty is more interesting as it doesn't change with seasons and weathers. Jacob believed that his flower would be even more beautiful in her natural milieu. She would have more room to bloom. Jacob apologized for limiting her freedom in his house. He had to abide with the code of society. He lived in an organized society with a well-established code of conduct. In that human society, people relate to one another as moral beings. People loved and respected one another. Anybody that breached to the code of conduct would be treated as an outcast. Jacob had to deal with Nikita as the outcast. He would let her deal with her infidelities away from his society.

He told Nikita to return Rosie to Shelton or Lacey. She refused to go. She had made so many friends who convinced her that her beauty would see her through. They did not want her away from them. Dickson, Juvenhack, Geram, and others informed her that Jacob had no power to send her back against her will. As always, she trusted them. She always listened to them and never to Jacob. Dickson had always been taking decisions in Jacob's house.

Jacob, however, swore not to let any idea from his rivals affect his private life. He let Nikita understand that he was the only master of the house and not her boyfriends. He had, therefore, to keep order and respect in his dwelling place. He refused the execution of Dickson's decisions in his house. He insisted that he was the one to make all decisions about his life. He did not trust Nikita anymore, and he would not let her keep screwing his life. Nikita started yelling on him. Jacob stood up and ordered her to cool down.

"Stop yelling on me. If you do it again, I send you back to Dickson. I will allow no more mess in my house. I have regained control of the situation. You should start packing your personal belongings and leave my house."

"You . . ." Jacob interrupts.

"I already made the decision and it is final. You have two weeks to leave this house."

Nikita, who had been complaining about jealousy, selfishness, and her lack of freedom refused to believe that Jacob would decide to break up with her. She had been planning with Dickson and Juvenhack to kick him out of the house in a fortnight. She would be free to do what she wanted with no man watching or controlling her. Following Dickson's advice, she decided that it was the time to kick Jacob out of his house. She moved closer to Jacob, screaming loud. She tied her hair, a way of showing that she was ready to use physical force to kick him out.

In the western society, the accusation of domestic violence is enough to kick a man out of his house. It is one of the great weapons effective in family destruction. Nikita knew it better. Thus, it would be easy for her to assault Jacob and force him out. If he resisted, he would be accused of domestic violence or sexual harassment and the cops would take care of him. When Jacob resisted, Nikita yelled so loudly that neighbors could hear her,

"I am not going anywhere. You are the one to get out of this house. I don't want you here anymore. Get out!"

Jacob cooled down for a while to listen to her. When she paused to breathe, Jacob asked her,

"Are you done? Is it the only thing you can say?"

"This house is not your place anymore. Go out," she yelled louder. Jacob inched closer to her, bowed his head, and spoke softly.

"Nikita, what are you saying? Did I hear you well? Can you repeat what you just said?"

Nikita grabbed him by the head and shook him, yelling even louder.

"I've told you to get out of this house, and I don't have to repeat it over and over again. I cannot tolerate your ugly face in here any longer. Get out, bitch!" she shouted vehemently while pointing at the door.

"I was a son of a bitch. Now I have become a bitch herself! Aren't I asshole anymore?" Jacob spoke jokingly.

"I told you and I repeat it once for all. Get out *now*. One . . . two . . . three . . . four . . ." She pointed to the door and started counting. Jacob laughed and helped her to count.

"Five . . . six . . . seven. How far will you go counting?"

"The stupid asshole is not listening. What are you still doing here? Get out, now!"

"You have put new batteries in your mouth, eh! Haven't you been able to watch your language so far? Can't you speak in a more kindly tone?" he asked.

The more she heard of him the angrier she became. She decided that the time to cast him out was right. She had been waiting for an opportunity like that and she would not lose it.

"If you don't go out right now, I call the cops to kick your ass out, bungling idiot. Get out, *now!*" she screamed louder. She stretched her arm to reach the phone. Jacob stopped her.

"Wait. You still have time to call. By the way, you don't have the right to use my phone anymore. It is my personal property. This house is not your home anymore. You have no more right to touch any of my personal belongings." He folded his arms.

Jacob had nothing to fear. He could not imagine anything worse than the life he was living. The cops had been saving him from her and Dickson's threats. They would only calm her down, but they would not return Jacob's dignity. The tragic fact was that Jacob preferred prison to life with Nikita Chissocco. If he were to be taken to prison, at least his life would be safer than in his own house. Still, now that Nikita wanted to call the cops to kick him out, he realized that he had been playing with fire all along. He rolled his shirtsleeves up and moved closer to her. This time, he spoke with authority. She could not meet his gaze.

"You want to call the cops on me!" He put a finger on his chest. Nikita quietened.

"Do you think that the job of the cops is to pack men off? They are there for the safety of everybody. They work for the common good of citizens. If they come here, they will get me out of this mess. Do you still want to call them? You still have one minute in this house."

Jacob picked the phone and handed it to her. She did not take it.

"Remember, this country is not Burundi. Our police are not Evildoers or Sans Echecs. There are no death squads here either. Even Geram, your Interahamwe, has no power to threaten people like in Rwanda. Will you call the cops now? No. It is too late now. One minute is over. Get out."

Surprised by this sudden change in Jacob's demeanor, Nikita learned to talk low and to listen to somebody for the first time in her life. She was used to kicking lovers and boyfriends out of her apartment in Olympia. She thought she was strong enough to do it all her life and in every country. If she did it successfully in Nairobi, Cotonou, and Olympia, it became impossible with Jacob. Not only was she living illegally in Canada, she was also in his house. She was still a visitor and she was known to police.

Jacob reached a point where he could not tolerate his enemies in his bed anymore. Nikita's way of life and her attitude had been ruining him. He had been struggling to prevent her behavior from destroying his life. The longer he waited, the more trouble he had. He explained to Nikita the reason for the decision to let her out.

"Nikita, I had very hard time dealing with you. You made a fatal mess here, and I don't want to live in it all my life. I refuse to be treated like a dishrag. I cannot let chaos rein in my life. If needs be, I will fight fire with fire. Do you get my point? I will fight fire with fire."

"What?" Nikita looked surprised.

"I will fight fire with fire," Jacob repeated.

"What do you mean?" she asked.

"There are evil spirits that dwell in your flower and in your unclean heart. Rosie is a devil. She is so powerful that she keeps tempting you to commit evil deeds. She has been luring you away from me and you followed her as if she were your head. She controls you and she takes you to the thick darkness of the Empire Studio 16 where you did awful things. I am bearing up under demons in my house. I must tell you that that game is over. You have to return to Auntie Sammie's gardens or else I will fight fire with fire."

"How do you fight fire with fire?"

"I don't need to give you an explanation. All I am saying is that I don't need you in my life anymore. Return your flower to the Home Depot *now*. From now on, the bees and butterflies will meet her there and not in my house. She is so beautiful that she will easily find buyers. Roses like yours sell like hot chocolates. You used your flower as a weapon. I don't want to be her victim. Good-bye, my Rose." He pointed at the door as he waved her out. She gave him a long wicked look before replying.

"I am not going anywhere," she cried.

She immediately realized that she made a terrible mistake by raising her voice again. She suddenly changed the mood and smiled to him. Her anger disappeared completely. She decided to refresh her love exactly like the first day they met in Olympia. She embraced him and kissed his lips. She pressed her breasts against his chest and wrapped her arms around him. She whispered a few words.

"Hon, I love you."

Jacob was so pissed off that he did not react. His heart started beating. Nikita reached for a couple of Kleenex and wiped tears from her eyes. She looked at him in the face and she smiled. In a low voice, she whispered again, "Don't you love me anymore? I love you very much."

Jacob withdrew from her arms and moved away in amazement.

"Come on! What do you think you are? Since when do you love a stupid asshole? Please, there is no time for witticism. Get out of my life. It is too late to love me now. By the way, how can you love a bungling idiot, a cold bitch, garbage among human beings, a motherfucker, a selfish and jealous son-of-a-bitch? Be honest to yourself. By escaping your onerous responsibility, you betrayed me, just as everybody predicted that you would. They were right."

"I am sorry, honey. I really love you. I promise to respect you all my life. I—"

"Stop that nonsense," Jacob interrupted her, standing on his dignity.

"Your behavior is destroying your dignity. You lost your self-esteem. You degraded me, and you made no bone about it. How did you dare bring those insane and unpleasant Evildoers in my life? You don't even realize how hard it is for a man to be cheated on like that. For how long do you expect me to support infidelities of that magnitude? I am sick of it. You are now depressing me every single day. I had never before felt as desperate as I feel with you. I am tired of this situation. You do not deserve to live in this house any longer. I refuse to throw myself under the train because of your adultery. Get out!"

"I don't love them. You are the only one I love."

"This is what I have been telling you all along. Don't lie that you ever loved me. You told everybody that you hated me. You said it hundreds of times to whoever would listen to you."

"Honey, don't think I am sort of a hooker."

"I am not saying that you are sort of a hooker. I would say you are a real one, not sort of."

"I am not a hooker."

"If you make bricks, people will call you a brick maker. If you lay pipes, you are a pipe layer. If you teach, people will call you a teacher. Everybody becomes what they do. With all you did, you can call yourself what you want, but like it or not, people will call you by what you do."

"Why are you always talking bullshit? Fuck you, son of a bitch! Oh, I am sorry. I didn't mean to insult you, honey. I love you," she apologized, realizing that it was not the time for insults.

"Call me whatever you want. I have had enough insults. You hate me so much that you can even kill me."

"I know that it is hard to believe me, but I really love you. I really do." She stared at him worshipfully. As her emotions were in riot, she rests her teary eyes and wet cheeks against his chest. She held him tightly when his spirits had taken a downward turn.

"Don't mess my shirt," he jerked her away.

She took some Kleenex and cleared her eyes. She let her dress fall open, and she tried to unbutton his trousers. Jacob did not let his anger go out at her suggestion. He had been inching toward getting rid of her since Dickson's mother-in-law's revelations. Any thought of Dickson with her was making him crazy. He jumped up in fury and threw her on the couch. She took off her clothes and pulled him toward her. She embraced him and gave him many noisy kisses.

"Hon, we didn't do anything for weeks. I want it on the couch," she implored. With that, she gave him a warm hug as she unbuttoned his trousers.

Jacob had no feeling of love left in him. He was not interested in love matters. He gave her a quizzical look, drew away, and recited a poem.

"Once upon a time, I loved a lady called Nikita. She used to be my lover. Now I am playing games with a mouse of slut. I wish I could find true love."

"I am your lover," she implored, opening one of her purses. She pulled out her engagement ring. She twisted it round her finger, showing that the ring was linking them together and forever.

"I am committed to you," she whispered.

Jacob did not even acknowledge seeing the ring. He did not care at all. "I don't want to hear your screeching shit. If I had a lover, I wouldn't be spending all my time discussing your boyfriends. There were many other things to talk about. You never seemed to belong in this house. If you were my roommate, you would at least pay the rent. I would not burn myself trying to keep you. Please, can you pack up your stuff and leave?"

"Honey, did you forget the promise to stay together all our lives? I will never default on that promise," she said reassuringly.

"Come on! We never walked together. You walked hand in hand with others, never with me. Please, leave me be and stay with them."

"Where do you want me to go? You are everything to me. I love you so much that I can't be away from you. I would rather die in your hands than be without you. Please, please, forgive me."

In spite of the excessive promises and apologies, Jacob did not change his decision. He had no more room for forgiveness.

"You gave me a lot of trouble, and you are not ready to put up with your bad behavior. You bamboozled me into fighting with the Evildoers when I had forgiven them for all the wrongs they did. Living with you is impossible."

"Please, forgive me. I promise to improve myself and treat you with dignity," she spoke through tears.

Unfortunately, the promises were useless now. She had no more room in Jacob's heart. Jacob responded with annoyance.

"Do you remember how many times I asked you to treat me with dignity?" he asked mockingly.

"Please, forgive me," she insisted.

"Come on! You never remained true to your vows. You destroyed my trust and confidence in you. I suffered too much because of your evil acts. How many times do you want me to forgive you? Please, go out."

"I don't have anywhere to go. Your house is my house. Please, give me another chance, I beg you, honey," she insisted.

Jacob had been counting on his courage and patience to accept the unacceptable. Now that he had regained his strength, he could not believe the unbelievable. In a flat voice, he went through the long chain of events that led him to the final decision.

"Abusive language, physical assaults, two babies lost, infidelities, what on earth didn't you do to hurt me?" he insisted on breaking the dangerous relationships.

He met with vigorous resistance on her side. And Jacob, who usually did not give up a fight until he had won it, admitted having lost the fight with Nikita's lovers.

"I had never imagined fighting a stupid war like this. Actually, it is not a normal fight. I was the one to support and tolerate a rebellion in my house. You rebelled against me and sold my secrets to the enemy. You went to the front line, and they provided you with ammunitions. How could I win such a war?"

"I want to stay here with you," Nikita implored.

"Nope. That is too much. You cannot treat me with derision and still want to stay with me. I cannot support a rebellion in my own house any longer. I already know that you are thinking of another man in your life. How many men do you need anyway?" he asked skeptically. "Every man will eventually be the right person to you. You have to leave my house," he concluded.

"Where can I go? Returning to Olympia requires several months of planning. And I don't want to return there," she said.

"I thought you had enough time in the Empire Studio 16. Do you need more than four extra hours at work every single day? Please, will you go out?"

"I told you I don't have where to go," she said with growing respect.

"I don't give a *dickson* where you go. I have been running after you for too long. I don't want to live with this tension forever," he concluded.

Nikita always told him to go to hell whenever she felt like it. Jacob reminded her.

"How come you have nowhere to go when you always send me to hell? You should go there yourself since you believe it is a nice place. Go to the hell of the Empire Studio 16. There are no more games with devils here. I will not let a whore to screw my life. How long do I have to suffer, being beaten at my own game! For God's sake, just leave."

"Honey, let me promise you something. If you give me a second chance, I will—" Jacob tapped on the table to interrupt her.

"Goodness gracious! A second chance? I gave you hundreds of chances and you refused to take any. Now you only want one chance!"

As Jacob talked with high voice, one of her sons understood that something weird might happen to his mom. He was used to hearing his mother yelling loud and Jacob remaining silent. They were not worried because their mom always had the upper hand. This time, it was the opposite. Nikita was soaked in tears speaking gentle and sweet words when Jacob was the one to yell louder. Nikita spoke in a very weak voice, and her child feared that she was in danger. He rushed to the living room to see what was going on and found his mother naked.

"Mom, what is the matter? Why are you naked?" he asked. Nikita turned against her son to push him back to the room.

"It is none of your business. Go back to your room and stay there," she instructed.

Still naked, she led him to the room and slammed the door behind him. She returned to Jacob to convince him.

"Hon, another chance will improve our relationship and we—" Jacob interrupted her again.

"Madam, I cannot let you stay here when I know that you cannot change."

"Why do you call me madam? You don't call me honey anymore. Do you have another honey in your life?" she asked.

"I am not playing games with you anymore. Get out!"

"You have another woman in your life. That is why you don't love me anymore. Can I know the name of the stupid lady who is taking my darling away?"

"Her name is Dickson, if you really need her first name. Her family name is Juvenhack. Do you want her middle name?" Jacob spoke ironically with a petulant look. Nikita took a deep breath and dropped her head.

"Sweetie, if you give me a second chance, I will—" Jacob interrupted her.

"Stop iffing as the dam is already broken. I gave you hundreds of chances and you didn't take any. Now you ask for just one." Nikita tilted her head up.

"Why are you doing this to me?" she asked with sadness in her voice, looking worried and exasperated.

"What are you still doing here? I am not Thomas, Kevin, Juvenhack, Dickson, and other slaves to your cunt. Leave my house as soon as possible," he said in a harsh and cruel voice.

"Where do you want me to go?" she asked in a trembling voice.

"Why is it that you don't want to go to your gigolo friends? I didn't know you were a sex tourist."

"Honey, they are not my boyfriends. I never loved them. They are only my sex friends. There is no true love between us. You are the only man I love in this world," she said respectfully.

Jacob was so pissed off that he buried his face in his hands and ran to his bedroom. He flopped on the bed and tried to pull himself together. Nikita's constant wittering got on his nerves.

By telling him that they were only her sex friends, Nikita implied that she wanted Jacob to know the truth. He had been accusing her that she loved them when there was no love between them. As the situation bothered him, she decided to make things clear.

Jacob equated having an affair to love. Nikita had to repeatedly explain that she never loved any of the men she was involved with. As he never believed her, she had to explain that having an affair and loving were two different things. There the problem lay as Jacob took one for the other and needed to be taught the difference. Nikita was going to elaborate if Jacob did not get mad.

As the guys were having her regularly, they took for granted that she would always be available for them. They took advantage of her weakness and stopped providing like before. Nikita came back to her senses and realized that what she was doing was a bit too much. She had never had four regular partners at a time. She realized that men were now taking her for a hooker, and she did not like it. She decided to control herself and take good care of her family. Turning back to Jacob was not in itself a bad thing. The problem was that she had kept him in the dark for too long and now he had found out everything at once. She would go and come as she pleased. Once she quit them, they doubled the amount of money they were providing and they won her again.

Nikita followed Jacob in the room and sat at the edge of the bed regretfully. She apologized desperately. For the first time, she looked guilty, worried, hangdog, appealing, and sad. She rolled Jacob's blanket down so she could kiss. She slipped her hand inside his shirt and moved it smoothly around his chest. She took her G-string out and started stroking his cheeks, pressing her breasts against his chest, and breathing harder and unevenly. She was suggesting lovemaking when Jacob's nerves were on edge. When she started unzipping his trousers, he jerked her hand away. He turned his head and fixed her a look.

"Nikita, this is not a romantic moment, and I am not ready to play your games. If you touch any part of my body again, you will regret it terribly. Please, take this as a last warning. You may not understand what I am saying, but I'd rather you didn't make me repeat it."

Nikita got out of him and slept beside him. He got up and fixed her a long look. Tears were welling in her eyes.

"It's no use crying over spilt milk. There is nothing left between us. I want to reset my life alone," he concluded.

Jacob had had enough. His tenderness and patience had finally expired. That day, the time to demonstrate his manhood and bravery had come. He decided to free himself from the evil spirits once for all. The danger needed to be removed not only from his house but also from Nikita, source of troubles. Jacob opened the door to let the evil spirits out of the house.

"If you need to live in a house of demons, Dickson's apartment is the right place," he told her. "You made a wrong choice by wanting to live with a jealous person."

Nikita ran out of the door, sobbing. She went straight to Dickson's apartment and complained to Dickson that Jacob did not want her in his house anymore. Dickson had always promised to take care of her if she kicked Jacob out of the house. Now that she was the one to get out, things complicated. He could not keep his wife and his mistress under the same roof. He could not even support another three children. He realized that he did not need her at all. Jacob called Dickson to confirm that he could keep her.

"Dickson, you needn't hide your affairs. She is free now. You can have her. If you don't agree with my decision, you can bring her by force. As far as I am concerned, there is no appeal to this verdict."

Dickson persuaded Nikita to call the cops and accuse Jacob of domestic violence. As she was doubtful about calling, Dickson himself called. Together with Nikita, they accused Jacob of violently kicking her out of the house. They described him as very dangerous to society. The cops arrived with all the equipment necessary to arrest a terrorist. When they arrived at Jacob's house, they did not believe it was the terrorist described by Nikita.

"Where is Jacob?" one officer asked.

"It's me, please, do come in," Jacob answered.

"Are you Jacob?" the officer asked hesitantly.

"Yes, I am."

"You don't seem to be the one we are looking for. Is there another person called Jacob in this house?"

"No. I am the only Jacob here."

"Are you Nikita's lover?"

"No. I am not."

"We are looking for Jacob. Where is he?"

"It is me. Nikita spent the night with another man, and she came back with a don't-give-a-shit attitude. I could not tolerate that anymore."

"You mean she is a sort of hooker?" he asked.

"I didn't say that, but she is in a way."

"So you kicked her out?"

"I just sent her back to her lover because life with her was not livable."

"From now on, you are under arrest." They ordered him to stand up, and they handcuffed him. They conducted him to one of their vehicles. He stayed with one police officer waiting for Nikita and Dickson's report. In the meantime, the officer noticed that Jacob was not as dangerous as Nikita led them to believe. He started talking to him as an innocent citizen.

The officer looked him up in the computer. He found how he had been regularly abused by Nikita who assaulted him six times in four months. Reports gave dates and hours of the events and how much Jacob was bleeding. Reports concluded that Nikita was a danger to Jacob's safety.

Jacob himself was speaking politely, what made the cop take a pity and treated him with more respect.

"She is not an easy person," he said.

"I always told you to take her away from me, but you never did. You decided to wait until she kills me so that you could react."

"This is not a police matter. We always told you to get a lawyer and start the process of getting rid of her. Somebody warned you that this lady would put you into a lot of trouble if you keep her in your house. I am surprised to see that she is still here. Now that you kicked her and the children out with and she called, we have no choice. We have to take you, and you will meet a judge tomorrow. But we will make sure there is no criminal record on you."

The officer did not see any reason they had to handcuff him. He trusted him that he was not a dangerous person as Dickson had described him. Jacob, however, did not want the handcuffs being taken off. He told the officer that there was a reason to handcuff him.

"You thought that I was a terrorist. So let me stay handcuffed to make sure I don't cause any danger."

"But they hurt you."

"It doesn't matter. They hurt less than Nikita. I got used to pain anyway. I just don't want anybody to think that I am a bad person when I am not."

"Please, will you allow me to take them off?" the officer implored.

"I'd rather you didn't until I get to jail. They liberate me from a terrible mess."

"We are not taking you to jail."

"I want jail. Life in jail will be much better than terrorism in my own house."

As they were talking, the officer who was taking report from Nikita and Dickson arrived. He was so furious that he would not give Jacob any chance to explain his side. He looked as angry as Dickson. He came with Nikita to take all house keys from Jacob. He did not even consider that Jacob had his hands attached in the back. It was not easy to reach his pockets. He wanted to treat Jacob with hostility. The other cop explained to him that he was not a dangerous person. In the meantime, one of the officers had gone through reports about Nikita. He showed to the other officers how many times police intervened in favor of Jacob. Jacob showed them scars on his arms and face when she scratched him. As they felt sorry for him, he asked them to take him to jail and keep him there until he was sure that she was no longer in Canada.

"If you can't send her back to Olympia, at least keep me away from her. I'd rather spend a year in jail than staying another week with her," he muttered.

As Jacob was the one to want jail, the officers understood that he was really in terrible mess.

"I had never seen a person who wants jail," one officer whispered to the others.

"He doesn't even want the handcuff taken off," another one added. "I say, he must have suffered a lot."

As police had no authority to send Nikita back to Olympia, they advised Jacob to find a lawyer that would deal with that situation. Before they could take him, they gave him a phone and a list of lawyers to call.

"Nikita wants you in the court. Do you have a lawyer to represent you?"

"I have my own lawyer, but he is not around and I can't just call him like that."

"We have a list of lawyers. You can choose one if you wish."

"I have only one lawyer and no other lawyer is higher than him. I don't need a phone to talk to him," Jacob spoke reassuringly.

"This is the only occasion to call him. You need him when you will see the judge." The officers were curious to know who Jacob's lawyer was.

"He will be there for sure."

"How will he be there if you don't call him?"

"He is always there for me."

"Did you have police cases before? There is nothing on your file."

"Never. This is the first time I am under arrest."

"Why do you have a lawyer, then?"

"My lawyer is not dealing with these kinds of cases."

"Who is your lawyer, then? And where is he?"

"My lawyer is Jesus Christ. He is in heaven. He will speak for me in the court. I trust him more than I would trust any other lawyer. He sees everything."

The officers looked at one another and gave him a little friendly smile. After a while, they asked.

"What is your job?"

"I am unemployed. I lost my job in this recession. That is even one of the reasons I am having problems with Nikita."

"What were you doing before?"

"I was working with Flexpipe Systems, doing the Quality Testing for the Pipe Production."

"What were you doing in your country of origin?"

"Well, I was doing something different." He didn't want to tell them.

"Were you a lawyer or something?"

Since they insisted, and they were being nice to him, he told them his brief life story. As they were sitting in the car, they asked him.

"What kind of music would you like to listen to?"

"I only listen to gospel," he said.

"Do you know any channel that plays gospel songs?"

"No."

The officer went through the channels but found no gospel.

"Jacob can do without music anyway," he said.

"We do not see you as a dangerous person who deserves jail. We advise you to let Nikita in the house for the moment, the time to follow all procedures to get rid of her slowly but surely. We ourselves are pissed off by the disorder she is causing, and the situation must end," a sheriff said.

"But I will feel better in jail," Jacob insisted.

"Sir, there is nothing wrong with you. You only need to do something about that woman. We cannot come for every stupid thing she does. You need to think about your future. You cannot choose to live like a slave in your own house. This is a country of freedom, and everybody needs to enjoy life with their beloved ones. All we ask you is to keep peace. If she assaults you again, call us and we will deal with her," the sheriff said.

Jacob disagreed with them. "You won't even do anything to her. You have been providing one-sided intervention. You only tell me to leave the house and return when she cools down. She should be the one to leave." The sheriff interrupted him.

"You are responsible for your own destiny. You did not ask police to choose you a lover. Don't ask them how to live with her. We only come when you call us. Don't tell us what to do. You have your own responsibilities as a man. No one else will build your dignity."

Jacob understood the message and thanked them. He promised that it was the last intervention in his house. The cops hoped that Jacob would finally let the slut out of his house. Once again, they told him to find another place to live for a few days until Nikita cooled down. Jacob swore not to go anywhere. The cops told Nikita to stay in Dickson's apartment at least another day before she could return home. She was comfortable in Dickson's apartment, and he had to fulfill the promise. She also counted on him for help. Dickson started panicking, thinking of how to deal with the situation. As he could not take care of her, he visited many organizations to ask for financial support. Wherever they went, they received the same categorical refusal. They were told that Jacob was the only one to help her. If he doesn't want her anymore, she had just to pack her stuff and return home.

"You cannot just cross the border to seek income support here. You need to return to Jacob or go back to your country."

Jacob had washed his hands clean. He would not accept humiliations and threats of all kinds anymore.

Three days later, Nikita sent a message of apology to when Jacob was still overwhelmed by the situation. He allowed her back home, but he refrained to listen to her. He did not wait a day to stuff the remains of what had once been the beautiful Rosie. He raked and gathered the dead leaves. He compressed and packed them into a black plastic bag. He dropped them in the trunk of his red Porsche and closed it. He opened the back door and ushered Nikita in. She sank in the backseat like a sick rat. Jacob did pretrip inspection of the vehicle before sliding in behind the wheel. He set the cruise control to 120 KMH and drove on Highway 1, Trans Canada, westbound.

He turned the radio on, cranked the volume as high as it could go. Dolly Parton's music flooded into the vehicle. He gunned the Porsche into the express lane and cruised straight to Vancouver where he connected with Highway 5 Southbound. He could only stop to fill the tank and have a coffee. After twenty hours of driving, he arrived in Olympia and unloaded the dead leaves in Sequoia Park. He proclaimed the declaration of Nikita's freedom in a dead voice. That final declaration marked the end of upsetting games.

"Ladies and gentlemen, the game is over. You have been crying for your freedom to shack up with whatever goes around. I cannot deny you freedom. Freedom is a good thing. I myself need it. When I carried a torch for you, I did not know that I was entering a bitter competition. If I had known that I had to deal with so many rivals, I would have practiced for the competition, and I might win the game. My competitors got enough practice, and they had no trouble defeating me. Now I am the one to get the rough end of the stick. I played games with devils and they defeated me with their skills and experience. I must acknowledge the defeat and congratulate the winners of your heart.

From now on, I am not in your life to control your freedom. The two-year long tyranny has come to an end. You have gained your freedom to do whatever you want to do and go wherever you want to go at your convenient time. You are free to pursue your enjoyment. I give you wings to fly so that you can fly as high as you can. You are *independent*, free to pursue the greener grass the other side of the fence." He squeezed her hand and sounded wistful when he said, "Good-bye, my *rose.*"

By taking Nikita back to Olympia, Jacob's intention was to give her more freedom to meet with her suitors away from him. He would no longer have to see, hear, quarrel, or interfere with other men's affairs in his house, the Empire Studio 16 or wherever.

After the declaration of Nikita's freedom, Jacob had to drive back to Edmonton. He could not drive another twenty hours. He stopped in Kelowna and stayed two weeks in a hotel, the time to pull himself together. He enjoyed and savored the peace he reclaimed. From Kelowna, he called Nikita's mother to let her know that he could no longer support her daughter. She congratulated him.

"My son, I was expecting it. I know my daughter well enough to know that it could never work. No man can handle her. If you had asked my opinion, I would never have advised you to waste your time on her. Unfortunately, she hid everything from me. She never wanted me to know about her life. She knew that I never tolerated her bad behavior. I feel sorry for you, but you didn't know her. She is not the kind of a person a man would put in his life."

As the load was lifted from his mind, the trouble was over. Jacob arrived in Edmonton and started taking down notes of all dramatic and upsetting occasions that led him from the land of the dead to the land of living skies. He compiled the incidents in a masterpiece that summarized the life of an innocent person betrayed in many ways.

Jacob was snowed under. He had to call maintenance department to fix the walls, doors, and everything Nikita and her sons had broken. The maintenance persons had to spend a hell of a week sanding rough spots and repainting not only the room but the entire house. Mopping the floor was a loss of time and energy. He had to hire a cleaning company to make sure the house was as neat as it was before the smell of the rotten rose.

If Jacob were to hate somebody, he would not hate Dickson and the other men involved with Nikita for doing their business in his bed. Jacob would rather hate himself. He should not have allowed an unclean heart in his life.

Jacob wondered what Ronald would say if he learned what Nikita did with members of the gang that sent him to the cemetery. Unfortunately, he is not alive to see it. There are so many of such disgusting situations in man's life.

People are just people. When Jacob escaped death a dozen of times, people got wind of it, but no one spread a word. The departure of Nikita Chissocco, however, was big news for the next two years. The event was like a great bolt of thunder. One would say a juicy event brewing in the cities of Edmonton and Olympia. The men involved with her became her spokesmen, diplomats, journalists, lawyers, and judges. They tried to make Jacob feel guilty of sending their mistress away. They claimed that he was stupid to let such a charming creature go away, whatever the reason. If they had media, they would have painted the event in living colors. They accused Jacob of kicking her out for just suspicions. In their eyes, she was so nice and kind that they did not want her away from them.

Jacob could not understand why so many men were affected by Nikita's departure. Their worries were reasonable. In fact, they were feeling twinges of loss with intense regret. They were going to miss her and were likely not going to see her again. They could no longer boast about their intimate relationship with her as she would no longer be around. She would not be showing up to seduce them. Now that they would no longer spend nights with her in the Empire Studio 16, they were grieving, as if heavens had fallen on them. They could bite Jacob to death.

People of good will understood that Jacob had no choice. He did the best he could do, and nobody could do it better. He did what every human being would have done in a similar situation. Those who condemned him were only ill intentioned.

As Paul Chissocco once said, loving any of his sisters was one of the most daring things man could do in life. Nikita was used to wild life. She was not the kind of woman to live with one man. Her flower required enough space to grow wilder and to bloom for everybody, not just one. If Jacob really needed a good flower, he ought not to go to the store. He would just grab a seed, plant it in a vase, and put it on his balcony. In that way, chances are that it would never chase everything that flies.

Days of a flower are counted. The rose was just a perennial plant. As a flower, Rosie could not last forever. Jacob had chosen her on April 18, 2007. He made the final payment on July 4, 2008. She was shipped in September of the same year. In April of 2009, she was already two years old, which was long enough for a perennial plant. But she was two months old in spirit. Once in Jacob's house, he became interested in the in-body while the bees and butterflies were only interested in the shiny and sweet things.

After the powerful remarks, Jacob felt a pang of guilt. He sat down, hung his head and started listening to his heart. He stretched out and relaxed. He had done all he had to do to make life enjoyable. He needed a sane and beautiful life. Now that he was done with Nikita, people say that he needed a seeded flower. In fact, everyone else had planted flowers, and they grew healthy. As Jacob was living in a Wild Rose Country, Jacob thought it would be a perfect environment for a *wild rose*. As the name implies, he thought she was native to the grassy area of his landscape. She would no more fight with evergreen trees to get oxygen. She would enjoy fresh air from the Rocky Mountains of Alberta. On the other hand, Jacob did not want the deciduous plant to lose her foliage in winter. In autumn, he put her in his room when trees were dropping their leaves. If he put her in the garden, snow would come and the ground would freeze. She would not survive the cold. Since the beginning of times, all flowers grew wild. Humans loved them and wanted them closer. They decided to corral them into beds. Jacob held no preference among flowers; to him, a flower is just a flower, whether wild or planted, black or white. Neither one has a soul or a diamond in it.

Now, when Jacob looks at the window, he feels sorry for the flower. He wanders aimlessly up and down the city streets, thinking of worms sucking Dickson and Juvenhack's leftovers. He wonders what he should have done to keep the flower alive. He had watered her every morning, and she asked for morning dew. Where could he find the morning dew on snow in minus forty degrees Celsius? When he watered her every evening, she needed proper rain twelve months a year. Who can get that rain in winter? Nikita hated the beautiful soft snowflakes. One cannot live in North America and still hate the beautiful snow. She was given Jacob's heart, and she still needed clouds and sky. Where could he buy those things? Even if money was not an issue, how can one buy clouds and sky? He gave her wings, and she needed more arms and legs. With only two arms and two legs, she did awful things by herself. If she got more arms and legs, no one would tell what would have happened with her gigolo friends. She would live in five houses at the same time.

11. The Rose Affairs in the Empire Studio 16

Jacob was dead with curiosity. He planned to see what the halls of the famous Empire Studio 16 looked like. He preferred to check by himself rather than asking

Dickson to describe the amphitheaters. He sent his résumé to the manager of the cleaning company, and he got the contract to clean the amphitheaters. In other words, he took over Nikita's contract. He had to clean the same halls and amphitheaters that Nikita, Juvenhack, and Dickson had been in. Jacob could now check on Nikita with other contractors. He soon learned that any contractor could enter the Empire Studio 16 with anybody they wanted. One did not have to report the visitors. They could come and go as they wanted. At night, only cleaners were there. Contrary to Nikita's claim, nothing prevented workers from letting in somebody to help them. There were some couples helping each other. In concrete terms, Nikita's statement that Jacob could not be let in was a big, *big* lie. She simply did not want him to discover the hidden affairs.

In the Empire Studio 16, Jacob discovered a lot about the Nikita-Dick business. One day, as he was eating his lunch, he spoke to Laetitia, his coworker. He knew of her because Nikita usually spoke about her. He was certain that the lady worked with Nikita, and she might have seen something. If he said that was too close to Nikita, Laetitia might not tell him the whole truth. She would be open to him if he lied that Nikita was just an acquaintance.

"Laetitia, how long have you been working here?" Jacob asked her.

"Almost a year-and-a-half now," she answered.

"Quite a long time, eh! You must know Nikita. She worked here until a couple of months ago."

"I remember her. Is she your sister? You really look alike. No one can doubt it. How comes she was so lazy and you are a hard worker!"

"Was she really lazy? She doesn't look like a lazy person."

"She would come with her husband, and they spent hours and hours in one room. Usually, each hall took Nikita forty-five minutes to clean. When her husband came to help her, it took them an hour and a half! I could never believe it. They worked as a team, and they were less productive. They never finished the work in time. To be honest, they were lazy."

"Why could it take them longer?" Jacob asked.

"I don't know why they came to enjoy themselves here at night. Rather than working fast and go home, they preferred to spend the whole night kissing each other. They are a strange couple."

Jacob listened curiously, but he could not catch everything she told him. His mind was lost, and Laetitia did not notice it. As Jacob's curiosity grew, he interrupted her to move to another topic. Yet every piece of information received embarrassed him more and more.

"What time would they usually finish to work?"

"I don't really know. I always finished my work at five, and I went home. They were still in that hall when I left."

"Maybe you speak of somebody else, rather than my sister."

"She was driving a red Honda Civic with the plate of the Evergreen State. Her husband is a tall dark man driving a black CRV, right?" Jacob took a deep breath.

"You may be right. I didn't know that her husband was working here."

"Actually, he was not working here. He only came to see her once in a while. Whenever he came, the work went slower. I don't know how you guys work. I thought many hands make light work, yet I witnessed the opposite."

"Are you sure that he was her husband?"

"What else could he be? She told me she was married. So he was her husband. Her husband's name is Dickson, right?" Jacob inhaled to hide embarrassment.

"I think he is the one she introduced to me as her husband. I saw them kissing too," Laetitia continued.

Jacob pretended he didn't hear the name of Dickson. He wanted to hear other names.

"Maybe he was just a friend."

"She did bring in others too. I remember one guy who met me at the front door. He himself told me he needed to see Nikita. I announced him to her, and she confirmed that she was expecting her friend. She hastened to let him in. What surprised me the most was that they jumped at each other and hugged in eagerness to show their affection. They exchanged more than just kisses. They glued themselves together like husband and wife who missed each other for a long time. Then they put their arms around each other, and they walked to Room 7, where she was cleaning. They were really in an affectionate mood."

"Can you describe the man to me? I am a bit confused."

"Actually, I did not pay much attention on him. I saw her with different men."

"How many did you see?"

"I can't really tell how many. I wasn't here all the time. Besides, I could not know if they were the same men as I could not tell which was which. I was not interested in details."

"Are you sure you saw more than one person?"

"I personally saw three. Most of the time, Nikita was the one to open for them. She only informed me that her husband or her brother would come. Laetitia saw vehicles but not always the persons driving them. They never came at the same time."

"So you think they might be more than three?"

"There is another one who drove a red Porsche. On some occasions, he would drop her off at night, but he never entered here. She never told me anything about him. He would pick her in the morning. I could not understand how she was with her husband all night, and he left at dawn. Then she would leave with the man with a red Porsche."

"How was the man in the red Porsche?"

"He waited outside, and he never got out of the car. And he didn't come as often as did the tall dark guy with a black CRV. He parked right there. The way they kissed, I believed he was her husband. When I saw a different vehicle, the guy told me he wanted to see his sister. I reported him to Nikita, and she came to let him in. Since I knew them, I could let them in myself. But I failed to understand how a brother and a sister embraced like lovers every day."

"He might have been her brother. We have a brother here."

"Her brother! Man, I wasn't born yesterday. I have eyes to see and ears to hear what is being said. By the way, a woman does not treat a husband and a brother the same way. Likewise, men don't treat their wives as they treat their sisters. You know what I am saying?"

"Her husband and her brother look like me. Don't you think they looked like me?"

"No. There in no way they can be your brothers. You and Nikita are light skinned. The other guys were very dark, and they looked really different from you. They might be brothers. The one with a Nissan Sentra was bald, and the other one was taller with long hair. What surprised me whoever came kissed her like her lover. They hugged and kissed every now and then. Even in their break time, they hugged and kissed as if they just met. Anyway, that is none of my business." Jacob coughed.

"One day, her brother, I mean, the guy with a Sentra, forgot to turn his lights off. As he was spending a lot of time here, I went to tell him that he left lights of his vehicle on. Being with his sister in the room was not a problem to me. I entered the big hall as usual. There was dead silence. I saw nobody as it was all dark. I wondered why they had to switch the light off when cleaning. I called, Nikita! Nikita! Nikitaaaa! She answered after the third call. To my great surprise, Nikita answered from the dark corner where I was hearing jiggle sounds from chairs. I saw Nikita pulling up her trousers before coming to ask what I was looking for. She emerged from that dark corner buttoning her shirt. Her trousers were still unzipped. She looked exhausted and strangely drained. I apologized for the disturbance and told her that her *brother* had forgotten to turn lights off. 'Okay. I will tell him. Thank you,' she said."

"Are you kidding or what? Go ahead," Jacob encouraged.

"The so-called brother remained hidden in the dark. He heard me talking about his car, but he remained silent in the dark corner. I wondered if I had seen her husband or her brother. When I exited the hall, I double-checked the vehicle and saw that it was the Sentra, rather the black CRV. After half an hour, the 'brother' went to turn the lights off. I checked him. He was the one who introduced himself as Nikita's brother, which Nikita herself had confirmed." Jacob took another breath, trying to remain calm.

"Are you bored?"

"No. I am listening to an interesting story. Go on."

"Since Nikita was rarely alone, I took the precaution of not to be entering the rooms unless I was sure there was no visitor. Even if I were told that the visitor was Nikita's own son, father, uncle, cousin or whatever, I would never believe her. If she could make love with her own brother, one would not trust any other relation."

"It is really interesting."

"Although I became more and more attentive, I always surprised her with different men. One day, as I had seen her coming alone, I entered one of the rooms as usual. I had not seen anybody coming, and I did not expect any surprise. To my great surprise, I heard Nikita giggling. I glanced in her direction and saw her wrapped in a man's arms. At first, I thought that I was wrong. But then, I double-checked and caught them kissing and caressing each other. The man dragged her to a chair with his prick sticking out of his trousers. He massaged her privates at the same time sucking her tongue. He helped Nikita to sit on the chair. He knelt down before her and buried his face in her legs. I slowly moved away without being noticed. Nobody knew that I saw them. The next day, I asked Nikita about her previous day. I said 'I didn't see you yesterday. How was work? Did somebody help you? I saw a vehicle outside.

"'I finished early because my brother came to help me,' she said. I could not agree that a woman could let herself being kissed by her own brother. But I pretended I didn't see a thing."

"Maybe they were just talking."

"How can a woman press her breasts against her brother's naked chest and unbutton her pants? No. He can't be her brother. Have you ever seen a man between his sister's legs or sucking her tongue?"

Jacob did not answer. He took another deep breath.

"If you haven't seen it, I did. A lot of things happened here, man," she concluded. "I know that they lied to me. I can't even believe that married couples should spend hours kissing each other at the workplace. This place is not more comfortable than their home. Can you imagine a husband and wife meeting here after midnight as if they had no home! Whoever her husband is, he is being cheated on. Nikita is your sister, but her behavior leaves much to desire. She is unfaithful to her husband."

As she spoke, Jacob was thinking of the discussions about her late hours and reference to Dickson. He never suspected that there were others who met her there. He knew that Juvenhack and Geram drove a Nissan Sentra of the same color. Both men were dark with bald heads. Jacob was sure that both men were involved with Nikita. Reports of their affairs were confirmed by many people, including Nikita herself. Jacob refused to believe that she was unfaithful to such a point that she would spend nights with different men in the Empire Studio 16.

Nikita had a stack of financial difficulties. She still had bills to pay in Olympia. Jacob was already spending a lot of money on her and her kids but did not pay her debts. She kept complaining about money, and some people promised to help. They made a budget for her. Jacob could not compete with them when he had lost his job in an oil company that had shut down. As one good turn deserves another, they received her services in return. In other words, her affairs were simple business. She could not put them down when love affairs were part of her life. Her flower had always seen her through financial difficulties.

Jacob already knew enough, but he was keen to hear more. He seemed to forget the revelations about Geram's test for HIV every six months and Dickson being at her workplace at night. He also knew that Juvenhack was having an affair with Nikita in the car. Now that more truth was revealed by another eyewitness that didn't even know Jacob, there was no more doubt about her promised unfaithfulness.

Jacob also knew that she had always been vulnerable to men. He had heard people describing her naked body. Whenever Jacob was with Geram or Juvenhack, he discovered signs that they knew her intimately. Still, Jacob needed to know which one was seen kissing Madam Chissocco in the dark halls of the Empire Studio 16. Juvenhack was a tall dark man with a balded head. Geram too was dark with a balded head. Both drove Nissan Sentra of the same color. But Geram was much shorter and fatter, and his face was round. They could be easily told apart. Thus, Jacob asked his informer to describe the man with a Sentra.

"Was the guy a short fat man?"

"He was a way taller than you."

Jacob was no longer in doubt. It could not be somebody else. Juvenhack was taller than he was while Geram was shorter. It was also known that Juvenhack always shared everything with Dickson.

Jacob sensed that his coworker might have seen more than she was letting on. She refused to reveal everything to Nikita's so-called brother. When Jacob entered the halls again, he only saw the image of Nikita wrapped in Dickson, Geram, and Juvenhack's arms. The amphitheaters were so big and so dark that there was no fear of being seen especially since no one was watching. The inside was a freewheeling place where they could do their business without fear of being caught. The choice of the place was really the right one. It was safer than any other place cheaters could imagine.

The revelations disturbed and struck Jacob with fresh force. He was so startled that Laetitia noticed that his exultant mood had swept away. She apologized for revealing her sister's affairs.

"Jacob, I did wrong to tell you about your sister's affairs, and I am sorry for that. I was not happy because they lied to me."

"It is okay. Thank you for the information."

Jacob was deeply disappointed. Laetitia noticed that he was irrevocably shocked by the information.

"How comes your sister's infidelities shock you so much as if it was your own wife! It has nothing to do with you. She is old enough to do what she wants."

"You know what? Nikita is not my sister. She was my lover."

"Don't tell me that. Are you serious? Why didn't you tell me before? I would never have told you everything. Please, don't let her know that I told you about her affairs."

"We are no longer together anyway. I knew everything. I wanted to find out what really happened here. She never allowed me to come here. I understood that she wanted to keep me away from what she was doing here. She got mad whenever I brought up the subject of helping her."

"Where is she now?"

"I don't care where she is. All I know is that she screwed my life. She is doing the same shit to somebody else, I am sure.

"If she was your lover, you are lucky that she is no longer with you. She is not a woman to be with."

As Jacob got the information he needed, he quit the job the same night. He had neither strength nor courage to continue working in the same halls that would remind him the dirty business. He was astounded, also ashamed to hear that Nikita was known to belong to other men—Dickson and Juvenhack at that.

Curiosity killed the cat. The information touched Jacob's feeling with a cold finger. He regretted why he waited so long to deal with the situation. Now that the cast was done, he tried to forget Nikita. He tried to erase from memory everything that reminded him of Madam Chissocco. Unfortunately, in the province of Alberta, all vehicles registered there were given a plate with the slogan Wild Rose Country. As the plate was at the back of every vehicle, Jacob was condemned to see the four-letter word every time. Selling his vehicles was not enough. He could still see all vehicles bearing plates with the same slogan. He sold the vehicles and started using public transportation. He decided to move to another place. When he had to sign the lease agreement, he noticed the word *rose* on the name of the street, Harvest Rose Park, North East. He exclaimed, "Jumping Judas! The ghost follows me everywhere! I don't want this place anymore."

He went to see his friend and found that he was living on High Park Rose. He decided to move from the province. He moved to Montreal and bought another vehicle. It was registered in the Province of Québec. The slogan on the plate, Québec, Je me souviens, bore no similarity with Wild Rose Country. However, while Jacob was trying to forget everything that would remind him of his upsetting experiences with Nikita, the Québec slogan meant "I remember." The slogan reminded Jacob of all occasions that marked his life. One day, as he was driving on the streets on Montréal, he checked an address and saw that he was driving on Rosemount. Then, he understood that the best solution was to love the name. The name is so beautiful that everybody loves it. The name does not do evil. Jacob had, therefore, to remember all occasions that marked his life.

Jacob lost his wild rose, not because of the greedy, ugly, and tall black sons of bees but because she was too fragile. Now that she was gone, Jacob can stand by the window and watch the world go by in peace. He can breathe fresh air and relax. He is finally liberated from the heavy load that fell on someone else.

NOTES OF THE AUTHOR

When I was living in the refugee camp, I seemed to have forgotten the misery I had gone through. I could not think about the past when I was struggling to keep my body and soul together. Besides, I was living with people who had suffered gravely. Their situation was a hundred times worse than mine was. I was now living in a peaceful country, yet I never felt free from the atrocities of the army of evildoers. Suffering nightmares every night, to me, one day seemed longer than a decade. I was only dreaming of a better place for my children.

Luckily, I managed to get my family to Canada. There, I was surprised but also shocked to see that some folks did not know the misery that Burundian people suffered for decades. When I told people some of the things I witnessed with my eyes, they were moved by my story and encouraged me to write a book. The idea of a book had never been in my mind. I hated to remember the past. As my coworkers kept asking me about my country, I was obliged to remember the horrors every day. Then I felt guilty for not being able to write a book and share my experiences with readers. To avoid repeating the same story over and over again, I decided that I should write my testimony. However, as I was working twelve-hour shifts, six days a week, and needed time with my family, I struggled to find time to write. I had four young children that occupied all my time. They needed a lot of attention as they were born in difficult situations. The first one came to this world in conditions that seemed impossible to live through. Only God knew that he would survive the killings. Others were born in the Kanembwa Refugee Camp, Tanzania. We were new in Canada, learning a new language and a new culture. Besides, wounds of oppression were still fresh. I still had nightmares about police and army killing my family and members of death squads running after me with butcher knives and machetes. Even in Canada, I would see police and run away. It was truly impossible to write a book in those conditions.

Few years later, I found myself forced to live a lonely life, away from my beloved children. With the misery we had gone through together and how I struggled through hell to keep them safe, I did not expect something to torn us apart. I began another struggle to adapt to a different kind of life, the hardest situation to endure. As I was living in solitude, I read books. Reading taught me a lot. I discovered how people went through situations similar to mine, which gave me courage and strength to move on. Thus, there was no reason I should not write a book especially that I had an important story to tell.

My next challenge was the language. Most of my life, I had lived in my home country and in refugee camps. Everything that I wanted to describe happened to me either in my mother tongue or in Kiswahili. I knew that I could write a good book in my first language. Still, being in Canada, I was well aware that no one would read it. My book had to be either in French, my second language, or in English, my fourth language. If I wrote in French, though, I would have to translate to my coworkers and friends that don't speak French. In addition, I myself hadn't spoken French for several years. Finally, as I was visiting the United States and gained friends that enriched my life experience, I decided that my original book should be in English.

The hardest moment of my life was when I started jotting down these lines. I had to practically relive all situations I went through since childhood. Fresh memories combined and would often cause storms of emotions. I would stop writing for several weeks as I needed time to pull myself together. Some passages gave me more troubles than did others. When I put the final stop, I blew out a deep breath, and with it, the memories went away.

Lucien Nzeyimana

Edwards Brothers Malloy
Thorofare, NJ USA
January 23, 2014